About the Author

Stephen Cowell was educated at UCL and Harvard and is an Honorary Fellow of Northumbria University. He lives in Northumberland and is the author of *Demise of the Military Hero*. A successful entrepreneur, Stephen's interests are now cricket and rugby, restoring gardens and walking his dog, Betty, in the wonderful countryside of Northumberland.

Broome Park

Stephen Cowell

Broome Park

Olympia Publishers
London

www.olympiapublishers.com
OLYMPIA PAPERBACK EDITION

First Published in 2020

Olympia Publishers
Tallis House
2 Tallis Street
London

Printed in Great Britain

Chapter 1
Trouble at Home

It is early summer 1900. Jane Dunhaughton is twenty-three years old and, as yet, unloved.

Jane was well named, for she was indeed plain. Plain not in intellect, curiosity or sensitivity, or even at times courage, but rather in appearance. She simply did not stand out. She did not dress flamboyantly or follow fashion, other than to appear modest. She was average height at five feet five, and average weight at nine stone. She did not have red, black or blonde hair, but rather mousey-brown unspectacular hair. She was not wild or eccentric but rather solid and dependable. She was not flirtatious or silly but considered and sensible. She did not cast judgement on others but reserved her opinions on all but the most testing of occasions. She always thought well of others or sought to find compromise if trouble was brewing. She was reserved, standing back in groups; on the periphery of conversations, hesitant to express a view strongly or forcibly.

Monday May 21st was the epitome of the perfect early English summer day. Dazzlingly bright and fragrant, the invitingly soft green landscape and wispy clouds high in the sky drew Jane to stand and stare as she opened the curtains. She loved this view, which spoke to her of tranquillity, permanence and security. It had become her comfort blanket and in recent times she had frequently found herself escaping into a safer world by standing at the window and losing herself in thought.

Today, though, Jane was more purposeful. She had an agenda and was determined not to be sidetracked. She opened her bedroom door and started to walk round the circular balcony which led directly from the main staircase, a superb stone structure which almost seemed to hang unsupported in mid-air. All the main bedrooms in Lainston House, where Jane had lived all her life, led off the balcony and this one feature alone gave the house real presence. It had an unexpected grandeur. The sandstone from which the balcony, the central hallway and staircase were carved looked as though each piece of stone had been lined up as in a jigsaw, so perfect was the match of the grains within the stone and so perfect the symmetry.

As she walked down the stairs, Jane was feeling far from grand. She felt distinctly uneasy and her stomach was both empty and queasy. She had not slept well, waking three or four times, wondering if her father had returned home and worrying if he had been drinking. As she neared the dining room door, which led off the central hallway, she paused, fearful of opening the door and discovering the truth.

She stood outside the door for at least ten seconds, during which she reminded herself that she must raise the issues that had been troubling her during the night. 'Right here goes,' she said to herself as she plucked up the courage to push open the door.

'Good morning, Father,' she said as she entered the delightfully airy and light room. The high ceilings and three large windows, each with a deep recess, made it a perfect setting for breakfast. A large oak-framed fireplace, elaborately carved, took up much of the wall facing the windows and provided a wonderful contrast of shade and form.

Her father, Irving Dunhaughton, was sitting at the table, a large oak multi-leafed beast that took up half the room and had clearly been made by the same hand that had fashioned the fireplace. He barely raised his head as Jane entered and spoke to him. A miserable grunt of acknowledgment reluctantly left his lips.

Jane was determined not to be put off. She followed the grunt with, 'It's such a lovely morning. The garden is looking splendid, isn't it?' She was going to try and engage with her father because they had much to discuss. She was going to be positive and cheerful and hopefully that would rub off on him.

'It might be lovely for some,' Irving snarled as he raised his head from the newspaper he had been pretending to read. Jane could see then that he looked dreadful: pale, thin, tired and hungover. His eyes appeared dark, with huge bags of reddish-black skin beneath them; in contrast, his cheeks were taut and pale. He was fifty years old but looked much older.

'Those with time to do nothing or those with nothing to worry about,' he continued. He looked directly at Jane as he spoke; he might as well have stabbed an accusing finger at her. It was just as Jane had feared as she came down the stairs: he was in a mood of self-pity and was determined to find fault with anyone who crossed his path.

'Father, you don't look well.' She had been about to add, 'Have you been drinking?' but held back, fearing that might be a step too far. 'Why don't you take to your room, have a good rest today and then maybe tomorrow we can discuss what we are going to do with the estate.' As soon as she said these words, she realised that she had given him an opportunity to put off the discussion she so wanted.

'What *we* are going to do with the estate? Since when have *we* decided what to do with the estate?' Irving responded aggressively. He switched his focus away from Jane, deliberately avoiding her attempt at eye contact. 'Some of us have work to do. We cannot *take* to our rooms,' he said mockingly.

'I am only trying to help, Father. I *could* help you. I would like to help with the farm and estate. I know how difficult it must have been for you since Mother died and I am worried about you and your health. We could work together, share matters, talk about things. That cannot be wrong, can it?'

She looked directly at him, speaking calmly and with a surprising amount of self-assurance, but he was not reciprocating. She had worried all night about this conversation, how to broach the subjects that had been building up inside her, how to find a way to make real contact. It seemed at the moment that her worst fears were coming true. He would not engage or treat her as anything but a child.

'What do you know about the farm or the estate?' asked Irving as he raised himself from the table. 'What can you do other than ride a horse? Stick to that, that's what you girls do best,' he said dismissively, turning away and walking unsteadily towards the door. 'You can't even find yourself a husband,' he said, more to himself than to Jane, but she heard him.

**

The Dunhaughton family lived in the family home, Lainston House, in Sparsholt, Hampshire, a few miles from Winchester. Jane's mother had died suddenly three years earlier from an unknown virus. Her death had started a steady and unremitting decline in Irving's attitude, health and well-being. The caring, sensitive, proud father had, little by little, become withdrawn, melancholy and negative. In recent weeks he had started to drink heavily and this accentuated the symptoms of depression Jane had seen growing gradually; it had also added another: aggression. Increasingly, and at a worrying rate, Irving was losing weight, control and friends.

As she sat forlornly at the breakfast table, Jane wondered what she could have done to have avoided the horrid exchange that had just taken place. Above all things she hated confrontation. She could not bring herself to say that the scene had not been her fault, for deep down she loved her father. She remembered him as he had been: tactile, sensitive and fair. She longed for her real father to return.

Mrs Squires, the housekeeper, entered the room, not from the door that Jane had used but from the one used mainly by the servants; it led into the small room used for plating up food before it came into the dining room. This prep room, as it was known, led directly into the kitchen. 'Is it all right for me to clear the table, miss?' she asked, even though she had already started.

'Is everything all right, miss?' she asked a few seconds later, surprised that Jane had not replied. Jane was one of the politest of people she knew.

Jane looked up. Mrs Squires could see that her eyes were watery and she looked dejected, certainly not the cheerful, steady Jane she had come to know so well in the fifteen years she had worked at Lainston House.

'Not really. I am worried about Father. He's so miserable and angry all the time. He will not talk to me.'

'He doesn't look well. I have noticed he is hardly eating. Not touched his breakfast,' Mrs Squires responded. She put down the dishes on the table and looked pityingly at Jane.

'I don't know what to do,' said Jane. 'I want to help but he will not let me. I've tried to stay cheerful and positive but it is no use — it just gets thrown back at me.' Her voice was quivering; she was having to work hard to hold herself together.

'I don't want to speak out of turn, and please excuse me if I am intruding, but I think you need to be firmer,' Mrs Squires said. 'Your mother was firmer, God bless her. Your father is not well and you need to stand up to him. Sorry for being so direct, miss, but I can see how troubled you are.'

***

Jane returned to her bedroom. It was her space, a haven of serenity, femininity and taste. It was surprisingly lightly furnished, given the fashion for heavy fabrics and dark colours.

Jane and her mother had designed the room together and chosen the fabrics, wallpaper and furniture shortly before her mother had died so suddenly. The throw on the bed had been made by one of the villagers specifically for Jane; its intricate and delicate tapestry depicted a field full of horses. The walls were covered in a lemon, lightly flowered paper that had been chosen to go with the throw. Light rugs surrounded the bed, at the end of which was a chaise longue upholstered in rich, bright yellow velour.

There were two floor-to-ceiling windows, both Georgian in style, with deep inlays and internal shutters. These shutters were never closed in the summer because Jane loved to lie in bed in the early morning and gradually wake, watching the sun rise and shine through the windows. She had frequently smiled to herself when she heard the phrase 'rise and shine'; to her it had the clearest of meanings.

A key feature of the room was the desk, which sat in front of the second of the two windows. It was exquisite, delicate yet surprisingly functional, with four drawers in which Jane neatly stored her stationery, pens and diary. On top of the desk to the right sat a framed photograph of her mother taken on her fortieth birthday, three years before her death. On the left side of the desk was a small vase of fresh flowers. Jane loved the garden and spent many hours cutting and arranging flowers.

On the bedroom wall near the desk were two paintings. Jane had painted one of them, a view of Lainston House, just over a year ago. It was acceptable but lacked conviction; the brush strokes were tentative and uncertain. The second painting depicted the Good Samaritan tending the injured traveller. Jane had purchased it from a gallery in Winchester, having been drawn by its compassion and sensitivity.

She entered the room and walked to the first of the windows, which faced directly south. The view was of a small expanse of lawn and a beech hedge, perfectly trimmed. Beyond this was a paddock of about ten acres, which sloped gently so that its boundary formed the horizon. To the right, two rows of lime trees rose majestically. They had been evenly spaced when they were planted and formed an avenue. The drive to the house wound its way between these trees.

To the left, Jane could see the church. It was so near that she could walk out of Lainston House grounds, cross a small track that was used only for access to the church, and be in the churchyard. She was a regular churchgoer and involved herself in village affairs through the church's activities. She was not particularly devout but she had a clear moral code; her catechism could be summed up simply as 'Do unto others as you would have them do unto you'.

As she looked out, she saw George, the church gardener, hunched over the flowerbeds. He had worked at the church for as long as Jane could remember; a more hardworking, meticulous yet doom-laden individual would be have been hard to find.

In the paddock Jane could see Woodly, her horse, contentedly grazing on the rich, green, early-summer grass. Jane was a skilled rider; it was the one area where she did stand out. She rode with passion, conviction and a great deal of bravery, always willing to take on the most challenging of jumps. Woodly was a special horse, recognised in the locality as such and easily the equal of any in the area. He had a special bond with Jane and other riders found him very difficult to control.

Riding Woodly, the church, Lainston House and its estate — these comprised the world that Jane knew. But this world was *all* she knew and increasingly she was beginning to realise that her experiences were circumscribed by what she could see from her room. She had begun to wonder if an invisible barrier lay beyond the window that was preventing her life from moving forward.

These thoughts had not just been growing but festering inside her. Unfortunately, or so Jane thought, they had intensified just as Jane's father had become more difficult. Jane knew that her emotions and her father's state were not connected; one was not the cause of the other. Even if all had been well with her father, Jane would still have been seeking greater challenges than she would find in the environment immediately outside her bedroom window.

Jane needed something to do.

Chapter 2
Friends Probe Deeply

Her father's comments had cut to the bone and Jane felt drained as she sat down at her desk. So much for worrying all night about asking to be allowed to manage the estate, or at least part of it. She had not even got past saying good morning. Worse still, her father had homed in on an aspect of her life that she had tried to hide from, but which she knew was not going away. She had no suitors or even the prospect of any.

It was eleven a.m. by the time Jane had composed herself. She changed into her riding clothes and walked out into the garden. She turned right towards the paddock. She did not need to call Woodly; when he saw her standing at the paddock gate, he sauntered over and pushed his head towards her. Jane instinctively moved her head closer and the two rubbed foreheads.

'What are we going to do Woodly?' she asked, moving her head slightly so that she could look him directly in the eye. 'What am I doing wrong? Is Mrs Squires right? Do I need to be firmer? I suspect that she is right — Father does need taking in hand — but what do I actually do? I can't twist his arm, can I?'

She moved her head forward again so that it was resting on Woodly. 'Why is he so cruel to me? Can he not see that I am on his side? What will happen to us if we do nothing? I can see the farm and estate going downhill. All these questions, Woodly, and you are not helping!' But the companionship was wonderfully therapeutic and Jane began to feel some spirit flow back into her veins.

'I sometimes think that I need to get away, see something of the world. Will you come with me?' She looked straight into his eyes again. He returned her gaze. 'I think you would if I asked you to. Come on, let's get you saddled up. I hope you've been listening. If you don't give me an answer by the time we come back from Lilly's, you will be in serious trouble!'

Jane had established a firm friendship with Lilly Baring, built initially on an interest in art and sketching and now on their growing interest in current affairs and politics. This aspect of their friendship was unquestionably fuelled by their shared belief in votes for women; they both believed women could do much more than they were allowed by convention and rules.

Lilly was Jane's age and her family were members of the Liberal Party establishment. Her father, Lord Baring, had been the local MP until he'd lost his seat to the Conservatives. He was, however, still chairman of the Hampshire Education Board and patron of numerous charities and worthy causes. The Barings lived three miles away on the other side of Sparsholt but the ride there was easy and pleasant, along little-used bridleways and farm tracks.

As they rode Jane and Woodly were as one. Completely synchronised together. Jane hardly touched the reins yet they rode at a fair pace, interspersing canters and trots. Their feeling of togetherness was complete.

'Hello, Jane,' said Harry, Lilly's older brother, as she turned into the courtyard of the Baring estate. 'Have you come to sell Woodly to me? I thought you'd come round soon enough.' He was smiling as he spoke, knowing full well that there was not the slightest chance of Jane selling her horse.

'Hello, Harry. Lovely day, isn't it?' she said, ignoring his question.

'It is indeed. Are you going riding with Lilly?'

'I hope so. It is not planned but it is such a wonderful day. Is Lilly in?'

'Yes, she is. Go on in. She's in the drawing room pretending to paint. She tries hard but she's hopeless.'

'No, she's not! She is very good,' Jane laughed.

She dismounted and let Harry take Woodly to the stables. She knew the house well and entered through the boot room into a narrow passage. From there she entered the surprisingly modest central hallway. It had nothing of the grandeur of the hall at Lainston House, despite the Baring estate being considerably larger. Jane crossed the hallway and pushed open the door to the drawing room.

'Jane, what a surprise! Do come in.' Lilly was sitting at an easel working on a painting. Jane could see the canvas on which there was an almost finished painting of three women lying down around a picnic laid out on the ground.

'Oh, you've nearly finished it,' said Jane. 'It is really good.'

'Do you think so?' Lilly asked, obviously searching for praise.

'I do. Much better than I could do. What are you going to do with it?'

'I'm hoping to have an exhibition in Winchester. Daddy said he would organise it for me.'

'I wish my father would help me,' Jane said wistfully.

'Oh dear, things still bad, are they?' Lilly asked.

'They are getting worse. He was really aggressive to me this morning and he looks so unwell. He is drinking and coming home very late.'

'Oh, Jane, I am sorry to hear that. Why was he so aggressive?'

'I don't know. Would you like to ride? We can talk as we go along. It is lovely outside,' Jane said, anxious to make the most of the day.

'Yes, let's do that,' Lilly replied.

They were soon out in the countryside and the gentle pace of the ride relaxed them both.

'Are you worried about your father?' Lilly asked.

'Yes, I am — and I'm worried about myself, too. I was trying to offer to help run the estate and farm but I never got the chance to tell him what we could do together. He says we girls should stick to riding horses!'

'I don't know what my father would say if I offered to run the estate. He might take the same line,' Lilly laughed. 'Men do tend to think we women are incapable of most things.'

'I doubt that your father would have spoken in such a patronising way. He is clearly trying to help you with your painting.'

'Yes, but he sees painting as a hobby. Actually working, doing a real job, that's different. That is the man's role. I think that's why they don't want us to have the vote. If women become Members of Parliament, they will see that we can do just as good a job as them.'

'Or better,' said Jane. 'I could manage the farm and estate accounts better than Father, even if he were well. I can see that we are being overcharged for supplies. Sometimes Father makes mistakes when the bills come in, adding them up wrongly or paying them twice. I spent a full afternoon in his office when he was out and he is very disorganised. Since Mother died, he has become careless.'

'Perhaps that's the problem — he no longer cares enough,' mused Lilly perceptively. 'By the way, are you going to the suffrage meeting on Thursday?'

'Yes, I am. I am more and more convinced that eventually the vote has to come to women.'

'Not if my father has his way. He is so against it — he says it will finish the Liberal Party,' said Lilly.

'I don't know why that should be so,' Jane replied.

As they rode along, mainly on Baring Estate lands, Lilly came back to Jane's problems at home. 'What are you going to do?' she asked.

'I don't know. I've tried my best but I can't get him to talk to me.'

'Have you *really* tried? Perhaps you need to be more forthright.'

Jane looked quite shocked. 'I was quite firm with him this morning but it seemed to make things worse.'

'Are you sure?' Lilly asked. 'You do tend to hang back. If we are in a group, you rarely let anyone know your real opinions. You are so considered and guarded. I think you are afraid of causing any offence'.

'I can only be myself,' said Jane.

Chapter 3
Broken Spode

The sun was streaming through Jane's windows when she awoke on Friday morning. It had rained in the night; the warm sun was drying the grass rapidly and there was a wispy vapour trail rising from the paddock and woodland. Jane watched, mesmerised by the beauty of the scene and its peacefulness.

Lilly's comments, and those of Mrs Squires, had never been far from her mind over the last few days. It was fine saying she had to be firmer, but how? She struggled to understand what she could actually do.

The previous night, she and Lilly had attended a political meeting in Winchester held by the local branch of the Women's Suffrage Movement. There had been lots of talk about direct action and the need to remain within the law. She wondered if there was any direct action she could take at home.

It was in this frame of mind that she went downstairs for breakfast, determined to make her father aware of just how much she wanted a real role in running the estate.

As she entered the dining room, Mrs Squires was picking up a broken plate. It was part of a pink Spode breakfast set.

'Good morning,' Jane said.

'Morning, miss,' replied Mrs Squires, rising from the floor.

It was then that Jane noticed food at the bottom of the wall and along the skirting board. 'What happened?' she asked.

'I am sure it was an accident,' said Mrs Squires uncomfortably.

'What was an accident?'

'I think you should ask your father, miss.'

Jane looked round. There was some post on the table next to her father's chair. 'Where is he?' she asked.

'He didn't say where he was going, miss.' Mrs Squires was trembling; she looked distraught.

'What is the matter? Clearly something has happened to upset you.'

'I just try and do my best, but it's difficult with your father as he is. He says I am dismissed and I must finish today.'

'What? Why? That's silly. Please, tell me what has happened,' Jane demanded.

'I really don't know. He asked for kippers but we didn't have any so he said he would have scrambled egg. He was reading the post when I served it then he suddenly threw the plate at me, saying I couldn't get anything right and that I was not to come back.' The woman was almost in tears.

'Oh, Mrs Squires! I am so sorry. It is not your fault.'

'I really need this position, miss. I don't know how I'll manage without it. I have always tried my best all these years.'

'Of course you have, and there is no possibility of you losing your job. I will speak to Father. Don't worry, everything will be all right.'

After Mrs Squires left the room, Jane looked at the correspondence which her father had left open. On top was a letter from Charles Tollerton, a local businessman who owned a brewery on the outskirts of Winchester. Jane had met him but did not care for him, finding him rough and dogmatic.

The letter, short and to the point, simply said:

Dear Mr Dunhaughton.

I am writing to remind you that the £100.00 I lent you is overdue for payment. I look forward to receiving it by return.

Yours faithfully

Charles Tollerton.

Jane did not know what to make of this. Why would her father owe Tollerton one hundred pounds? She was pondering on this and on the broken plate as she helped herself to fruit. She had only just sat down when her father burst back in to the room. The door swung on its hinges and banged hard into the wall. He looked agitated; he was red in the face and breathing heavily.

'Morning, Father,' she said. He did not respond but walked straight to the pile of papers on the table. 'Father, is everything all right? Mrs Squires is very upset.'

He father picked up the papers then turned to Jane. 'She can't get anything right,' he said angrily. 'Hopeless woman.'

'She said you have dismissed her. She is really upset. Why did you say that?'

'I said it because I wanted to say it. It's my house and I will say what I like.'

'Father, why are you so angry? Mrs Squires has been with us for fifteen years — she is almost part of the family. She works very hard.'

He did not respond, but clutched the papers tightly in his hand. He stood looking at Jane and, for the first time in her life with him, she began to feel uneasy.

'Has something come in the post that has upset you?' she asked, wanting to lessen the tension. Even now she could not bring herself to ask why he owed Charles Tollerton a hundred pounds. She shied away from the question, still anxious to appease him.

'What is in my post has nothing to do with *you*. Nothing,' he repeated very loudly. He moved towards the door.

As he did so, Jane, taken aback by the ferocity of his response, found the courage to speak as loudly as she could, though her words were still little more than a whimper. 'I have told Mrs Squires that everything is all right and that she is not dismissed.'

Her father turned round sharply. For a moment Jane thought he was going to explode with anger, but he looked at her dismissively and said, 'Do what you want.'

Jane sat for a good ten minutes before she moved. She had been quite frightened for a few seconds; this was something quite different, a feeling she had never experienced before. As her breathing returned to normal, she realised this was a pivotal moment.

With the broken Spode still on the sideboard, with the gentle sobbing of Mrs Squires faintly audible from the plating room, and her own breakfast untouched, Jane accepted, with the quiet determination that she was capable of, that things must change and that she must change as well.

Chapter 4
Political or Ethical

The general election was taking up all the local and national newspaper coverage. The war in South Africa dominated debate across the land; fierce argument raged between those who saw themselves as patriots and supported the war and those opposed to it, who were seen by the patriots as unpatriotic.

Winchester was not immune to the schisms in both town and countryside. These schisms divided not just Conservative and Liberals but caused divisions within the parties themselves. Viscount Baring was very much against the war but most of his party were, if not jingoistic, supportive of it. His son, Harry, was a fierce supporter, much to his father's chagrin. Viscount Baring, although not really intending to do so, threatened to cut Harry off; Harry, with equal lack of intent, threatened to join the Lancers.

It was with eager anticipation that Jane and Lilly awaited the speakers at a Liberal Party rally in Winchester. They had arrived at the Corn Exchange some ninety minutes before the start and were glad they had, for within half an hour the venue was overflowing. The trading floor had been filled with temporary seating brought in from local nonconformist churches. There were not enough chairs and the aisles were full of men, mostly middle aged and well dressed, although there were also many younger, casually dressed men, mainly tradespeople. Of the two hundred present, only twenty were women and these were almost exclusively elaborately dressed and young to middle aged.

As they sat at the front, Lilly said to Jane, 'I wonder what he is like. I've heard he is most handsome.'

'Who are you referring to?' replied Jane with a quizzical look.

'Why, Edward Hemmerde of course,' Lilly exclaimed. Edward Hemmerde was the Liberal Party candidate for Winchester.

'I really don't know. I'm not sure it is important — though I am interested to hear what his views are,' Jane said.

'Oh Jane, you need not be so serious all the time,' Lilly laughed. 'He might be quite a catch. He is coming to the house tonight. You are most welcome to join us.'

'I have read that he is against the war. If that's so, I'm surprised that he has been selected because the people here seem to be right behind the government.' Jane responded. She was always uncomfortable when a conversation moved to men and marriage; her reply was intended more to turn the conversation from eligible catches than to discover Edward Hemmerde's views.

'I suspect most of the discussion will be about the war but I am much more interested in his views on women's suffrage,' said Lilly, suddenly becoming more serious.

'So am I,' agreed Jane enthusiastically. 'The war is important but it doesn't really affect us, or indeed the majority here. It is so remote. Votes for women, though, affects everybody.'

'I agree, but we are British and we must look after the Empire. I just don't understand why the Boers hate us so much. Why are they willing to die for their beliefs? They must know they can't win.'

'I've been thinking about that,' said Jane. 'I think they hope we will not care enough about South Africa to see lots of our soldiers killed. The Boers must read our press and see how divided we are. Perhaps they hope that there will be a change of government and a new government will be willing to compromise about somewhere so far away.'

'Goodness,' said Lilly, clearly very impressed. 'I think they should get you to give the speech tonight.'

By now there was a real buzz of chatter and anticipation, which suddenly stopped when Edward Hemmerde walked through the substantial wooden doors that led onto the trading floor.

He was twenty-nine, tall with black hair, imposing, strong and confident. He was a Cambridge man, a keen and successful rower, and he knew Winchester, having been at school there.

Lilly nudged Jane. 'Told you so,' she whispered.

As Hemmerde walked onto the platform, accompanied by his agent and a number of local Liberal grandees including Lilly's father, Jane's attention was caught by the only woman in the group. Aged about forty, she was strikingly soft and feminine. To Jane, she was inexplicably magnetic. She was not glamorous, yet she had presence; she was not tall, yet she had height; she had not spoken, yet Jane could imagine her voice. She imagined that it would be sensitive and caring. She nudged Lilly back, asking who the lady was. Lilly did not know.

It was not until the chairman, Lilly's father, called the meeting to order and introduced the party on the platform that she learned the identity of the woman. She was introduced as Emily Hobhouse, secretary of the South Africa Conciliation Committee. This did not mean much to the audience, and there were murmurs of 'Who? What?'

Edward Hemmerde spoke eloquently and powerfully, as befitted a future leading barrister and QC. There was occasional heckling, put down by the rest of the assembly, but the audience was quiet when he turned his attention to the war. They listened uneasily; they were respectful but concerned about his message.

The honourable course for Britain to take, Hemmerde argued, was one of magnanimity. 'As the world's leading power, we could find a just solution without the need for war, bloodshed and death. It is not just the Boer army who are suffering but civilians, including women and children.' At this point he introduced Emily Hobhouse.

Hobhouse rose and, to a perfectly silent audience, explained that as secretary of the women's branch of the South Africa Conciliation Committee she was in touch with ladies in South Africa such as Catherine Courtney, the wife of Leonard Courtney MP, and other concerned politicians and welfare campaigners. In recent days she had received distressing news that large numbers of Boer women and children were being held in camps created specifically for them after the British forcibly moved them from their homes. She'd had reports that the conditions in the camps were very poor, with no sanitation, no running water and little food.

Emily spoke quietly, at times a little too quietly, but with obvious concern. The audience, however, did not want to hear suggestions that Britain was imprisoning and starving women and children; there were cries of 'No! No!'

Hobhouse stood her ground and spoke in a louder voice. 'I understand that some of you will find these accounts distressing and hard to believe, but I have every confidence that the women writing to me are telling the truth. They are not Boers or Boer sympathisers, but humanitarians and good Christians.'

She ended by saying, 'I could not support a candidate for election who wanted to continue the war and win by inflicting unnecessary suffering, particularly on women and children. For that reason, I fully endorse Edward Hemmerde and hope that all righteous and well-meaning Christians will feel the same.' She sat down to complete silence.

A spark had been lit in the tinder-dry recesses of Jane's troubled mind. She wanted to hear more from Emily about South Africa. Something did not seem quite right and she wanted to learn more. She was glad she had accepted the invitation to go back to Lilly's home. This would provide the opportunity she was seeking.

It would also change her life.

Chapter 5
Two Magpies

The Barings' house was overflowing. All the grandees from the evening's event had gone back there, as had Edward Hemmerde and Emily Hobhouse. A splendid cold buffet was laid out with salmon, beef, ham joints and pies of every description, accompanied by salads, fruit, cheese, bread, wine, lemonade and beer. There was a great deal of chatter and tittle-tattle, as well as some serous politicking.

It was clear that the house was divided between the moralists on the one side and the pragmatists on the other. The moralists, Viscount Baring, Hemmerde and Hobhouse amongst them, were convinced that it was their duty to oppose the war and to use every possible method to bring about peace. The pragmatists argued that this was all very well but what was the point of pursuing this argument if it was clear you would lose the election, fail to gain power and therefore have no influence? Better to fudge, say you supported the army and then, when in power, negotiate a peace.

Jane was fascinated by the discussion that took place between individuals who knew each other well and who joked and mocked each other mercilessly; she was even more fascinated by the fact that Emily Hobhouse was, whilst not in the centre of the debate, certainly a party to it.

The group moved outside and sat in the late evening sun. The garden was beautiful, the herbaceous borders radiating fierce yellows and reds, crimson and burnt orange. The lawns had been freshly cut and there was the feeling of a cricket match to the occasion. Play up, play up and play the game, thought Jane.

She desperately wanted to meet Hobhouse and understand more about what was going on in South Africa. She found an opportunity to ask if she could join her table when a seat was vacated. Emily smiled warmly and beckoned her to sit down.

Jane started by saying what a wonderful evening it was and how enchanting the gardens were.

'Indeed they are,' replied Emily. She held out her hand and introduced herself.

'I was at the Corn Exchange and was troubled by what you were saying,' Jane said.

'In what way?'

'Surely it cannot be right that women and children are rounded up and kept in camps!'

Emily mellowed visibly. 'I am afraid I have to be careful what I say. People have such entrenched views and at times simply do not believe me, or suggest that I am exaggerating for effect.'

'Does that mean that what you have seen is worse than you described to us?' Jane asked.

'In my view, yes. I have heard the most distressing tales, even of children dying of hunger as well as disease.'

'But why? What is the reason for this?'

'My South African friends are of the clear view that it is Kitchener's policy to force the Boers to surrender by depriving them of their homes and lands. They will be starved into submission.'

Jane shuffled uncomfortably in her seat, arching her back stiffly.

'But that's terrible,' said Jane her face agitated but totally engaged, her eyes fixed on Emily who seemed remarkably composed and assured.

'Indeed, it is, and that is why we must do all we can to stop it,' came the reply.

Jane and Emily talked at length, Emily about how she came to be involved in the South Africa Conciliation Committee and Jane about her problems at home. She was almost pleased to hear that Emily had suffered some serious financial loss due to being misled over investments, for it meant that she understood what Jane was going through.

They were deep in conversation when Lilly and Harry joined them. Jane introduced them. 'These are my best friends,' she said.

As the sun disappeared, a chilling mist seeped across the immaculate lawns. Soon the white garden chairs were vacated, leaving them like sentries barring the mist from rising up the steps into the house itself.

A magpie perched on the first-floor balcony immediately above the entrance to the garden room. Jane instinctively looked round for a second magpie saying, 'One is for sorrow.' She did not see a second bird before she went inside.

By now people were leaving and she was anxious to speak with Emily, if only to determine if they might meet again. Harry arrived and asked if Jane would like to be taken back to Lainston House; Edward Hemmerde and Emily Hobhouse were going back to their hotel in Winchester and they would be passing her home. Jane thought there must have been a second magpie!

As they sat in the carriage, Jane said she was really interested in the work Emily was doing and admired her for the strength of her convictions. She was really asking if she could be involved.

Emily recognised this. 'Would you like to meet for coffee at my hotel in the morning?'

Jane seized the invitation with alacrity.

The next morning, she was positively excited as she went into the Old Vine Hotel. She told the wizened man behind the small but elegant reception desk her that she was there to meet Emily Hobhouse.

'In the lounge,' came the blunt reply. 'She's expecting you.' Even this staccato response pleased Jane as she would have been seriously disappointed if the meeting had not taken place.

The Old Vine Hotel was an eighteenth-century coaching inn situated in the very heart of Winchester. Its garden and terrace looked directly at the cathedral. The inn's oak beams had the effect of lowering the room heights and provided a cosy, intimate, atmosphere. It was raining heavily outside and the log fires created a sense of warmth beyond the heat they generated.

Jane looked nervously around, trying to identify the direction of the lounge until a 'Through the door' bark from the man at the reception desk provided guidance. Jane immediately saw Emily and Edward sitting by the window overlooking a terrace where the rain was cascading down the steps into the garden.

There were smiles and handshakes all round and coffee was ordered. Emily was more business-like than the previous evening, yet still appealing and sensitive.

They quickly moved onto the work of the South Africa Conciliation Committee and the need for money to help its work.

'We are dependent on one or two key supporters, including Lord Courtney,' Emily explained. 'But we need to obtain assistance from other sources, not just because the need is so great but because this will most likely give further impetus to the aims of the committee.'

Jane was interested to note that Edward was clearly comfortable with Emily doing most of the talking; most of his interventions were to support or endorse what Emily was saying.

The Conciliation Committee were organising a women's march against the war, which it was hoped would lead to more publicity about the devastating effects the war was having on women and children.

'Will you not be seen as unpatriotic?' Jane asked.

'We have a moral duty to oppose wrongful actions,' Emily replied. 'And once people know what is going on, Christian Britain will surely change tack.'

'We are fighting to keep South Africa in the British Empire,' Edward said. 'We believe that negotiating a peace with the Boers is by far the best way to secure this.'

As the discussion progressed, it was clear to see just how convinced they were that right was on their side.

Jane was somewhat in awe. She had never before met people who had a national or prominent role. The vicar or bank manager were the most senior people she could think of, other than those she met through Lilly's father, and she met these only in a social setting with the chat at best perfunctory. She was taken aback by just how normal Emily and Edward seemed, yet amazed by their zeal and conviction.

She was nervous about expressing her views too strongly, fearing that she would put her foot in it by saying something unwise or, even worse, utter rot. She chose her words carefully, sounding them out in her mind before uttering them; she mostly asked questions rather than expressing opinions. Later, when she reflected on the meeting, she likened it to an interview except that the roles were reversed, with Jane wanting acceptance but asking all the questions. She desperately wanted acceptance; she was not clear what form that would take but, for the first time in her life, something out of the ordinary had jumped out at her and she wanted to capture it.

They had been talking for an hour. The waiter brought more coffee; more people came into the lounge, generating a noisy but welcoming buzz, nothing shrill or loud but a noise conducive to frankness. As the meeting progressed though, Jane began to retreat. The buzz could not break down her inhibitions or self-doubt; she wanted the meeting to end not because of who she was with, or what they were saying, but because she was afraid. Afraid of failure; afraid of failing to make the most of an opportunity.

She need not have been afraid. Emily, sensing a drying up on Jane's part and conscious that she and Edward needed to catch the train back to London, smiled and touched Jane's arm. 'Would you like to be involved in our work?' she asked. 'I am sure you would find it most satisfying and there is so much you could do for us.'

The deal was sealed with little, if any, negotiation.

'Yes, yes, I would like to be involved,' Jane said simply.

'Then I will write to you setting out what you can do and how it might be made to happen.'

There was a clear magnetism between Jane and Emily and they parted in high spirits. Jane was convinced that the opportunity to break through that invisible barrier was presenting itself, and Emily felt that she had unearthed a solid and dependable rock.

Chapter 6
A Long Wait

Jane found the next week interminably long. She tried to keep occupied by riding, tending to Woodly, arranging flowers for the church, reading and following the news about the war. She met with Lilly and told her all about the meeting in the Old Vine Hotel. But the most important thing she did each day was to check the post.

She checked the post the very next morning after her meeting with Emily, even though she knew that there could not possibly be a letter after such a short time. By the end of the week she was in despair, convinced that the offer to be involved had been just a convenient way to end the meeting. She began to question her own abilities. Why did she think she could get involved? What had she done to show her worth? Nothing!

On the eighth day after their meeting, the 31st of August, Jane surveyed the post with dread, hardly daring to look through the assorted bundle of letters, bills, newspapers and church news. There was nothing. Nothing, simply nothing.

A sickness deep within her stomach began to flare up and she felt nauseous. Every single moment of each day had been spent waiting for the non-existent letter. It had occupied her whole mind, her whole being, and its effect was debilitating. She had no control over events and, irrespective of the feverishness of her mind, there was nothing she could do.

She could weep though, and for the next four hours Jane floundered in her room like a fish gasping and gawping on the decks of oblivion. Hers were not the overly emotional sobs of the disappointed or the low wailings of the broken hearted, nor the uncontrollable tears of the bereaved. Her weeping was silent; it came from within. Waves of anguish thundered against the breakwaters deep inside her soul. Her home life was in turmoil; her father aggressive and ill; she had no role, she had achieved precisely nothing in nearly twenty-four years, and nobody wanted her. She had not kissed a man in earnest, never mind secured a partner. She had no role, no plan and no future.

The 1st, 2nd and 3rd of September brought no relief, but the anxiety of waiting for the letter started to wane as hope and expectation evaporated. The cheerfulness and eagerness of the young woman who had skipped up the lane to Lainston House after her conversation with Emily had gone, replaced by a vacant dolefulness. The days dragged.

On the 4th September 1900, two letters arrived at Lainston House, both for Jane. The first was hand-delivered; the second was from London and the address was written in delicate copperplate handwriting. Jane instantly drew a deep breath. It must be from Emily, she thought.

She opened the hand-delivered letter first, wondering who it was from. It was from Reverend Shell, the vicar of Jane's church, the one literally at the bottom of her garden. In the letter was a formal invitation inviting Jane to be his guest at the Mayor's Ball on the 29th of October. Also enclosed was a handwritten note saying that he hoped Jane was able to accept; if so, they could travel together with Mr and Mrs Field, who were also attending. Jane knew the Fields well as they were regular churchgoers.

Jane was taken aback. She had no expectation of such an invitation and certainly not from Reverend Shell. He had been in the parish about three years but was still seen as a newcomer. He was about thirty, short and slightly overweight, and had an unkempt look about him. He was fearsomely intelligent and well-read, to the point where his language was obtuse at times; Jane was not the only parishioner who frequently failed to understand his sermons. When she had infrequently talked to him on a one to one basis, she found him irritating. His habit of closing his eyes as he spoke, and turning his head to one side, as though summoning up from the deepest recesses of his mind some long-lost morsel was slightly more than irritating. It was off putting and Jane was not the only person who avoided personal contact if at all possible. She was taken by surprise by the invitation for although she had seen him only a few days ago at church and also in the village, and he had given no indication that he wanted to invite Jane to a ball.

'Perhaps he could find no one else,' she thought as she put the invitation down, desperately wanting to open the second letter.

She had opened the first letter with interest and curiosity; she opened the second with eagerness and anticipation but, above all, with foreboding. She feared it would be a disappointment.

It was with some difficulty that she forced herself to read past the first paragraph which she convinced herself was a preparation for bad news.

My Dear Jane

I am so dreadfully sorry to have taken so long to write to you. It seems so long since we met and talked so earnestly at the Old Vine Hotel. I am afraid I have been ill, confined to my bed for three days and then lacking any semblance of energy or industry. Please forgive me, for I feel sure you must have felt I had forgotten you when I got back to London. I can assure you that this was far from the case.

I was on the point of writing a few days ago with a suggestion that you come to London and help with the work of the committee. There is so much to do and so few hands. However, I then received an offer to go out to South Africa to set up an organisation to help with the orphans of the war. I am very keen to do this.

I instantly thought about our conversation and your desire for new experiences and challenges, something removed from Hampshire country life. I could not help but think you might be interested in coming with me as my assistant, and my friend.

I know this will come as a complete surprise and shock but I am convinced it is right for you. Can you come up to London so that we could meet and discuss what it would mean? Do say yes. Please let me know by return when you will come. I will not take no for an answer!

Once again, my apologies for the delay in writing but in some ways the delay has been for the better.

Your dear friend,
Emily

Jane stood transfixed, quite unable to take in what she had just read. She felt unsteady and placed her hand on the large coat stand that stood proudly guarding the entrance to the boot room. She needed to sit down and moved into the dining room where she sat at the table.

A few minutes went by as she collected her thoughts. Her eyes did not move from the painting of huntsmen on the wall but she saw nothing. Tears of relief formed and gently trickled down her cheek. She wiped her eyes and started to smile. Her hands came together and she squeezed them almost in a prayer of thanksgiving.

She was not thinking of South Africa. She was not thinking of the war, or the logistics of the journey, or the impact at home. She was thinking that she had not failed. She had impressed; there was nothing wrong with her, she had something to offer. She sat for some time, not so much collecting her thoughts as collecting herself, putting her emotions in order and regaining a semblance of normality.

She went upstairs and sat at her desk. She was very meticulous and neatly filed all her correspondence, receipts and invitations in separate folders. There was never an occasion when she could not find a particular paper. Her organisation, though, could not help her write a satisfactory reply. Despite every effort to calm down and think rationally, the first seven attempts at a response were discarded and went into the basket under the desk. It was over an hour before she was content with what she had written.

Dear Emily,

I was so thrilled to receive your letter. Of course I will come up to London. Would a fortnight tomorrow, Tuesday the 22nd, fit in with your commitments?

I plan to be in London by twelve noon. Shall we meet for lunch? Can I suggest we meet at Claridge's Hotel? I can get a cab from the station.

Your true friend,

Jane.

Chapter 7
Wanting to Impress

The 22nd arrived in a flash. There was not a moment when she did not think about Emily's letter and its implications. Her initial, joyous reaction, the careful drafting of the reply, the dash to the village post office to make sure that the response went that day, gave way slowly to the consideration of what going to South Africa with Emily would entail.

As she settled into her seat on the 9.37 train to Waterloo from Winchester, Jane took out the notebook that contained the checklist of issues she needed to consider. She was organised and neat; each item on the checklist had a follow-up page. There were hundreds of notes, which she had made over the last few days.

As the days had gone on, she had become more and more practical and started thinking about clothes, equipment, money, travel documents and all the things necessary for international travel — about which she knew nothing. She had confided in nobody, not even Lilly, not knowing if she was at liberty to mention the work of Emily and the South Africa Conciliation Committee. She was determined not to be run out without facing a ball, even if it was incredibly difficult not to tell Lilly what was transpiring.

Jane had increasingly turned her attention to organisational issues rather than emotional or family matters. Initially her father had featured prominently in her thoughts but, as the week progressed, she moved away from trying to scale the alpine cliffs of family breakdown when she concluded she had no hope of reaching the summit. Rather, she would tackle the substantive issues of Emily's offer. Only when those were resolved would there actually be a family matter to deal with.

In any event, the last week had simply reinforced the decision she had taken after her father had broken the Spode and shouted at her. Her father's demeanour had been almost unbearable. Mealtimes were a trial, an endurance, his staccato mumblings delivered in pitiful, sour-faced anger as he wallowed in self-indulgent melancholy. Jane remained composed, offering constructive comments when she felt able but they were not welcome.

She had only been to London half a dozen times. She'd had tea at the Ritz with her mother for her birthday, which she had thought magnificent. She had also visited the Natural History Museum with her mother. With Lilly she had been twice, once Christmas shopping and once to see *Romeo and Juliet*.

As the train journey progressed, Jane thought of her mother and realised just how much she missed her, not just for maternal guidance, the warm shoulder and the comfort of home, but also for the companionship. She was sure they would have made lots of trips up to London together.

The noise and smells in and around Waterloo hit her forcefully as she queued for a cab. The number of horse-drawn vehicles of every description was hard to take in, as was the resulting manure on the roads. The hustle and bustle of the street sellers, beggars, top-hatted businessmen, newspaper sellers, cabbies, sandwich-board men, prostitutes, waifs and shoeless children numbed her senses. Given that her home was little more than an hour away, the contrast to Lainston House and rural life in Hampshire was remarkable. It could have been a different world.

She was nervous now, more nervous than she had ever been, and she began to feel unwell as the cab neared Claridge's. What if Emily had changed her mind? Jane was sure that her friend would be there because Emily had confirmed the meeting straight away, but what if this South Africa plan had evolved into something new or been abandoned? Things seemed to be happening so fast; one minute Jane was filling her days riding and gardening, the next meeting politicians and visiting London to talk about going to South Africa.

She was a good ten minutes early and not sure where to go. She went to the reception desk, telling them who she was and that she was expecting to meet Emily Hobhouse for lunch. She was shown into the lounge and offered coffee, which she accepted. Her hand shook as she poured it.

As she looked around, she could not help feeling insignificant. The hotel was busy, with an endless stream of people coming in and out, being introduced and shaking hands. Confident calls of 'Waiter!' and 'My man!' rang out. Everyone seemed to feel at home.

She drank the coffee in a gulp and was pouring another cup when, to her relief, she saw Emily come in. She stood up so that she would be noticed.

Emily smiled warmly and quickly crossed the room. She put her arms around Jane; it was as if they were best friends who had known each other for years.

'Jane, I am so pleased to see you. It is so good of you to come up to town — and with so little information from me. You're looking splendid.'

'Thank you,' Jane said modestly, looking down for a second. 'I was thrilled to get your letter and I have so many questions.'

'I am not sure I can answer them,' replied Emily. The waiter came and they ordered more coffee. 'What I can say is that the need for decent honest people to help in South Africa is very clear and urgent. Yesterday I received more letters from South Africa describing terrible things that are going on. I have learnt that hundreds of Boer women have been impoverished by the military operations and are being herded like cattle, moved from pillar to post. There is a real danger of disease breaking out if nothing is done.'

'What *can* be done?' asked Jane. She could see that, for Emily, this was not something that *might* be happening; Emily believed to her core the reports that were coming out of South Africa from the Conciliation Committee.

Emily's concern was not mere rhetoric or posturing; she was deeply affected and, as she spoke of the conditions, Jane could see the moisture glistening in her eyes. She was a true humanitarian, who could not comprehend the actions of one group against another. 'I know there is a war and that war leads to dreadful events, but they should not be deliberate. They should be consequential.'

'I don't understand, Emily. Is all war not deliberate?' said Jane.

'Yes, but the suffering should be a *consequence* of the war not a deliberate part of it. I don't believe one side should deliberately try to inflict punishments on those who are not directly involved.'

It was clear from her expression that Jane still did not understand the point Emily was making.

Emily continued. 'My view is that if there is a battle and there are casualties on both sides, each side should look after the casualties, even if those casualties are not their own men. It is simply human decency. What they should not do is deliberately seek to cause casualties in those not directly affected, such as women and children on the other side.'

There was a pause as Jane reflected on this. 'And you think this is what we are doing to the Boers?'

'I believe the Boer women and children are suffering — I am convinced of that. I do not know if it is deliberately planned or a consequence of other things. All I know is that I must do something to help them. This is not about being anti-war or unpatriotic, it is about helping those who cannot help themselves.'

It was impossible not to be swayed. It was not her eloquence or power of her argument but Emily's visible sincerity and emotion that convinced Jane that she too wanted to be involved. She recognised that her own thinking was nowhere near as advanced as Emily's; she had not thought about war or its consequences. She had followed the Boer War with Lilly but it was almost like following a football team: 'How are our boys doing?' The deeper analysis had not been there, and she had certainly not thought about the human suffering involved. She felt, if not ashamed, humbled. 'I have not thought about it in that way. I can see that it is quite different.'

The waiter called them through for lunch and they left the lounge and went into the richly furnished restaurant. There was a comforting warmth and conviviality inside and an atmosphere of orderliness and efficiency. Waiters glided like sailing ships, holding large trays that seemed to act like sails, blowing them across the deep-pile carpets.

'This is such a splendid choice,' said Emily. 'I have never been here before.'

'Neither have I,' said Jane. 'I wanted to impress you.'

'You have,' replied Emily as she reached out and squeezed Jane's hand.

As lunch of tomato soup, lamb cutlets and apple-and-blackberry tart came and went, the two were immersed in deep conversation. It was not the conversation of ladies who lunched and gossiped but that of the busy and concerned. It was not all about the war; there was talk of family, the past, votes for women, problems at home, Emily's failed marriage — but above all it was South Africa that dominated.

'I can understand your concern. I am sure I would feel the same way if I had your knowledge. But I am not sure how you intend to help. What is it that you will actually do?' asked Jane.

'Not what *I* will do but what *we* will do,' said Emily. 'It is that question that sums up why I would like you to be involved. You are so organised and sensible. You are exactly the person who can ensure that I don't miss the obvious. The fact that you have come so well prepared with pages of notes and lots of questions simply confirms my initial impression. I, *we*, are going to set up a distress fund for South African women and children. We are going to go out to South Africa and use the money we raise to help those in need. We will use my connections with the Conciliation Committee and politicians here and in South Africa to arrange for us to visit the areas most in need. We will organise delivery of food, medicine, clothing and tents. We are going to create publicity for this most worthy cause and we are going to do good things of which we can be proud.' It was not said with arrogance or self-importance but with humility and tenderness.

It was this contradiction that entranced Jane; Emily's belief that she could make a difference was expressed in the softest of tones, yet with genuine feeling and concern.

'And you really think I can help?' Jane asked, seeking reassurance.

'I do. And the sooner we start the better,' replied Emily. 'I know you will have things to sort out, not least with your father, but the sooner you can let me know that you will come with me, the sooner we can get down to some serious planning.'

'I can let you know now.' A broad smile crossed Jane's face. 'I would love to be involved. I think I will be lost at first, so you will have to be patient.'

'The first thing for you to do is to come up to London. The committee will easily find lodgings for you, or more likely put you up in one of the member's houses. Lord Courtney is very helpful. You need to meet people and get involved, and you cannot do that in Hampshire. Today is

Tuesday. Do you think you could arrange to come up two weeks from today? That should give you time to sort things at home and get organised.'

Jane took a deep breath. The enormity of the venture was immediately clear; she was being invited to leave the family home, in which she had lived all her life, and move to the busiest city in the world. 'Well, yes. But I am a little worried about some matters.'

'What are they?' Emily asked. 'Let's deal with them now.'

'I don't know how to say this. I have never been in this position before.' Jane looked at Emily, hoping for assistance, hoping she would raise the issue for her.

Emily simply opened her hands; she was willing to catch what was coming but she was not going to throw the ball. For the first time there was a gap in the conversation and a feeling of awkwardness. 'Come, Jane, out with it. What is your concern? I am sure it can be overcome, whatever it is.'

Jane mumbled, 'I am a little concerned about money. I do have a little, but I am unclear what my expenses will be.'

Emily reached out for her hand. 'Jane, all that will be taken care of. The committee have agreed to fund the two of us to go out to South Africa and have put money aside for our expenses. We shall, of course, be expected to raise further funds but, given the clarity, simplicity and necessity of our mission, I have no doubt at all that we will secure them. We have some very influential friends in South Africa who will help.'

'Oh, I see,' said Jane, feeling like a schoolteacher had told her not to be so childish.

'So it's agreed you will come here in two weeks' time?'

'Yes, it's agreed.'

Chapter 8
Friends and Family

As she travelled home on the 5.17 from Waterloo to Southampton, Jane was staggered how quickly the time had passed, just how much had been covered and how much she had learned. She had not realised how naïve she was, how much of a sheltered life she had lived, how little she knew of the world and how it operated.

Emily was sixteen years older but could have been much more for she had done so much. She had travelled extensively to the USA and to Mexico, been engaged, lost money and learned from it. She had been involved in charity missions before going to Minnesota to help Cornish mineworkers there. Her commitment to humanitarian ideals was not a theoretical exercise of philosophy, it was founded on giving practical, meaningful support to people in need. Jane, in her organised, neat way, tried to write down what she herself had done. She could think of nothing.

As she travelled home, her overriding feeling was one of bewilderment. Could all these things really be happening? Was she in control or was some larger force pushing her down this river? If it were, she did not feel that the river was a gentle stream but rather a raging torrent racing towards an unknown and uncharted destination.

As her cab from Winchester station approached home, her bewilderment turned to trepidation. What would she say to her father? How would she say it — and how would he react?

She was clear that the sooner she told him the better, otherwise she would not be able to concentrate on the hundreds of things she had to do in the next couple of weeks. Her notebook was already organised into tasks for each day: visiting friends; seeing Reverend Shell; sorting clothes; directing post; finding a home for Woodly. This last item caused her anxiety above all. She loved Woodly and she would worry about him constantly while she was away.

There was no question in her mind that she was going to South Africa, but not for one moment had she considered that she might not come back. She was going to London for a few weeks. Emily had mentioned travelling to South Africa in December and being in Cape Town for Christmas. If they were in South Africa for six months, Jane would be back within the year. That was how she would describe it to all those she would meet in the next week, not least her father.

The cab dropped her at the front door. It did not appear that anyone was at home. Enid, the fourteen-year-old scullery maid appeared from the back of the house and told Jane that her father had gone out about an hour ago.

It was now eight thirty p.m. and Jane was hungry.

'Enid, is there any food in the kitchen? Anything at all, nothing special. Could you have a look and bring it to my room? I would be so grateful.'

She would not normally have asked, she would have gone into the kitchen herself, but she was exhausted. She had never before concentrated so intensely for such a long time.

A plate of ham, with some potatoes and salad was brought up by a timid, insecure Enid. It was beautifully presented. Jane looked at the girl with some surprise. 'That looks lovely. Thank you, Enid.' The tension lessened and Enid's face relaxed as she moved away downstairs.

'I must tell Mrs Squires about Enid,' thought Jane. 'She can clearly do more than clean.'

There was no point waiting up for her father. He may well have been drinking; if he had, it would not be a good time to tell him about South Africa. She would wait until the morning.

Despite being deeply tired, Jane could not sleep. Her thoughts jumped from the endless list of things to do to her father. She ran through imaginary conversations with him over and over again without ever feeling confident or in control. Her mental exertions kept her awake most of the night and it was not until five o'clock in the morning that she dropped into a deep sleep.

She did not wake until eight thirty. From that moment, she was at action stations. She quickly washed, dressed and went downstairs. Her father was sitting at the dining table, newspaper in front of him together with a half-eaten breakfast.

She jumped straight in, fearing that if she prevaricated her courage would evaporate and the moment would be gone. 'I went up to London yesterday, Father, and met Emily Hobhouse. You recall I told you I had met her and the prospective Conservative MP at Lilly's house.'

Her father looked up but said nothing, clearly anticipating that more was to follow.

Jane carried on. 'She has invited me to go to South Africa and help with the poor women and children who have been made homeless and destitute as a result of the war.'

'Plenty of destitute here need help. What could you do, anyway?'

'There is much I can do. So much needs to be done.' Jane had rehearsed this bit; she was keen not to get into detail but to focus on going to South Africa and being away from Hampshire for a year.

'The key issue is that I shall be away for about a year. You need not worry about money as the South African Conciliation Committee will be paying all our expenses.'

In her rehearsals Jane had thought that this was the crucial point to make, and she was pleased it had come out so easily.

'South Africa Conciliation Committee!' he said dismissively. 'So are you saying you have decided to go? With someone you don't know!' He widened his eyes, looking aggressively at Jane.

'Yes, yes. I have given it a great deal of thought and I am convinced that it is the right thing to do.'

'Can't be that much thought. You only met yesterday!'

This response had not been rehearsed and Jane felt on the back foot. 'Emily is very well connected and everything has been thought through. It will be good for me to see more of the world than Sparsholt and Winchester.'

Her father was now looking down at his plate. He pushed it to one side and rose from the table. 'So be it. Good luck to you.' There was no real aggression or anger, more a

'Well, you're deserting the ship as well' tone. He walked purposefully out of the room and Jane heard him climbing the stairs.

She sat for what seemed like ages, doing nothing, not thinking, planning or reviewing, just sitting. It was as though the brief two minutes with her father had sapped every ounce of energy from her body and left it lifeless and immobile. Only slowly did her thinking powers return; these were given a sudden jolt into action by Mrs Squires coming into the room and asking if she wanted breakfast.

***

The next week shot by. She visited Lilly first and was made to recount every detail of her conversations with Emily and with Edward Hemmerde.

'What was he like?' Lilly asked, stirred and stimulated by Jane's news. 'I'm sure he was really charming, a real gentleman. What did he say? Did he think he would win the election? Is he going to remain in Winchester?'

Caught up in the excitement of the moment, Jane failed to register just how interested her friend was in Edward.

Lilly was more than supportive of Jane's plans. 'You must, you must go! I wish I could go too. I am so envious!'

The most serious business between them was not about South Africa, politicians or family breakdown but about horses, more specifically Woodly.

'I could be away for almost a year,' Jane said. 'I need Woodly to be well looked after or I won't sleep for worry. I know it is forward of me, but I was hoping you might be willing to look after him. I suspect Harry would not mind the chance to get to know him better.'

There was no question of Lilly turning down Jane's request. 'Of course I will. We have lots of stabling. It is no trouble — in fact, we will love having him.'

'Oh, thank you, thank you so much! That is such a relief to me.' Jane's face visibly brightened; it was an enormous relief and her spirits lifted considerably as a result.

'Well, that's Woodly taken care of,' Lilly said. 'What about your father? Have you told him?'

'I have,' replied Jane. 'I didn't really get a response. He looked at me as though I was deserting a sinking ship. If he had said "Et tu, Brute" I would not have been surprised.'

'I would,' said Lilly. 'I don't think your father has read Shakespeare.'

'He has. He used to recite it a lot, pretending to be Richard the Third or other characters.'

'I didn't know that. I've only known you these last three years and he has never been like that.'

'No, you are right,' said Jane. 'He has not been the same person since Mother died.'

'Maybe you going will be just the jolt he needs to bring him to his senses,' Lilly remarked.

'Maybe, maybe not. We shall see,' said Jane.

It was clear that Jane had moved on. Underneath the genuine compassion for her father, there was a steely determination that she had a life to live as well.

The next few days passed quickly. Jane was her usual organised self, sorting clothes, writing letters to distant relatives, visiting various folk in the village. She spent two full days in the library at Winchester reading all she could find about South Africa — the war, the politics, what the ships were like that would take her there, what the weather was like — anything that might be useful and help her prepare.

Her mood had now changed from excitement to practicality. She found that she was not worrying about her father and she saw him infrequently. There was little, if anything, she could do; it was clear that, even if she stayed, there was no guarantee that things would improve.

A remark that Edward Hemmerde had made when they met at the Old Vine Hotel came back to her. 'Everything changes, it is life's cycle. We all have to change if we are to avoid permanent conflict.' He was talking about the British attitude to the Boers but he could equally have been talking about society in general and families in particular. Jane reflected that he was right; she could not plan to live at Lainston House for the rest of her life and expect everything to remain unchanged.

She made a particular effort to go out riding on Woodly and enjoyed two lengthy hacks with Lilly. On the final one, Harry joined them and took time out at the end to walk Woodly before taking him to the stables and rubbing him down.

Entering the stables, Jane walked over to Woodly who was eating some oats. She put her arms round him and hugged him tight.

'Now, Woodly, I am going away for some time. Not for ever but longer than I have ever been away before. I want you to be a good boy and do as you are told. I don't want to hear you have been difficult! You will be well looked after.' She spoke at length to him, whispering in his ear, stroking his neck. She lowered her voice, not wanting to be overheard and also to emphasise the tenderness of her message.

'I want you to pray for me, Woodly. Pray that the Lord keeps me safe and that my journey proves worthwhile. Pray that I can make a contribution and don't become a burden to Emily. I want you to pray for my father as well. Pray that whatever is afflicting him recedes and his old self returns. I shall be praying for you, praying that you make good friends whilst you are here with Lilly. She will tell me all about you, so don't think you can misbehave and get away with it.'

Although Jane was doing her best to be light-hearted, her words revealed not only her love for him but her persistent self-doubt. As she left the stable, she looked back and caught Woodly's eyes following her intently. She pressed her lips tightly together as the pressure behind her eyes reached breaking point.

That moment was captured in her memory; she was to remember it many, many times.

Chapter 9
Preparations

The day before she was due to go back up to London, Jane called on Reverend Shell. She had been twice that week, taking the short walk to the vicarage from home, but on both occasions he had been out. 'I cannot say I am disappointed' she thought to herself as she walked back to the House. 'He is so strange.'

On this occasion, Monday morning, Jane crossed the garden and walked down the lane to the vicarage straight after breakfast rather than waiting until mid-morning, which was the norm for house calls. When they met in the morning room, Reverend Shell breezed in looking confident and bright. It was a lovely summer morning and the dahlias and hydrangeas in the garden were displayed perfectly through the French windows.

'So good to see you, Jane. You are bright and early. I understand from Mrs Davies that you have called twice.' Mrs Davies was his housekeeper and far and away the leading gossip in the village, if not the county. 'I am sorry I was out. The Bishop has had us all running around, I am afraid.'

'That's quite all right. I just wanted to tell you my news. It is quite exciting.'

'I am all ears,' said Reverend Shell as they sat down.

Jane had decided to be brief. She had seen George Shell many times but always in connection with the church and she could not say that she really knew him.

'I have been offered an opportunity to help families badly affected by the war in South Africa. I will be working with good Christian people and will be going to South Africa to help distribute food and clothing.' She stopped there disconcerted by the closed eyes and the head turned away. She was not certain if Reverend Shell had been listening.

'Well, I don't know what to say, other than that opportunity has come your way and you seem to have grasped it. I certainly hope everything progresses as you hope,' he said, looking disappointed as he opened his eyes and turned towards her. 'Does this mean you will not be able to come to the Mayor's Ball?'

'Oh no! It was kind of you to invite me. I will be working in London for some weeks and so I will make a special journey back. I have already booked a room in Winchester for the night of the ball.' Jane received few invitations to balls and she knew she was going to come back to Sparsholt if only to see her father. She wanted to go — not least because she wanted to know why Reverend Shell, or George as he asked Jane to call him, had asked her.

Mrs Davies showed her out. Jane was on the point of saying that she would be away for a while but then thought better of it. She did not want to go through the story again, and she was certain that she would be pressed to do so if she offered the slightest opportunity.

The rest of the day was spent packing and unpacking, sorting and discarding, all undertaken with enthusiasm and blissful ignorance of what was really needed. Mrs Squires tried her best to be helpful, giving advice about what clothes to take and what to leave behind, but the furthest she had ever been was to Southampton.

Most of Jane's clothes were being sent in a trunk to Lord Courtney's house in Cheyne Walk, Chelsea. A brief letter from Emily, which had arrived that day, advised that this was where Jane would be staying until they left for South Africa. Jane found the news reassuring; going to London and staying in a hotel on her own would have been quite daunting.

Jane's research had brought up the fact that Lord Courtney's wife, Catherine, had founded the South Africa Conciliation Committee. Lord Courtney was a supporter of votes for women; he was also from St Ives, where Emily had said she was brought up.

Jane was beginning to appreciate how important and influential these networks were. She was meeting and becoming involved with people who really mattered. It made her feel less inhibited, somehow more assured.

Her father was not at dinner that night and she began to worry that there would be no further opportunity to say goodbye to him before she left. At breakfast there was no sign of him and Mrs Squires informed her that he had not been home the previous night.

There was little Jane could do other than write a heartfelt note, which she left with Mrs Squires with firm instructions that she was to give the letter personally to her father. She was afraid that simply leaving the letter on the dining-room table would give him the opportunity to say that she had left without a word.

In the letter she explained where she was staying, how she could be contacted and when she would be going to South Africa. She also said that she would be at Winchester for the Mayor's Ball; if he would like to see her before she left, that would be an excellent opportunity. She told him she had booked a room at the Old Vine and dearly hoped that he would call and see her.

Did he care what she did? Jane tried to convince herself that he did. She could not bear the thought that he was indifferent to his only child, who had lived with him all her life.

Above all, though, she was upset. Why was life so cruel in throwing up these trying circumstances just when she was entering into the biggest period of change in her life? A comfortable and loving home would be a sound platform from which to launch herself. She wondered if the lack of firm foundations would impact on her ability to cope with whatever lay ahead.

***

She arrived at Claridge's at twelve noon, just as she had on her previous visit. Just two weeks! What a lot has happened, she thought, as she entered the hotel.

Emily was early this time and was waiting in the hotel foyer. After a warm greeting, they went into the lounge and ordered coffee. The first time Jane had been to Claridge's she had taken in so little, being so focussed on the meeting with Emily. Now she was much more conscious of the opulent surroundings, the unmistakable atmosphere of dignified ostentation, the feeling that 'we, the members of the club, are at home — no bounders in here'.

The waiters were efficiently invisible, gliding and sliding, serving and swerving. The maître d', resplendent in morning coat, wafted his hand here and there and, through an invisible cord, young waiters were not so much pulled as drawn, rather like a skilled fly fisherman gently but inexorably bringing home the catch. It was quite mesmerising; Jane could easily have spent an hour or so watching this theatrical show.

Emily, though, was soon down to the business in hand. 'I will come with you to Cheyne Walk and introduce you to Catherine Courtney. You are bound to like her, everyone does. I have told her all about you. She and Lord Courtney are delighted that you will be staying with them until we go.'

'Go?' said Jane naively.

'Yes, to South Africa. The passage is booked. We leave on the 7th of December.'

'Sorry, I am being slow today. So much has happened — is happening — it's hard to keep up.'

Jane felt slightly uneasy but Emily soon put her at ease. 'Not at all. I am amazed that you have been able to sort out your affairs so quickly. How did your father react?'

'There has not really been a reaction, just a grumpy show of indifference. It was quite upsetting that he showed no real interest.' Jane looked down and her shoulders sagged slightly. She noticed a speck of dirt on her shoe and bent to wipe it off.

'I know he is difficult and he has some serious problems but he is my father. He is the only close relative I have. He could have said goodbye,' she said as she looked up. She looked lost, like a little girl whose pet cat has been missing for a few days.

Emily again came to her rescue. 'I am afraid it is simply part of life and growing up. You have coped well up to now, remarkably so. Remember you are not going for good. When you come back, I guarantee that your father will be more appreciative of what you have done for him and what you needed to do for yourself.

'Believe me, when I was in America and my partner broke my heart and my bank balance, I thought the world had ended. But you have to get on with things and tell yourself repeatedly that, at the end of the day, you are responsible for your own affairs and happiness. You cannot buy it in a shop or get these waiters to bring it. You have taken some big decisions in the last week or so, but these are just the beginning of a whole new world for you. Everything will be fine because you can make it so.'

They held hands briefly. At that moment they both realised that the future months would be shaped not just by a common purpose but a genuine friendship. 'Let's have some lunch then go on to meet Catherine,' Emily said.

***

If Jane was plain, Catherine was a serious challenge to the eye. What she lacked in physical attractiveness, however, was more than made up for by the warmth of her personality, her ability to see only good in people, and her willingness to use what she saw as her good fortune to help those in need.

Her marriage in 1883 to the Liberal former cabinet minister Leonard Courtney had not only opened up a significant seam of money but also a vibrant, active network of social champions. The Webbs, Charles Booth, Henrietta Barnett and Octavia Hill were already known to her through her welfare work in the East End; now that she had some money and her husband's contacts in government and among his many wealthy Quaker friends, her problem was not who to help but how to prioritise the many calls upon her time that arrived almost daily.

Fifteen Cheyne Walk was an imposing four-storey town house with basements, fashionably close to Westminster, the Houses of Parliament and the hotels and restaurants of London frequented by the political class. It was to be Jane's home for the next month.

Emily and Jane were shown into the drawing room on the first floor by a maid who clearly knew Emily well. The drawing room had floor-to-ceiling windows that looked out onto the street; a neat, black, iron rail fronted the balcony. There were many books and magazines on tables, and a magnificent desk. It was a comfortable room, light and airy; Jane felt that it had the feel of a professor's home or that of a judge or lawyer. It was a room for serious conversation or contemplation.

Catherine breezed in, confident yet welcoming. She was fifty-three but looked seventy.

'Gosh, she could be my grandmother, especially as she is dressed in a black smock with no shape or style,' Jane thought.

'Emily, how are you? And this must be Jane. I have heard all about you. Let's have some tea and get you settled in. I do want you to feel at home whilst you are here,' Catherine said.

For the next ten minutes they exchanged inconsequential pleasantries but, once the tea had arrived, Catherine moved the discussion on to weightier matters, particularly the Distress Fund for South African women and children.

'We have already raised £1,500, mainly from Quaker families, but the critical issue in the next few weeks is to double that at least. What we need is for the three of us to work out a clear plan and make the most of our time. Jane, what do you think? How would you like to get involved?'

The spontaneous and immediate invitation to contribute came as a thunderbolt to Jane. This was real, not playtime. Jane was learning fast, though, and she parried the question. 'You are so much more knowledgeable than I am. But I am convinced that if people knew what I have learnt since meeting Emily, there would be a great deal of sympathy for the cause.'

'The cause. I like that,' said Catherine. 'Yes, the cause.'

'We need to publicise the cause,' said Emily, smiling as she emphasised the words. 'At the moment we are talking amongst ourselves and to our friends, but we need put our message to the wider public. That is what we should concentrate on.'

Paper and pens were taken from the desk and the three began to make notes as to how they could raise awareness of 'the cause'. Jane was very much the observer because much of the discussion concerned the utilisation of the networks Emily and Catherine were involved in. Lord Courtney was going to be critical, especially if he found ways to raise the issue in the House and get valuable press coverage.

Over the next hour a plan began to emerge and they divided up the responsibilities. Jane would shadow Emily for the first couple of weeks, which would be a good way for her to meet people and see how things worked.

'It's not just awareness,' said Emily. 'We must offer real help. How are we going to make sure the donations help? We need people working now, so that by the time we get to South Africa we can see what is effective and how to make it even better.'

'Quite right,' said Catherine. 'We must get Betty involved in appointing people to help us. We can send some money now.'

'Betty?' enquired Jane.

'Betty — Elizabeth Molteno — is a key member of the committee and lives in Cape Town. She is vital. Her father was the first prime minister of the Cape region.'

They talked and planned for a couple of hours, by which time Jane had voluminous notes and was more than a little punch drunk. All this was new to her, not just the information about endless names, but the whole process of planning and organising. It was a revelation to see how high the expectations were of this group. A few weeks ago she'd had no idea that this sort of activity went on; she'd never had reason to think about these matters. She had thought that you elected an MP and they got on with it. This now seemed ridiculous; nevertheless, that was how she had thought of political matters and she supposed that she was not alone in holding such views.

They broke off and Catherine took Jane upstairs to her room on the third floor. It was at the back of the house and overlooked a small garden. The room was spacious and decorated with thick green wallpaper with a bold flowery pattern. There was a desk, wardrobe, dressing table, one easy chair and a single bed. Jane found that her clothes had been unpacked and placed in the wardrobe or drawers and she took some time rearranging things to her liking.

Lord Courtney joined Catherine, Emily and Jane for dinner which was served in an elegant dining room, rich but homely. Jane found him to be the perfect gentleman, kind and concerned. He was as she had imagined, studious and considered. His eyesight was very poor and he carried a large magnifying glass. When he spoke, his words formed neatly structured sentences that, in themselves, made a cogent argument.

Jane liked the Courtneys; she could see that they were a perfect match, their conversation intertwining seamlessly. They elaborated on each other's words, correcting, adding to, but rarely questioning.

When Jane retired, she was exhausted both mentally and physically. Keeping up with Emily and the Courtneys was no easy matter. She slept deeply and contentedly, the sleep of the engaged and busy.

***

The next few weeks passed at a frantic pace and left Jane wondering what she had been doing all her life. Now having something to do had meaning: meetings; coffee mornings; cajoling; haranguing; arranging; distributing; talking; sweet-talking; promoting; counting; filing, and banking. Above all else, they were anxious to stick to the cause and concentrate solely on the relief of distress for the women and children.

It was Jane's idea to stress that some of the women and children could be British, as quite a number had travelled with soldiers to South Africa. If they emphasised support for this group, they were less likely to be accused of siding with the enemy, the Boers.

They did get some of this criticism, however, and Jane saw just how quickly a crowd could turn if incited by an agitator. A public meeting in Islington was terrifying. One lone male heckler, about thirty, well dressed and clean shaven but for a curling moustache, started shouting out harmlessly enough, trying to be funny and witty. He was neither, but each time he stood and raised his voice he became more angry, and abusive.

'Why should we give money to people who kill our troops?' 'What do you toffs know?' 'You women would have our boys killed.' 'You need a good slap! Get off home.' No one tried to stop him and others joined in, smelling blood and excitement. The noise of the hecklers totally drowned out the speakers.

It was then that things began to get out of hand and fruit was thrown. Tomatoes rained down on the stage and one hit Jane on the shoulder. She backed away, seeking refuge, amazed at how things could turn so suddenly but also astounded at how courageous Emily was, standing at the front of the stage staring down the hecklers, not taking one step back, and shrieking that they should be ashamed. How dared they call themselves Englishmen?

'Never let them see you are frightened,' she counselled Jane. 'If you do, they have won. Give as much as you get.'

'We are only wanting to relieve distress, not fight,' said Jane, clearly agitated, frightened and uncertain.

'But that's the point. Most of those making trouble — and it's only a handful of people — think we are on the side of the Boers. Anything but total and unconditional support for Kitchener and our boys is, by definition, fighting for the enemy.'

The only release from this hectic schedule came on the 29th of October when Jane returned to Winchester to attend the Mayor's Ball. She had given little thought to Reverend Shell and what would have been a big day for her had she not become embroiled in the Distress Fund activities. Now the ball scarcely registered on her many 'to do' lists. Even on the train going back to Winchester, her mind was occupied by the work they still needed to do before they set sail on the 7th of December.

Once she arrived at the hotel and checked in, it was not Reverend Shell who occupied her thoughts but her father. Would he come to see her? She hoped so, if only to see that she was well. He had not responded to the two letters she had sent from Cheyne Walk.

She dressed in her finest frock, a black-lace outfit she had purchased at Harrods. She put on a diamond necklace and matching earrings that had been her mother's and were her most precious possessions. Reverend Shell and his party were due to collect her at seven p.m. At six thirty, she went down to the reception area of the hotel, hoping beyond hope that her father would call. She was already disappointed she had not had a knock on the door from a bellboy saying her father was there.

As the minutes ticked by, she started to pace the foyer nervously. On two occasions she asked reception the same question as to whether a Mr Dunhaughton had arrived or left a message. By the time Reverend Shell appeared, Jane was quite agitated and somewhat downcast, a state that was not unrecognised by the vicar.

'Jane, you are looking splendid. It is simply wonderful of you to come tonight.' He waited for a response.

'Thank you. You are very kind.'

Reverend Shell had expected more. There was an embarrassed silence; neither was used to escorting members of the opposite sex to formal dinners and both waited for the other to make the next move.

'Is everything all right, Jane? You seem rather preoccupied,' the reverend asked. It was not an unreasonable observation given that Jane's eyes were darting around the foyer, constantly checking any movement in and out of the hotel. As she was not the only guest being picked up and taken to the ball there were many comings and goings to check, and her eyes barely touched upon Reverend Shell's face.

'I am sorry but I was expecting to meet my father before we went off to the ball. I am so disappointed that he is not here.'

'Would you like to wait a little longer? He may have been delayed.'

This was instantly seized upon, with Jane throwing out a net to capture the opportunity almost before the words reached her ears. 'Oh yes, could we? I really would appreciate just another few minutes. I won't get another chance to see him before I go to South Africa.'

'That's fine,' said George. 'It will be quite all right. I will go outside and tell the coachman and the other guests that we will be delayed a few minutes.'

It was more than a few minutes during which time Jane and Reverend Shell hardly spoke, so intensely was Jane focussed on her father. It was no good, however; with great reluctance, Jane had to concede that her father was not coming and she could keep the others waiting no longer.

The evening was ruined. No amount of attempted small talk from Reverend Shell, which he was very bad at, the Fields or the other couples on the table could bring Jane back from her disappointment. Nor could she convey to the others the excitement of working on 'the Cause' or her impending journey to South Africa. She told them about Emily, the Courtneys and the meetings, but her tone was flat, detached and hardly invited follow-up questions.

The evening seemed interminably long. There was a boring speech that went on and on, its only virtue being that it interrupted endless courses of a meal that Jane had no interest in. She did take to the dance floor twice but it was with leaden-footed embarrassment.

When the time came to leave, she knew she had not been great company and said quite timidly, 'I am so sorry. I have not been my normal self. I am so distressed that I've had no news from my father, and I will not have another opportunity to see him before I travel. I don't know what to do.'

'Would you like me to call on him tomorrow and let him know your concern? Does he know where you are staying?' asked Reverend Shell.

'Oh yes, that would be so kind. Would you write to me and let me know what he says?'

'Of course, Jane. Of course I will,' he replied with a tenderness that had been missing on both sides for the whole evening.

It gave George Shell a glimmer of hope that he would have reason to stay in touch with Jane, and it gave Jane a glimmer of hope that she would have news from her father.

***

The next week was spent in final preparations, packing and writing letters to supporters in South Africa. The committee had raised another £1,000 and arrangements were put in place for Lord Courtney to transfer this money into a bank in Cape Town. They would use it to buy provisions, clothes and food, particularly for babies and children.

As the time for departure approached, Jane thought less often about her father. She was deeply hurt that he had made no effort to contact her despite George Shell calling upon him. Jane had received a letter from the reverend saying that he had called at her family home, as she had asked, but had been unable to make contact with her father.

As she got into bed the day before they were to set sail she prayed silently, 'Lord, please forgive me if I have done wrong in leaving Father when he is so troubled. Give us both the courage to overcome adversity and to face whatever lies ahead with strong hearts and firm resolve.'

Chapter 10
Arrival

On the 7th December 1900, Jane and Emily boarded the SS *Avondale Castle* from Southampton, which departed in mid-afternoon for the open sea. They were not due to reach Cape Town until the 29th December.

Jane found the sea passage and the *Avondale Castle* invigorating. It was all new to her and to the other passengers as the ship had only commenced on the South African run as part of the Union Castle line that year.

The public rooms, restaurants, lounges and library were opulent, and richly furnished. They all made substantial use of wood panelling, which was ornately carved to engender a feeling of comfort and security for the passengers. The food in the restaurants was prepared in the belief that the passengers had nothing to do but eat and then walk off the effects by promenading along the decks. The menus were elaborate and pompous.

A lot of time seemed to be taken up in the sumptuously furnished dining room with its highly starched tablecloths. As the voyage progressed, Jane began to think that the tablecloths reflected the atmosphere among the travellers:

stiff and formal. She did not like the fact that they were allocated a particular table at which to sit; mealtimes became an endurance test of false small talk with pompous and arrogant businessmen who had no time for Jane and Emily once they discovered the purpose of their visit to South Africa.

If the public rooms rivalled those of grand hotels, the cabins failed miserably to match those of even the most basic inn. They were small to the point of inducing claustrophobia, forcing the travellers out onto the decks or into the lounges. Even so, for Jane the journey was an exhilarating experience which she tried to capture by sketching life on board and the seabirds that landed on the decks.

Emily found the journey tedious and uncomfortable. 'If I have to walk round the deck of this ship once more, I think I will throw myself off it,' said Emily. 'It's like a mathematical formula: the more days you are on this wretched boat, the more agitated you become.'

'Oh I don't know, the first week was very pleasant,' said Jane, not certain how serious Emily's dislike of the journey really was.

'Maybe for two days but not for a week. But at least all this time has allowed me to solve the problem of what to do with serious criminals.'

Jane looked at her expectantly, awaiting pearls of wisdom.

'Make them spend the rest of their lives walking round these decks!' They laughed then Emily added, 'Seriously, I cannot stand another day. Thank goodness we should arrive tomorrow.'

'Well, at least we have learnt some Boer language, so it has not all been wasted time.'

'That's typical of you, Jane, always finding the positives. But you are right, even a smattering is bound to be a help.'

The SS *Avondale Castle* sailed into Table Bay, Cape Town, at four a.m. on the 30th of December. Emily and Jane were bowled over by the overpowering magnificence of Table Mountain and the nearby Devil's Peak and Lion's Head. These, and the long range of the Blauwberg Mountains, were made all the more magnificent by being seen for the first time as the sun rose, changing the light by the second and sending shimmering rays of gold cascading down the cobalt-blue slopes. It was a sublime moment.

'Gosh,' said Jane.

'Yes, indeed! Gosh,' replied Emily.

It was a brief interlude, for soon they had to board tugs to get to shore as the docks were too full to allow the ship in. Landing immediately brought home the fact that they were in a war zone. The docks were overflowing with military equipment, forage, long lines of military trucks and swarms of khaki uniforms.

They saw few women and even less of their luggage, which they could not trace amidst all the confusion. After two hours of hopeless enquiries, they decided to come back the next day when hopefully the baggage would have been sorted out and they could be reunited with it.

It had been arranged that they would stay with Elizabeth Molteno, who they found to be nothing like the upper-class Victorian woman they had expected. They soon realised that 'Betty', as she insisted on being called, was not interested in normal social conventions. She was forty-eight years of age, unmarried, and had until recently been fully engaged in teaching and running a school she had founded in Port Elizabeth. She had been forced to close the school as parents in the very British Port Elizabeth objected to her 'pro-Boer' stance on the war.

When they met, Betty was wearing a rough, badly fitting long skirt and drab grey blouse, covered by a stained smock. The cheapness of her clothes did not detract from the striking beauty of her face and the presence of her personality. She was tall and stood upright, looking proud and independent. Her hair fell down onto her shoulders in a free-flowing cascade that emphasised both her femininity and her independence of spirit.

'It is so good to see you,' she said, almost jumping with enthusiasm. 'We have been so looking forward to your arrival. You must be exhausted. I find it so tiring being cooped up on a ship — nothing to do but eat and make inane small talk with people you don't know or like!'

She spoke quickly and enthusiastically, creating an atmosphere of spontaneity and familiarity. The warmth of Betty's welcome matched the searing heat of the day, which was becoming a challenge for Emily and Jane whose heavy clothes were quite unsuited to the South African summer. All of a sudden, the deck of the *Avondale Castle,* with its cooling sea breeze, seemed highly desirable.

Their discomfort was not unnoticed by Betty. 'You must be very hot. You will need some lighter clothes. Some of mine will fit you.'

Soon they were having tea. It was not long before the talk moved away from the journey and the weather in England.

'News from Johannesburg is that there are more than four thousand women and children in one camp alone,' said Betty. 'Some English officers on leave in Cape Town told us of their loathing for the deliberate burning of the Boer farms. Do people in England know this is going on?' The jovial Betty who greeted then had quickly become the passionate outraged campaigner they had heard about. 'The women and children left homeless are being deported and housed in great camps, which simply cannot cope. Conditions are terrible.'

'I must get to these camps, see for myself what they are like and use the money we have for food and clothing,' said Emily. 'That is why we are here. Our cause is to relieve distress.'

'Yes, I agree — but getting to the camps will be difficult,' said Betty. 'You will need a pass and at the moment I cannot see Kitchener — or those doing his bidding — giving you one. Martial law operates once you leave Cape Province, and the further north you go the more restrictions apply. Moving around is very difficult and non-military personnel are treated with great suspicion. And you are a woman!'

'Well, I have an ace up my sleeve,' said Emily. 'I have an introduction to Alfred Milner from my aunt, Lady Hobhouse. Her husband knows Milner, they were friends at Balliol College. I am hoping he will agree to me travelling to the camps.'

She looked at her host, seeking approval, but Betty replied, 'He might, but he has no authority outside the Cape. It is the military that count and, by all accounts, Kitchener is answerable to no one. We need to get to Kitchener.'

Jane was pleased that her time in the Winchester library was paying off. She knew all about Milner and had felt able to discuss his role many times whilst she was staying in Chelsea and again during the passage out. As the High Commissioner for South Africa, he had a great deal of say in determining British strategy; he also controlled the flow of information back to London. By all accounts he was exceptionally bright, a Classics scholar, a gentleman in all ways, but extremely ambitious and ruthless. His own interests weighed heavily in his thinking on any matter — or at least this was the view that Jane had formed from listening to Lord Courtney, Caroline, Emily and others.

The next week was spent meeting friends of the Distress Fund and the Conciliation Committee. They moved from Betty Moltano's home to that of the Currys because many people wanted to help and also hear first-hand news of England. Their home was also larger and more comfortable. Jane was captivated by the beauty of their garden. Grapes were ripening, and there were peaches and apricots everywhere. The flowers in the herbaceous borders were brilliant oranges and reds, colours that could not be seen in England.

'I could live here,' Jane said to Emily.

'Really? Would you not find it too claustrophobic, a bit like your village but warmer? I think you would soon suffocate. I know I would.'

'I don't know. It seems incongruous that it is so peaceful and settled, the weather is divine and people don't seem so driven, yet I know there is a different world outside.'

'Indeed, there is,' said Emily. 'Tomorrow I am meeting Milner and I don't think I have ever been so nervous in my life. If I don't win him over, there is no chance of him asking Kitchener for our permit to travel outside of the Cape. If we don't get the permit, our journey will have been a total waste of time.'

'That's too harsh,' said Jane. 'At least we will have tried and done our best.'

'I am not even going to contemplate failure. Leonard Courtney has just sent me a letter. All it says is: *Emily, re your meeting with Milner, be prudent, be calm. Affectionately yours, Leonard Courtney.*' She handed the letter across for Jane to see.

'Sounds like good advice,' said Jane.

'Indeed,' replied Emily, looking more worried than Jane had ever noticed before.

Jane started to grasp just how significant this meeting was to her friend. There was quite a pause, during which Jane was sure that Emily was mentally rehearsing the meeting with Milner.

Suddenly, though, Emily turned to Jane. 'Whilst I am at the High Commission, will you go and visit the wounded Boer prisoners in the camp at Wynberg? Lady de Villiers has a pass so she and some of the other ladies can help. You may pick up useful information about what is happening up north.'

'Of course,' Jane said uneasily.

Up to that point she had merely accompanied Emily, mainly meeting well-meaning Christian women supporters. It was now clear there were far more camps than they had first realised and that many were substantially larger than they had imagined. Jane was keen to be more than Emily's shadow and to do something herself, but the prospect of visiting wounded prisoners made her feel inadequate. She had never seen anyone with a bad injury other than one or two riders who had broken bones whilst out with the hunt. 'I hope I don't find it too upsetting.'

'You will, but remember not to show it,' said Emily. 'The purpose is to make them more comfortable, so we need to act as though they are fine.'

The following afternoon Jane went with five other women to the prisoners' hospital. She braced herself before they entered the ward; it was fortunate that she did, for she had no idea that there would be more than two hundred wounded prisoners laid out in four long lines.

In effect, the ward was four large tents put together. The wounded lay on wooden beds that were little more than packing cases with a mattress on top. The linen was clean, though.

There was complete, eerie silence. No one was talking and there were no cries of pain or shouts for assistance. Two nurses, both South African volunteers, were the only people in the ward. They were both young, not more than Jane's age, but they seemed organised and diligent. The matron who accompanied Jane and her group explained that the surgeon came round twice a day and there were always two nurses on duty.

The most seriously injured lay in the first line. The matron did not want Jane or any of the other ladies to talk to them. 'We do not want to disturb them, they need total rest. Feel free to talk to patients who are awake, but don't wake anyone up.'

Jane was hesitant about talking to any of the wounded. She had never been in a hospital before, never mind one full of 'enemy soldiers'. She was at a loss as to what she should say, how to start a conversation, and she found herself hovering behind Lady de Villiers. Fortunately, that lady had no hesitation in asking each patient she stopped by, 'What are your injuries?' When told, she followed up with the question, 'How long have you been here?' This, in turn, was followed by, 'Where are you from and do you know where your family are?'

It was a blunt interrogation with little apparent warmth and no attempt at pleasantries, but it was remarkably effective. All those Lady de Villiers stopped next to spoke willing and openly, and the women obtained a lot of information.

Jane was transfixed, watching intently, listening and learning. The last question to everyone was always the same, and again was short and sharp: 'Do you lack anything?' Most replied that they were well looked after but those that did say they were lacking mentioned only one thing: water to drink.

As they moved to the next part of the ward, Lady de Villiers turned to Jane. 'Right, your turn now. No point hiding away. Remember, make it easy for them. Simple questions, don't pretend to be their friend. We are here to make sure they are comfortable. They trust us more if we are direct.'

It was a girl full of trepidation who stopped at the first bed in the new section. The soldier was sitting up. His arm had been amputated above the elbow; he looked dreadful, his face hollow and yellow with fear written all over it. His eyes stared straight ahead and Jane was not sure if he was conscious of their presence.

She tentatively asked, 'What are your injuries?' but got no response.

'Speak up, he can't hear you,' said Lady de Villiers. Jane asked the question again this time moving into the patient's eye line. 'What are your injuries?'

His eyes met Jane's. 'What's it look like?' he asked aggressively.

Jane stumbled; she could not answer or think of a follow-up question and she shrivelled visibly.

It was Lady de Villiers who came to her rescue. 'You have lost your arm. Not the end of the world. Accept it, or life will be very bad for you. Come on, Jane. There plenty are more patients who are not feeling sorry for themselves.'

As they moved on, she said, 'Come on, Jane, try again. You got a bad one there. There is always one.'

They walked well away from Jane's failure, for that is how she saw it and how she felt: a failure. But she was not allowed to wallow in self-deprecation for Lady de Villiers put her hand against the small of her back and pushed her firmly towards a bed where a boyish patient was propped up.

Lady de Villiers waved at Jane, making it clear that she expected her to ask some questions.

A deep breath later, and a totally inaudible question withered and fell unheard onto the wooden planks of the floor. 'Louder,' came the voice behind Jane, and the hand once again pressed into her back.

'What are your injuries?' This time Jane asked the question audibly, if not confidently.

'I cannot walk. I was trying to escape and fell from my horse, hurting my back.'

'Oh, will you be all right?' Jane had departed from the script and it did not go well.

'No. Doctor says I will never walk again.'

Again, Jane stumbled, her legs wobbling, her head wanting to turn in any direction so she did not need to look into the poor boy's eyes. She would have turned and run if it had not been for the hand pushing the small of the back.

There was a silence that seemed to last hours but was in fact less than three seconds before Jane blurted out loudly and quickly, 'Where are your family?'

'They are in a camp near Bloemfontein. Farm was burnt down and they have nowhere to go.'

'How many are there in your family?' Jane asked decisively.

'My mother and five brothers and sisters.'

'Your father?'

'Dead. Been dead five years. I worked the farm.'

'Is there anything you lack?' Jane asked. It dawned on her that she must not respond to the patient's questions. If she was to get through this, she must ask and listen but not comment. Her brain was working feverishly, not so much on listening or looking at the injured soldiers but on controlling her own emotions and giving her the strength to stand by the bed and appear engaged.

'I need water to drink,' came the reply.

Jane and Lady de Villiers both nodded, signalling that they had received and understood the request. They began to move away; as they did so, they heard a plaintive cry: 'And news from my family.'

As the visiting party came back together, the matron asked if everything was all right.

'The patients are asking for water,' replied Lady de Villiers.

'Oh yes,' the matron replied. 'There is a shortage. It has to be transported here and we simply don't get enough.'

'And what are *you* doing about it?' asked the now-agitated Lady de Villiers. She had a true gift of making clear her expectations by way of succinct questioning and prolonged emphasis on the 'you'.

'I have asked the supply officer a number of times but nothing has happened.'

'Not good enough!' came Lady de Villiers' reply. She was now on a mission. 'Make a fuss, have a tantrum, go with a cart yourself — but it is your job to sort it out.' Turning to the other ladies she added, 'I think we are done here. When we come back next week, I am sure we will find that Matron has solved the water problem.'

She turned to the matron and did not so much look her in the eye as throw a net round her and draw her close. 'I have every confidence in you,' she said.

***

When Jane met up with Emily later that evening, they recounted their respective experiences. Jane started by saying she had been afraid at first but had learnt a great deal from watching Lady de Villiers. 'She is quite formidable, very direct and challenging, yet I think it is all an act. Outside the hospital, she is so sweet and gentle. She told me that she was just like me at first but learnt that getting things done when there is a war on requires a no-nonsense approach. You have to be very clear so there is no room for doubt or prevarication.'

'It sounds like your visit was worthwhile.'

'Indeed,' said Jane. 'But how did you get on with Milner?'

'Very well indeed,' Emily replied. 'I was the only lady at lunch with eight men, mainly officials. There was one military man, a captain in the Welsh Guards. Afterwards I met privately with Milner, as we could not really talk over lunch. He admitted that the farm burning was a mistake, and he agreed that something needed to be done to improve the condition of the women and children. He told me that he had seen truckloads of women and children coming down from the north and they were in a pitiful condition. Anyway, to cut a long story short, we had quite a strong exchange of views for over an hour — but he did agree to our request to visit the camps. And he also agreed to supply us with two railway trucks to fill, one with clothes and one with food.'

'Oh, that's good,' said Jane. 'Are they ready now?' As an afterthought she added, 'How will we load them and fit them on to the train?'

'We will find a way,' said Emily. 'No, we can't go yet because we still need Kitchener's approval. Lord Milner has written — he dictated the letter supporting our request whilst I was there. I think he is a very amiable man, but weak. He is sharp and clear-headed but narrow, blinkered even. Everyone says he has no heart but underneath I think he does care and is worried about the long-term effects our policy of burning and destruction will have on England's reputation.'

'Is Kitchener really his boss?' asked Jane. 'I thought that Milner was the High Commissioner and that soldiers reported to politicians.'

'Good question, Jane,' said Emily. 'In my view, Milner has decided to make his life easy by siding with Kitchener on all things. Reading between the lines, I think that he is afraid that falling out with Kitchener won't do his career any good. He mentioned that Kitchener ruined Lord Curzon in India.'

'When will we hear?' asked Jane.

'Tomorrow, hopefully, but the day after at the latest.'

It was actually two days later that a telegram arrived from Government House. '*Kitchener agrees. Please call in to discuss details. Milner.*'

Jane and Emily hugged each other and rushed downstairs to tell the Currys. They were like teenagers, excited and girlish. 'Now our real work starts,' said Emily.

Chapter 11
Into the Camps

The next few days were taken up with buying food and clothes. Their money did not go far; the price of provisions had risen massively because the army was buying nearly everything available. Keeping 400,000 troops fed and watered was a huge logistical task, and most food had to be imported as South Africa simply did not have enough. It was not just the men who needed feeding; the aarmy relied on large numbers of horses and they needed food and water.

For Jane and Emily, finding their way around the suppliers was daunting. They found blatant opportunism from those wanting to milk the military cow for all it was worth, and outright hostility for what was seen as an attempt to assist the enemy. The most common reaction, though, was incredulity that a couple of English ladies would be going into the war zone to give out food and clothing.

Fortunately, Milner had made a couple of officials available to help Emily and Jane obtain supplies and they increasingly fronted the operation. The two women divided the work: Emily talked to officials and raised awareness and money, whilst Jane prepared for the trip to the camps. The two officials were invaluable; they not only found and negotiated with suppliers but also helped load the trucks.

It was the evening of the 22nd of January 1901 when Jane and Emily boarded a train for Bloemfontein. As well as the two trucks, which had been loaded onto the train, they carried a few possessions that were to prove invaluable in the weeks to come.

The first was a kettle lamp for making tea and cocoa; the second, a box of tinned foods that could withstand the heat once they left civilisation. Apricot jam was to become a treasured luxury as they sat in total darkness in the wilds of the South African Karoo, seeking the next camp. These small but precious gifts had been provided by the many friends they had made in Cape Town over the last few weeks. It was a tearful and frightened group that saw them off.

The third possession was altogether different but perhaps even more valuable for their mission: it was a signed letter from Alfred Milner.

Dear Miss Hobhouse

I have written to General Pretyman, the military governor of the Orange River colony, asking him to give you any assistance in his power.

Personally, I am quite willing that you should visit any refugee camp in either TV or ORC if the military authorities will allow it. As you are aware, Lord Kitchener is not prepared to approve of you going farther than Bloemfontein at present. But, as he has expressly approved of your going as far as that, I do not think there can be any difficulty about your visiting the camps either there, or at any place on the railway south of it.

In any case, you can show this letter as evidence that, as far as I am concerned, such visits are authorised and approved.

Yours very truly,

A Milner (High Commissioner)

Jane and Emily stood at the carriage window, watching as the crowd of well-wishers slowly melted from view. They said nothing to each other for some time. Jane wondered if Emily felt as frightened as she did.

As soon as the platform party disappeared, she began to feel alone; for the first time she became conscious of the fact that they were the only women on this packed train. The preponderance of soldiers in uniform with rifles and packs brought home that they were about to enter a war zone. She worried about language and the basics of where they would live, wash and eat. What had seemed an exciting adventure whilst they were travelling from England, or undertaking more detailed planning in Cape Town, now seemed not quite so jolly.

Jane was desperate not to reveal her feelings to Emily; she did not want to let the side down. She need not have feared, for exactly the same thoughts were going through Emily's mind: she was also determined not to show how frightened she was.

As the afternoon turned to evening and then dusk, the train moved slowly north, leaving the fertile valleys of the Cape. The view from the window metamorphosed into a still blackness. The night was darker than they had ever known before, and its blackness compounded Jane's unease and nervousness.

There was nowhere to sleep and the night seemed endless as she struggled to get comfortable on hard wooden seats in a carriage full of British junior officers. They were neither friendly nor approachable, and Jane felt distinctly that she and Emily were not welcome. Other than initial introductions, the officers asked no questions but eyed up the two women, perplexed as to why they should be on this train and in their carriage.

When dawn arrived, it was well received by the restless and aching pair. The rising sun seemed to lift the uneasy tension in the carriage and revealed a totally different landscape. They had now reached the arid plateau of the Karoo. Jane had never seen desert; its vastness, the sweep of the land and the sky, mesmerised her. In the distance flat-topped hills, which Jane later learnt were called *koppies*, glimmered with a burnt-orange tinge.

Emily interrupted the disconcerting silence. 'It's as if even the plants are antisocial.'

Jane smiled, for she had been thinking just the same thing as she tried to come to terms with the vastness of the landscape. The desert plants, spreading endlessly before their eyes across the dusty reddish-yellow terrain, were always yards away from each other

'Just like our friends here,' Jane said, looking at the slumbering soldiers.

It took two more days to reach Bloemfontein. The train was dreadfully slow, crawling through steep passes, stopping frequently for water and to allow the hundreds of soldiers to eat and have 'comfort breaks'. It was a great shock for Jane to see scores of soldiers relieving themselves by the rail tracks.

'Better not look out the window when we stop, miss. Not a pretty sight,' said one lieutenant.

Jane's naivety and upper-class upbringing were sorely tested, as was her patience at having to queue for what seemed like hours in the fierce heat for meals at the station stops.

As they progressed, passing through Beaufort West, De Aar and Naauwpoort, the landscape took on a more sinister, desolate appearance. The Nuweveld Mountains provided relief from the monotony of the lower Karoo. The Valley of Desolation was well named, its craggy outposts and searing cliffs making it an impenetrable barrier. As they neared Bloemfontein, there were more alarming features. Animal carcasses were everywhere, mules, cattle, horses, and there was no sign of life. The occasional burnt-out farm dispelled whatever doubts Jane might have had about the truth of the stories she had heard, as did the desolate appearance of the farms that were still intact. There was simply no one around.

'It's like the ghost towns I saw in Colorado,' Emily said. 'But at least there was some animal life there.'

'It's quite eerie, isn't it?' said Jane. 'I did wonder if all these reports we've had were exaggerated but they aren't. People have been moved out.'

'I agree,' said Emily. 'In some ways I wish the reports had been exaggerated. I have an uneasy feeling it's going to be worse than we heard.'

When they eventually reached Bloemfontein, they were desperately tired and dirty. The second day in the Karoo had seen fierce thunderstorms and violent dust storms. The sand, a toxic red, took no heed of windows and carriage walls; it penetrated everything, leaving everyone covered in a fine powder, and it irritated eyes and noses. Any food they ate tasted gritty, and Jane was embarrassed at having to keep emptying her mouth into her handkerchief. No one cared by this time; no one was looking at her.

Everyone wanted to get off the train, not least because the further north they went the greater was the danger of attack from the Boer guerrillas. Jane had not really worried about that, thinking she was well protected by a train full of soldiers.

It was the same lieutenant who had told her not to look out of the window who brought alarm to her face by saying, 'Sooner we get to Bloomy the better. We're sitting ducks on this train.'

'Surely they won't attack a train load of soldiers,' said an incredulous Jane.

'Miss, it is precisely because we have a train load of soldiers that they would want to attack.'

From that moment, a panic-stricken Jane scoured the horizon for men on horseback sweeping down towards the train. Her mood was not improved when the same lieutenant said laconically, 'They attack at night — usually.'

It was late afternoon on the 24th that the train arrived in Bloemfontein. Jane and Emily could not get to the inn they had booked fast enough, but the desire for a wash and change of clothes had to wait until they had ensured that the two trucks were safely delivered to the army depot so it was dark by the time they reached the inn.

Jane was too tired to eat much, although she did drink two whole pots of tea. 'This is the best-tasting tea I have ever had,' she said to the pretty young waitress who served them. The girl did not know how to respond and simply smiled. 'I know I should be hungry but I am too tired to eat. I must go to bed,' Jane continued.

'Yes, of course,' Emily said. 'Tomorrow I will go and see General Pretyman. We should plan to go to the camp the day after.' She also looked tired as she pushed back her chair and stood up from the table. She tried to brush the dust from her clothes but it was a half-hearted attempt, and she realised it was a futile act.

Jane was watching her and said wearily, 'I think we will need some new clothes. I have never been so dirty.'

'I agree,' replied Emily. 'Clothes first, then General Pretyman.'

The moment Jane's head hit the pillow, she entered a sleep so deep that no dream could penetrate the inner sanctum of her mind. She was as close to hibernation as any human can be. The hotel was very basic, the room at best could be called rustic, but its clean sheets and lumpy mattress conveyed Jane to nirvana. She had never in her life been anywhere near as tired and she hardly moved for nine hours.

She was woken by persistent knocking at the door. 'Yes?' she called out.

The pretty young waitress who had served them the previous night, who was in fact the owner's daughter, answered that Miss Hobhouse was at breakfast and wondered if Jane would be joining her.

Jane opened the thick heavy curtains, which acted as a blackout, and saw that it was a hot bright day. Lots of people were about. 'What time is it?' she asked, speaking through the door.

'Ten o'clock, miss,' came the reply.

'Please tell Emily I will be down in ten minutes.'

She washed as best she could, using the large bowl on the dressing table, and then took her only change of clothes from her small case. How she badly needed more underclothes and lighter dresses! Nevertheless, when dressed she felt a hundred times better than the night before — clean and, if not smart, at least presentable.

She went downstairs into the dining room, the only public room in the hotel other than a very small reception area. Emily was sitting with a woman in her mid-fifties. As Jane entered the room, they both rose.

'Jane, can I introduce you to Mrs Caroline Fichardt? Caroline, this is Jane Dunhaughton, my true friend and help.'

As they sat down and ordered tea and toast, Emily explained that Betty Moltano had written to Caroline outlining the purpose of their visit and wondering if she could help.

'I am very keen to help in whatever way I can,' Caroline said. 'I think what is going on is quite deplorable. I will gladly do whatever I can for those poor women and children.'

Jane asked if Caroline had been to the camp. She was somewhat taken aback when Mrs Fichardt replied that she had not as she could not get a permit. 'You see, the British think I am, if not a Boer spy, at least a Boer sympathiser.'

'Oh,' said Jane, looking shocked and turning to Emily for guidance. 'Are you?'

Caroline sat bolt upright and replied firmly, and with the authority of someone used to being obeyed. 'I want to see peace. I have many friends on both sides and it distresses me to see so much killing and destruction. It is not beyond hope that the two sides could agree a settlement that would stop the terrible things that are going on.'

Jane was learning to read between the lines and recognised immediately that Caroline had not answered her question. It registered in her mind.

The three talked intensely and at a great pace. It transpired that Mrs Fichardt was a wealthy widow, her husband having built up one of the largest farm-supply companies in the Orange River area. He had died some two years earlier from a heart attack. Many of their friends were farmers or ranchers and nearly all had now been displaced. 'It makes me weep to hear of the conditions the women and children are in, not just here in Bloemfontein,' Caroline said angrily.

'We have been trying to find out how many camps there are but have not had much success,' said Emily.

'They are opening new camps all the time,' Caroline replied. 'Kitchener is being far more aggressive than Roberts. I am told that in the north they are simply rounding up everybody and burning all the farms, not just the farms of known Boer fighters. The conditions in the camps are dreadful and people are dying.' She spoke with a strange mixture of sadness and anger, resolve and despair. 'It's the young children who are suffering most. They are too weak to fight off disease.'

Emily and Jane had not heard these views expressed with such obvious anger before. In comparison, the ladies in Cape Town now seemed to be just concerned humanitarians, decent Christian people doing the right thing. Caroline came across as someone who wanted to go much further than simply handing out food and clothes or ensuring prisoners were well treated. She had fire in her belly, and was angry that she lacked the means to do anything about the cruelties she believed were being unjustly perpetrated.

'The least I can do is to offer you accommodation at my home whilst you are in Bloemfontein,' Caroline went on. 'But I am afraid to do so unless General Pretyman authorises it. You don't want to get on the wrong side of him.'

'Well, I will go and see him now,' Emily said. 'Jane, can you get some clothes for me as well? No time to lose.'

***

When Emily came back that afternoon, she seemed bright and confident. 'I got on well with him. He is from Cornwall and our families know of each other. That helped, but he does not care for Caroline. His face turned very sour when I said we were intending to stay at the Fichardt house.'

'Really?' said Jane, wanting to hear more.

'Yes. He sees her as a Boer supporter and very bitter.'

'Perhaps we should stay somewhere else.' Jane was nervous about appearing to be on the side of the enemy, and deep down she was uncertain about Caroline. Jane was clear that she was for England; she did not want to be thought of in any way as someone who acted against British troops or interests. It had never crossed her mind that helping women and children was anything more than that.

'It's all right. Pretyman came round when I said that maybe Caroline would be less bitter after we had stayed with her.'

Jane thought about this for a few moments and then said, 'Depends on what we tell her once we've seen for ourselves what the conditions are like.'

'Perhaps, but for the moment General Pretyman is on our side. Not only that, he is going to have two soldiers help us get the trucks to the camp. Did you get some clothes?' Emily asked, looking down at her own dirty dress.

'Yes, I hope they are all right. They are in your room.'

Later that day a carriage came to the hotel and took them to Kya Lami, Caroline Fichardt's home. The house and grounds were very grand: imposing, yet welcoming. The sweeping drive, lined by white-painted stones, could well have been in Hampshire but the wonderful tall podocarpaceae and ocotea trees towering into the air, their tops lost in the brilliance of the sky, were authentic South African. Xerophyta bushes interspersing the taller trees radiated a brilliant lilac blue and drew the eye to a spectacular display of bolusanthus, which marked the end of the drive that opened out into a gravel courtyard.

As the carriage stopped in front of the veranda of the colonial house, the doors were opened. Black servants, immaculately but informally dressed in blue trousers and white shirts, helped them down. As they entered the hallway, their eyes were drawn to the stunning marble floors that provided welcome coolness, as did the ornate shuttering on the windows.

In her room, as Jane placed her things on the sumptuous bed with its crisp linen sheets, she wondered if this was the norm for European families in this part of South Africa. Whatever misgivings she had about Caroline, it was certainly a very comfortable place for them to base themselves.

The gardens were large and colourful and, for the first time in many days, Jane was reminded of home. There was a large number of gardeners, all black, who seemed to melt into the background as she strolled the grounds before dinner. Sweeping lawns, wonderfully green, had what appeared to be yew trees providing shimmering shade. Rich borders of deep-red and yellow daises, red-hot pokers and tall grasses merged seamlessly into the lushness of the lawns.

The garden's appeal for Jane lay not just in its intrinsic beauty, its softness and its shade, but the contrast it provided with the harsh, barren earth of the world outside its gates and walls. It was indeed an oasis of tranquillity. In days to come, Jane found it hard to reconcile the difference between this heavenly spot, which she would have been happy to call home, with the altogether less appealing sights in the camps.

The next morning Emily and Jane were taken down by carriage to the goods yard where the trucks had been left. They had been told that there would be two soldiers at the yard office at ten a.m. who, if they introduced themselves and showed the pass General Pretyman had provided, would take them the three miles out of town to the Bloemfontein camp.

When Jane and Emily arrived, the two soldiers were waiting. After some difficulty understanding what they were saying, so broad were their Geordie accents, they all boarded the first truck and set off.

It was slow going; the roads were bumpy and stony and there were many deep ruts where heavy, horse-drawn goods carriages had repeatedly been driven. The heat was oppressive even at that time of day and there was no shade.

'Wish we had an umbrella,' said Jane.

Emily made no comment, looking intently ahead.

At last they came to the top of a long low hill that looked out over what seemed to be hundreds of miles of flat plain.

There were no trees and little vegetation, only occasional small clumps of grass on the yellowish-red earth.

The only thing that intruded on the vastness of the plain was the whiteness of the hundreds of bell tents that were pitched in uniform rows. Immediately in front of these tents were three larger buildings with flat walls and roofs. 'Hospital,' said the squaddie.

Even though there were hundreds of tents, they appeared like white ants stuck on a giant yellow canvas. The lack of fences, trees or bushes added to the feeling of openness and space. But it was not a kindly space; it appeared unforgiving and bleak.

The trucks eased their way down the gentle slope towards the camp. As they neared the camp gates, details came into focus. Groups of women were bunched around the entrance to some of the tents and many small children were sitting strangely still and quiet. Each row of tents had been given a name, Kent, Sussex, Hampshire and so on, and these signs were painted roughly on white canvas sheets.

The hospital buildings were made of corrugated iron, as were the camp office and store. Emily and Jane felt hundreds of eyes looking at them as they made their way to the camp office and introduced themselves to the commandant, Captain Nelson. He was tall, well over six feet, with a square chin and a thin wispy moustache that did not fit well with his face.

His right hand was heavily bandaged; as he approached the two ladies, he went to offer his hand to shake and then withdrew it, shrugging his shoulders and smiling. 'Cut myself on my own sword. Nearly lost my hand. Still, mustn't grumble. Would you like something to drink or eat?'

'We would like to talk to some of the women first,' Emily said. 'We want to find out what they need.'

'That's fine. Feel free to walk around. Do you want me to unload the trucks?'

'Would you mind if we walked around first?' Emily asked.

Jane and Emily spent the next three hours walking among the tents, down Kent Avenue, up Sussex Drive and back down Hampshire Avenue. What they discovered was shocking, even though they had been prepared by the many reports that had filtered back to England and by the strong views expressed by the committee members in Cape Town.

They sat in the tents, talking as best they could to the Boer women including a Mrs Raal, a Mrs Roux and a Mrs Pienaar, among many others whose names they could not remember. They remembered these names because all three women told them they had 'lost two children' whilst in the camp.

At first Jane thought the children had literally been lost and it took some time for it to dawn that 'lost' meant dead. The matter-of-fact way the women described their loss was quite staggering.

It was only over the course of the next few hours that Jane and Emily came to understand how these women, these mothers, could be so phlegmatic. What these mothers had learnt from misery and grief was that wailing and lamentation would not improve their situation. They had to think first of their children who were still alive; they had to give them hope, keep their spirits up, to think of tomorrow and not today. They were trying, but the effort exhausted even the fittest and bravest of them; outward signs of emotion, other than cuddling their children, were a waste of precious energy. What they struggled most with was the relentlessness of the misery and the fact that there was no end in sight.

Mrs Raal spoke just like all the women, in an expressionless heavily accented voice.

'We all fear more deaths. We can do nothing about the conditions. During the day the burning heat inside the tents makes them unbearable, yet outside there is no shade. We either boil inside or burn outside. At night the temperature drops below freezing and we don't have enough blankets. Most of us don't even have a bed. We sleep on the floor. If it rains, the water sweeps off the hard ground into the tents, wetting everything; if it rains for more than a few minutes, the water penetrates the canvas and flows down the inside of the tents.'

She did not speak with bitterness or anger or despair or even submission, but rather with resignation and the acceptance of the inevitable. There was still pride, effort and fortitude simmering underneath the lid of oppression.

'Do you have enough to eat?' asked Emily.

'We receive food rations twice a week,' she replied. 'The problem is not the amount — we are not expecting luxury or even home comforts — but in what we can do with it. The meat comes raw, uncooked. We have flour for bread and biscuits, tea and coffee, lentils and oats, but we have no wood to light fires or to burn on the few stoves we have. Most days, we have no means to cook.'

As she spoke, Jane looked around. The raw meat was attracting thousands of flies and the inside of the tents was covered in a moving, black, noisy wallpaper that frequently leapt and swirled and enmeshed anyone unlucky enough to be in its path.

Mrs Raal noticed Jane's watching the flies. 'The flies bite, they cause sores and spread disease. We would probably be better off without the meat,' she said.

Jane and Emily found the women's stoicism truly remarkable, but it was the weariness and the pain on the blackened faces that brought tears to their eyes. These women's farms were burnt; they had no animals for fresh meat, eggs or milk. They did not know where their husbands or brothers were.

It was, though, the suffering of the children that hit the hardest. The children, deprived of all stimulation, cold then hot, scared and starving, were often too weak to eat and susceptible to all manner of illness, particularly typhoid. They lay around the tents with nowhere to go and nothing to do, weak and demoralised. The mothers tried their best to offer stimulation, encouragement and hope but, one by one, day by day, they saw their children collapse then be taken to the camp hospital where the sole nurse, a badly overworked Boer girl of Jane's age, fought a losing battle to bring some comfort.

After three hours of listening and asking questions, Jane and Emily could take no more.

'Let's go, Jane,' said Emily. 'I think we have seen enough. I am so angry that we British can be doing this. I am at a loss as to how we can call ourselves Christian if we treat people in this way. What is worse is that all the stores we have brought will not make any difference. These women need wood, shelter and mesh to keep the flies away. They need tinned food, not clothes.'

As they walked back to see Nelson, Jane said, 'This cannot be right. These people are all going to die if nothing is done.'

'It isn't right, it's an outrage,' said Emily, fighting hard to remain composed.

It was mid-afternoon and the sun was bleaching the fabric of their dresses. Their skin was already burnt and beginning to smart. The backs of their necks had been exposed the most; the necklines of the dresses Jane had bought in Bloemfontein the day before exposed only a few inches of skin, but the sun attacked any chink with venom. They had been sitting on the ground, talking to the women with their backs to the sun; the exposed skin on the backs of their necks had suffered an unrelenting attack and was already sore. It would get much worse.

'Are all the camps like this?' Emily asked Captain Nelson pointedly.

'I don't know. This is the only one I have been to,' came the reply.

'Well, are you happy with the conditions? Is this what you want?'

'We are doing our best in the circumstances,' he said, offering two large glasses of water to the parched English ladies. 'There are simply too many refugees for us to cope with.'

'We understand there are two thousand here alone,' said Jane. 'Can they not be moved further south? It's much cooler there. Or allowed back to their farms? Some have told us their farms are still intact.'

'Miss, I don't make the policy. You will need to see Kitchener, not me,' Captain Nelson replied.

'We will,' said Emily angrily.

Captain Nelson sighed and sat back. He looked over the heads of his two flustered, hot, unwanted visitors. 'If I could offer a little advice... I am sure you are well meaning and have decent, honourable intentions. Personally, I share your view: I think these camps are a mistake and will do us no good in the long term. But they are here, and it will not help your cause to fall out with junior officers. You need to work with us, not attack us.' He stopped and looked into Jane and Emily's faces. 'I will work with you and help where I can, but we have to work with what we have.'

The women looked at each other. They did not want confrontation; they simply wanted to help women and children whose conditions had to be experienced to be understood.

It was Jane who spoke first. 'You are right, Captain Nelson. Our intentions are honourable and we have come simply to help. Any assistance you can give us will be greatly appreciated.'

Emily said nothing, her mind having already moved on. She realised the hopelessness of the cause if there was no end to the policy of concentrating the women and children in camps.

Jane's intervention, made without reference to Emily, was an important event in their relationship. It marked the first time Jane felt sufficiently confident to speak up before her friend. Up to that point, she had been guarded, at times uncertain, always conscious of her lack of experience. She now realised that she had an invaluable role to play; her friendship with Emily had reached the point where she knew Emily's views without being told.

The intervention also marked the point where Emily focussed her attention not just on the distribution of goods to the needy but on solving the underlying cause.

They agreed with Captain Nelson that the trucks would be unloaded and that the women in the camp should be asked how best to distribute the food and clothes. What they had not anticipated was that the wooden packing cases, in which the goods had been carefully stored, would prove to be the most sought-after items. Within minutes, the cases were being broken up and chopped into kindling for cooking fires. Each small piece of kindling was treated like gold dust; each avenue agreed to have just one fire and to cook with as few pots as possible.

In the next few days Jane, in particular, was to learn lessons from the pragmatism of the Boer women that would prove invaluable as she visited other camps.

They journeyed back to Kya Lami in silence, exhausted physically and emotionally. They left the two Geordie soldiers at the rail depot where Caroline's carriage was waiting for them. They soon found themselves in their rooms, stripped to the waist and washing in cool, freshly drawn water. At first Jane luxuriated in its coldness, repeatedly lifting the water with her hands to her face and shoulders. She gently dabbed the back of her neck and tried, without success, to see how burnt she was by bending and turning in front of the small mirror on her dressing table. After many minutes she sat on the bed and dried herself, not just her face and shoulders but also her eyes from which tears of incomprehension were seeping silently and continuously down her cheeks.

They said little at first to Caroline; they described the camp and how it was laid out, the numbers of 'refugees', Captain Nelson and his views that the camps were a mistake, the heat and lack of shade. They did not, however, detail the horror of the flies, the lack of beds and bedding, the spread of disease, the overworked nurse, and the baleful, drawn look of the disconsolate and dejected children. They were mindful of General Pretyman and did not want to give him any more ammunition by stoking fires within Caroline.

Over dinner and breakfast the next day, they began to put together a plan as to how they could best help the thousands of women and children in the camps. It was now clear to them that the problem was much greater than they had realised and it was getting bigger every day; more farms were being burnt and more land cordoned off so that it was impossible for the Boer commanders to revisit and stock up on supplies. The magnitude of the scale of the British military operation was far beyond what they had expected, as was its ruthlessness.

'We cannot hope to visit all the camps,' said Jane. 'There are simply too many. We can't get into the ones in the Transvaal, or even the ones north of Bloemfontein. And even if we could, what can we do? The supplies we could give out would make no real difference.'

'They would make a difference to those who got the food and clothes. Every bit helps,' said Caroline.

They were sitting on the veranda after breakfast; the garden, with its soft sweeping lines, drew the eye forward across the manicured lawn to the tall bushes that guided the eyes to the right, where the garden path slithered through a yew hedge and on out of sight. An unattended wheelbarrow provided a focal point as the path disappeared.

'It's so green and soft,' said Jane. 'It's hard to imagine that just four miles from here the land is so harsh and open and stretches for what looks like hundreds of miles with no trees. I agree that some could benefit, but this land in its vastness reflects the scale of the problem.'

Emily raised her head at this comment. She had been reading a letter from Catherine Courtney, which had arrived from home that morning. She could see before her eyes that Jane was growing in understanding, in ambition and in practicality.

'Catherine Courtney says the committee have transferred more than £2,000 to the account in Cape Town and this will now be transferred to Caroline here in Bloemfontein,' said Emily. 'We can use this money to stock up the trucks and we can go to any camps, as long as they are not further north. I think we should give out as much as we can but, whilst doing this, gather as much information as we can about the camps and the plight of the poor people. We will send this information back home, with photographs, and campaign at the highest levels to get Kitchener's policy changed. We can go back to England and support the campaign both in raising money and awareness. Jane is right: we cannot make much difference here on our own. Whatever we do will simply be a drop in the ocean. Our efforts now have to be about getting the policy changed.'

There was general agreement about this and the next few days were spent in a hectic schedule of sourcing goods, particularly food that did not need cooking: tinned food, corned beef, fish, jam, biscuits. They bought firewood and whatever medicines they could find.

'I wish I knew more about medicine,' said Jane to Emily as they came out of the only pharmacy store in Bloemfontein. 'I really don't know what we should be looking for.'

'Me too,' said Emily. 'We could do with a doctor on our team.'

Chapter 12
Kya Lami

On the morning of the 10th of February 1901, Jane and Emily set off to visit Norval Pont and Aliwal North camps. They were better organised this time, more prepared both mentally and physically, having been well rested in the wonderful luxury of Caroline Fichardt's home.

Jane's suspicion of Caroline was weakening by the day and she had started to warm to her. She had noticed that underneath the tough front that Caroline presented there was a hidden warmth and genuineness. It was kept in the background but was nevertheless an ever-present component of her makeup.

Jane first saw it when Caroline noticed that one of the gardeners had cut his knee on a sharp shrub. She immediately went inside and came out with a bowl of water and some bandages. She personally washed the knee of the black gardener, Philip, and wrapped the bandage round his knee. 'Don't be so careless in future or your leg might have to come off,' she said, in a feigned show of disapproval.

Caroline's underlying sensitivity surfaced again that same evening when she asked if Jane had heard anything from her father. Caroline was aware of his difficulties, as Jane had confided that she was worried what state the estate at home would be in when she got back.

'If only we had a good manager to look after things,' she said wistfully. 'Maybe Father would listen to a man.'

'Does he need to listen?' Caroline asked perceptively, sensing that all was not well at Lainston House.

Jane opened up, telling of her father's problems; she was clearly still upset when she recounted that her father had not said goodbye to her when she left for South Africa. Neither had he replied to the two letters she had sent him since leaving.

A few days after this conversation, Caroline asked if there was any news from home. 'Not yet,' said Jane.

'I shall pray for your father and the family well-being,' Caroline said, putting her arm round Jane's shoulder as they walked into the garden.

The lack of news from home had initially not been a problem for Jane. The excitement of the trip, the adventure, the new surroundings, new faces, being busy, all helped suppress the longing for even a morsel of news from her father. She had exchanged a number of letters with Lilly in which she described in detail the days in South Africa, the people and the countryside. She had not spelt out the horrors of the camp at Bloemfontein but had given sufficient clues for Lilly to ask searching questions. In return, Jane had asked Lilly if she had news of her father and was now eagerly awaiting the response. The sense of hurt at not having anything from home grew and was beginning to gnaw and corrode her self-esteem. What had she done wrong?

She dashed off a letter to Lilly explaining that they would be away for what might be a couple of weeks visiting more camps and distributing clothes and food. She would not be able to pick up mail but was eager for news of home.

She also took the unusual step of writing to Mrs Squires at Lainston House. It was a short letter, explaining where she was and what she and Emily were doing, then asking how everything was back at home, explaining that she had not had any letters from her father.

Jane gave the letters to Caroline and asked if she would post them.

'Of course,' Caroline replied. 'They will go today.' Looking at the letters, she saw that they were both addressed to Hampshire and one to Lainston House. 'I did pray,' she said. 'Chin up.' Such a simple remark from an upright, proud woman had an immediately uplifting effect on Jane; she was more alert when she got into the carriage, and her inner self-doubt was replaced by pragmatic optimism.

The journey to Norval Pont was just over 200 miles and was far from pleasant. The train was overcrowded, hot and dirty. Guerrilla attacks on the line resulted in frequent delays as the track, which had been blown up, had to be replaced. Twice they passed trains that had been attacked and set on fire. Jane and Emily were scared, constantly on edge, thinking that they might be attacked, injured or killed. They tried to make light of it.

'Are you a good shot Jane?' Emily asked, with a smile on her face.

'Don't joke, Emily. I can't help being afraid.'

'We all are,' replied Emily. 'At least you will be able to jump on a horse and ride away to safety. I am a hopeless rider!'

For much of the journey the bald-headed guard, a measly shrivelled specimen about fifty years of age, who wiped his nose constantly on a grubby rag, let them sit in his van as all the carriages were grossly overcrowded with soldiers. The van was cramped and full of paraphernalia, and he made things much worse by frequently reminding his only female passengers how many trains had been attacked in the last year.

Both Emily and Jane were deeply suspicious of him. He shuffled around, much too close for their liking, and he smelt dreadful. The only mitigating factor that made his company remotely endurable was the fact that the van had a toilet, for which they were grateful. Their experience on opening the toilet doors in the carriage had made Jane physically sick; even Emily turned away in disgust at the revolting sight.

When they reached Norval Pont, they discovered that there was no town or village. It was simply a railway junction on the south side of the Orange River. The camp had been set up on open land just a mile away from the station stop. It was sited on land that sloped gradually down to the river, beyond which, in the distance, there were a number of small hills. On the far horizon high peaks shimmered in the fierce heat.

They had great difficulty getting the truck unloaded from the train; they simply did not have the strength to undo the fastenings and could get no one to help. Their frustration quickly turned to panic as the train began to move off. The screams of 'Stop! Stop the train!' from a hysterical Emily secured the immediate attention of a British officer on horseback who, quickly sizing up the situation, galloped up to the front of the train and rode alongside the engine, shouting at the driver to stop. Emily and Jane were more than grateful for this same officer ordering a very reluctant group of squaddies to help get the truck off the train.

Having had the truck rescued from imminent disappearance, they were forced to leave it by the side of the track and were deeply worried for its safety. The screams, shouting and general hullabaloo had attracted the attention of every petty official in the area and they were taken, in a none-too-friendly fashion to the camp commandant, by what they judged to be the most ignorant soldier they had ever met.

From that moment on, Jane and Emily were met by scores of petty officials or junior NCOs who were either incredulous that two English ladies were out in the Karoo at the height of summer, or deeply suspicious of their motives. At every turn they had to produce passes and letters of authority; even those from Kitchener and Milner were inspected and turned over time and time again by disbelieving interrogators.

However, Captain du Plat, the camp commandant, turned out to be the very opposite. Suave, well-spoken and considerate, he soon had Emily and Jane drinking lemonade in his tent and offered them any help he could. His tent was large and obviously used as a meeting area as well as his private quarters. It had a large table and six chairs; at the far end was a canvas sheet that marked the demarcation with his private quarters. The heat inside the tent was almost unbearable, and there was fine dust covering everything that made everyone immediately feel dirty.

As at Bloemfontein, Jane and Emily walked around the camp talking to the women. It was soon clear that things were well organised and conditions were altogether better. The river was used solely for bathing and washing clothes; times were strictly allocated for adults or children to bathe, and separate times allocated for washing clothes. Drinking water came from a spring nearby and there was plenty of fresh, clean, cold water for everyone in the camp.

The mood, as well as the physical environment, was quite different. The women were angry at being 'imprisoned' as they termed it, but they did not have the dejected, pathetic faces of the Bloemfontein women, and the children were far from lifeless. They were occupied every day with school, organised games, and in helping bring water to the camp.

It was a much happier Emily and Jane who settled down that night into a tent made available for them by Captain du Plat. They had eaten in the camp mess, discussed the war, how long it would go on and its lasting effects. They had been offered advice on where they should go and assistance in bringing the truck to the camp.

'Let's not leave it overnight at the station,' said Captain du Plat. 'I will have it brought up here. In the morning you can organise how the goods should be distributed.'

'What a difference between here and Bloemfontein,' said Emily. 'I really believe that here we can make a difference.'

'We need to make a list of all the reasons that make this camp so much better. Then we can try and ensure that they adopt them in all the camps,' replied Jane.

'You will need to create a new list in your book,' Emily said in a friendly, mocking manner.

Jane's lists had become a standing joke between them but now Emily, as much as Jane, relied on ticking off items in order to measure progress.

'We can start now and the first item will be beds,' said Jane. 'All the tents have beds and the women and children are not lying on the hard or wet ground.'

'And item two is the water,' interrupted Emily. 'Separate bathing and drinking water.'

They went on for an hour, adding and adding to the list. They were excited, prodding each other to think of one more point. Who would have thought, as they dined in Claridge's, that a few weeks later they would be sharing a tent in the desert, unwashed and dirty and surrounded by soldiers and prisoners? They slept soundly that night.

In the morning they woke and went outside the tent, emerging into bright sunlight which had them shielding their eyes. As their focus adjusted, they noticed long lines of women down by the river, undressing and walking into the water to bathe. Emily and Jane looked at each other, both clearly thinking that they would love to bathe in the cool water. The train journey had been horrible; their hair was matted, and they had slept in the clothes they were wearing.

'Yes,' said Emily, 'we must.'

They rushed down to the riverbank and quickly undressed, joining hundreds of other women. There was no embarrassment, just utter bliss as they ducked their heads under the water. One of the Boer women came up and offered them a bar of soap.

'Soap,' said Jane. 'That's for the list as well.' It was the first time that she had ever been naked in front of other people.

The morning was busily spent unpacking the truck and working with four or five of the women to decide which of the goods had the highest priority and how to distribute them amongst the 1,500 refugees in the camp.

'It's no wonder they are so bitter,' said Jane. 'The woman in that tent, over there,' she pointed at a tent about fifty yards away. 'She was not allowed to bring anything whatsoever. The only things these women have are the clothes they were wearing at the time they were moved out. Not only have they nothing here, but they have nothing back at their home as the farm was burnt down. She said the aarmy said they were giving assistance to the Boer commandoes but that was a lie.'

'A lie?' said Emily.

'That's what she said,' replied Jane.

They stayed another night. They washed the clothes they were wearing, having taken a change of clothes from the supplies they had brought to give out. Jane felt strangely guilty about doing this, wondering if it was theft. It was not just the change of clothes that worried her but the relative orderliness of the Norval Pont camp and the well-being of the refugees. If the other camps were like this and not like Bloemfontein, then maybe the internment policy could be justified.

She made the mistake of saying so to Emily. 'Maybe things are not as bad as we feared. Everything seems in good order here.'

Emily scowled instantly. 'Good order? I don't call imprisoning civilians, burning their homes and making children live in these dreadful tents good order.'

It was the first time they had ever differed or exchanged contrary views. Jane, ever seeking to avoid confrontation and not wanting in any way to seem to be at odds with Emily, immediately retracted. 'Oh yes, I agree. I was simply meaning relative to Bloemfontein.' Nevertheless, she felt chastised, and for the next hour or so she was guarded in what she said.

Captain du Plat provided them with a pass for travel to Aliwal North camp. When he handed it over, he said it was one of the largest camps and growing rapidly. He made a point which neither Jane or Emily had considered. 'The people in the camp at Bloemfontein are Boers; they have been moved because they are considered to have been helping the insurgents. The people in this camp have, in the main, come because they fear attack from the Boers. The camp at Aliwal will be full of people who also fear the Boers and feel they need protection. Other camps in the Cape Colony will be full of Dutch speakers. The army think of Dutch speakers as the enemy. They can't get their mind around the fact that speaking a different language is not a sign of guilt. Dutch speakers are therefore seen as people who are already helping the enemy, or who would help them if they got the chance. I sometimes think our policy and actions are making it a self-fulfilling prophecy; the more we destroy their homes, the more likely they are to become our enemy.'

'I wonder if that explains the difference between the conditions we have seen,' said Jane.

'We shall see,' Emily responded. There was a slight hint in her reply that she was not going to allow any wavering on Jane's part.

The journey to Aliwal was horrendous and at times the pair seriously questioned the wisdom of what they were doing. Mentally Emily was the stronger of the two. She was intent on gathering information that she could take back to England and use to get the policy of concentrating civilians in camps ended. She was already fully aware that giving food or clothes out would make no meaningful difference, but she needed a reason to travel in the military zones.

Jane, though, was not on the same page as Emily; whilst she was desperately keen to be thought of as useful, supportive and caring, she was not thinking of the bigger picture but rather the opposite. Her mind, in the tedious hours spent sitting at railway sidings in the boiling sun, always moved to the suffering of the individuals she talked to in the camps. She genuinely felt for them and, in her darkest moments, she could not escape the image of the lifeless children lying idly and forlornly in the camp at Bloemfontein.

It took them two days to reach the remote and inconsequential Aliwal North. They endured severe privation, lack of food, water and sleeping accommodation. The trains were dirty and the stops lacked any toilet facilities. They were depressed, hungry, dirty and worn out when they arrived at Aliwal. What they found there was a mirror image of Norval Pont and once again they questioned why they had come all this way to see more of the same.

They were well received by the camp commandant, Major Apthope, who did his very best to make Jane and Emily comfortable. He cleared out a large tent and provided linen, water and soap. He gave them both nurses' uniforms so that they could change and wash the clothes they had been wearing.

Aliwal was not a prison and the people there were free to go into town and buy provisions, if they could find any to buy. They could use the post office and communicate with the outside world. It was just as Captain du Plat had indicated: these people had come into the camp of their own volition, and they were treated as well as resources allowed.

'I think they have deliberately sent us here,' said Emily. 'They want us to think that these camps are nothing like the stories we have heard.'

Jane was about to say that she thought that was a bit harsh but she bit her tongue, remembering Emily's reaction the last time she had shown anything but total opposition to the camps. She allowed a few minutes to go before saying, 'They still need soap and fuel, and there is no food for them to buy.'

They talked to as many women as they could, took photographs and distributed clothes and tinned foods, which were well received, especially the jams. Most of the women were thrilled that two English gentlewomen had come out to help and seemed genuinely pleased with the support Emily and Jane could offer. Even so, when the two friends started their journey back, they were in a reflective mood.

'What do you think we have achieved?' asked Emily, staring out of the carriage window.

'Well, we have helped quite a lot of people. Hundreds now have better clothes and the tinned food must really have helped,' said Jane.

'Yes, that's true, but there are thousands and thousands in the camps and we have not been to the ones in the north.'

It was a mightily relieved pair of anything but gentle-looking upper-class Englishwomen who arrived back at Caroline Flichart's house three days later.

Caroline was aghast when she saw them and quickly ushered them into the house. 'Good grief, you look absolutely exhausted! You need to get to bed straight away.'

'Not before we have drunk a gallon of lemonade and eaten everything you have,' said Emily.

'Oh, have you had nothing all day?' Caroline asked.

Jane, running her fingers through her dust-covered, matted hair and looking down at her filthy dress, replied matter-of-factly, her voice lacking any emotion, 'Not for two days. The army are on the move, marching in thousands in long columns and I am afraid we were in the way. Apparently, from what little we could pick up, Kitchener has ordered a major assault on the Cape Colony and is determined to catch De Witt and the other Boer leaders.'

'At least you are back safe and uninjured. I don't suppose the army wanted to be bothered with you if they had other things on their mind.' Caroline took large jugs of lemonade from a tray brought in by a very young black girl.

'The soldiers don't want women at all — unless they are injured in hospital and then they are more than happy for us girls to look after them.' Emily screwed her face as she emphasised the words 'us girls'. 'Do you know, if the world was turned upside down and generals were women and men did the nursing, I am not sure there would be any wars. They would not be able to stand the sight of what war meant. It would no longer be a game.'

Emily was tired but angry, and her bitterness, which had been brewing for days, was coming to the boil. She continued. 'Do you know, they would not let us on one train which was the last out of Norval Pont yesterday, even though there was room? "Don't want the chaps distracted," was what one pompous twit of an officer said. We had to sit all night in a filthy shed being bitten by horrible insects with nothing to eat or drink.'

'At least you did what you set out to do. You visited two more camps and gave out the food and clothes. It was not a waste of time,' said Caroline.

'They deliberately sent us to the camps that are the best organised and have plenty of clean water. There was no disease, like there is up the road. The commandant of Norval Pont more or less admitted that.' Emily was leaning forward tapping the arm of her chair in quite an animated manner. Her tiredness was no match for the intensity of the opposition she felt for the army's strategy. 'I know people in the army think that we are supporting the enemy but we are not. All I see is that we are destroying the very thing we want to keep.' Her voice was full of emotion, rising and falling with every point.

Caroline could see that although Emily was full of adrenalin, Jane was exhausted, withdrawn and uneasy. She sought to move the conversation on. 'Your letters back home, Emily, are having quite an effect. The committee in Cape Town received another £2,000 yesterday and £1,000 whilst you were away. This is on top of the money in the bank when you left. You will be able to really stock up and plan where you would like to go next. If the army is really on the move, it might not be easy. In any event, you need to rest for a few days.'

'Is there any mail for me?' asked Jane softly. It was a plaintive cry, drawn from the depths of her inner self. She was not asking in anticipation that there would be any mail, nor was there any sign of nervousness over what the answer might be. This was not a ritualistic enquiry of no real significance, being asked for the sake of appearance; it was the real Jane with her heart on her sleeve. However undemonstrative its delivery, the question sought the slightest morsel of affection from her only known relative.

The manner and timing of its delivery, amidst the tales of war and soldiers and privations and politics, when she was tired beyond sleep, summed up Jane. The caring, sensitive girl, now caught up in events that she struggled to understand, asked the question that meant most to her. She had heard that there was more money; she had heard the emotional cries of defiance and of reason from Emily, and she had framed responses to them all. But what came out was not what her conscious mind was guiding her towards, but what her moral core implored her to ask. The despair of the women in the camps, the lifeless children, the illness and the deaths, had simply reinforced her view that, above all, family ties had the strongest knots. Seeing so much suffering brought home to her the lack of true affection in her life.

'Yes, there are two letters, Jane. They are in your room,' said Caroline.

They went to their rooms. Jane decided she would bathe and change before opening her mail. She did not recognise the writing on one of the envelopes but noticed that the postmark was from Oxford. The second letter was clearly from Lilly.

She sank into the bath and closed her eyes. As she wiped the dust and dirt from her face, she could not help but think of the women in the Bloemfontein camp and the impossibility of them ever lying full length in a bath in such tranquillity.

When she had dried herself and dressed, she felt composed and ready to open the letters. She held each one, weighing which to open first. She found it a remarkably difficult choice; she did not realise it, but her tiredness was making even the simplest of tasks challenging. For no reason that she could remember afterwards, she opened first the one from Oxford.

It took her some time to register who it was from and even more to take in what it was saying. She re-read it three times. It was not long, just one and a half pages, but its content was unexpected and she needed to understand it fully. She began to think she was too tired to take it on board.

She opened the second letter, the one from Lilly, with a mixture of hope, dread and resignation. What news would it contain — good or bad?

The letter was short, just two pages, but it did contain news of her father. Lilly said she had decided that direct action was needed and called at Lainston House. She had called twice, in fact; the first time Jane's father was not in. The second time Lilly had told him that Jane was upset at not having seen him before she left or having heard from him since. Lilly said she had told him that Jane was fine and in good health. Jane re-read the next few lines:

Jane, you will not be able to guess what happened next. He sat down and said, 'I am trying to appear tough, hard, as though I don't care. But I do. Jane leaving has made me think about my own behaviour. I have been trying to write but I cannot get the words out. I did not want to make things worse. Will you tell her I hope she is well and I am thinking of her?'

Jane, I gave him a hug and said how much that would mean to you.

Even Lilly did not know how much it meant. There were no tears, no sobs or shouts of joy. Jane stood in front of the mirror and raised her chin. 'Chin up,' she said to herself, taking a deep breath and slowly allowing a huge beam to light up her face.

She went back to the first letter. It was from the Reverend Shell. It enquired about her, hoped that all was well and that she was finding her work useful and rewarding. It went on to say that he had decided to leave Sparsholt and take up an appointment with the East Africa Missionary Society. He would be based for the first few months in Oxford so he could better understand the aims and ways of the society, but then he would be taking up work in Kenya. He ended with the sentence Jane had struggled with:

When you are back in England, do feel at liberty to contact me. I would so much like the chance to hear of your adventures and hopefully you will be interested in mine.

Your true friend
George

Was this as innocent as it sounded or was he really indicating more? Jane, heartened by the news from Lilly, looked more

127

carefully at the letter. It was addressed to Miss Jane Dunhaughton, Care of Mrs Catherine Flichart, Bloemfontein, Cape Colony, South Africa. How did Reverend Shell know she was at this address? Lilly had not said that she had told him.

'Why me?' she said to herself. 'I have nobody asking me to functions or writing to me other than George Shell. She felt uncomfortable as she thought of him. The way he closed his eyes and looked away when talking, was very off-putting. She could not imagine spending any length of time with him.

She was still puzzling over how he knew the address as she went downstairs and met Caroline on the veranda. 'Do have a gin, Jane. It will do you good. Was it good news?' Caroline asked in her no-nonsense way.

'It was. My good friend Lilly Baring called round to see Father and he is well and apologised for not writing. But he said he was thinking of me.' Jane gave a huge sigh of relief. 'From what Lilly said, my leaving may have had just the effect I was hoping for.'

'That's good, really good,' said Caroline. 'Well, now you can have a large gin!'

The next few days were spent recovering strength and energy, writing letters and planning what to do next. No garden could have had better restorative qualities. Jane became familiar with all its nooks and crannies. She moved round with the sun, marvelling at the design and how the size and shape of the plants wonderfully complemented one another, no matter the time of day. The abundance of colours from the dianthus, snapdragons and belladonna merged perfectly with the evergreen camellias and strelitzias. Nowhere was the heat from the sun overpowering and shade-loving plants thrived. In the evenings, the veranda became the gathering spot; the day's progress was recorded and the plan for the next day or days mapped out.

It was agreed that they would make a trip to the Cape Colony. They would need to travel back to Norval Pont and then on to Naaupoort, where they would catch a train to Kimberley. Going back to Norval Pont filled them with dread but there was no alternative. It was, according to Caroline, the hub of the rail network in the Cape Colony and all trains passed through or started there.

They were uncertain as to how difficult travel would be in the Orange River Colony, but they reasoned it could not be worse than in the Cape Colony where they had just been. They could not go north of Bloemfontein, so they either stayed where they were or went west. They chose west, primarily because of Emily's desire to gather as much information on as many camps as was physically possible.

They had filled the trucks with clothes and tinned foods, and had sufficient money to fill half a dozen large packing cases and have them taken to the station ready for loading onto the train. Caroline's servants were a great help, and once again they were grateful to Captain du Plat who made available soldiers to help load the trucks and have them placed on the trains. He updated their passes but, in doing so, advised Emily that things were probably much worse than they had encountered before. The army had been given new orders from Kitchener and was ruthlessly depriving the Boers of land and means of support. It was no longer just Boer farms or Boer sympathisers who were being targeted; all land was being ransacked and made uninhabitable. The Boers were going to be forced to surrender through starvation, deprivation of supplies and contact with their families.

Emily and Jane sat down for dinner with Caroline on the 3rd of March determined to press on — but with a great deal of apprehension.

Chapter 13
For Want of a Donkey

It took eight days for Jane and Emily to reach Kimberley. They were better prepared for the journey this time, with changes of clothing, water in canteens, and some food. Both took lots of paper to write and draw on. They knew the journey would be at best tedious, but was much more likely to be dangerous, unpleasant and deeply boring.

A few hours into the first leg of the journey, Jane tried to sketch the landscape, something she had occasionally done at home. She found the scale, the lack of defining features, the low sparse vegetation and the absence of trees hard to recreate. She found the landscape atmospheric and the animal life scarce; the light was blinding during the day, making it hard to focus for any length of time.

She liked the mornings, despite the crowded train and its uncomfortable carriages. The mornings had a captivating beauty as the plains were slowly opened up and lit by the rising sun. Early morning, with its quite pleasant temperature, lulled the innocent into a false sense of tranquillity, which was sent tumbling into oblivion by mid-morning as the heat rose inexorably. By lunchtime, though, Jane was bored with the same view and frustrated that there would be endless more hours before it would change.

They made a stop at Springfontein, which was nothing more than a railway stop but which had been chosen by the army as a place to base a new camp simply because it was near the railway. They were made welcome by the commandant, Major Gostling. He did all he could to help but the materials he had were woefully short and becoming immeasurably fewer day by day. The apparently endless stream of new arrivals, forcibly transported from their homes on the high veldt, had seen the camp grow from 200 in its first week to 1,200 some six weeks later. The camp, its infrastructure and those sent to work there could not cope; it was clear to Jane and Emily that those in charge had, in reality, given up.

The conditions they discovered were far worse than at Norval Pont or Aliwal. The refugees had nothing, and clothing was terribly short. Some women had taken blankets to use as skirts, and many children had no shoes and badly blistered feet. They seized upon the three cases of clothes that Emily and Jane gave out with a strange, dispirited frenzy. But it was the lack of fuel that was the major problem; there was simply nothing to burn to keep warm at night or to cook with.

Whilst these material privations were upsetting, it was the mindset of the women that made a lasting impression upon Jane and was diligently recorded by Emily. The women were shell-shocked, not literally but in every other sense. The burning of their homes, the forced movement to the camps, had left them paralysed with fear. They were past tears, voiceless.

Jane came to realise what the phrase 'drained of emotion' really meant. It was as though a tap had been applied to the women and left open so that what remained were zombies, walking but barely conscious of the world outside their own bodies. If they did have any emotion, it was used to hide the utter despair that came into their eyes when they heard the pleas of their children for food or relief from the pains they had to endure.

It was not the start Emily and Jane would have liked and things did not improve; they got worse. They travelled further and further into a land of utter destitution, of suffering and illness, of pain and hunger. As they travelled from Springfontein to Naaupoort, then De Aar and Belmont, they passed newly dug graves alongside trenches and ramparts. Major battles had taken place the previous year as the Boers had tried to stop the British army from moving north. There had been little effort to remove the evidence of these futile encounters, both large and small, from the landscape. The noisy train compartments, full of bleary-eyed soldiers, went quiet each time the train, moving at a snail's pace, passed the white crosses, burnt-out waggons and military detritus.

Jane and Emily arrived at Kimberley on the 12th of March 1901.

'It's much bigger than I imagined,' said Jane. 'And more prosperous. Just look at the store over there.' She took Emily's arm and turned her ninety degrees so she was facing a brick-built, three-storey general store.

There were other shops on either side of the street, which ran at right angles to the station. There were numerous offices and a post office. The streets were full of well-dressed women wearing large hats and heavy full skirts, as well as male office workers in suits and formal hats. Delivery men in both horse-drawn waggons and motor waggons were running here and there carrying impossibly large loads.

To Jane's surprise, there were fewer military personnel than she had seen in Cape Town or Bloemfontein but there were large numbers of black males sitting on the pavement in groups, seemingly lost and certainly looking hungry and in need of clothes to replace the rags they were wearing.

Kimberly was booming; it had been built on the back of wealth from diamond mining. 'This reminds me of the American West,' Emily said to Jane. 'The buildings are very similar and about the same age. It has the same busy feel and yet there are lots of people with no work.'

'How do you know?' asked Jane.

'I can see,' said Emily, looking surprised but shifting her eyes towards the groups of black men. 'They are hoping to get work, probably in the mines. The men in Colorado sat around just like this when they had no work.'

'They are all black,' said Jane with naïve innocence.

'Yes. In Colorado they would have been a mixture of whites, Blacks but mainly Chinese,' Emily informed her.

'Chinese?' Jane was puzzled. 'I didn't know there were Chinese in America.'

'There are. Tens of thousands who went firstly to the gold mines in California and then, when they closed down, they moved on to Colorado. I went out to Colorado to help the miners from Cornwall, who had gone out there hoping for a better life. But they, like the Chinese, did not find it. They were exploited and used, and many lost everything.'

'They could not have lost as much as all those poor people in the camps,' said Jane, looking for agreement from Emily.

'No, that's true,' replied Emily. 'But many suffered badly.'

They were able to stay at the Queen's Hotel which, given the discomfort of the last eight days, appeared as would a lifeboat to a shipwrecked seaman. They were overjoyed at the cleanliness, the bedding and the wide choice of food in the restaurant.

In some ways it was hard to recognise that they were in a war zone. Everyday life seemed to be going on as normal. There were business people having meetings, errand boys, women meeting friends. People were, in the main, well dressed and well fed.

They were introduced by the hotel manager, who had been made aware of their arrival by Caroline Fichardt, to a number of local women who did voluntary work at the camp. They had their own committee, which was trying to raise funds, and they marvelled at the amount raised by Emily in London.

'I shall arrange for £500 to be transferred from Cape Town to you here. That should help,' said Emily.

Both Jane and Emily were concerned at the reports provided by these women. 'Conditions are simply appalling. If only people knew how bad they were, or could see the suffering, I am sure it would stop,' said a Mrs Newman, who appeared to be in charge of the volunteers. 'People are dying daily and disease is spreading,' she continued. 'There are too many here and no hospital facilities. They say there is a hospital but it's just a tent where the sick people are taken.'

Jane and Emily agreed to meet Mrs Newman the following morning after breakfast. She was about forty years old. Her husband was a Welsh mining engineer. They had been in Kimberley for three years, but she was unhappy and wanted to get back to England as soon as possible. 'Alun earns very good money and we have a house far better than we could afford at home — with servants — but I can't settle. I miss the greenery and my family.'

Mrs Newman kindly arranged for her own servants to pick up the trucks from the station and take them to the camps. Emily and Jane travelled to the camp with her.

What Mrs Newman and the other Kimberley ladies had told Jane and Emily about the camp was far from encouraging, but it in no way prepared them for the horror of what they discovered.

The camp was just two miles from the town, just two miles from the offices, shops, hotels and obvious prosperity, but it could have been on a different planet. It was situated on a small field of not more than twenty acres, totally surrounded by barbed-wire fencing. There were guards at the gate and patrolling the perimeter.

'Why are there guards and a fence?' asked Jane as they pulled up at the main gate. There had been none at the other camps they had been to.

'We don't know,' replied Mrs Newman. 'It's not as though the people here have anywhere to go. Their homes have been burnt!'

There were more than 1,200 people in the camp. The tents were closely packed together and there did not seem to be any organisation or routine. There was no river to wash in, and no drinking water supply. The toilet facilities were unimaginably filthy.

Mrs Newman introduced Jane to a Mrs Snyman who could speak perfect English and who acted as interpreter as they toured the camp. Emily went off to talk to the commandant and discuss the distribution of foodstuffs and clothes whilst Jane talked to the 'refugees'. It was not easy. The bitterness and hatred of what the English were doing to them kept spilling over.

'You won't believe what they have done to us,' Mrs Snyman said. 'We used to own a farm, a wonderful productive farm, but your army burnt it, burnt it along with the farms of my neighbours. All the animals were killed. Senseless.'

Jane was speechless, not knowing what to say when confronted by first-hand accounts. Nothing in her upbringing had equipped her for suffering on such a scale. She found it hard to reconcile the England she knew — Christian England, love thy neighbour, Good Samaritan England — with the reality of what she was hearing. This was not a newspaper report that could be questioned for bias or impartiality, not a third- or fourth-hand tale from someone who knew someone. This was real, spoken by those personally affected.

Jane knew that affected was not the right word. Traumatised, brutalised, maybe. But for what? What was it that England, her England that she cherished so much, wanted to preserve that it was willing to inflict such suffering? Or did England really know what was going on?

She remembered the hostility of the public meetings back at home, where people did not believe — or did not want to believe — the tales of brutality and suffering. What would they say if they saw and heard what she could now see and hear?

As she toured the camp, hearing more cries of despair and despondency, she wondered if it really was a collective responsibility. Was it really England doing this? No one she knew would support such a policy, she was convinced of that. Could it be an individual's responsibility? Was it Kitchener or Milner, or both?

They stayed at Kimberley for three days. Each day they met with Mrs Newman and Mrs Synman. Jane could not help but compare the two. They were the roughly the same age; they were both intelligent, caring and well read. Mrs Newman was neat and Presbyterian tidy, fresh-faced and lively, a middle-class woman wanting to better herself. Mrs Synman, until a few weeks ago, had been prosperous, wealthy even. She had toured Europe, visited art galleries, churches, castles. She had stayed in the finest of hotels and travelled first class. Now she looked little better than a tramp. Her dress was filthy, her face and hands black from the sun and dirt. Not dirt that could be washed off with a rinse but deeply engrained, dirt that had built up day after day and nothing would remove. No wonder she was bitter.

Emily worked hard to record carefully all that she saw. It was vital to take home to the people of Britain a picture of what Kitchener's policy meant in reality. This was not a war game, where everybody got up after the game was over; people were dying in the Kimberley camp every day. The recording was vital to her, and she was already planning the campaign she would organise and lead when she got back.

Both Jane and Emily did everything they could to mitigate the suffering that they saw. They tried to raise morale by talking to and encouraging the women. They brought more clothes and foodstuffs but it was nowhere near enough to make an impression. They helped nurse the sick, even though they were afraid of catching typhoid or dysentery.

Each day they nursed the baby of a Mrs Loeuw. She had been brought into the camp some two weeks previously, having been forcibly moved out of her home, which had been burnt before her eyes. The baby girl, just seventeen days old when she was taken into the camp, was desperately ill; she would not take any food and now she was starving to death. From the moment she was born, her mother had fed the child on milk from a donkey that the family had on the farm. Donkey's milk had fed all her children. When they arrived at the camp the donkey, which had travelled with them more than 200 miles, was taken from them. Mrs Loeuw and the volunteers pleaded for it to be returned so the baby could be fed, but the camp commandant refused to pay any attention. Day by day, the baby wilted and shrivelled. Only after ten days, when a new camp commandant took over, was the donkey found and brought to them but it was too late. The baby died in her mother's arms.

Jane, Emily and the mother hugged each other but they did not cry. All three of them felt the same emotion, deep and intense. It was a feeling of repugnance yet resolve, shame yet sympathy, despair yet determination. Jane, who had never nursed a baby before, would never forget the hollow pitiful eyes of Mrs Loeuw, nor the slow, silent way she put down the body in the bone-hard earth.

Jane looked skywards as she prayed silently for the soul of the tiny, wrinkled bundle of bone-dry skin that lay on the ground before her.

In the hotel that night they were subdued, reflective and sad. They pitied Mrs Loeuw and all the other women in the camp who had lost children or who would lose them if nothing was done. They railed against the injustice and despaired of their inability to do more. Emily poured her anger into words, letters designed to stoke up flames of passion in the drawing rooms of liberal England. Jane, in the watches of the night, sought solace through prayer and a commitment to right the wrongs she had seen through her own good deeds.

The next morning, they woke hardly refreshed but with clearer minds. Over breakfast, they decided they would continue as planned to visit the camp at Mafeking and then return to Kaya Lami. It was a major effort of will, for both had an overwhelming urge to turn back, not wishing to see any more distressing sights.

It was Jane, though, who pulled them round. 'If we go back now I suspect that in weeks to come we will feel that we have let down all those in the camps. We still have clothes to give out and whatever we see will be useful to you, Emily, when we get back.'

'I agree. You are right. I am afraid I feel my courage is deserting me. I am tired, not because of the travelling or lack of sleep but because of what we are seeing. How much upset can we take?'

'Did you see Mrs Loeuw's face when she laid the baby down?' asked Jane.

'I did. I wish Kitchener had seen it too,' Emily replied, screwing her napkin into a tight ball and throwing it onto the table. 'Just look at us, eating breakfast in this nice hotel whilst not two miles away people are being starved to death.'

Chapter 14
Strange Cargo

The next three days were spent preparing for the trip to Mafeking. They bought more clothes, stocked up with as much food as they could get hold of and loaded the trucks, or Mrs Newman's servants did. They wrote letters home and to the committee in Cape Town, and advised everybody where they were going.

They boarded the train on the 5th of April. As usual, they were met with disbelief, suspicion and antagonism. The train was overcrowded but they managed to find a compartment with three English nurses travelling back to Mafeking. It was a relief, for Jane and Emily had been dreading the hours of frosty silence with English squaddies, who would clearly not want these 'ladies' in their carriage because it would limit what they could say and what language they could get away with.

Throughout a thoroughly miserable and uncomfortable 300-mile journey they witnessed long processions of 'refugees' going south, together with hundreds of animals. Cows, pigs and horses were all being driven by military personnel on horseback. People, animals, waggons of every description were densely packed together, a tidal wave of misery. The lack of water was having a disastrous effect. The noise from the animals, desperate for a drink, was a squealing cacophony. Many could go no further and sank to the ground exhausted, but it was their death knell for then the horsemen rode alongside and shot them.

'Oh my God, what are they doing?' said one of the nurses, a thirty-year-old Scottish woman with a broad accent that Jane found hard to understand at times.

'They are under orders not to slow up the columns. My bloke's in the Cheshires and he says they have been told to shoot any animal that can't keep up,' said the second of the nurses.

'Should shoot the people as well, then they won't keep attacking our boys,' said the third nurse.

'Oh that's terrible!' said the first nurse. 'You cannot mean that. You're a nurse, for Christ's sake.'

'I am a nurse for our boys,' said the third nurse, a rough, thin-faced woman of about thirty-five with very short hair. 'I don't see why I should nurse traitors or those who won't fight proper.'

'What do you mean fight proper?' asked the Scottish nurse.

'I mean ambushing, sneaking up and attacking trains. Stand up and fight if you want to fight, I say.'

At that moment the train pulled into a siding just outside the small town of Warrenton and jolted to a stop. The nurses, Jane and Emily were thrown forward into each other. No one was hurt but the argument was not continued for, at that very moment, with a frosty tension in the carriage, they passed a sight no one had ever seen before.

A goods train, pulling about forty open coal waggons, passed them on the right-hand side. The waggons did not have coal in them; they had people. Hundreds and hundreds of Boer families, mainly women and children but with some aged men were crammed in. All had haggard faces, and all looked wet and cold with drenched clothing and damp, lifeless flattened hair. The women, nearly all hatless, held babies and young children in their arms. There was not a spark of life in any one of them.

Every waggon was the same, crammed with pitiful people at a loss to understand what was happening to them, all staring into the train they were passing but seeing nothing. They were dirty and many appeared to have weeping sores on their arms, necks and faces.

'Do you want to shoot them?' asked the Scottish nurse, looking directly at the hard-faced nurse. Even she looked appalled, barely able to comprehend the horror of what they had just seen.

There was a poignant silence, broken only when the hard-faced nurse said, 'No, that's not what I meant.' It was clear that she was contrite and her eyes toured the carriage seeking forgiveness. Her gaze landed on Emily and, in a remarkable transformation, the nurse's face changed to one of supplication, almost pleading for acceptance.

'Those poor souls deserve our sympathy and help,' said Emily, still reeling in shock from the nurse's comments and the sight of the goods train from hell.

Chapter 15
A Big Decision

Jane and Emily arrived in Mafeking on the 9th of April 1901, nearly a year after the siege had ended. The camp was some six miles out of town and it took a great deal of effort, aided by a generous donation of pound notes, for the station master to arrange for the trucks to be unloaded and stored in a local warehouse. They hired a local merchant to transport the goods to the camp in a horse-drawn waggon. For some reason they could get no one to drive the truck. They were reluctant to drive it themselves as they didn't know the route or what the road would be like.

They spent three intense, draining but driven days at the camp. It was better than Kimberley but still lacking in sufficient tents, soap, medical supplies and basic foodstuffs. They gave out what they could and helped the only nurse who was working there. They knew that they could not bring any meaningful improvement to the patients but the nurse, a very pretty eighteen-year-old South African girl, was heartened by their visit and their genuine desire to bring some relief to the camp prisoners.

'What do you need most to help the prisoners here?' asked Emily. They had just come out of the hospital tent and were walking back to the administration tent where the commandant had his desk.

'We can't call them prisoners,' said Doris, the young nurse. 'The camp commandant does not like it. He insists they are refugees being given protection.'

'Well, they didn't want to be brought here and they have nowhere to go to and are not free to leave, so it seems to me that they are prisoners,' Emily retorted.

'I'm only saying what I've been told,' Doris replied. 'I am just trying to help. It doesn't matter to me what they are called.'

'Of course, that's why we are all here,' said Jane, looking at Emily disapprovingly.

'Soap,' said Doris. 'And bleach to keep things clean. Oh, and blankets — we don't have enough and it's so cold at night.'

When they got to the tent, they made a list of the most urgent requirements and promised they would bring what they could from town the next day. They realised that they would only be able to obtain a fraction of what was needed.

As they left and travelled back to the town on a military waggon, Jane took issue with Emily. 'You were quite hard on that young nurse. She is so young and doing her very best. We need to encourage her as much as possible.'

'You are quite right,' replied Emily. 'I was just letting off steam. Doris is lovely, and it's remarkable how organised she is.' She looked directly at Jane and took her hand, squeezing it lightly. 'It's very hard for us all and I find it so difficult to keep my temper. If you weren't here, I would be upsetting everybody, and that would do no one any good.'

They went back the next day and gave out the remainder of the goods from the truck. They had made a special effort to get soap and blankets for Doris from the general store in the town.

Emily took them to her personally. 'Doris, we have brought you some soap and bleach,' she said, intent on repairing the impression she had created when they first met. 'Probably not enough, but hopefully it will help. You are doing such good work here and with so little.'

'Oh, thank you!' Doris gave a huge smile. 'I've been asking the official here for weeks and nothing happens. You have done it in a day!'

'Isn't it amazing how someone so young can keep so cheerful amidst such atrocious conditions?' said Jane, as they said goodbye to Doris. 'That smile is so infectious. It makes me sad to think her youth is being spent in such circumstances. She deserves better.' Jane was heartbroken six months later when she discovered that Doris had died of typhoid that she'd caught in the camp.

They retraced their journey back to Bloemfontein, stopping en route at Kimberley. They visited the camp again but there was little change and little they could do. They had exhausted their supplies. They arranged for money to be sent to the volunteers, and Jane made a special effort to say goodbye to Mrs Newman, who she visited at her home. She was made most welcome and they had tea and cakes. It was all so English and civilised.

'I know you are here with a specific purpose but I am so pleased to see you,' said Mrs Newman. 'I wish we were meeting in rather more pleasant circumstances. I like to see people from England but I am afraid that does not happen very often.'

'Do you miss home?' asked Jane who had warmed to Edith's honest simplicity and openness. 'Do you have family back in England?'

'I have three brothers but we are not close and I rarely hear from them. My two sisters and I keep in touch as best we can. My mother is still alive but very frail. What I miss most is not seeing the nephews and nieces growing up.' She looked down and then into the distance. 'It would have been nice to see them growing up. We so wanted children but it is not God's will.'

'I am afraid I have so little knowledge of children. I have no brothers or sisters but I grew up wishing that I had. Would Alun like children as much as you?' It was rare for her to have such personal conversations but she felt a gentle force pushing her to probe a little deeper.

'Yes, he would. We talked about children a lot when we were first married, whether we wanted boys or girls, names for them, what they would do. All the usual things. When nothing happened, he stopped talking about them. I have not said this to anyone but I sometimes think he blames himself.'

'Oh, I see,' said Jane. Actually, she did not see. She was deeply aware of her lack of any knowledge about the workings of the human body.

It was Edith who moved the conversation along. 'I received a letter from my sister Amelia last week. She referred to people in her church saying there were camps for civilians affected by the war, and she was asking if there were any near here. They have no idea back home, do they? Poor Mrs Snyman is quite ill and very depressed.'

'People are only told what the government want them to hear. If they could see what we can see, they would feel differently,' Jane said passionately.

When Jane left, she did not expect to meet Edith again. As she shook her hand and gave her a hug she said, 'I hope you manage to get back to England before too long. I can tell how much it means to you.'

Jane and Emily left Kimberley on the 18th of April. They were delayed constantly and had to change trains frequently. They slept in station master's office on camp beds at De Aar; at Norval Pont, the railway station officer gave up his tent so that the two English ladies could have somewhere to sleep.

They reached Kya Lami on the 23rd of April. It was a very welcoming sight to Jane, who had been thinking throughout the journey of its greenness and tranquillity. When she went through the gates it was not the garden or the trees or shade that impressed upon her but an indefinable feeling of stability and certainty. The ability to wash, change, comb her hair and remove all the dirt from her nails provided the most basic yet immeasurable pleasure.

Her ablutions over, Jane bounded downstairs eager to wallow in conversation with Caroline and to sit in deeply cushioned chairs rather than on the hard train benches. She wandered through the house onto the veranda, where she found Caroline reading.

'You look better! What a difference a bath can make!' She beckoned Jane to sit down beside her.

'I actually feel quite sprightly, given the journey we have had. I think your home is lovely. The very thought of it has been a comfort to me whilst I have been away,' said Jane.

Caroline sensed that Jane wanted to say more. She waited.

'When I volunteered to help Emily, I had no conception of what it would actually involve. I had no knowledge to draw upon which would have enabled me to understand what it would be like. I had never been further than London. What I have seen has been a real shock and at times it has been deeply upsetting. But I know that if I was offered again, the chance to come and help Emily, and I knew precisely what it would be like, I would have no hesitation in accepting.'

'I am sure that is true,' said Caroline. 'And it is heartening that there are young people like you with such good inside them.'

Jane reflected on this for a moment. 'I think it is not just about doing good or what we think Christian people should be doing. It's also about myself. Coming here and seeing such suffering has made me appreciate just how lucky I am in being born into such privilege. It is so easy to take living in a big house with a farm with servants and plenty of food as the norm. I am a better person for now having a better understanding of how ordinary people live. I used to think that I lived an ordinary life but I now realise I do not.'

'No one is ordinary, Jane, and you most certainly are not. Everyone has something to contribute, but often they are not given the opportunity.'

'I certainly feel that is true back at home. Women cannot even vote — but I am certain that if we did, lots of new opportunities would open up and not just for those with money.

'That may be so,' said Caroline. 'But I think you are right to reflect on the luck of birth. I wish more would do so. I often wonder why I have this house and estate and all these black people around us have nothing.'

'I think they are very happy working for you,' said Jane.

'That may be true, but it is all relative. If they did not work here, they probably would have no work at all.'

'I had not considered that aspect. Whilst I have been travelling to the camps, my thoughts have been more about myself. I am not a politician, nor could I do what Emily does, but I now know that it gives me quiet satisfaction to be helping others.'

'Is quiet satisfaction enough?' said Caroline.

'I am not sure I know what you mean.' Jane looked puzzled.

'Would you find helping others as rewarding if that meant you had to live in poverty all the time? You need to have people with money to help, just like the Good Samaritan.'

Jane did not respond and felt no pressure to do so. The two of them sat pondering those thoughts as a servant brought out a tray with lemonade.

Over dinner that night, Caroline brought Jane and Emily up to date with what was happening in England. 'It appears that your letters and reports are having a major impact. Apparently, the newspapers are full of information drawn from your letters home. Your supporters, Emily, have been asking questions in the House of Commons. John Ellis — do you know him? — confronted the Secretary of State for War,

St John Broderick, demanding to know if the accounts were true. By all accounts, there is growing concern in the government because the international press is portraying British actions in a very unfavourable light. Some are saying the British are conducting a systematic and deliberate scorching of the earth leading to the deaths of hundreds, if not thousands, of civilians.'

There was a long silence, broken only when Emily said, 'I have been told the same. I have just opened letters from my brother and from Lord Courtney, which say much the same thing. The trouble is that all this might cause us real problems here in South Africa. If Milner and Kitchener see me as the source of these reports they will almost certainly try and put an end to the Committee's work.'

'They will target you, not the Committee,' said Caroline. 'They will not be overly concerned about what South Africans say but an Englishwoman is different. You will be seen as a troublemaker, but you must have known that!'

Rather naively, Jane jumped in. 'I don't think so. We came out to give relief to women and children. What can be wrong with that?'

'If only it were so simple,' said Caroline. 'What you have discovered is that the only truly effective way to relieve the suffering is to close the camps. Milner, Kitchener and all the others involved in promoting the war will oppose that because the camps are central to their plans.'

Emily straightened her back and, as though addressing a public meeting, announced, 'I must get back to England. I can do more there than here. We need a change of government policy if we really want to help these poor souls and I now have the evidence to make people take notice.'

'I think that's right,' Caroline agreed. 'I share your view that only the politicians in England can stop this dreadful policy. You can use your connections and what you have learnt here to better effect back home.'

The dinner was coming to an end. They were all tired but pleased with what had been achieved and the decisions made. The commitment to the cause had been reaffirmed. It was Jane who had the last word. 'I would like to stay here. I feel I can achieve more here than I can back home,' she said, looking at Emily. 'There is so much to do and it is getting worse day by day.'

Chapter 16
Precious Gift

After a few days of much-needed rest, Emily made preparations to travel back to Cape Town and onwards to London. She did not know how long she would have to wait for a berth on a ship but assumed at least a week. Given that she would have at least two weeks on board, she could not envisage being back in England before the 1st of June. She sent off letters to committee members throughout South Africa, and to her friends and family back home, and set off for Cape Town on the 1st of May.

For Jane, Emily going back was quite a moment. She had always looked up to her friend, sought her advice and followed her lead. Whilst the age gap between them did not suggest a mother-daughter relationship, that was a more accurate description than that of sisters.

Jane had recognised and accepted that Emily had far more experience of the world, had travelled extensively and been part of a well-connected network of politically involved people. Jane knew that if she had not met Emily she would not now be in South Africa. She knew also, from the moment she had started working with Emily in London, that she,

Jane, was on a steep learning curve. Nevertheless, she had learned fast; her confidence had grown and she felt that day by day she was being accepted as an equal.

Jane did not worry about how she would manage, what she would do and how she would organise things after Emily went back to England. She was comfortable with her ability to distribute effectively the substantial amounts of money that had already come in to the Distress Fund and what was likely to continue to come in. She had already determined to make much more use of the local South African volunteers and seek to recruit more across the country. No, for Jane it was not the work or her ability to do it that caused concern, it was the loss of companionship.

For nearly a year, she and Emily had been together every day; they could now read each other's thoughts, finish each other's sentences, predict how each would react to new events. Above all, Jane worried about who she would talk to. Caroline Fichardt and Elizabeth Molteno were just two of the many women she had met, but they could not replace Emily's companionship.

Emily had said that she would be back in South Africa in six months, no later than the end of October. By that time, Jane thought she too would be keen to go home. Already she was thinking occasionally about what she would do when she got back to England. She knew she would need to find a worthwhile occupation, perhaps helping the disadvantaged, even if it was on a part-time or voluntary basis. And what about home, her father and her income? How would these look by the time she got back?

Three days after Emily left for Cape Town, Jane went down for breakfast. The mornings were colder now;

temperatures in the evening dropped to freezing and, whilst the daytime reached a pleasant twenty-one degrees, mornings had a chilly, almost frosty feel.

Jane wrapped a thick shawl round her shoulders and went onto the veranda. It was too cold to sit out but she stood for a few minutes watching the gardeners tidying already impossibly neat borders and sweeping irresponsible leaves which had, without authority, blown onto the immaculate lawns.

Jane loved this space. Lainston House garden was wonderful by any standard, but it did not have the colour or variety of Kya Lami. Nor did they have as many gardeners, and the two they did have had to do lots of other jobs as well. It was clear there was a strict hierarchy of servants at Kya Lami and that the gardeners felt that they were at its pinnacle. They took immense pride in the garden and in their own appearance; Jane never once saw a gardener with dirty clothes. How did they keep so clean, she wondered?

She went inside to the dining room. Caroline was sitting at the table reading letters. 'Morning,' said Jane cheerfully.

'Good morning,' replied Caroline. 'You are looking very fresh today. I take it you slept well.'

'Indeed,' came the reply. 'I must be catching up with all the hours' sleep I missed on those wretched trains.'

She sat down and helped herself to a bowl of fruit. 'It's my birthday,' she announced to Caroline.

'Oh, is it? You never said last night. Happy birthday. We will have to make a cake for dinner tonight.' Caroline paused for a moment and then said, 'Better still, why don't we go into town and eat in the hotel? It will make a nice change and I will ask one or two of the others to come along.' She did

155

not specify who these others were; it was taken as read that 'the others' were people well known to Jane, which of course they weren't.

'If I can be rude, Jane, how old are you?' asked Caroline. She put down her spoon and the letter she had been holding and looked directly at Jane. It was not a perfunctory question and Jane knew instinctively that there would be a follow-on. Caroline never deviated from the straightest line in obtaining the information she sought.

'Twenty-four,' she replied.

'Twenty-four. I see. And is there someone waiting for you back home?'

'Waiting for me?' Jane asked in a surprised tone. She did not say it but her voice implied: 'Are you playing a game with me?'

'Yes, a man. Someone you're fond of.'

'No, no one.'

'Well, it's time that there was. You will have to work harder.'

Jane did not reply. Caroline did not require a response; she had pronounced on the matter and that was that.

Jane spent the rest of the day resting and walking in the garden. She thought occasionally about Caroline's instruction and found herself smiling. 'I wonder how you work harder at finding someone,' she mused. 'Reverend Shell is the only person who has shown any interest in me and I did not work hard with him. I simply knew him through church. Maybe that's it — I simply need to know more people.'

These thoughts flitted through her mind yet they were not random or unstructured; it was just that the soothing ambience, the tranquillity and restfulness of the garden, did not summon urgent thoughts. It did not demand beginning, middle and end arguments, all carefully sorted and sifted. Yet it was a place where the seeds of ideas could be watered, fed and arranged, so that gradually carefully considered, mature thoughts arrived in full bloom.

It was so with Jane. On this day, her twenty-fourth birthday, she set out, albeit without knowing, to work harder at finding someone who would wait for her.

The evening was a great success. Caroline invited three other ladies from Bloemfontein and they had dinner in the Free State Hotel. It was a long time since Jane had been out purely for social reasons and she relaxed totally, finding herself quite at ease even though the company was new to her. She found the South African women more direct, less fussy and a great deal less pompous than the English.

After dinner, a decorated cake arrived and Caroline orchestrated a chorus of *Happy Birthday* for a smiling and content Jane.

The next few days were spent obtaining supplies and filling a waggon to take the goods to the camp. Jane only filled one waggon, having decided that it would be easier to manage if she was on her own.

Philip the gardener, who had cut his leg, provided immeasurable assistance particularly in lifting and carrying. He told Jane that he was married with four children, the oldest a son of eleven years of age. Philip had worked for the Fichardts for eleven years; he had started when his son was born and was very happy at Kya Lami. He was well treated and had more money than most of his neighbours, many of whom had no work.

The next morning, they laboriously transferred all the goods from the waggon into another waggon, as the first one had an axle that looked likely to break off its mountings. It was Philip who noticed its poor condition and pointed it out to Jane. She knew that it would be a major problem if the waggon broke down en route; the road was badly rutted and the axle was unlikely to survive such a journey. Reluctantly Jane, Philip and two other servants moved the goods; Jane was glad that it was so much cooler, for it was heavy work.

Eventually they were ready to travel the four miles to the camp. As they set off, Jane remembered the searing heat and the flies inside the tents when they had first visited. She hoped conditions had improved.

When she reached the top of the hill and looked down across the plain, she was shocked to see that the camp was twice the size it had been when they were last there. The tents had spread out so much that it was no longer possible to see all of them at once. She was also alarmed to see that a high fence now surrounded the camp; she could just make out the profiles of guards walking round the perimeter.

On the far horizon she saw a large column of horses and waggons that, although she could not be certain, appeared to be heading towards the camp.

She reached the camp gates and was stopped by a guard. She showed her pass and asked if Captain Nelson was available.

'Captain left last week. Been posted to Pietermaritzburg,' said the guard.

'Who is commandant now?' asked Jane, disappointed that someone who would almost certainly have been helpful and considerate was no longer there.

'Captain Llewellyn, but he is away until Thursday.'

'I am here to provide assistance to the refugees and distribute food and clothes. Is there someone in charge I could talk to? I came a few weeks ago and Captain Nelson was most obliging.' Jane spoke clearly and confidently.

The guard stared at her, bemused. After twenty seconds or so he shouted out, 'Private Jones, take this woman to the lieutenant. Tell him she wants to give out clothes.'

Jane climbed down from the waggon and followed Private Jones for about 250 yards. The ground was hard and barren. Strangely, there were few people about but Jane did notice a number of much larger tents that had not been there before. The first one had a large red cross outside.

'Is that the hospital?' asked Jane.

'Yes, ma'am,' Private Jones replied.

She was taken to the camp commandant's office. It was not the same one that Captain Nelson had used; this was much bigger and was clearly made up of a number of tents joined together. The right-hand side adjoined a wooden-sided building that was built on low stilts. In this part there were a number of desks; on the walls were maps and charts.

Jane heard Private Jones explain to the guard at the door that the lady wished to see the lieutenant. The guard disappeared through a flap in the tent to the left and reappeared a couple of minutes later with the officer.

'What is your name?' he asked brusquely.

'My name is Jane Dunhaughton. I was here a couple of months ago and met Captain Nelson. He kindly assisted us in giving out food and clothes to the refugees. I have more food and clothes to distribute.' Jane deliberately used the word

159

'refugees' and pointed to the waggon, which was still at the main gates.

'You should have asked before you came. There is a lot of sickness here. It is no place for a young woman. Are you from England?' he asked, looking puzzled.

'Yes, I am. I am here to help the Distress Fund for South Africa give out money that has been donated by people back in England.'

'I thought you said it was food and clothes,' the lieutenant said. He was now moving towards the main gates.

'We use the money to buy food and clothes,' Jane said, scurrying to keep up with him. He was small, not much bigger than her, and looked not more than twenty-one. He was certainly younger than her.

'Why?' he asked. He stopped abruptly and looked at her suspiciously.

'Why?' she responded, not understanding the question.

'Yes. Why are you buying food and clothes? The refugees receive rations.'

'The rations are insufficient and people are suffering,' Jane said, looking directly at him.

The lieutenant resumed his quick march to the main gate. He stopped when he arrived at the waggon and looked aggressively at Philip, who was still holding the horse's reins. 'Who's this?' he demanded, pointing with the cane he had been tapping against the side of his boot.

'He is helping me,' Jane said, annoyed at the lieutenant's aggressive tone and demeanour.

'He can't come in. No blacks in this camp.'

'He is here to help me lift the cases from the waggon. He is not going to stay.'

'Doesn't matter. He cannot come in. Anyway, neither can you. I will need authority to admit you. Come back the day after tomorrow.' He turned and started to walk back to the tent.

'Excuse me,' said Jane running after him. 'We have come all this way. Let us unload at least.'

'No,' the lieutenant said, marching past her. 'Come back the day after tomorrow, if you must. But if I were you, I would stay away. There is a lot of disease here.'

By now he had turned his back and quickened his pace, increasing the distance between himself and Jane, who had stopped in her tracks.

She stood for a few minutes, wondering what to do next. She looked around. There were certainly substantially more tents, many of which were clearly part of the infrastructure of the camp rather than tents for the refugees. Yet there were fewer people, hardly any walking around or sitting around the tent openings. She could not understand this.

Reluctantly she turned, went back to the main gate and climbed back onto the waggon. 'We will have to go back and come back the day after tomorrow.'

Philip said nothing, but expertly turned the horses round and they set off back in silence. The roads were very dusty, hard and deeply rutted; unlike the journey out, when Jane was full of anticipation and enthusiasm, on the way back she felt every bump and grind. The landscape only added to her frustration. She found it depressing in its lack of vegetation, colour and its monotonous flatness.

Jane recounted what had happened at the camp to Caroline and also aired her concern at the lack of people, despite the growth in the size of the camp. 'Where are they getting water from for so many? And what about toilets? There is no river nearby, not like in some of the other camps we have been to.'

She spent the rest of the day writing letters to Emily, Lilly, Betty Molteno and Catherine Courtney. As the day drew to a close, she began to think more analytically about the lieutenant's reaction to her visit and his references to disease in the camp. Maybe he was angry about being there with the risk of getting ill himself. Maybe it was worse than she'd imagined. Was that why there were so few people about?

Jane and Philip made the same trip two days later. They followed a long convoy of horse-drawn and motor waggons from the town to the camp. There must have been fifteen waggons in the convoy and they settled in behind the last of the vehicles. Most were civilian waggons carrying what looked like bags of food, but two of them were carrying logs, which Jane assumed were for burning on stoves.

When they presented themselves at the gate, Jane was pleased to see that Private Jones was on duty. 'Hello, you back again?' he bellowed in an almost friendly manner.

'Yes! May I see Captain Llewellyn, please? My name is Jane Dunhaughton and I would like to distribute clothes and foodstuffs to the refugees.'

Jane got down from the waggon and followed Private Jones, exactly as she had the on her previous visit. She was made to wait outside the administration tent for what seemed an eternity until the captain appeared. He was totally different to the lieutenant she had met previously; he was older, around thirty, and much taller and heavier. He looked friendlier. 'Jane Dunhaughton?' he enquired.

'Yes, that's right,' she replied.

'You came yesterday.'

'The day before yesterday,' Jane corrected him and was about to explain her purpose when he interrupted.

'It is very good of you to try and bring supplies for the refugees but there is a lot of sickness here and I don't want you to get ill as well. I cannot let you wander round the camp. If you want to unload and tell us what you have, we will arrange for it to be distributed.'

'That is very good of you, but I would appreciate the opportunity to talk to some of the women and get a feel for what things they need.' She paused and waited for a response, but she could sense that Captain Llewellyn was not going to engage in a drawn-out conversation. She added quickly, 'Captain Nelson found the reports very useful.'

'I am sure he did, but when you came last the camp was less than half the size and there was not an outbreak of typhoid and dysentery. I cannot let you go round it.'

Jane could see that there was no point in arguing the point. 'All right, I understand. Where would you like us to unload the goods?'

They were told to put them by the camp store and Private Jones was instructed to take them there. They climbed on to the waggon. Private Jones told Philip to turn round and follow the perimeter track for four hundred yards.

Jane could not help staring at the perimeter fence. Its stark brutality crushed her spirit; what would it do for the prisoners, for they clearly were prisoners now? The barbed wire at the top of the ten-foot fence was a cruel and unnecessary sight for the already dejected refugees.

As the waggon turned, Jane's eyes focussed on another one coming towards them. This one was loaded with five coffins, two abreast with one placed on top.

'Are many dying?' Jane asked Private Jones.

'Yes, a lot. Over fifty this week. It's the children. Going through them like nobody's business.'

'Is there a doctor?' asked Jane.

'Yes, but there's little he can do. Too many people, dirty water — and it's so cold in them tents at night.'

'Any nurses?' Jane asked.

'Some of the women help out.'

'Which women?' Jane asked quickly.

'The pris—' he stopped himself. 'The refugees.'

They unloaded the waggon. Jane had the cases with the warm woollen clothes placed separately and pointed these out to Private Jones. As Philip and Private Jones stacked the cases neatly into foodstuffs and clothes, with the children's clothes placed in a separate pile, Jane looked down the long rows of tents. Outside one tent, about a hundred yards from where she was standing, a group of women were gathered. There were two old men with them. Impulsively Jane decided to go and talk to them.

She hurried as fast as she could. Private Jones had not seen her go and she was soon at the tent. Her instincts had been correct: she had recognised one of the women. Hurrying towards her, Jane tried desperately to think of her name. As she arrived at the tent entrance, it came back to her.

'Mrs Pienaar. Remember me? Jane Dunhaughton. I came about two months ago.'

Mrs Pienaar was holding a small child, a baby certainly not a year old. She was in clothes that were little better than rags and her face was engrained with dust and dirt. She looked dreadful, a terrible apparition; the hollowness of her eyes and their emptiness were a definition of misery.

Mrs Pienaar looked at Jane but made no sound. She nodded and acknowledged that she knew who Jane was, but then turned her back and went inside the tent, followed by one of the old men.

One of the other women touched Jane on the arm and asked, 'Sorry — who are you?'

Jane replied that she was here to give out food and clothes that had been provided by the Distress Fund for South African women and children. There was a look of utter contempt from the two women who had turned to talk to her. They said something to each other in Dutch, which Jane could not understand. Then one of them spoke in English. 'You English burn our farms and then come to hand out food. Damn you. You're not welcome here.'

Jane was sent reeling by the onslaught; she was not prepared for it. She sputtered a weak reply. 'I am sorry. I think it is all wrong. It's the only thing I can do. I want to try and help.'

'Mrs Pienaar's child died today in the hospital. That is the third of her children to die here. How many more?' The woman was screaming at Jane. 'Answer me! How many more? How many more?'

Jane was surrounded by angry women and she was frightened, really frightened. She looked round for help but her mind was scrambled and she could not focus on where she had come from or see the waggon or Philip.

'I have come to help. It is not my fault and I am so sorry all this is happening. What can I do but try and help? Nobody made me come. I am so sorry.' Jane looked as though she were about to burst into tears. The only words that would come out were, 'I am so sorry.'

'You're right, it's not your fault — but it's your country's fault,' the angry woman said. She kept switching into Dutch, talking in a very fast and heated manner with the other women. 'Mrs Pienaar has lost her third child. Just one to go now. Just one more. It will die soon. You say you want to help, then help. Save the child.'

Jane did not know what to say. She could not think properly or clearly. Her heart was pounding. 'I can come back with medicine. I will bring medicine,' she said quickly, thinking this was the answer. 'Yes, medicine. That's what is needed.'

'No, the child will die here.' The angry woman turned and went into the tent. Jane was left surrounded by four others, all bonded by the utter misery on their faces and their abject, pitiful condition.

No words were spoken and there was an edgy silence, not broken until Mrs Pienaar appeared at the entrance to the tent with the baby still and lifeless in her arms. Jane was mortified. She could recognise instantly that the child was near death yet she felt inept and hapless.

The angry woman took the child from Mrs Pienaar then turned and came over to Jane. 'Take the child. You want to help, so take the child. Look after him.'

She held out the baby and pushed it gently towards Jane's breasts. Jane's arms were down by her side but one of the other women came up behind her and raised them, so that the angry woman could place the child in them.

It was like a dream. Jane was helpless, overtaken by events. She looked desperately at Mrs Pienaar, thinking that she would put a stop to this, but she simply nodded her head and said, 'Go. Go now.'

The women turned Jane round and pointed her towards the direction from which she had come. The waggon was at the end of the avenue of tents; it had not moved. Jane stopped a couple of times and tried to turn round but the angry woman's voice had changed. 'Courage,' she said. 'Do what is right and save the child. He will die here. You can save him.' She moved in front of Jane. 'You want to help. Take the child.'

They were now just twenty yards from the waggon. Philip was holding the reins but there was no sign of Private Jones. The woman put her hand in the small of Jane's back and pushed her towards the waggon.

In a trance, Jane released one hand from the baby and grabbed the handle to pull herself up. Philip looked at her, bemused, and then at the woman who was gesticulating at him to go. 'Go, go now,' she said, and pointed towards the main gate.

Philip, not knowing what to do, was waiting for instructions. Jane sat, looking straight ahead, unable to speak. She was shaking with fear and shock. She was holding a lifeless, silent baby. What should she do? What if the baby died in her arms?

It was only when the angry woman came round to Jane's side of the waggon, reached up and pushed Jane's leg hard that the trance was broken. Jane looked at her and heard her shouting and pointing at Philip, 'Tell him, tell him to go!'

Philip was also looking at Jane and repeatedly asking, 'What do I do, mam? What do I do?' He looked very worried. Being inside a British concentration camp and having people shouting and gesticulating at him was a nightmare. He was expecting soldiers to arrive any minute. 'Please, mam, what do I do?' he asked again.

Jane was not looking at him. She could not hear him for now the only thing she could see was the lieutenant from her previous visit walking along the perimeter road towards them. His cane smacked the ground with every stride; he clearly was not out for a stroll.

Jane came out of her trance, heard Philip's imploring questions and felt the woman pushing her legs. She looked down at the baby in her arms, still lifeless. She looked up; the lieutenant was now only a hundred yards away.

'Philip, let's go. Let's go now.' Her eyes met those of the angry woman and both knew at that moment that Jane was committed. They nodded to each other as Philip got the horses moving.

Within a few seconds, they were level with the lieutenant who held up his cane. 'You were told not to visit the refugees,' he bawled. 'What are you doing?'

'Sorry, I saw someone I knew. Just had to say hello. Going now. All is well.' Jane was calmness itself. 'Come on, Philip.' She signalled to Philip, whilst looking at the lieutenant. 'Don't want to overstay our welcome.'

'No, it's not all right!' He moved to one side so as to be next to Jane rather than in front of the waggon.

At that point, the angry woman came up to him. 'We need water,' she demanded. 'And we need the clothes that they have dropped off.'

168

By the now the waggon was ten yards past the lieutenant. He turned to follow it but the woman ran in front of him. 'We need them now,' she said.

Jane and Philip did not look back as the waggon picked up speed. They came to the main gate and saw that the barrier was open because another waggon was leaving. They carried straight on until they reached the top of the hill.

'Stop,' said Jane. She was shaking; the adrenalin was pumping through her and her legs were like jelly. All her strength seemed to have evaporated. 'Let's just stop a while,' she said.

They sat for ten minutes without saying a word. At first Jane did not move. She was not certain if the last fifteen minutes had really happened. Had she imagined them? Slowly, though, she began to function and as she did the baby in her arms stirred. The sheer enormity of what had just happened began to register.

'Oh Philip, what do I do now?' came the plaintive question.

Philip was not certain of his place and how much he could say. He was not certain if he was really being asked or if this was a question to the air, as he called thinking aloud.

'I think we should go back home,' he said.

'Yes, so do I,' said Jane.

Little was said on the four-mile journey. Jane tried to nurse the baby boy who was now crying. The cry was not loud or shrill but more of a whimper. She felt inadequate, not knowing how to nurse a child. Why had she taken it? Surely it was wrong and she should have been stronger? As these thoughts were forming, though, she thought of Mrs Pienaar's desperation. Would she, Jane, not have done the same if she had been the child's mother? What was she supposed to do now?

As Kya Lami came into sight, Jane recalled the image of Mrs Loeuw placing her dead child on the ground. 'Oh please, Lord, let this child survive,' she prayed.

When she got back to Kya Lami, she immediately called out for Caroline. One of the servants went to fetch her and she found Jane sat in the dining room with the baby on her lap.

Caroline looked in amazement; she could see Jane was traumatised by whatever had happened. She heard the baby whimpering and coughing with a dry wispy sound.

'I need your help, Caroline.' Jane looked up and her eyes pleaded for support. 'I really don't know what to do.'

Caroline put her hand on the baby's face then moved the shawl in which it was wrapped and felt its body. 'The baby is cold. We need to get some warm clothes immediately and some warm milk. And then you can tell me what has been going on.'

A servant was called and Caroline asked for warm milk and a spoon. 'Did Philip go with you?' she asked.

'Yes, but he is back here now.'

Caroline asked the girl who brought the milk to find Philip and ask him to come and see them. As she did so, she took the baby from Jane and sat down. She immediately started to spoon-feed the child, who took the milk hungrily and without fuss. Caroline instinctively started talking in warm soft tones, asking the child what his name was, how old he was. It all seemed so orderly and natural.

When all the milk was gone, Caroline nursed the child, gently swaying him from side to side. 'Go on then, tell me what has happened,' she said.

Jane recounted the whole tale, from arriving at the camp, unloading the goods, seeing Mrs Pienaar, being accosted and then urged to take the child. She explained that Mrs Pienaar had lost three children in the camp already and looked in a dreadful state. She told Caroline of the fifty deaths that week.

'So this is Mrs Pienaar's baby?' Caroline asked.

'Yes,' replied Jane.

'And Mr Pienaar?' Caroline raised her head to look at Jane.

'Dead. Killed in a raid some six months ago.'

'Well, that makes it easier. He won't be saying you stole his child.'

At this point Philip arrived. He stood at the entrance to the dining room until Caroline summoned him. 'We have a new guest, Philip, as you have seen. You have some young sons, don't you?'

'Yes, three, and one girl.'

'Do you have any clothes and nappies that would fit this child?'

'Yes, mam.'

'Well, if you would be so kind, go and get some and bring them here. You will be paid for the clothes and anything else that you can spare that would be useful. Off you go, and hurry up. No time to lose.'

Jane was in awe of the clarity and speed of Caroline's decision making. 'What are we going to do?' she asked.

'We are going to make the child comfortable, feed him and then decide what to do in our own time. We both need to calm down, think rationally. There's no need to do anything for a few days. What you have been through today just confirms what I have heard from some of the other ladies in town: the camps are literally death camps. I can understand poor Mrs Pienaar not wanting to lose a fourth child. God, I hope Emily can get things done back in England. We will have to tell her about this urgently. A mother giving up her child so it may live. That should sway a few hearts.'

Chapter 17
No Things Stranger Than Folk

There was no specific time when Jane realised that she knew what to do. It did not come as a bolt from above; there was no divine inspiration. Nor was it the result of prolonged, detailed, analytical thought. It was not the result of prompting or suggestions or any sort of conversation whatsoever. She did not wake up one morning and say, 'That's it.' Nor did she remember a dream, which pointed her in the direction of travel. When she knew she could not say, but know she did.

Sitting on the veranda, wrapped in a thick blanket but enjoying the winter sun, she looked at Caroline and said, 'I know what to do. I know what is right.' She said it positively, with pride and conviction. There was not a hint of self-doubt. There was a calmness and certainty about her demeanour that was reassuring. Despite the cold, almost frosty morning with its breathless stillness, she looked warmly at Caroline.

A red-eyed dove sat on a branch of a giant ana tree, looking down on them, not moving or singing, but clearly listening. It wanted to hear what Jane knew, and it focused intently.

Jane did not seem in any hurry to disclose what she knew, and Caroline was in no hurry to ask her. Both recognised that it was important but whatever it was would not disappear like the vapour rising from the lawn as the sun moved round and warmed the heavily dewed grass.

Jane took Caroline's arm and moved it so it was pointing at the dove. As she did so, its mate joined the dove as though summoned to come and hear something interesting. The birds sat on the branch, eyes not blinking but studying, watching, recording a snapshot of time that would not be repeated but would never change.

Jane and Caroline sat watching them for a good few minutes, not wishing to disturb the beauty of the moment. Then one of the doves broke the impasse when it hopped from side to side on the branch.

Jane smiled and said, 'It knows as well.'

'I think it does,' said Caroline very calmly. She did not, as most would have done, ask what Jane was thinking. She knew the answer would come but it would not be forced or prompted. She did not have long to wait.

'I will give the baby to Mrs Newman who I met in Kimberley. She will bring up the child.' It was a matter-of-fact statement; there was no equivocation, no question mark, no angling for confirmation or support.

Her statement was treated as such by Caroline. She did not ask 'Are you sure?' or 'How do you know she will have the child?' or, more cuttingly, 'What makes you think she would take the child?' She accepted the statement for what it was, a statement of fact.

It was not until the next morning at breakfast that the matter was raised again. The servants had taken great pleasure in looking after James, for this was what Caroline had called the child. She had not initiated a debate on the subject of a name. She knew that Jane had brought the child home and James was as close a name to Jane as she could think of, so James it was.

As Jane helped herself to eggs and toast, Caroline asked for James to be brought in. She had not asked Jane if she was happy with the child's name, nor did she on this occasion. She did not need to for, as she sat down with a full plate of three eggs and a mountain of toast, Jane said, 'I need to build myself up if I am going back to Kimberley.'

'When are you going?' asked Caroline.

'I don't know yet, but I have written to Mrs Newman and will post the letter today. I thought I would send a telegram as well. I will go into town after breakfast. We need to ensure that James is strong enough for the journey.'

It was the first time she had used the baby's name in conversation. Its use confirmed that he was James from now on.

Jane rode into town on one of Caroline's horses. It seemed an eternity since she had ridden, and her mind instantly went back to Woodly and the paddock at Lainston House. A perfect picture appeared and she could see every detail, smell Woodly's breath as he nudged up to her. She needed confirmation that he was well. As she trotted on the unpaved dirt track down to the Bloemfontein, she decided to write to Lilly and also to her father. She hoped all was well and that the next news from home would be as positive as the last.

She sent the telegram from the post office, the first she had ever sent. She had four or five goes at drafting the message and was far from happy with her final effort, but she decided it would do. The letter she was sending was far more important.

Her telegram read: *Must meet urgently stop Have set out all in letter stop Will set off to you on 20th stop Send telegram if unhappy stop Jane*

She was not sure about the word unhappy but found all substitutes even worse. How could she set out a life-changing proposal in a telegram?

The letter would have to do the job: engage, stir emotions, offer hope and fulfilment. She was happy with it. It had not taken many drafts, in fact no drafts at all. She had recounted the whole day — the journey out to the camp, the guards, the unwelcoming attitude of the military, the angry women, poor Mrs Pienaar, being chased by the lieutenant — it all just poured out. Every word was heartfelt; the excitement, the bewilderment, the sense of hopelessness, the despair on the faces of the women. She caught it all.

The crunch came when she wrote:

Edith, I am going to make a proposition to you which I know is totally unreasonable. It will change your life, and what right do I have to take such a liberty? On the other hand it is my moral duty to ask, for I believe beyond doubt that you and your husband could give James a wonderful life and that he would bring joy to you both.

If you do return to England, as I know you desperately want to, he will have a loving home and a sound Christian upbringing. If he stays here in South Africa, in an orphanage, who knows what sort of life he will have — but it will certainly be one without the love you could provide. If he has to go back to the camps there is a good chance he will die.

You impressed on me how much you wanted a child but that it was not to be. Here is an opportunity to overcome the pain I know you have felt. He is a lovely looking boy, so strong given what he has had to endure. Please help him grow; nurture and love him. He will, I am sure, make you and your husband happy.

I will set off with James for Kimberley on the 20th May. I will fully understand if you are not willing to accept my precious gift. If it is too much for you, please send a telegram to reach me before I leave.

Your true friend,

Jane.

'The telegram has gone; the letter has been posted. The die has been cast,' Jane said to Caroline when she got back.

'Well, we must sit tight and wait until we see which way the wind is blowing,' Caroline replied. The exchange of metaphors lessened the palpable tension between them. Both knew it would be an anxious few days' wait.

Jane occupied herself writing letters to Lilly and her father and in reading her own correspondence. She had received a letter from Emily posted from Cape Town, which advised that she had managed to get the last berth on the RMS *Saxon,* a Union Castle Line passenger ship which left for England on the 8th of May. She had a first-class berth; it was either that or wait for three weeks, and she felt it was vital that she get back.

She intimated, but did not go into detail, that Kitchener and Milner, who was also a passenger on the *Saxon,* had

177

become very hostile as a result of the press coverage and debates in the House. The Secretary of State for War, St John Brodrick, had apparently been asking Kitchener and Milner to refute the allegations that were being made.

In her letter, Jane asked Lilly what the mood was like back home. Was it true that Emily was getting a bad name?

Jane also spent some time riding. There were miles of open space for her to roam and she enjoyed the freedom and exhilaration of a true gallop. She took pleasure in watching the many types of animals, all so different from back home. Gazelles and springboks, jackals and ostrich and birds of colours and varieties that were almost bewildering. The contrast of the open spaces with the garden at Kya Lami never failed to register and made her appreciate even more the genius of the original garden designer. Now that was a good vocation, she thought to herself.

'Where is James?' she asked a young servant girl, when she had returned from riding. On being told that Ruth, another one of the servant girls, was looking after him, she said:

'Oh, do you think it would be possible for Ruth to bring him down? I would like to hold him.'

When Ruth appeared a few minutes later she was carrying James in her arms, wrapped in a large white linen towel. For the first time Jane held James in a relaxed comfortable manner, not now frightened with the responsibility and nervous of the situation she was in. The ride had allowed her the time to free her mind and consider what was to happen to James and what would his future hold.

'What are we going to do with you?' she said tenderly, gently rocking to and fro. 'Early days I know but we do need a plan,' she said to herself.

On the fourth day, a telegram arrived. It was eleven a.m. Jane and Caroline were still in the dining room after breakfast, discussing the correspondence that had arrived from Betty Moltano and the Currys. A large sum on money had been received for the Distress Fund, which was good news. However, the bad news was that there was growing unease amongst the Cape community that the numbers in the concentration camps were still growing and that Kitchener, believing his strategy was working, was redoubling his efforts at cutting off all sources of support for the Boer commandos.

He had built long lines of fencing stretching hundreds of miles. He had positioned blockhouses along these fences, which were manned by soldiers who were in visible range of the next blockhouse so they gave each other firing support. He had also introduced roving patrols of troops on horseback who took on the Boer commandos at their own game, staging ambushes, attacking supply lines and generally being a nuisance to the insurgents.

The size of the allied forces in South Africa, now over 600,000 troops, meant that the whole economy of the province was geared up to supplying them. Large numbers of military officers were in Cape Town, either on leave, in transit or arranging supplies. There was little attempt at secrecy and both Betty Moltano and the Currys had commented that it seemed to be a deliberate policy to make it clear to the civilian population how effective the strategy was. They, and Jane and Caroline, wondered if this was meant to get back to the rebels, discourage them and bring them to the negotiating table.

The telegram was addressed to Jane Dunhaughton, C/O Kya Lami, Bloemfontein. A servant brought it into the dining room on a silver tray.

Caroline took the telegram, looked at it and nodded. 'This is it,' she said, and handed it over to Jane.

Jane took a big breath then puffed her cheeks as she expelled the air from her lungs. She stood up as she opened the telegram and discarded the envelope.

Jane received letter stop Need to see child stop If all well yes. Letter on way Edith end.

Jane read the telegram two or three times and then shouted, 'Yes, yes, yes! I knew I was right! Yes, she will have James.' She jumped in the air and hugged Caroline.

She was simply ecstatic; a whole host of thoughts and emotions were flooding through her mind and body. She was doing good; it was the right thing, James would be looked after, Edith would have the child she so wanted, and Jane would not have the worry about what to do with him. At no time had she ever thought she could bring him up herself; it had never entered her mind. She twirled round and then steadied herself on the dining-room table.

'I wonder how she defines "all's well",' Caroline said, on reading the telegram herself. 'Better calm yourself, Jane. This is not a *fait accompli*.'

Jane froze at the unexpected response. Her joy and excitement were extinguished like a match being plunged into a bucket of water.

'What do you mean? She has said yes,' Jane said imploringly, desperately seeking an explanation that would relight the embers of her enthusiasm. 'She would not say yes if she did not mean it. I know her.'

She might as well have said, 'Please don't say that. Please say everything will be fine. Please say how pleased you are.' Caroline could see that and felt for her, but it was because she sympathised with Jane that she knew she had to introduce a note of caution. That is all it was, but notes of caution from Caroline were succinct and blunt.

'It is good news, Jane, excellent news. But let's see what the letter says before we rush into making plans.'

The letter arrived three days later. It was a long three days, which Jane found difficult. However, she looked at it, she could not help but feel annoyed. She saw Caroline's reaction as negative rather than pragmatic, sour-faced rather than cautious.

She did not say anything to Caroline and tried her best to act normally as she did not want them to fall out or argue. She was sure the letter would settle matters and put things back on an even keel. Even so, it was a long three days.

***

Jane took the letter to her room and sat on her bed. She opened it hopefully, and with every expectation that any seeds of doubt would be cast aside. It was a long letter, some three pages, rambling and almost incoherent at times. It was not well written, lacking care in its composition and structure. It would have been half the length if Edith had taken twice as long to write it.

The first page added nothing of substance; it was not until halfway through the second page, by which time Jane was having great difficulty not skipping to the end, that the real issues were addressed:

Alun would like a son and he would love to bring up James but needs to know he is all well. I have told him you have said he is, but he needs to see for himself that the child has two arms, two legs — you know what I mean — and has his wits about him. Alun could not bring up a half-wit.

The next truly important part came at the top of page three.

Alun says we can only bring him up in England. He knows I want to go home and has already written for jobs, one in Northumberland in the mines, the other in Kent, again in the mines. They are good jobs, well paid. He would be a boss with a good house.

If all's well, then we will go back home. Alun wants to have few days' holiday and go to Cape Town. We've never been to Cape Town as we came in to Durban. Can you go to Cape Town and meet us there? Then we will go home.

Your loving friend
Edith
P.S. Thank you from the bottom of my heart.

Despite her confidence that Edith would take James, it was a greatly relieved Jane who put down the letter and went over to the window. The wind was blowing strongly and leaves and twigs were swirling around, dropping to the ground only to be picked up when the next gust funnelled its way through the trees. A giant pile of leaves was being created at the base of a hedge running along the west side of the lawn. Jane stood at the window watching as it grew before her eyes. Slowly she began to take in what Edith had said in her letter.

She would have to go back to Cape Town. She could stay with Betty Moltano or the Currys, or one of the other supporters of the Distress Fund. If she went back to Cape Town, would she base herself there or come back to Bloemfontein? She liked it at Kya Lami. It was a special place but it was not in the centre of things and she felt rather isolated. On the other hand, it was certainly nearer the camps than Cape Town.

She took the letter downstairs. Caroline was sewing in the drawing room and looked up as Jane came in. 'Well, what did she say?' she asked in her straightforward way.

'She says yes, as long as they can see for themselves that James is well. They are going to take him back to England. Edith's husband has applied for jobs back home. I knew they would, I just knew it. I am so relieved and pleased. I am going to have to go to Cape Town — they want to meet there and then go home if all is well.' As she spoke, her relief showed on her face. She wanted to say, 'I told you so,' but refrained, not wanting to dampen the moment. She was looking for Caroline to say something positive and supportive.

'If all is well?' Caroline asked, looking puzzled. She had not shown any response and her face was quite inscrutable.

'Yes, they want to see for themselves that James is well.'

Caroline appeared to ponder this statement for a while; after quite a pause, she appeared to settle things in her mind and stood up. 'Well, that's good then. Well done, Jane. I did not think it likely they would take James, but I admit that I have never met them and you have.'

It was smiles all round and there was an immediate change in the atmosphere. Caroline went to the drinks cabinet and pulled out a bottle of gin. 'Let's celebrate. It's not every day you find a home for a baby you have saved from certain death.'

The next week was spent planning the trip to Cape Town. Jane replied to Edith, saying how pleased she was and that she was certain it would be the best decision they had ever taken. She said that she planned to be in Cape Town in mid-June and asked if they could be there by then. She fully understood if they needed more time.

Ten days passed between Jane finishing the letter, posting it and getting a reply. These ten days did not seem as long as the three days spent waiting for the initial telegram from Edith; nevertheless time dragged, not least because Jane could not finalise her plans until she knew when she would need to be in Cape Town.

She was not short of things to do and she was both mentally and physically engaged as she waited. There were many letters from the committee and the Distress Fund. When not dealing with these, she spent time in the garden and rode. Her worst fear was that James might become ill and be unable to travel to Cape Town but, as the days passed, he appeared to get stronger and stronger.

Jane did not know how old he was but guessed not more than six months. She was annoyed with herself for not having found out when she was in the camp but, when she recalled the pattern of events, she realised there had been no time to ask questions. A cold shudder went through her every time she thought of the angry woman thrusting James into her arms and the look of utter misery on Mrs Pienaar's face. What must it be like to lose three of your sons and give the fourth one away because you thought he would die? Jane wondered about going back to the camp and finding out more about the child but, on reflection, thought it better that she stayed away until she had settled James's future once and for all.

When the reply came, it was agreed that Jane would meet up with Mr and Mrs Newman on June 15th. They would be staying at the Grand Hotel on Strand Street, which was all Jane needed to know in order to begin preparations for her own journey to Cape Town. It was not something she was looking forward to; the journey had been difficult enough when she had travelled up with Emily but now she would be on her own. Well, not on her own for she would have James with her. She remembered how uncomfortable the train journeys were and the thought of having to look after James as well filled her with dread. She had no experience of babies; at Kya Lami, the servants took care of him.

She discussed as much as she could with Caroline but found her not particularly helpful. 'You will manage,' and 'It will soon pass,' were amongst the few words of encouragement that she received. Caroline appeared more interested in sorting out Jane's time in Cape Town; she sent off letters to Betty Moltano and the Currys advising of Jane's arrival.

Jane was keen to discuss with them how she could best contribute to the work of the relief fund and use some of the money that was continuing to come in.

On the day of her departure, a wonderful crisp bright cold day, Jane breakfasted with Caroline. She did not feel hungry and picked at a small bowl of fruit. She felt very nervous and the pit of her stomach ached with tension.

'You need more than that. Eat properly. You might not have another meal for a few days,' said Caroline.

'I am so nervous,' Jane said, looking embarrassed.

'Nonsense! Once you are on your way you will feel better. Have you finished packing?'

'Yes, everything is ready. I have ticked everything off.' Jane had compiled the most meticulous of lists, asking the servants what she needed for James and received precise instructions about how and what to feed him. Carrying three days' provisions for him was the most difficult logistical task: the tins of milk were heavy. She was going to take three cases: one of paraphernalia for James, one of food and one for her clothes. When she saw the cases and tried to lift them, she decided to discard her own clothes and buy new ones when she got to Cape Town.

When she was due to leave, Philip loaded the cases onto the carriage ready to take her to the station in Bloemfontein.

Standing at the entrance to the house, hands together, looking confident and assured, Caroline took away whatever small amount of wind Jane had left in her sails by saying, 'If it does not work out, I will bring up James.'

Jane looked at her in amazement. 'Really?' she asked Jane.

'Yes, so don't worry. You have a back stop.'

'Oh, thank you. That is so reassuring. It has been a worry what I would do if they pulled out.'

'Well, now you know, so off you go.' Caroline moved down the steps and almost pushed Jane into the carriage.

Jane nodded to Philip; he flicked the reins and the horses started forward. She turned and saw Caroline skip up the steps into the house. She began to question if she was doing the right thing. Would Caroline have liked to bring up the child? Should she turn round?

These thoughts danced around in her mind and the short journey into town passed in a flash. She wanted to go back — but what about the Newmans? Was she not committed? Surely Caroline, confident and brusque as she was, would have said if she wanted to bring up James. It was not as though she was shy in coming forward. No, Caroline was simply being helpful and giving Jane peace of mind. Yes, that was it, Jane none-too-convincingly decided.

The train was already in the station when they arrived and there was a great deal of activity loading the trucks attached to a very small old engine.

Jane climbed down from the carriage, holding James in her arms. She felt very strange and uncertain as she thanked Philip for handing down the cases. 'Wish me luck,' she said, as he turned the carriage round.

'Good luck,' he said. 'Will you be coming back?'

'Yes, I will be back but I am not sure when,' Jane replied.

As she stood on the platform watching the carriage move away, she wondered if this was true.

To the right of where Jane was standing with her two cases there were a large number of flatbed waggons on a track parallel with the one that came into the station. These were loaded with boxes, packing cases and bales of straw and hay, all due to be taken north into the Transvaal. There were four or five empty flat cars; on these sat a large number of troops in khaki uniforms. They looked bored and scruffy.

A fat, uniformed railway official came up to her and asked where she was going. When she said Cape Town, he looked at the baby in her arms. 'Best of luck then. It's a long journey at the best of times, never mind with the war. Have you got a ticket and a pass?'

It struck Jane like a clap of thunder. She had failed to get a pass. Up to now Emily had dealt with getting the passes and they had been given in her name. *Allow Emily Hobhouse and companion Jane Dunhaughton free passage within the Cape Colony.* She could see in her mind's eye the official letter and also the accompanying note from Milner's office as Colonial Secretary. Inwardly she trembled. She felt a complete idiot. She had not even started her journey and she had run into a monumental problem.

She did not know where her response came from, or how it even managed to escape her lips. She calmly looked down at the cases and then at the baby in her arms and said, 'Oh yes. It's in the case. I can get it out if you like.' She started to bend down and exaggerated her difficulty in holding the baby.

The official said, 'It's all right but keep it handy. You will be asked for it on the way.' He waddled off, his trousers massively too long and catching under his rubber-soled boots.

Jane breathed a sigh of relief. She looked at James, who was fast asleep. 'Gosh, James, lucky escape. We are going to have to have our wits about us, I can tell.'

There were only two passenger carriages on the train and, as she had expected, they were far from first class. The floors were dirty and the seats covered in dust. There was no glass in any of the windows, nor did it look like there had ever been. There were three male civilians in her carriage dressed in black, rough-looking suits with waistcoats. They wore bowler hats, which they raised when Jane got in.

She had James under one arm and had lifted one case into the carriage when one of the men stood and said, 'Hey let me help you ma'am.' He jumped down and picked up the remaining case, placing it in a single movement onto the overhead rack. He did the same with the first case and, before Jane had settled into a seat, was looking intently at her. He was about thirty years of age, tall and strong looking, with a black moustache. He had remarkably clean, shiny leather boots.

As Jane settled down, feeling very self-conscious and well aware that all eyes were on her, he boomed out in a stentorian voice, 'Hi, my names Silverton, Arthur Silverton, and these two no-good vagabonds are not to be trusted. I would not speak to them, if I were you.' He looked at the other two with a wide grin.

One of them took off his hat and threw it by its brim at Arthur Silverton who caught it expertly and threw it back.

'My name's Silverton, John Grassington Silverton. I'm his brother,' the other man said, pointing at Arthur. 'And this is Henry. Henry has not got a second name.'

Henry blurted out, 'How many times do I tell you?'

'Told you, he does not have a name. Just call him Milker.'

Henry looked at him with disdain and shook his head. 'Excuse him, he thinks he is funny.'

'No, it's you who are funny,' John replied quickly.

'Well?' Arthur said in a loud deep voice, leaning forward and looking straight at Jane.

She was not sure what was expected. She was not used to this style of banter and quick jovial remarks.

'Well, who are you, where are you going, where have you been, how old are you, what's your mother's name and can you cook?' He smiled, a great grin from one side of his face to the other. 'Like I said, don't talk to those two. They are dangerous. Don't worry, I will protect you.'

This light-hearted jesting was a novelty to Jane but she knew instantly that she liked it; the lack of formality and stiffness was uplifting. She found herself smiling in return and feeling more at ease.

'My name is Jane Dunhaughton. I am travelling to Cape Town.'

'Cape Town? Well, so are we, as long as we don't get ambushed along the way.'

It was the start of a three-day journey that was made all the easier by the presence of these three roguish but very likeable young men. It turned out that they were farmers from a small hamlet some thirty miles from Bloemfontein. They were going to Cape Town to travel on to the United States. They wanted to see more of the world than the dreary Karoo, and wanted to be in a place with more girls. They had passages booked on a liner to England and then to New York.

'So the woman in the camp just gave you the baby and you are now going to give it away?' said Arthur, incredulity in his voice.

190

'Well, I wouldn't say give it away. Mrs Pienaar was doing what she thought best. She was worried he would die in the camp.'

'We know all about the camps and the burning of farms, don't we?' Arthur looked for support from his two companions. They nodded. 'I have to say, though, I've not heard of babies being given away but I do know there have been a lot of deaths. What I can't understand is you also giving the baby away. Do you not feel responsible for him?'

Jane hesitated before responding. 'I feel totally responsible but I can do two good turns. I can save the baby and give him a good home and I can bring joy to another couple.'

'You know, my mother used to say there was nothing stranger than folk. This tale is sure strange. I can only hope all goes well,' said Arthur. This did not stop the three of them, at times they thought Jane was asleep, questioning the veracity of her story. They found it hard to believe the picture she had painted. Why would someone so posh go to the disease-ridden camps and ride on these awful trains? Jane heard Arthur say, 'My mum would certainly have said that girl is strange.'

The exchange made a mark on Jane. Arthur's comments made her realise she was dealing with a helpless child who needed her. By the second day, she found that she was more confident in her dealings with James. She was less uncertain that she was doing things right, and more conscious of his personality. She played with him, watching his eyes follow a rattle as she moved it in front of him. She observed him holding a set of keys that Arthur rattled in front of him and looked closely at his tiny fingers.

Despite their uncertainty over the validity of her story, the three fellow passengers were perfect gentlemen and constantly helped her. At the stops they made sure that the toilet was clean before they let Jane in; on more than one occasion, they got a bucket and cloths to clean the washroom. They held James at times, and helped Jane open tins and prepare food. At one stop they persuaded the guard to let Jane sleep in the guard's hut whilst the baby slept outside, with the three young men in a tent they had with them. Throughout the journey they pointed out the landmarks and the wildlife. They could not have been better companions.

Jane particularly liked Arthur: his humour, adventurous spirit and inquisitiveness, along with his lack of pomposity, appealed to her. In the many hours they sat on the train over the three days, she wished she had met young men like him at home. She wondered if the United States was attracting many such young men who were seeking adventure and escape from routine and ordinary lives. Was that not what she herself was doing?

Despite the companionship and assistance from Arthur, John and Henry, Jane was very relieved to get to Cape Town. She was tired and desperately in need of clean clothes and a long soak. She was thrilled that James had not only survived the journey but looked to be thriving. He had put on weight and was alert. She did not think there was any reason why the Newmans would not think that 'everything was all right'.

As they neared Cape Town, and the men started to sort their possessions, Jane placed James in the corner of the carriage, wedged between the window and the back of the seat. She stood up, pulled down her own case and took out her notebook. She carefully wrote out her name and English address, and also the hotel address where she was staying in Cape Town. She gave it to Arthur, together with a note which simply said: *Thank you for all your help. I have greatly enjoyed your company and I wish you and your brother and Henry the very best of luck in the United States*. She folded the note, placed it in an envelope and handed it to Arthur as the train came to a stop.

'Just in case you are ever in Hampshire, do call,' she said.

Chapter 18
Brief Encounter

The station had plenty of porters and, in what seemed like less than a minute, she was in a cab being taken to the Grand Hotel. The hotel was a splendid colonial refuge. It could have been anywhere — Singapore, Hong Kong, Kenya, Nigeria or any number of the Caribbean islands. The same people would have been coming in and out, looking fresh, clean and superior.

It was, therefore, a sheepish Jane who approached the check-in desk. To do so, she had to cross a magnificent mosaic floor emblazoned with the coat of arms of the Cape Colony. She had James in her arms, was looking distinctly travel worn and was very hungry. She felt out of place and uneasy.

The clerk looked at her suspiciously and asked in a mocking tone, 'How can I be of assistance?' He expected that the vagrant would soon be leaving.

'My name is Jane Dunhaughton and I believe you have a reservation in my name,' Jane said quietly.

The clerk looked surprised but said he would check. 'Yes, it appears we do,' he said, without looking up from the large ledger that lay open before him. 'I will get the porter to take your bags.' He waved his hand and, as a porter emerged from nowhere, pointed to Jane. Then he contemptuously wafted her away, hoping she would never be seen at his desk again.

The room was lovely, light and airy, with pine furniture, cotton sheets, a large double bed and a separate area for dressing and washing. A very large bowl with an even larger jug of water was positioned on a dressing table with a mirror. There was a note on the table that said that guests who required a bath should ring for a maid. This was just what Jane did, but not before she had arranged for room service to go to the nearest store and purchase two skirts, two blouses, underwear and a new coat.

The clothes were waiting for her when she emerged from a very, very long soak. The hotel clerk might have been snobbish and aloof but the room-service staff could not have been more helpful in getting Jane what she needed and also in looking after James whilst she lay in the bath.

It was an altogether different Jane who approached the hotel desk after breakfast. It was June the 15th and she looked pristine and prim in a black full-length skirt and white high-necked blouse with a long black woollen cardigan that the room-service girls had given her, saying it had been left by a guest more than a week ago.

There was a different clerk at the desk. She asked him if the Newmans had arrived. It took a surprisingly long time for the clerk to find the answer. Having looked for ages in the ledger, he excused himself and went into the back room.

Jane began to panic, thinking they were not coming; they had cancelled, had second thoughts about the whole idea. She was starting to tremble and looking intently at the door where the clerk had disappeared when she felt a slight tap on the shoulder and a quiet, 'Jane, is that you?'

She turned round and there was Edith Newman, accompanied by a thickset, bowler-hatted, moustached man in a three-piece suit.

'Oh, I am so glad you have arrived. We have been worrying that you might not have been able to get here, what with the war and all. We arrived last night. Terrible journey, but I suppose you know all about that. Oh, this is my husband, Alun. Alun, this is Jane.'

Edith was clearly very nervous and her speech was five times faster than normal. She was moving her weight from foot to foot. As Jane shook Alun's outstretched hand, Edith continued, 'Is everything all right?'

'All right?' replied Jane, the first words she had been able to get out.

'Yes, you know, with the baby?'

Jane hardly recognised this woman. Her speech pattern was quite different and she was on edge.

Alun interrupted. 'Please excuse Edith's impatience. You must think it very rude of her firing off these questions before we have been properly introduced.' He looked at Edith in a 'calm down, for goodness' sake, woman' way. 'Truth is, since we got your letter Edith has not been herself.'

Jane began to fear the worst. They were nervous because they did not want James but knew they had to come and tell her personally. They wanted to be away as quickly as possible, get it over with. It had been a silly idea — had Jane really expected just to give a baby away?

It was staggering how many negative thoughts could go through a brain in a fraction of a second, especially when that brain was looking for any sign, no matter how trivial, that the thing it was seeking more than anything was not going to plan.

'Oh, I understand. James is fine. He is upstairs sleeping in my room.'

'We are not staying. We are in another hotel not far away. Not as expensive as here.'

'We are not staying' sent a great thud into the pit of Jane's stomach like a kick from a horse.

'I see,' came her reply. She was uncertain; not one minute had passed since they had met and now, she was on guard, hesitant about how to progress matters.

'Can we see the baby?' Alun intervened. 'I would really like to move things along as best we can.' He seemed impatient and nervous, and he occasionally glanced around the room as though he might be seen by someone he knew.

'Why, of course,' said Jane. 'Would you like a coffee first or some tea?'

'No, thank you, we have had breakfast. We would like to get this over with, you know. Then we'll know for certain.'

Edith was hanging back. Jane noticed Alun look straight at his wife as he spoke. 'Edith is finding this difficult and would like to get it over with. That right, isn't it, Edith?'

Edith nodded and added a quiet, 'Yes.'

'I see,' said Jane, perplexed by the lack of warmth in the conversation. She struggled to find the right response.

'Shall we go up to your room?' Alun turned and moved toward the inner lobby. 'Are the rooms this way?'

Jane felt herself being herded towards the stairs but was powerless to impose any element of control on the proceedings. She was being railroaded, but it was the unexpectedness of the way that things were unfolding that was inhibiting her. It was not as she had rehearsed it in her mind.

In no time they were up two flights of stairs and walking along the corridor to room 212. Jane fumbled for the key and let the Newmans in.

James was lying on the bed, wrapped in a blanket. Jane picked him up and held him in her arms. 'This is James. He has been as good as gold. He has grown and put on weight. You would not know now what a difficult start in life he had.' She looked intently at Edith and Alun expecting some genial friendly response but none was forthcoming.

'Would you mind if we took off the blanket and laid him on the bed?' asked Alun. 'I had four brothers and two sisters, all younger than me.' That statement was clearly meant to explain all to Jane but she did not know what its relevance was.

Again, she gave a feeble, 'Oh, I see.'

Alun took the baby from Jane and laid him on the bed. He removed the blanket and lifted the baby's white, full-length cotton shirt. James was wearing a nappy, which Alun unfastened. He looked at the baby carefully and then refastened the pin. He touched James on the side of his face and watched as the child moved his eyes and turned to the side. Alun turned him over and held out his arms. James started to cry.

Edith and Jane were mere spectators. Jane had no idea of what he was doing; she had no experience of babies. She was not sure what Alun was doing, only that he had taken control.

'Boy seems fine. All there,' Alun said, looking straight at Edith.

'Really?' said Edith, a clear sense of relief in her voice.

'Yes, the boy seems fine,' Alun repeated, this time looking at Jane. 'If you don't mind, we would like to take him now. Get things over with.' He wrapped James in the blanket, picked him up and handed him to Edith. 'We will go now.'

He turned and moved towards the door. Edith looked at Jane; there was fear in her eyes, and nervousness. Jane was now concerned, indeed worried.

'You are going to look after James? I mean really look after him and love him? It is not too late to say no. I will fully understand.' Her voice trembled. 'Where are you staying? I would like to keep in touch. I will want to know how James is getting on.'

Even as she was speaking, Alun was ushering Edith through the door into the corridor. He turned to Jane. 'It's best this way. Get things over with. He will be fine. He is James Newman now, and always was.' As he said the words 'always was', he nodded his head, clearly wanting Jane to confirm that the baby had always been James Newman.

Jane was mesmerised; as though through thought-transference, she started to nod. Yes. James Newman.

As they scuttled down the corridor with Jane scampering to keep up, she called out. 'Edith, I have put my trust in you.'

This made Edith stop. She turned and came back towards Jane. In a low whisper, clearly not wanting Alun to hear, she said, 'Don't worry, Jane. James will have a loving home.' She turned and walked back towards Alun, who had moved further down the corridor. As she did so she turned again and with unmistakable tenderness and sincerity she said, 'Thank you, thank you.'

***

It took Jane a good hour to recover. Never in a hundred years would she have envisaged that the handover would be so functional, so businesslike, so impersonal. She did not understand and, as she sat on the bed, she could not rationalise the Newmans' behaviour.

The only redeeming aspect of the whole brief episode was the look she had seen in Edith's eyes. They had told Jane that she would look after James and would love him.

Even so the rest of the day was little more than a blur. She failed to hear what people were saying to her; she was trapped in her own world of bewilderment. The only other emotion that she had, which struck her forcibly when she entered her room after dinner that night, was a feeling of emptiness. By the side of the bed lay the case with all the paraphernalia she'd needed for James. The Newmans had not taken it, as she'd assumed, they would. Lying there, it reinforced the feeling she had of there being a void.

She recalled the feeling she had as a child when her pet dog had died and his bed lay empty in the kitchen. It upset her to see the vacant bed and confront the reality that it would not be filled again. The kitchen was always alive and warm but then it seemed cold and austere. This was the feeling she now had. She felt she should have been pleased because her plan had come to fruition. She had dreamed on the train of celebrating the handing over of James and sharing a toast with the Newmans to his future happiness. All she could hear now was an empty silence. Had she made a terrible mistake? Would James have been better being brought up by Caroline?

She tossed and turned during the night and, as she rolled from left to right, she reached out to touch the child who was no longer there.

Chapter 19
Cape Town to Durban

Jane spent three forlorn, introspective days at the hotel reliving those five minutes of confusion. As she dwelt on the sequence of events, she began to feel used and coerced. It should not have been like that. She should have been stronger, more forceful. A happy and joyous event had become memorable for all the wrong reasons and she blamed herself.

She worried now about James and his welfare. Had she been wicked in handing him over to people she hardly knew? She prayed for him to be safe. It was only incrementally over the next three days, during which she did not venture out of the hotel, that she began to leave the world of self-absorption and re-join the community, which, she reminded herself, was looking to her to alleviate some of its own wrongdoings. Rest and sleep played a major part in her recovery.

On the fourth day, June the 19th, she ventured out of the hotel for the first time and sauntered without a specific purpose along the streets of Cape Town. The contrast with the interior of South Africa, Bloemfontein, Kimberley and the minor railway station stops she had seen was even greater than that between London and Sparsholt. This impression was heavily influenced by her taking her first ride on an electric tram, an event that amazed her.

She stayed on the tram for over an hour, going round the city twice, taking in the buzz and vibrancy that was everywhere. The docks smelt heavily of fish; large numbers of men and women could be seen packing them into drums or gutting them on the dockside. It was some time since she had been somewhere new and not had to worry about passes, disease, petty officials and the suffering in the camps and this helped further lighten her mental turmoil.

She jumped off the tram at Adderley Street and walked down the sidewalk until she came to a large department store. She bought more clothes and shoes and two hats, and asked for them to be delivered to Betty Moltano's home.

In the hotel she was amazed to discover that a telephone service had been installed in Cape Town in 1884 and there were now more than four hundred registered users in the city. She used the hotel phone to ring Betty and was astonished to be able to speak to her. She realised how little she knew of the world.

What Jane did know was that she was very short of money. She had not really spent anything since she had arrived in South Africa; everything had been provided by her hosts at the houses in which she had stayed. Train tickets, goods for the camps and subsistence had all been paid for by money drawn from the Distress Fund. Betty, the Currys or Catherine, had simply given her money. Now Jane wanted some money of her own.

She entered the Standard Bank, an imposing neoclassic building built in 1891. It had a grand banking hall, with very formal stiff-suited tellers situated at the back of the hall. On either side there were desks with chairs where customers could explain what they were seeking to the four under-managers and four clerks who sat, with intimidating uniformity, looking out into the hall.

Jane had learnt much in the few months since she had left Hampshire and strode confidently up to the first of the desks.

'My name is Jane Dunhaughton. I am visiting friends here in Cape Town. I live in England. I would like to draw some money. I have my cheque book with me.' She pulled the cheque book from her bag.

'It is a pleasure to meet you, Miss Dunhaughton,' said a pleasant, clean-shaven young man of about her own age. 'May I ask where you are staying?'

'I am at the Grand Hotel but I am going to stay with my friend, Elizabeth Moltano,' Jane replied.

'May I ask if Mrs Moltano banks with the Standard Bank in Cape Town?' asked the clerk.

'I really don't know,' said Jane. 'Is that important?'

The clerk looked puzzled. 'Would you excuse me for a moment?' he said and went across the room to an older gentleman. The pair of them returned and the senior bank official addressed Jane.

'Miss Dunhaughton, I am the assistant manager. I understand you are seeking to draw a cheque. Is that correct?'

'Yes, that's right. I am visiting Cape Town from England.'

'I am afraid that without identification or a letter of introduction we would have to telegraph your bank in

England for authority. That could take some time. How long will you be in Cape Town?'

'I am not entirely sure. Perhaps a few weeks,' Jane replied, starting to feel that getting some money might be more difficult than she had envisaged.

'We can telegraph, but getting a response from the right person is always problematic. It does get sorted out eventually but it's not something that can be done in a hurry.' The assistant manager offered these words hoping Jane would go away. He had a dozen forms to fill in to authorise transactions drawn on another bank. 'Do you have a relative or friend who banks with us? They could draw a cheque on your behalf.'

'Oh yes,' said Jane seizing the chance to escape from this embarrassment. Two other customers were now waiting for attention and Jane felt her every word was being listened to. 'Yes, that's a sound idea. I will do that. Thank you.'

Jane almost ran out of the bank. She felt belittled for no obvious reason. She had committed no faux pas or misdemeanour; she had explained things clearly and with confidence; she looked smart and clean. Nevertheless, the Jane who came out of the Standard Bank on Adderley Street was a foot smaller than the one who went in.

Her confidence was based on small steps, small successes. She had come a long way in the last few months but those small steps had taken her to a ledge on a precipitous cliff. A small slip could soon have her tumbling back down. She was conscious that it was ridiculous, that all she had done was go into a bank and make a reasonable request, but nevertheless she felt diminished. The feeling would soon go, but it lurked deep down, waiting for the next slip.

***

Jane spent the next three weeks with Betty Moltano. Betty did exactly what the assistant manager had suggested. Jane made out a cheque to her and in return Betty gave her twenty British pound notes that proved to be more than sufficient for her needs.

In those three weeks, Jane attended numerous meetings with members of the committee and gave her first-hand account of conditions in the camps, what she had seen on the train journeys, the burnt-out farms, animals being driven to their deaths, people in open trucks. The other ladies always listened in silence and, on more than one occasion, tears could be seen being wiped from the faces of the well-meaning, sincerely concerned but out-of-touch Cape Town upper classes.

What Jane did not recount was anything about Mrs Pienner, James or the Newmans. Something told her that she should keep this quiet as she was certain that the ladies of the committee would question her deeply about James if she raised the topic, and she did not see what this would achieve. For all she knew, James and the Newmans might well be on their way back to England. She was slowly coming to terms with the episode and, rather like the Newmans, was now going to act as if it had never happened.

Jane started to write letters to a wide range of members and supporters of the committee in various parts of South Africa. She began to organise a network of volunteers who could take clothing and foodstuffs to the camps and who would have the advantage of being, if not local, substantially nearer than she was. She was provided with letters of introduction from a number of the Cape Town group and always enclosed one of these with her own letter.

The Distress Fund committee had an office on Darling Street. Jane went there most days, occupying herself by helping with the post, preparing food parcels and writing to the press seeking free publicity for their work. She was methodical and organised, keeping detailed lists of who she had written to, recording when she received a reply and its content. She had her own box in which she filed her correspondence, again in her trademark organised fashion. She knew she would not be there long and wanted to ensure that whoever took over from her when she went home would be able to follow the thread.

Whilst she was writing letters for the Distress Fund, she became concerned about her personal correspondence. Any letters for her would probably go to Bloemfontein and she was worried that her frequent changes of address meant that they would go astray. She had received no recent news from home, or Lilly, and wondered what was happening. The lack of correspondence from England amplified the growing call of home. She was beginning to understand why Mrs Newman had so desperately wanted to go back.

In the third week of July, a meeting of the Distress Fund in Cape Town decided that they needed to coordinate activities with the work that was going on in Durban on the west coast of South Africa, itself a substantial port and distribution centre. There was a large British community in Durban and the city had a thriving commercial sector. Leaders of the Cape Colony Committee, including Lady de Villiers, Dr Andrew Murray and Sir Bisset Barry, all very prominent members of the community, lent their names and support to a campaign to coordinate all relief activities under a single umbrella. Due to the publicity generated by Emily, they had received a massive increase in funding not just from Britain but from across the world, and relief activities were springing up in many areas.

The Cape Town press was full of reports from London of the fierce arguments that raged as a result of Emily's report on conditions in the camp and the bitter denials emanating from the government, and the Secretary of State for War, St John Brodrick, in particular. *The Times*, the mouthpiece of the British government, sought to belittle Emily, portraying her as an agitator and interfering amateur. On the other hand, Sir Henry Campbell-Bannerman, leader of the Liberals, made a speech in which he said, 'When is a war not a war? It is when it is carried on by methods of barbarism in South Africa.'

This followed a meeting he had had with Emily on the 13th of June. Four days later, David Lloyd George moved that the house debate the situation in the camps as a matter of urgency. His statement that the death rate of twelve per cent a year was tantamount to 'a policy of extermination' was like an incendiary bomb, and government supporters intensified their personal attacks on Emily.

'I do hope Emily is well and coping with all these horrid statements about her in the press,' Jane said to a group of volunteers in the office 'I fear for her safety.' She remembered clearly the anger at some of the public meetings she had attended before leaving for South Africa. She was, though, immensely proud that the struggles they had gone through together were having a major effect. 'It is good, though, that her work is having such impact. I do hope it will lead to a change of policy by the government and stop Kitchener's policy of farm burning and concentrating the civilians in camps.'

Jane noticed that the press was full of praise for Milner, who had received every available accolade when he arrived back in England. She wondered how this could be, and how so many decisions were taken by politicians who had no understanding of the actual position.

As she continued to read the press, one article reprinted from *The Times* in London, caught her eye. It referred to an announcement in Parliament by Sir John Brodrick that a committee of six women, headed by a Mrs Millicent Fawcett, would report on conditions in the camps. The article said that they had already left for South Africa. Jane knew of Millicent Fawcett, one of the leaders of the women's suffrage movement in England. Jane had been with Lilly to hear one of her speeches but she struggled to remember much else about her.

'I say,' said Jane quite loudly to the whole room, 'I think we should all read this article, it is very important.'

It did indeed arouse serious interest.

'A committee of women: that must be a first,' said one of the ladies.

Another said, 'It will be a whitewash. It is what they always do to cover things up and buy time.'

'I am not so certain,' said another. 'Once Fawcett and her colleagues see the camps, surely it will lead to conditions being materially improved if not to them being closed.'

Jane introduced a note of caution, 'I worry that they will only visit the well-run camps. Emily and I visited some which were, on the whole, quite reasonable. If they only go to the good ones, the report will be without value.'

She repeated her concerns privately to Caroline Murray, a senior member of the Distress Fund committee. They agreed that they must do all they could to meet with the visitors and take them to all the camps.

Later in August, Caroline arranged a meeting with Millicent Fawcett when she arrived in Cape Town but she did not persuade her on any points. Millicent Fawcett was a very forceful personality and she had clear ideas as to how the committee would be organised; local people were not going to interfere with her plans.

On the first day of August 1901, Jane left Cape Town for Durban with a party drawn from members of the Distress Fund committee. She was pleased they were travelling by ship, not by train. The journey took three days but it was, as Jane kept telling the delegation, immeasurably more comfortable than the train journeys she and Emily had taken. She actually felt quite privileged.

The delegation was made up of wealthy people, some with their servants. They had first-class berths and everything was quite splendid; it was a jolly sea cruise with wonderful food, clean and comfortable cabins. What a contrast to the terrible conditions Jane had endured on those seemingly endless train journeys! Even so, the relative opulence of the journey, the expectation of the party that this was how they would travel, and the remoteness of this from the families in the camps made Jane uneasy. She did not say anything but she wondered if this was what their campaigning was really about.

She was also uneasy that the one time she raised the issue of the separate camps, which had been set up for black people displaced by the burning of farms, she was met with bewildered expressions. 'Why would we be interested in the black camps?' was the attitude. She did not raise the issue again.

The meetings in Durban were business like but repetitive. They talked about the same things they had in Cape Town, discussed the same issues, and agreed much the same as had been agreed at Cape Town. It was all very much at arm's length; they talked about how to distribute the significant sums that were coming in, but no one at the meetings thought about taking the goods themselves.

They did visit a hospital for wounded officers and addressed a number of small meetings, but Jane found the work superficial; it did not communicate the suffering that was going on. It seemed far too nice and restrained, a few well-meaning and caring people raising a few pounds to help less-important people.

When the opportunity came to do something more practical, Jane jumped at the chance. Everyone agreed that the real need was in the Transvaal. There was little information about conditions in the camps there and, given the scale of the resources they now had, the committee wanted to get the support of the army to distribute goods there. Jane agreed to travel to Pretoria, some 333 miles from Durban, to talk to senior commanders and try to persuade them to help on the ground. All the committee members agreed that this needed a personal presence otherwise, although agreement might be obtained, nothing would happen.

Jane helped draw up this plan and pointed out how helpful it could be having a local contact such as Captain Nelson. She was pleased that she was going to do something practical. She also intended going to Pretoria and coming back via Bloemfontein so she could see Caroline Fichardt before going back to Cape Town. She hoped Emily would be back in South Africa by then and she herself could prepare to go home.

Events, however, interfered with this plan. Unknown to Jane, or anyone in South Africa other than those in Kitchener's or Milner's private offices, plans were being made to prevent 'that dammed woman', as Kitchener described Emily, from setting foot in South Africa again. They'd had enough of the trouble she had caused them and they were determined she was not going to add fuel to the fire.

Kitchener and Milner were fully supported by the government, which was reeling from the international condemnation of the concentration-camp policy and from the bitter attacks from Lloyd George, Campbell-Bannerman and other leading Liberals. The last thing they wanted was Emily Hobhouse getting in the way of the women's committee they had sent out to South Africa.

Millicent Fawcett could be relied upon; she was one of them, a 'sound chap'. She might be a leading light in that votes for women movement, but on Britain's place in the world she was fully behind the war and its motives. Even better, rumour had it that she was no friend of Emily Hobhouse who, it appeared, had been siding with tenants in a bitter dispute with their landlord — none other than Millicent Fawcett. Millicent was not one to forget those who crossed her path.

Chapter 20
Gunshots and Poetry

Jane left for Pretoria on the 10th of August. This time she was armed with all the appropriate passes. She may have been uncomfortable with the Cape Town delegation but they did have the right connections. The Transvaal was under martial law but many of the senior officers came down to Cape Town for leave and stayed with the wealthy elite or had family who had immigrated to the Cape. These connections were used to good effect; Jane was authorised to travel on the railways to Pretoria. The pass, however, made it clear that she must not travel outside the boundaries of Pretoria town itself. Jane was quite happy with that, as much of the area was frequented by Boer guerrilla fighters and there were frequent clashes with the British forces.

This journey was different in one respect from the last train journey she had made: she did not have the responsibility of James and her load was substantially less. She had no truckloads of clothes and food to load or unload and she felt slightly ashamed that she found this liberating. She had nothing to worry about other than herself.

The train journey from Durban to Pretoria was far easier and shorter than the journey from Cape Town to Bloemfontein, or so she had been told, and took just one day if all went well.

The train from Durban was unlike the trains leaving Cape Town for the north. Whilst there were a number of normal carriages with seats, most of the train was made up of specially adapted goods waggons. These had high metal sides and every few yards there were holes from which soldiers could fire rifles. They were, in fact, armoured cars and Jane had never seen anything like them. As soon as she saw them the feeling of liberation disappeared.

There were also a significant number of horseboxes into which five or six horses were crammed. Jane was aghast, as she looked at the terrible conditions, they were being kept in. 'Let's hope they get lots of water,' she thought.

It was a lovely twenty-two degrees with low humidity when they left Durban. If only winters were like this back home, she thought, but as the journey commenced, she began to change her mind, feeling that she rather enjoyed the contrast between the seasons.

She was surprised at how different Durban was from Cape Town in all aspects, not least climate. The dryness of the winter made it more appealing, and the flowers and birdlife added to its general impression of being a most attractive town. The large-leafed dragon trees, with their great lime-green leaves, and the numerous cabbage trees looked ancient and weathered, rather like the yew trees Jane was familiar with. They provided a rich, tropical backdrop to the city.

Durban was clearly affected by the war, for the station had a lot of soldiers boarding or embarking trains. When she got off the boat, the docks were dominated by ships bringing in supplies and thousands of horses.

She settled down in a carriage with a well-dressed elderly man and two young women around her own age. They nodded but made no effort to engage in conversation and there was a slightly uncomfortable atmosphere that lasted for some time. Each person was wondering what the others were doing.

The two girls must have known each other, or so Jane assumed, but there was little evidence of it as they barely talked. Jane played a game with herself, guessing what each person did. She decided that the old man (old was a bit unkind as he was certainly not sixty) was a farmer. He had huge rough hands and broad shoulders. She could see him manhandling sheep. It turned out that he was a railway engineer and he was going to Pretoria to supervise the construction of more marshalling space on the line.

Jane assumed that the two girls were nurses going back to the front after leave. Her assessment turned out to be correct.

The train had been moving along at irregular speeds for some eight hours when it came to a stop. The light was sinking fast and shadows from the track-side trees stretched what seemed hundreds of yards away into the distance. The birdlife was noisy and the occasional woodpigeon called out in a dejected, unanswered dirge.

Jane, who was sitting by the window, leaned out to see what had caused the train to stop. Looking toward the engine, which was not in view, she saw solders jumping down from the trucks and running out in a line away from the track. Whistles were being blown and officers were barking out orders. A cacophony of orderly confusion pervaded the still emptiness of the terrain.

Jane turned to her travelling companions, all of whom seemed not only unruffled but also uninterested when she announced, 'Looks like something is wrong. The soldiers are running up the banks.'

'The line has probably been cut,' said the old man.

'More likely they want to relieve themselves,' said one of the nurses.

'Yes, much more likely,' said the other girl. They did not look up from the books they were reading.

The intensity of the shouting and the number of men running along the side of the track and disappearing over the bank increased second by second. It fuelled the blood in Jane's veins and she felt her heart pumping faster. Her eyes traversed instantly a whole 180 degrees as she desperately sought to know what was going on. Then she heard crack after crack, much louder than anything she had ever heard before, totally unlike the guns at a shoot with which she was familiar. Then she heard not just cracks but pings as bullets hit the train, not once but time after time.

Jane froze, not able to move a muscle as she listened to the whoosh of bullets ricocheting and thudding into the hard bank side or the gravel on the track. The adrenalin inside her reached fever pitch but she stood motionless other than her eyes which were darting across the skyline incessantly.

'Get down, you, stupid woman!' barked a soldier from the track side. 'Get down on the floor.'

Jane jumped and turned back into the carriage. The two girls and the old man were already lying full length on the floor. She dropped like a sack, falling on the legs of both girls, neither of whom said a word.

Jane lay there for what seemed an hour at least but was, in fact, less than five minutes. She put her hands over her head in a ridiculous attempt to protect herself. She tightened every muscle in her body, trying to make herself as small as possible, curling her back so that her head bore down into her lap. Her head pounded from within.

Then the carriage door burst open and Jane screamed. An officer, with his revolver drawn, looked down at them from his imposing six-foot height. He had to stoop to get through the door. Surveying the bodies on the floor, at first he thought they had all been shot. 'Anybody hurt?' he asked in a plummy, upper-class accent. 'Come on, answer there!' he shouted. 'Anybody hurt?'

'I don't think so,' said the old man, pushing himself up into a sitting position.

'Believe me, if you had been shot you would know. You girls, come on, get up. No good lying there. Party's over.'

'What happened?' Jane asked feebly. She was still shivering uncontrollably.

'Line was cut and a few bandits fired at the train. Lads soon saw them off. No need to worry.' The officer was still holding his revolver, which he waved about as he moved his arms to illustrate where the line had been cut. He saw Jane looking aghast at his gun and slid it into his holster. 'Still not fired a shot,' he said to himself, clearly disappointed.

The train did not move for the next two hours. Jane and her fellow travellers decided to get out of the carriage and jumped down onto the track side. A number of fires had been started and troops were brewing up and making the best of the delay. It was only on seeing this that Jane began to calm down, her shivering gradually subsiding.

'You were right,' she said to the railway engineer, whose name she still did not know. 'It was a cut line.'

'Yes. It might be some time before it is repaired as the light has gone now. Don't know if they have the equipment to repair it. Should have — and plenty of men here to get it done.'

'Perhaps they will need your help,' Jane commented, trying to make eye contact with him.

'Yes, they might. I will see.' He marched in a sprightly fashion towards the front of the train.

Jane and the two girls continued to amble along the track side. They were not certain what they were doing or where they were going, but they felt much better being close to the soldiers who seemed quite at home, relaxed, joking, preparing tea and frying up.

'Hey, girls, come and join us. Fancy a bite?'

'I'd fancy a bite!' shouted another soldier and there was a burst of laughing and muttering.

Somewhat startled, Jane and the other two women looked in the direction the invitation had come from. A large group of soldiers in somewhat unconventional uniforms, more like the Boer commandos than the British soldiers, were sitting around a camp fire that blazed strongly and threw up a light that illuminated half of those round the fire.

'Come on, we need someone to do the washing up,' a wit shouted, followed by more bellows of laughter.

'Come on, girls, join us. We're going to have a long wait.'

The soldiers' accent was unusual. Jane could not place it but it was not English or South African. The two nurses whispered in each other's ears then moved towards the soldiers.

'Righto, make room for your betters,' one of the nurses said, stepping over outstretched legs and making towards the centre of the group.

'Better at what, love?' shouted a youngish-looking lad with a wide-brimmed hat. His tunic had a high collar with black felt edging around the neck. He had a wide belt wrapped over his shoulder, which went down his back where it was fastened to another belt around his waist. His boots came up to his ankles and his leggings up to his knees: Jane was to learn they were called puttees. He stood out from the others because of his age: he looked younger, more innocent.

'Better at things you don't know about,' interjected the second of the nurses.

'Whoa!' cried the soldiers. 'She's got you sussed already.'

There were a few other comments that Jane could not make out but which aroused much hilarity and further banter.

A couple of the soldiers stood up. They had made some impromptu seating from the packs they were carrying and they offered them to the girls. 'Sit here, love. Make yourself at home.'

'Here, have a cup of tea,' offered another soldier.

The two nurses climbed over numerous kitbags and backpacks and sat down amidst the group. They were soon drinking hot tea from tin mugs. Jane was amazed that these two uncommunicative and aloof individuals had been transformed in an instant into gregarious, high-spirited companions.

She was standing at the side, unsure what to do, when another soldier addressed her. 'Come on, come and join us.'

He stood up. He was about five feet ten inches tall and clean shaven, except for a finely shaped moustache that tapered into thin points. He wore a wide-brimmed hat with a black band, and over his shoulder he had a large belt with a number of pouches where he kept bullets, a knife, a corkscrew and other bits and pieces. He looked to be in his mid-twenties.

Jane did not move at first. It all seemed a bit irregular. Was it appropriate to sit with soldiers around a campfire? She noticed the rifles neatly stacked in small circles with their barrels facing upwards.

'Come on, I'm not standing all night. You too posh to sit with us?' He held out his arm, summoning Jane. As though drawn by an invisible magnet, she moved towards him and dropped onto a large kitbag, on top of which was a rolled-up blanket. In no time she was handed a tin mug and a tin plate holding a huge bacon sandwich.

'Go on, help yourself,' the soldier said. 'There's plenty more and we might be here some time. My name is Handcock, Lieutenant Handcock, Bushvelt Carbineers. What's a posh girl like you doing out here in the bush in the middle of the night and the middle of a war?' He spoke in the accent that Jane had not recognised.

'Oh, I am travelling to Pretoria to provide assistance to those who have to live in the camps.'

Handcock mocked the formality of her reply. '*Oh, I am travelling to Pretoria.* Hey lads, listen up — this gal's *travelling* to Pretoria, just like us.' He stressed the word 'travelling' and then, looking directly at Jane, said, 'But you've not told us what a posh girl like you is doing here. We want the facts, the whole facts and nothing but the facts.' Turning to face the circle of soldiers, he added, 'Don't we, lads?'

There was an instant cry from them all. It was clearly some ritual they had going on. 'The facts, the facts, nothing but the facts,' they shouted, followed by lots of laughing and banter.

'Come on then, let's be having it,' Handcock said. 'First of all, your name, rank and number.'

'I'm Jane Dunhaughton and I come from Hampshire in England. I am helping the Distress Fund for women and children suffering from the war.'

'More,' said Handcock. 'We need more, don't we lads?' Again, the cry went out: 'The facts, the facts, nothing but the facts,' but this time chanted like a musical ditty. The two nurses joined in towards the end, shouting out, 'Nothing but the facts!'

'Well, I'm not sure there is anything else,' Jane said.

'Not sure there is anything else!' Handcock exclaimed in mock exasperation. 'We haven't started yet, have we, lads?' He raised his arms repeatedly with his palms facing upwards, encouraging the circle of onlookers to repeat the chorus.

'The facts the facts, nothing but the facts!' the soldiers roared, the ditty becoming even more tuneful. Even Jane saw the funny side and began to laugh.

'That's better,' said Handcock. 'No need to be formal with this lot.'

'Where are you from? I can't place your accent,' Jane asked, relaxing as she absorbed this new experience.

'Well, we're from all over. Quite a few Aussies, me included, some Canadians. The Breaker over there, he's English but been in Australia for ten years or more.' He pointed out a solid-looking chap in his late thirties with sharp features, dressed in the same uniform as the others. 'The Breaker, he's a legend back home.'

'Why?' asked Jane.

'Best horseman in Australia bar none, and hard as nails. Never fails to get the better of any horse. Need it breaking in, then you call for The Breaker. Poet and singer as well. Top bloke, from a posh family like you. But don't get on the wrong side of him.'

'I will try not to,' Jane replied uncertainly. 'Can I ask how you are all here in South Africa? Are you in the army? Your uniforms look more like the Boer commandos we see pictures of.'

'Adventure, see the world, good pay, good mates, get paid for riding horses all day. Can't be bad.'

'Do you ride horses all day?' Jane asked, not believing him.

'We will when we get up to Pietersburg. Our horses are already there,' Handcock replied. He took a hefty chunk out of his sandwich.

'But what do you do, riding all day?' Jane's question illustrated her almost total lack of understanding of military matters. She could not picture why the men were here in South Africa and what they would be doing.

'We are part of the Bushveldt Carbineers, a new regiment which Kitchener has set up to copy the tactics of the Boers. Take them on at their own game, give them a taste of their own medicine. We track them down, ambush them and cut off their supplies. Go deep into the country. The British need people like us, hard country folk used to living in the outback, good on horses. We don't operate like the main army, all those old stuffy blokes with their endless rules. We just get on with it.'

'I see,' said Jane. It was abundantly clear that she did not see at all when she asked, 'So do you actually fight the Boers?'

'Hey, lads, posh Sheila here wants to know if we actually fight.' He emphasised the word 'actually' mocking Jane's upper-class accent.

'No, we just run away!' one of the soldiers shouted dismissively.

Jane was uncomfortable yet intrigued, on edge yet curious. She was a little frightened of these hard, irreverent men yet eager to find out more about them. There was something about their demeanour that reminded her of the three lads she had met on the train going to Cape Town when she'd had James with her. Handcock was similar: less reverential and more spontaneous than other men she had met. They were more worldly wise than she was, maybe because they had to be. They seemed more quick-witted than the farm boys and stable hands back home, and certainly more adventurous.

'Why do you all chant "nothing but the facts"?' she asked, trying to piece things together.

'Our last commanding officer, right bastard — and I apologise for the language but he was — always kept interrupting us whenever we made a report. "Just give me the facts," he kept saying. So we started mimicking him. We all hated him, pompous twit.'

'Oh,' said Jane. She had never heard anyone speak so directly before.

The group around the campfire broke into separate, smaller groups. The two nurses drifted, or were manoeuvred, apart into two different bands of soldiers, each with half a dozen chaps. They were the centre of lustful looks and barely concealed innuendo, which they seemed more than capable of handling.

Another group, which included The Breaker, sat writing or looking at maps. Handcock stayed talking to Jane and slowly the conversation became less flippant, less casual. They asked each other many questions and started to form pictures of each other. Handcock was intrigued to discover that Jane was a skilled horsewoman; Jane was even more intrigued to discover that Handcock had a love of the countryside, nature and poetry. She would not have guessed that soldiers and poetry went together.

It was only later that she discovered that there was a strange connection between the two.

A couple of hours after she had joined the group, singing broke out. This time it was not mass chanting or little limericks but a gentle ballad. Accompanied by a soldier with a recorder, The Breaker sang the tale of a lone bushman who had lost his love and spent long days and nights yearning for the chance to right his wrongs and win her back. Jane found it magical and she shared smiles and deep glances with Handcock.

At the end of the song, The Breaker got up and walked over to Handcock and Jane. 'Well, Handcock,' he said, 'this must be Kitty.' He started to recite a poem and picked up a shovel that lay on the floor not far from Jane's feet, holding it like a broom.

When Kitty glides into a room
There I contrive to stay,
And watch her whilst she with her broom,
Sweeps all the dust away.
For bright-faced, slender Kitty's
Such a comely sight to see,
She grasps that broom with magic touch,
And waves it willingly.
And with her white and shapely arms,
Where dimples love to play,
She wields that magic wand and charms
Dull care — and dust — away.
All this life's care and sad concerns
No longer darkly loom;
All shadow into sunlight turns,
When Kitty does the room.
Along life's thorny path of gloom
I'd wend a cheerful way,
Did Heaven send Kitty with her broom
To brush the briars away?

The performance was wonderful; Jane was enraptured. Throughout the poem The Breaker looked directly at Jane, yet constantly swept the briars away.

This was a new emotion for her; it was not the exhilaration of jumping over a fence at speed, nor the contentment of looking out over the parklands of home or hearing laughter with her friend Lilly. This was a new sensation: being serenaded by a skilled womaniser but also a wonderful actor and poet. She wanted more of it.

'Well, Handcock, you can't keep Kitty to yourself all night. She needs to sing with us.'

'It's Jane. She's from your area, Hampshire.'

'Well, Kitty's a Hampshire lass. I am from Devon, a much superior county. Come, Kitty, what are you going to sing?'

'Oh no, I can't sing at all.'

'Nonsense, everyone can sing. Come on, name your song.'

'I can't! I really can't!'

'Do you go to church?'

'Yes.'

'Well, there you are then. I bet you sing in church, don't you?'

'Well, yes.'

'A hymn. We will sing a hymn. *Onward Christian Soldiers* — you must know that. Everybody listen up,' The Breaker shouted out. 'Kitty here is going to lead us in singing *Onward Christian Soldiers*. Full voices now.'

He turned to Jane and signalled for her to stand up. Handcock rose as well. The soldier with the recorder blew a few discordant notes and, after a number of false starts, the recognisable tune of *Onward Christian Soldiers* whistled through the air.

The Breaker shouted out, 'One, two, three,' and indicated to Jane to start singing. This happened twice; Jane stood there, not making a sound, embarrassed and dreading even attempting to sing alone.

'Righto, lads, all together.' The recorder started up and a loud, yet surprisingly tuneful choir of twenty soldiers burst into song. As they did so, they began to march. 'Onward Christian soldiers, marching as to war.'

They turned and marched anticlockwise round the campfire. The Breaker moved Jane and Handcock to the front of the procession and the recorder player joined them. Now Jane started to sing, hardly noticeably at first, but as they continued verse by verse, she grew in confidence. Feeling less self-conscious, she relaxed.

As they came to the end of the last verse, The Breaker shouted out, 'Now, Kitty, first verse from you.' She continued to sing; the other voices died away as The Breaker furiously signalled to the men to stop singing. Jane hardly noticed that she was singing alone until well through the verse, so immersed was she in the pleasure of the moment.

At the end there was wholesale whooping and laughing. Jane and Handcock held hands and jumped into the air two or three times. She might have been frightened to the point of rigidity just a few hours earlier when the bullets had hit the train but now, at this moment, with these soldiers, these hard men, she was truly happy.

She was less happy when word came down from the front of the train that they could not start work getting the line fixed until the morning. It was another three hours until dawn, then it would take at least four hours to bring track to replace that which had been blown up.

The day's events were beginning to take their toll and Jane felt desperately tired. The long eight-hour journey, the bullets and being frightened like never before, the campfire, the banter and the singing had made this truly a day to remember.

She reluctantly made her excuses, left Handcock and went back to the carriage, which was empty. She made a pillow from her bag and stretched out full length on the seat. She had no difficulty in getting to sleep, imagining as she drifted away what the hills around Adelaide were like, for Handcock had mentioned them specifically. If they were like Handcock, they would be very fine indeed.

The next day dragged on. It took far longer than anticipated to reconnect the line. The commander of the troops other than the Bushveldt Carbineers organised patrols and a makeshift kitchen serving up hot food and tea. Latrines were built for the troops and, on the other side of the train, a latrine with canvas around it was made for the ladies.

It was mid-afternoon by the time the order came for everybody to pack up and get on board. Jane sat in the carriage sketching, writing and thinking, thinking of Handcock and just how wonderful she had found his camaraderie, banter and, most surprisingly, his sensitivity.

It was when the railway engineer entered the carriage that the day went downhill at an alarming rate. It appeared that the engine was useless. A bullet had passed through the water tank; slowly the tank had drained dry and there was no way of making steam. They needed a replacement engine to pull them to a siding or all the way to Pretoria. The driver would have to send a party out to the next station stop that had a telegraph. They were closer to the main station at Kroonstad than the one at Ladysmith, but perhaps the smaller stations at Bethlehem going north or Harrismith going back towards Durban would have a telegraph. The driver was certain they did. Either way, there would be a long delay of perhaps two days or more.

There was nothing to do but make the best of it. Camps were set up again. Fortunately, the train had passed the Wilge River a few miles to the south around Swinburne, hardly a place, just a mark on the map. A party of troops was despatched to walk the line north and another party went south.

In the meantime, the line south was reconnected with the line on the north side. After another three hours, a party of troops was put in a carriage; this was de-coupled and pushed down the line until they came to the river. The soldiers collected as much water as they could transport in the carriage and brought it back to the stranded train.

The weather was fine, dry and clear, which was a blessing. At least it was not the hottest time of the year; that would have been unbearable. As the day dragged on, Jane made a special effort to find Handcock, which was surprisingly difficult as she was reluctant to ask anyone where he was.

The two nurses seemed to know a great deal about the Carbineers and had not come back to the carriage the previous night. Jane did not ask where they had slept.

It was not until dinnertime, when the campfires were glowing fiercely in the rapidly dwindling light, that Jane came upon Handcock. He was sitting on his own reading, with a plate of potatoes and beef. Tents had been erected all along the line and soldiers were sitting outside the entrances eating, sleeping, cleaning weapons and generally wasting time as best they could.

'Hello, Kitty,' said Handcock.

'I prefer Jane,' she replied.

'That's fine, Jane it is.'

They both said how much they had enjoyed the previous evening. Handcock said that companionship, fun and laughs with your mates were the best parts of being in the military. There were downsides, like when your mates were killed, but everybody knew the risks when they signed up.

'What are you reading?' Jane asked.

'Wordsworth. *Lyrical Ballads*. Do you know it?' he asked.

'No, I am afraid I don't. I should but *Daffodils* is all I know.'

'There are better poems than that. Let me read you one.'

He put down his plate and took up the book. He started:

If from the public way you turn your steps
Up the tumultuous brook of Greenhead Ghyll,
You will suppose that with an upright path
Your feet must struggle; in such bold ascent...

He read the whole of the poem *Michael* to a transfixed Jane. When he had finished, which took him almost fifteen minutes, he put the book down and looked at her. She was wiping a tear from her eye.

'That is the saddest and yet most beautiful poem I have ever heard,' she said.

'Yep, all of life is in that poem. I am glad you liked it.'

'I did. I really liked it.'

'Well, I like you too, Jane Dunhaughton,' he said, taking hold of her hand. 'I thought about you last night after you went to bed. Thought you were the sort of girl I would like to settle down with.'

'But you don't really know me,' she said.

'I think I have a fair idea. I could always get to know you better.'

'I would like that,' she said.

He leaned forward, kissed her gently and stroked the back of his hand across her face. It was her first kiss, and to say that it did not disappoint would be an understatement. It was utter bliss.

She looked down at the ground and then, after what seemed a long time to Handcock, she said, 'What are the Adelaide Hills like? Is there utter solitude there?'

'There is. I am sure you would like them.'

'I am sure I would.'

They were interrupted by a group of soldiers coming to sit by the fire and eat their dinner. For the rest of the evening Peter, for that was Handcock's first name, asked Jane an endless stream of questions. She did not feel she was being questioned; she felt that someone was taking a genuine interest in her.

He listened intently as Jane told him everything about herself, her background, family, friendships, and how she came to be in South Africa. She told him about the baby, James, and Emily and everything else that came to mind.

It was eleven p.m. when Jane and Peter said goodnight. They had hardly moved all night. He kissed her again as she stopped at the carriage door. 'Sleep well,' he said.

Jane woke early the next morning. She had tossed and turned in the night, thinking hard about Peter and how she might meet with him again — and soon.

Once again, she had been alone in the carriage. At one point she sat up, looking out into the blackness of the night. There was no doubt in her mind that she could fall in love with Peter. He was a hard, rugged soldier, one of the lads, full of banter and good fun; yet equally he was the most sensitive person she had ever met. She believed him to be honest, open and sincere, and his love of words astonished her. On a number of occasions during the evening he had recited lines of poetry, not to show off but to add depth to a particular point he — or more likely she — had made.

It was mid-afternoon on the next day when the train started to move again. Jane walked up and down the track, hoping to bump into Peter but he was not to be seen. Nor were any of the Carbineers. She began to worry that she would not see him again when the train hooted, signalling it would soon move off. But then he came walking purposefully along the track, looking into the carriage windows. She leaned out and waved and he hurried towards her.

'Jane, who knows when we will meet again but I do so want to. Give me your address. At the end of the war, which hopefully will be soon, I will find you. I will come to England if need be, or you can come to Australia.'

'Yes, I would. I would come straight away.'

There was no question that they both meant it. Jane reached into her bag and drew out a pen and paper. She wrote out her address carefully and also her two addresses in South Africa.

As she handed the paper to Peter, she said, 'Do take good care of it.'

'Don't worry, I will. Take care.'

He turned and walked away. He did not turn round until he reached a bend in the track, then he stopped, turned and waved.

The train started shortly after that, pulled by another locomotive from Kroonstad. Seven hours later they were in Pretoria.

Jane got off the train with the nurses and railway engineer. She noticed Peter standing on the platform with a group of officers, engaged in animated discussion.

He moved quickly towards her. 'I am afraid there is a bit of trouble and we are having to move out quickly. I will find you, so don't worry.'

'Peter, take care. Please.'

'I will.' He turned and went back to the officers' meeting.

Chapter 21
Biding Time

Jane busied herself as best she could on Distress Fund business but her mind was only half engaged. She thought constantly of Lieutenant Peter Handcock. What was he doing? Was he in danger? When would they meet again? Would she go to Australia? She kept telling herself that she was jumping the gun, that she hardly knew him, and that the war might go on and on. But it was no good. She had now one overriding objective and that was to meet him again.

It was not easy for her in Pretoria. She was staying in the Grand Hotel in Church Square. The hotel, which had seventy rooms, was only ten years old and was a fine, imposing, Germanic-looking building. The standards were high but after a few days she tired of being in a hotel. It did not compare to the home comforts of Kya Lami or being with Betty Moltano in Cape Town. She began to resent having to go down to the restaurant for meals and the chambermaids constantly moving her things in her room. She did not like the bathroom arrangements, which lacked the privacy she was used to.

Pretoria was not Cape Town; it was nowhere near as well developed. Most of the streets were unpaved and it had a distinct outback feel, which was matched by its inhabitants, many of whom made Jane feel distinctly uncomfortable.

She also found great difficulty in making progress with the issue she had come to Pretoria to deal with. The Distress Fund wanted the support of the army to distribute aid to the camps. They thought this would be far more efficient and economical than trying to do it themselves. The fund had far fewer contacts in the north of the country; roads and railways were less developed and, most importantly, there was far more military activity. However, the army did not appear to have a similar view.

Jane, despite the introductions she had, found it almost impossible to see senior commanders. She could not gain admittance to Kitchener's headquarters where the senior officers were based.

Lieutenant Colonel Birdwood, who later became a field marshall, and Kitchener's ADC Frank Maxwell were the two names Jane had been given, but neither responded to her letters. When Jane turned up at the headquarters, armed with her letter of introduction, she was made to wait more than two hours in a dingy side office and saw no one other than a junior lieutenant.

What Jane did not know was that, at the highest levels, the work of the Distress Fund was being viewed with considerable suspicion and even hostility. The politicians back home were under intense scrutiny from the world's press. Emily was tearing round the country, making speech after speech, and the Liberals were making life a misery in Parliament. Milner, Kitchener and increasingly Chamberlain, the Colonial Secretary, saw the Distress Fund as the source of the problems, accentuated by the personal accounts of that wretched Miss Emily Hobhouse. Now the army was having to organise and prepare for visits from the investigating committee led by Millicent Fawcett. So when Jane presented herself, she was not sowing seed on fertile soil; indeed, it would have been hard to imagine a rockier, more barren patch.

Jane was no politician and she did not see the bigger picture. She did not even try to work out why she would not be seen. Had she not done some good work in the camps? Were the materials she had distributed not helpful? She felt very much alone; not being able to go home at night and talk to Caroline or Betty was a major handicap. She wanted to help in a practical, positive way. The camps had upset her and she genuinely thought the work she had done was morally right.

She was not a campaigner; she could not, nor did she want to be, an Emily. She could in no way cope with the personal attacks that Emily had to deal with, nor would she be comfortable with seeing her name in the press, other than if she had won a point-to-point race.

She had been in Pretoria a week and had little to show for the time she'd spent there. She had met a few people but come across major resistance to her visiting any more camps. Even Distress Fund supporters felt that, given the imminent arrival of the investigating committee, this was not the time to interfere. Jane tried to argue the point that they would simply be giving out aid but she made little headway. The general line was that she was assuming aid needed to be given and, in any event, travelling to the camps would not be allowed given the fighting that was going on.

It was now the 21st of August. Jane felt trapped, unable to travel outside of the centre of Pretoria, unable to speak to senior officers, unable to confide in friends and unable to see Lieutenant Handcock. She was also missing in action for now no post came to her, and she was worried that, if it did, she would have moved on again. She decided that she would go back to Cape Town, wait for Emily to come back and then prepare to return to England.

With this plan in mind she went to the railway station, a short walk from her hotel, and asked about the next train to Cape Town. She started to despair when confronted by obsequious but duplicitous officials who feigned helpfulness but practised obstruction.

'Wish we could help but have you no pass? Will you get a pass? Why are you travelling? We are looking after your interests. It's dangerous on the railways these days, especially for a lady on her own.'

She spent two hours being passed from pillar to post and making no progress. She could not find out when the next train was leaving.

She was totally exasperated when she said, 'I have tried my best to obtain information from you. I simply want to go back to Cape Town and then go home, I have these letters of introduction from prominent men and I will see to it that your names are made known to them. I will go back to my hotel and come back with my case. I will sit here until the next train comes and I will get on it. If you try and stop me, I will ensure that you answer for your actions.'

It was the most un-Jane-like performance. She tried her best to appear strong and forceful. She pointed her finger at the senior railway official and stamped her foot. It was an act but it worked.

'I suppose we could make an exception. I see that you did travel up here from Durban.'

The official went away and left Jane for another half an hour. She had shot her last bullet. What would she do now? She was saved, however, by the official coming back with papers and tickets for the train, which would leave at three p.m. on the 24th.

The official, a thin slimy weasel with thinning hair and a greasy uniform, added to complete Jane's day, 'Be prepared for a long wait as all the trains have been subject to severe delays, what with the ambushes and derailments.'

As it turned out, the train left Pretoria station at four thirty p.m. on the 25th of August. Jane was glad to be leaving; she had seen nothing, accomplished nothing. The only good thing — and that was very good indeed — was that the journey to Pretoria had resulted in her meeting Peter Handcock. She rarely thought of anything else as she wearily made her way back on another long, boring, uncomfortable train journey.

She sent a letter to Betty the day before she left Pretoria telling her she was on her way back. It was only when she was on the train that she thought she would probably arrive back at Betty's house before the letter arrived, as it was almost certainly on the train with her. This proved to be the case.

At breakfast on the 29th, Betty, opening her mail, announced to Jane, 'Oh, I understand you are leaving Pretoria on the 24th and should be with me on the 27th or 28th.'

They both smiled and engaged in some light-hearted self-mockery. It was the first homely conversation Jane had indulged in for some time and she realised just how relieved she was to have left Pretoria.

One morning after breakfast, Jane and Betty went into town to do some shopping and have lunch. It was in the Grand Hotel that Jane let down her inner defences and opened up.

'I met someone on the train that I really liked,' she said. It was after the ambush. The soldiers were all sat around drinking tea and playing silly games. They were singing and at one point we all marched round the camp fire singing *Onward Christian Soldiers*. I sat next to a soldier a lieutenant. I was amazed at just how sensitive he was. He read me poetry.' Jane was looking at her feet unable to show he face but her words were meant to be heard. There was a soft silence which rung loudly and connected the two.

'It seems he made a real impression on you,' said Betty, her antenna quickly picking up the seriousness of Jane's comments. 'Will you be seeing him again?'

'Yes, most certainly,' Jane replied instantly. 'I am sure he will be in touch. I gave him my English address — and yours and Caroline's in South Africa. I do hope he is safe.' She looked up and caught Betty looking directly at her. Betty reached out across the table and took hold of Jane's hand. She squeezed tenderly as she said, 'I am sure he will.'

Chapter 22
Winds from the North

What Jane did not know was that on arriving at Pretoria the Bushveldt Carbineers embarked immediately for Pietersburg, where they were to meet up with their horses and undertake a number of missions attacking known haunts of the Boer leaders. They were under direct instructions from Kitchener, who thought he had the Boers on the run and who was determined not to give them a chance to regroup.

Kitchener believed that, if his plans came to fruition, the Boers would have no choice but to enter negotiations by the end of the year. His strategy envisaged, that if he had captured or killed the Boer leaders, they would be enfeebled at any peace talks through a lack of direction. To this end, he placed the Bushveldt Carbineers under the command of a Captain Taylor, who had come to prominence because of his ability to speak not only the Boer language but also Zulu and other tribal languages. Taylor was an Irishman who had lived in Africa for more than ten years and had earned a reputation for brutality.

Captain Taylor was under orders to be ruthless and show no mercy. The Bushveldt Carbineers were to operate secretly, without pomp or fuss, and outside the normal channels of command. It was not a good place to be in August 1901, if you wanted to stay out of trouble.

Jane stayed with Betty during August and September. It was pleasant and comfortable but she felt the tide had turned. She did not want to visit any more camps or do any more travelling on those horrible trains. She knew that she and her kind were not wanted, not only by the army but also by Millicent Fawcett and her investigating committee.

Millicent refused to meet with members of the Distress Fund in Cape Town, saying that she preferred to reach her own conclusions. It was a terrible snub for the well-meaning, compassionate group that made up the committee. For Jane, it confirmed the opinions that she had formed since being in South Africa, and particularly since her visit to Pretoria. The establishment knew best and did not need foreign chappies telling them what to do.

The days began to drag and she felt a distinct lack of purpose. She was becoming homesick. She had received no news for some time and questions began to accumulate. How was her father? Was he managing the estate? Was he sober? How were Lilly and Emily? How was Woodly?

These questions grew in importance as the days passed; even greater were her worries about Lieutenant Handcock. When would she see him again? *Would* she see him again? She bought a copy of Wordsworth's *Lyrical Ballads* and found herself reading *Michael* time after time. She had a perfect image of Peter's face as he sat reading the poem to her and could remember the blissful feeling that had run through her as she sat, mesmerised by the beauty of the language. She read more of the poems and wondered why she had not been introduced to them before. They spoke to her directly.

It was Betty who noticed Jane's change in demeanour, the lack of spark, spontaneity and inquisitiveness that had been a central part of her makeup. 'Are you missing home?' she asked.

This question came because Jane had hardly responded to Betty reading aloud an extract from *The Times,* which included an open letter from Emily to St John Broderick, the Secretary of State for War. The letter, published on the 29th of September, had caused quite a sensation. It castigated Broderick for inaction and asked if the thought of the 3,245 children in the camps, who had closed their eyes forever since Emily had last seen him, would not spur him to do something.

Despite the power and anger in the letter, Jane hardly blinked and seemed indifferent. This was not her view — far from it — but her initial enthusiasm for the cause had been severely tested by the establishment's ability to sidestep or distort what seemed to be common sense.

'I don't know what I'm doing here now. I don't seem to have a purpose.'

'Would you like to do something or do you want to go home?' Betty asked, moving to the window and looking out on to the street. Her apartment was light and airy, with large windows, and the afternoon sun was making it difficult to see. She adjusted the blind.

'I don't know. I was planning to wait for Emily to come back but now I can't think why. It seems that things have changed, what with the investigating committee and the increased opposition to our work. If Emily does come back, I don't think she will be able to go round the camps like before. I wonder if we may have made things worse.'

'Oh now, that is nonsense. If you and Emily had not gone to the camps in the first place, the terrible conditions would have been just rumours. Your work changed everything.' Betty was getting quite animated; she was clearly unhappy that the work of the Distress Fund was being questioned by one of its champions.

'I am not sure it has changed anything. It was the fact that the death rate in the camps continues to rise that led Emily to write that letter. I think in some ways it has made things worse. We are not seen now as honest, decent people, telling the truth and doing Christian acts, but rather as Boer sympathisers. Poor Emily is taking such a lot of abuse, yet all she is doing is trying to end wrongdoing by telling the facts. I don't want to be seen as an enemy, which is how many people now see her.' Jane made these remarks in a flat, understated way; this had the effect of dampening the growing tension in Betty, who sat down again.

'Jane, I am afraid that once you get into national politics, which is what Emily and you have done, there is no such thing as truth. What you see as fact supporting a stance that you have taken will be seen by others as fact supporting an opposite view. Truth changes according to the beholder,' said Betty.

'I'm not sure I follow that. All I know is that I have seen things with my own eyes — they are facts,' Jane said with rather more animation.

'They are to you, Jane, but others will see the same images and have quite different views,' said Betty. 'You have seen that yourself. You see a starving disease-ridden child and you conclude it is because of the camps. Someone else sees the same child and blames either the father for going away to fight, or the mother for not looking after the child. For me, the only thing I believe to be undeniably true is that truth belongs to those in power. They manipulate it. Anyway, this does not answer the question of what you are going to do. I can see that you are lost at the moment.'

'Yes, I am. That's right, I am lost,' Jane said, suddenly brightening.

'Well, I have a plan. There are lots of children orphaned by this terrible war. They need homes — but they also need schools. I plan to open a number of schools where these unfortunate children can learn some basic facts.' She emphasised the word 'facts' and smiled, remembering Jane telling her about the Carbineers chanting about 'The facts'. 'Reading, writing, arithmetic, that sort of thing. If the army and the Empire do not want our money for the camps, we can use it to give children a basic education. You would be good at that and, whilst we are doing it, you can decide when you are going home.'

Betty stood up and walked to the drinks' cabinet. She poured two gin and tonics and handed one to Jane. 'Is that a plan?' she added.

'Yes, it's a plan. It's a good plan,' said Jane.

A few days later, in early October, a number of letters arrived addressed to Jane. They had been redirected from Bloemfontein. Jane opened them eagerly. The first was from Emily, dated the 10th of September, and went into considerable detail about her activities since she had arrived back in England, her speaking engagements and the

244

government's response. It was dated before her letter to *The Times* and so made no mention of that.

The real news was at the end of the letter when she announced that she had booked a berth on the *Avondale Castle* that would leave Southampton on the 5th of October; she would arrive at Cape Town on the 27th. This was news that Jane welcomed. Emily was actually on her way by now.

It was not until later in the day, when she pored over the letter again, that she began to wonder what Emily planned to do when she got to South Africa. There was no mention of this at all. Maybe Emily was not aware of how things had changed, thought Jane.

The second letter was from Dover. Jane looked at the envelope and could not work out who had written it. When she opened it, she was surprised to find that it was from Edith Newman.

Dear Jane,

I do hope that this letter gets to you and that you are well. I worry that you will have moved on and it will miss you.

You must think us terribly rude rushing off like that and hardly a word spoken between us. Alun wanted to get it over with. We intended to come straight to England and didn't want any complications. We didn't want the hotel wondering why we arrived on our own but then had a child with us, so we stayed in a different hotel for a few days before we got the boat to England.

Alun has a job managing a mine in Kent and we are now living there. No one knows that James is not ours and we shall keep it that way. He is fine and doing well. Please don't

tell the mother what happened to him. We don't want any
complications.

When you are back home do come and see us. We were
hoping you would be his godmother. It seems right.

I hear bad things about the war and am so glad we are
back home. Do let us know when you are coming back.

Your dear and most grateful friend,
Edith

Well, thought Jane, I didn't anticipate that. She was pleased
that they were home and settled. She understood why they
wanted to pretend that James was their child. She would be
thrilled to be his godmother and she would write that day
confirming that she was pleased with the way things had
turned out.

The third letter was from Lilly. Jane opened it with eager
anticipation but also some nervousness. She was right to be
nervous for the letter contained distressing news. Lilly said
she would come straight to the point: Jane's father was not
well; indeed, he was quite ill. He had fallen badly when
drunk and lain for many hours before the housekeeper
discovered him. He had a broken leg but it had not healed
and had become infected. It was getting worse. '*Jane I hardly*
dare say it but I fear the worse.' Lilly went on to say that
there were rumours that her father owed money to local
businesspeople and that was why he was drinking.

She ended by saying:

'*I am so sorry to have to deliver such bad news. Do you know*
when you will be returning home? You are sorely needed.'

For Jane it was simply too much. The self-doubt about her worth in South Africa, and whether she had made things worse there, was compounded by a terrible wave of guilt. She immediately blamed herself for her father's dire predicament. If only she had stayed in England. She looked at the date on the letter: the 15th of September. She stumbled and had to steady herself as she realised that her father might already have passed away. She must go home as soon as possible.

She rushed down to find her friend. 'Betty, I have to go home. I have received really bad news from my friend Lilly. My father is ill and there are rumours he has incurred debts. I need to go home!'

'Then you must go,' Betty responded. 'Family comes first and I suspect you are needed more back home than here. You need to go down to the port and see about booking a passage.'

The Victoria and Albert waterfront buildings contained the offices of all the shipping companies with scheduled services to the UK. Beach Road, which led to the quay area, was exceptionally busy with dozens of waggons and carts coming and going from the quayside to load and unload the ships in the dock or those at anchor outside the harbour waiting for a berth. The military presence was substantial, with quartermasters and their staff checking and re-checking huge bundles of papers containing the shipping lists.

There were few, if any, respectable ladies around the area but there were many prostitutes hoping to pick up customers from the scores of bored and frustrated seamen coming ashore. Officials tried their best to keep them out of the docks but many climbed fences to get at the newly embarked.

The first berth Jane could get was not until the 1st of November on the *Roslin Castle*, a Union Castle Line mail ship that offered a few passenger berths. Booking a berth and being issued with tickets and a receipt made Jane feel better only in the sense that the journey home had, to all intents, started. It would be a long couple of weeks before she embarked, and even then, it would be fifteen days before she was back in Southampton. What would she find when she got home?

Once back in Betty's apartment, she began to make a list of all the things she needed to do before she set off. She needed to write to numerous people telling them of her plans, amongst whom Lilly was first and Emily second. She would leave a letter for Emily with Betty in case they did not meet up when Emily arrived in Cape Town. She remembered her friend was due to arrive on the 27th of October. If there was any delay in Emily's journey Jane might already be on her way home.

She wanted to go and see Caroline but could not face the prospect of travelling all the way to Bloemfontein and back by train. Of all the places she had been in South Africa, Kya Lami was by far the one where she was most at home and somewhere she could have envisaged living permanently — but only if she had a wider purpose.

Jane also needed to respond to Edith Newman and accept her offer of being a godmother. She would visit them in Kent when she was back in England.

The days did indeed move slowly. Jane did her best to keep busy but really she had nothing to do but wait. She wrote at length to Caroline, detailing all that had happened to her, updating her about Emily and mentioning Lieutenant

Handcock. She wrote to Edith, accepting the offer to be godmother with genuine affection and joy. She advised her of her return and said she would call as soon as she could.

She pretended to help Betty plan the new schools but she was uncertain what she could do now that she was committed to leaving. She read, but found her progress was ponderous as her mind constantly wandered to thoughts of Lieutenant Handcock and her father. She started to feel the first thrust of anger at her father building up inside her; she understood that his downward path had started when her mother died, but was it not everyone's duty to bear the slings and arrows that life brought?

Eventually the 27th of October arrived. It was a mild day with a slight breeze and no prospect of rain. The *Avondale Castle* was due to berth that afternoon. Jane had planned to meet several of the Distress Fund members mid-afternoon to welcome Emily back to South Africa.

Jane and Betty took the tram to the quayside where they met Caroline Murray and Mrs Curry, who had both come into town specifically to meet Emily. They waited patiently for two hours as the other passengers disembarked — but there was no sign of their friend. On making enquiries, it transpired that Emily was not being allowed to get off the ship and set foot in South Africa.

They were all aghast but Dr Charles Murray, Caroline's husband, was not shocked. 'They don't want her back. They would prefer her out of the way, especially as the investigating committee is still at work.'

'But what right have they to stop her? She is British just like us,' said Jane, agitated and anxious.

'They can because South Africa is under martial law. Kitchener can simply order that she should not be let ashore,' replied Dr Murray.

Indeed, this was the case. The Foreign Office had been alerted that Emily Hobhouse was on the *Avondale Castle* and soon telegrams were pulsating down the wires between Milner and Kitchener. They agreed that Emily Hobhouse should not be allowed to disembark and gave instructions accordingly.

They left the quayside and went back to Betty's apartment, trying to plan what they should do next. There was a general air of hopelessness and despondency, coupled with simmering anger.

Betty and Jane contacted the press and tried to get them interested in the story of Emily being held under arrest, but they came up against apparent indifference. What they did not know was that Milner's office had already been in touch with editors of the local press threatening dire action if any story appeared about Emily Hobhouse.

The next couple of days passed in an impasse. Emily was held on the ship and told that she would be placed on the next ship back to England. It so happened that this was the *Roslin Castle*.

When Jane boarded the *Roslin Castle,* she was aware that Emily was on board. Emily had been moved by armed guards, who had carried her from the *Avondale Castle* across the quayside and onto the *Roslin*. What Jane was not prepared for, however, was Emily's appearance.

When they met in Emily's cabin, Jane was aghast. The impressive, magnetic presence that had mesmerised Jane at the political meeting in Winchester little over a year earlier was no more. Emily looked seriously ill, literally worn out by the campaigning, the travelling, the discomfort of the trains. The personal abuse and, at times, physical attacks had taken a heavy toll. She was pale and drawn, had lost weight and appeared ten years older.

Jane was taken aback not only by her physical appearance but also by the fact that Emily had brought a nurse with her, a Miss Philips. Forty years old, heavyset with short hair, Miss Philips was pushing Emily in a wheeled chair.

'Oh Emily, what has happened? What is the matter? You didn't say you were ill.'

'Just a chest infection, Jane, and exhaustion. I will get better but all the fuss over getting back into South Africa has not helped. I despair at the effort and trouble they will go to stop the truth getting out.'

'Never mind the truth, Emily, it is you we must worry about. You're going to have to let others fight your battles. The authorities are not going to let you on shore,' said Jane.

'I know. I thought when I met Milner that he came across as a decent chap with sound views, but he runs with the fox and rides with the hounds. He will not stand up to Kitchener; he is more interested in being courted and knighted. Never mind him, come and give me a hug. It is so good to see you again.'

Jane bent down and hugged Emily, who felt frail. 'Are you eating properly?' she asked, looking directly at Miss Philips who shook her head indicating clearly that Emily was not.

'So much has happened in such a short time. It seems a different age from when we set off from Southampton just over a year ago. So much has happened in the last three months, and still the government prevaricates. The worry has made me ill. Children are still dying every day in the camps, and we deny there is a problem. One day the truth will get out and then Kitchener will have to answer for his crimes.' Despite her physical condition, Emily spoke with emotion, nearly breaking down as she uttered the words: 'answer for his crimes'.

'Well, that may be the case but right now I think rest is what you need — and something to take your mind away from worrying. Let us get comfortable in our cabins and have some tea. There is so much to catch up on.'

The journey home was melancholy, grey and subdued. The embers of Emily's fire were slowly dying; any mention of Kitchener, Milner or the camps, simply threw more water on the embers — water which turned to steam.

If Emily was angry, Jane was worried; if Emily was resentful, Jane was anxious. The closer they got to home, the deeper and more intense her anxiety became. She wanted to engage with Emily, rediscover her spirit of adventure that had been so prevalent but now seemed so far away.

Wordsworth's lines, *'Whither is fled the visionary gleam, where is it now, the glory and the dream'* jumped out at her from the page as she sat reading in her cabin, trying her best to pass the time. The lines hit her forcibly. 'Where is it indeed?' she thought.

She might have wanted to engage with Emily but she could see that, at the moment, talking about anything that remotely approached the problems of the camps only made matters worse. All the time they had spent together, all their shared experiences and the very reason they had met in the first place, had been driven by their intense commitment to relieve suffering. Now it was difficult to find any subject that did not touch on the very issue that was causing the melancholy. It was a long journey home.

The weather deteriorated steadily as they progressed north. The swells in the Bay of Biscay did nothing to reduce Jane's anxiety. For two days and two even longer nights they were more or less confined to their cabins. There could be no pleasant strolls around the deck as the waves buffeted the sides of the ship, tossing it violently.

Even experienced crewman started to show some concern — but not as much as the passengers when an 'all hands' cry went out from the bridge. A fire had broken out in the boiler room. It was soon dealt with, but the sight of crewmen running with fear on their faces did nothing to brighten the dense blackness of the sky.

It was not until the *Roslin Castle* entered the Western Approaches that the storm began to abate and the ship steadied to an even keel. Jane, Emily and Miss Philips had all been sick. Two days of dehydrated misery had them longing for home but, as they neared it, Jane's nervousness grew.

They reached Southampton on the 26th of November 1901, and inched into the docks at first light. By nine thirty a.m. the passengers had started to disembark. It was a strange and subdued parting for Jane and Emily.

Emily was being pushed in a wheelchair by Miss Philips and was by no means on the way to recovery. She took hold of Jane's hand and said, 'I do hope all is well at home. I am praying for you.'

'I know you are, Emily. And I wish you a speedy recovery. Please stay away from politics for a few weeks.' Jane looked pleadingly at her.

'I shall try,' Emily said, and managed a rather weak, insipid smile.

Chapter 23
The Gates are Closed

Jane took a hackney cab from the port terminal to the railway station. She was struck by the greyness of the sky and the bitter cold sweeping in from the Channel. The port, as always, was busy with hundreds of porters and dock workers scurrying around, all dressed in dark, heavy trousers and jackets and with their flat caps pulled well down. There was a fine mist of rain that added to the depressing picture and contrasted starkly with the clear, pristine, blue skies she had become accustomed to over the last year.

It did not seem much of a homecoming. She had never been away before for more than a week. Although she did not admit it, Jane felt that if all had been well at home there would have been someone at the docks to welcome her. Emily had been met by her brother, Leonard, and Catherine Courtney; why was there not someone to meet her? Why was she not close enough to anyone to the extent that they would be here at the docks?

The grey, drab surroundings, the bone-numbing cold and the lack of any welcoming party filled her with dread. There was simply nothing to brighten her gloom. Seeing Emily being wheeled away, clearly most unwell, reinforced her mounting anxiety. Would her father be in a wheelchair if he had broken his leg? It was perverse but she rather hoped so, for that would mean he had survived the infection.

She caught the 12.32 train to Winchester. She had entered an empty compartment but soon a number of other people drew back the door and entered. Looking out of the window of her first-class carriage, she could not help but contrast the luxury of the compartment with the horror of the trains she had been on in South Africa.

Jane kept looking for uniforms, expecting to be asked to show her pass or told the train had been derailed. She thought about Lieutenant Handcock. Strangely, she could not dwell on his memory. The bliss of their short encounter did not fit with her mood or with the drabness of the day.

When she got to Winchester, she hailed another hackney cab and asked to be taken to Lainston House. As they moved along the quiet country lanes, Jane could hardly lift her head. She stared down at her feet, not wanting to recognise how near they were to arriving home. She was unable to keep her hands still; they tapped relentlessly on her lap.

Her trepidation almost got the better of her when they came to the entrance to the estate. She wanted to turn round and escape; she simply could not face what lay before her. She was, though, unable to issue any revised instructions to the cabbie. She was literally petrified, and unable to utter a word despite the frenzied thoughts rushing through her.

The road took the cab through the avenue of lime trees, then round the side of the house; they would have come into the large courtyard had the gate not been closed. Behind this inner gate was the main entrance to the house; either side of the courtyard were impressive single-storey buildings and a conservatory. Jane could see nothing, however, for the gates were closed.

In a trance she climbed down. There was a notice pinned to the gate and she moved closer to read it.

Following the death of Mr Irving Dunhaughton,
Lainston House is closed.

All enquiries should be directed initially to Messrs Simpson and Simpson, Solicitors, High Street, Winchester.

Jane stood transfixed. Her eyes wide open but seeing nothing. She did not read the notice a second time for she was unable to do so. She felt unsteady and reached towards the gate but then she was on her way down, her legs buckling and giving way completely. She hit the ground with a heavy thump and her head cracked hard on the ground.

The cabbie, who had been watching and wondering if they were going in through the gates or not, saw her fall and jumped down. He pulled her up, trying to get her into a sitting position, but she was a dead weight and he wondered if she were alive.

'Are you all right, love?' he kept saying, completely lost as to what to do. He looked round but there was no one in sight. He ran back to the cab, pulled the cushion from his seat and brought it back, placing it under Jane's head.

'Come on, love, come on!' He sounded desperate as he tried to see if she was breathing. He looked round again and shouted, 'Help! Anyone there? Help!'

It was with mighty relief that he noticed a flicker in Jane's face. Her eyes twitched and then slowly opened. 'Are you all right, love? Thought you were a goner. Gawd, I did!'

She had been unconscious for only a few seconds, certainly not more than ten, but to the cabbie it seemed like ten minutes. The tension in his body and mind visibly lessened, like a cat ready to spring relaxing once the danger had passed.

Jane did not reply. She did not hear him but saw his rough face mouthing words at her. She tried to sit up but struggled; she felt incredibly weak, and her head pulsated with pain.

It was another thirty seconds before she said anything. 'I am sorry, so sorry. My legs just gave way.'

'Nothing to be sorry for, love. Must have been some shock.'

Jane could not bring herself to say what had happened. She did not want to repeat the words on the notice. The notice, the notice on the gate... Her eyes moved, pointing towards it.

The cabbie moved over and stared at it. 'Afraid I don't read too well, love. Was it this that was the shock?'

Jane sat up, rubbing her throbbing head, a vicious kicking pain pummelling her. Already a huge lump was appearing. She was white; all colour had gone from her face and she looked bereft.

'Do you live here, love? You need to go inside and lie down. You don't look too good. I could go and get a doctor, if you like.'

Jane was not listening. The only noise she could hear was the thumping in her head, as though a horse was repeatedly kicking her.

'What do you want me to do, love? Do you know anyone who can help?' The cabbie was getting desperate and started looking round again. He spotted an old man walking slowly towards them and he beckoned. 'Hey, over here, over here!'

George, the gardener, never moved in a hurry but there was a noticeable increase in the pace of his steps. As he got closer, he realised who was sitting upright but looking groggy.

'You know her, mate?' said the cabbie. 'Just collapsed all in a heap. Thought she was a goner.'

'Yes, it's Jane. She lives here with her father but he's just died. She's been away.' It was the longest sentence George had spoken in years.

By now, Jane was becoming aware of what was happening around her. She felt embarrassed at being on the ground and tried to push herself up but she was still unsteady.

The cabbie grabbed her arm. 'Careful, love. Don't want to fall again. Come and sit in the cab, it will be more comfortable for you.' He and George took her arms and helped her back to the cab. It was a struggle for her to step inside but, with an ungentlemanly push to her backside, they helped her into the seat.

'Take her to vicarage,' said George to the cabbie. 'They will see to her, get the doctor.'

'Where's that, governor?'

George told the cabbie it was just round the corner. Then with some difficulty, he climbed onto the cab and sat next to him. They slowly turned round and followed the road to the vicarage further along the lane.

For Mrs Davies it was an absolute godsend: Jane arriving home; George all in a tether; Jane needing attention; the cabbie needing paying; doctor needing to be called. She could see weeks of gossip accumulating in front of her eyes. She was efficient, though, and soon had Jane lying on the couch in the morning room.

By the time the doctor arrived from Sparsholt, having been summoned by an agitated Mrs Davies, Jane looked much better; some colour had come back into her face, she was attentive and talking. The doctor pronounced that she would be fine but would have a sore head for a few days. He gave her some aspirin.

'I saw the notice on the gates,' she said. She did not need to say anymore.

'Your father died three weeks ago. He was buried ten days ago. People did not know what to do, not knowing where you were.' There was more than a hint of criticism in Mrs Davies' comments, amplified by the fact that she did not express her condolences. She was factual but cold; a keen observer would have suspected that Mrs Davies did not approve of Jane off gallivanting whilst her poor father was left at home, what with all his troubles.

'Will you be staying at Lainston House tonight, Jane?' Mrs Davies asked. 'I could get Mrs Squires to come over, get some fires going and bring in some food.'

'I am not certain,' replied Jane, who was desperately trying to recover her senses. 'Do you think you could send a message to Lilly Baring saying I have arrived home and could I come and see her?'

'Of course,' replied Mrs Davies, who was simply delighted to deepen her own involvement in the adventure.

Two pots of tea later, Lilly arrived. She and Jane burst into tears when they met and hugged each other.

'I am so sorry, Jane. It must have come as a great shock. I wrote telling you your father was in grave danger, but I suspect you had already left by then.' Lilly was walking round the room, feeling awkward. Her best friend had come home to find a note on her gate saying her father had died. Could she have done more to prevent that happening? She thought so — but what?

Lilly was also uncomfortable about asking what would happen next. Did Jane now own the estate? If not, what would she do? She had thought about this many times since Irving had died. She was glad she was not Jane.

'I received your letter saying Father was very ill, so I was slightly prepared, but seeing it written up on the gate was such a shock.'

'I'm sure it was. What will you do now? Why not come back home with me? Stay with us for a few days, get some rest and find out about your father's affairs when you have recovered.'

Within half an hour, Jane was in a carriage with Lilly, having put up no resistance to her suggestion. As soon as they reached the Barings' house, she was ushered into a guest room. She was deadly tired, drained by the worry that had increased in intensity as she had neared home and by her fall. Her injury, whilst not serious, hurt incessantly. She undressed, got into bed and silently wept the tears of the lonely.

Chapter 24
Fires Need to be Relit

Even without her father's death Jane would have been tired, but Irving's demise compounded her weakness. She found it difficult to give serious thought to the many issues she faced and when she did, her mind soon wandered. More and more, she thought not about Irving but her mother. 'If only...'

On the third day she felt stronger and spent it talking at great length with Lilly, who wisely and with great finesse got Jane to open up, so that she told of her experiences in South Africa and of her fears for the future.

'I am not sure if there is a will and, if there is, what it says. It's only now that I realise how little I actually know of the family's financial affairs. I am worried that I might have nowhere to live. I really don't know what debts Father has left.' Jane was sipping coffee in the drawing room. She noticed that the Lilly's painting of the three women having a picnic was hung to the right of the door.

'Did you have an exhibition?' she asked, looking at the picture.

'I did,' said Lilly enthusiastically. 'I sold four paintings but do you know what the gallery owner said?'

'What did he say?' replied Jane, not really interested.

'He said I should pretend to be a man and then my paintings would be taken more seriously. I was so annoyed with him.'

'I am not surprised you were annoyed and I am not surprised that he said that,' Jane responded drily. 'They simply don't accept that we can do just as well as them. If Father had just let me run the estate perhaps all this would not have happened.'

'That may be, Jane, but from now on you have to think about the future, not the past.'

They sat for a couple of hours, alternating between local news and Jane's experiences and concerns. Lilly was skilled at making gentle remarks that invited a response. She was an attentive listener and recognised that it was some time since Jane had been able to express her true feelings and anxieties. Jane admitted that she really missed her mother now.

When she was describing the train journeys and the appalling images of the Boer refugees in the open trucks, she seemed to lose herself in another place. She closed her eyes and described the scenes with clarity and with perfect recollection.

Lilly got out an atlas and they pored over the maps of South Africa. Jane marked out the journeys she had taken and the sites of the camps. She told her friend about being handed the baby, James, and how she had given him to an English couple. Lilly was transfixed, amazed at the number of adventures, incidents and lucky escapes that her friend had experienced.

When Jane told her about Lieutenant Handcock, the singing, the silly antics and the poems, Lilly could tell immediately that this was more than a chance encounter for Jane. It was clear the lieutenant had struck chords deep inside her and that she longed to see him soon.

Her opinion was confirmed when Jane offered up the comment, 'Now that Father is dead, it is more important than ever for me to see him again. I would happily go to Australia, if need be. Have you ever read Wordsworth's poem *Michael*, Lilly?'

'No, I'm afraid I haven't,' came the reply.

'You must. It is so sad it will make you cry. I have a copy I will lend to you. You will see why it impressed me so much.'

'Are you sure it was the poem that impressed you and not the person reading it?' asked Lilly.

'Both, probably,' replied Jane wistfully. 'How is Woodly?' she asked, changing topics abruptly.

'Woodly is fine. Would you like to see him?'

'Oh, I would! That would be wonderful!'

They put on coats and boots and went out through the boot room into the courtyard, then across to the stables. Jane recognised Woodly instantly in the far box and he saw her as well, raising his head and kicking his door. Jane ran over to him and reached over the half door as he stuck out his head. She kissed him and hugged him tightly, whispering how much she had missed him and how she hoped he had behaved himself.

Lilly was convinced that Woodly was actually smiling as Jane smothered him with affection. She went over to the corner of the stables to a box of apples and handed one and then another as Jane fed them lovingly to her horse. It was the best therapy imaginable.

The next day Jane went to the offices of Simpson and Simpson in Winchester. She had walked up and down the high street hundreds, if not thousands, of times, past the corn exchange, the butcher's, baker's, milliners and every other shop, hotel and inn. She had looked in every window but she had never noticed the solicitors' offices. She'd never had reason to; the eye only sees what it is looking for.

The sign on the wall simply said :Simpson and Simpson, Solicitors, 32 High Street, Winchester. The door was open and led to some rather steep steps up to the offices on the first floor.

When Jane entered the dark outer office, she turned immediately towards the window that overlooked the high street. It was small and let in insufficient light for the size of the room.

A confident, strong voice asked, 'Yes, can we help you?' The voice was that of a youngish man, probably around thirty, who was sitting at a desk piled high with papers and files.

Jane explained who she was and that she needed to see someone about Lainston House and Irving Dunhaughton's estate. She was asked to wait. The young man knocked on the inner office door and went in, closing the door behind him.

He was gone for a good few minutes, leaving Jane uncertain about what was happening. Her uncertainty was reaching the point of irritation when the door finally opened again and the young man appeared, followed by an older, shorter man with a large beard. He introduced himself as Edgar Simpson and invited Jane to come into his office.

The inner office was even darker than the outer one. There was no window, just a skylight in the roof. It was only eleven a.m. but a gaslight burned, as did a gas fire on the far wall. The room had just one desk, again covered in papers and files. Two walls were filled with bookcases, which had large numbers of boxes and papers in every available space.

Mr Simpson was pleasant and offered his condolences. He wanted to know where Jane had been and when she had last seen her father. He was sympathetic and understanding but also very slow and meticulous. It took well over an hour for him to come to the essential points Jane had come to find out. Did her father have a will? If so, what were its terms? What was the extent of the estate and were there any debts? Above all, Jane wanted to know the process that would have to be followed.

Mr Simpson was thorough, explaining all the steps and making sure that she understood. After seventy-five minutes, Jane tried to push things along by asking if she could see her father's will.

This seemed to cause Mr Simpson a real problem. He mused and stroked his beard. 'Yes, yes, I see that you will want to know the contents. I have it here and I can summarise it for you, if you like. Full of legalese. You know what these documents are like.'

Jane did not know what they were like and she dreaded listening to a summary from Mr Simpson, which she assumed would be far longer than the actual document. She asked again if she could see it.

'Yes, yes, of course.' Mr Simpson handed it to her. 'I am afraid you cannot take it away. I must keep it here,' he added.

Two minutes later, Jane handed back the document. 'I am afraid I cannot make head or tail of this. What is it saying?'

Much to Jane's surprise, she received a succinct and clear answer. 'It says that all your father's assets on his death pass equally to his children, other than for Lainston House and the estate which, in the event that he died without having a son, pass to his brother.'

'I did not know he had a brother,' said Jane, somewhat shocked. 'You said "equally to his children". I am his only child.' She sat bolt upright and gripped the arms of the chair.

'Indeed, indeed,' said Mr Simpson. 'It's all very confusing but I am not aware of any other children. So unless someone pops up, all his assets will be yours — except the house and estate as you are not a son.'

'But did he have a brother?' asked Jane, a hint of desperation in her voice.

'Oh yes, most definitely. But no one knows where he is or if he is alive. It seems he went off to India when he was in his early twenties and little is known about him other than that. Did your father never mention him?'

'No. I never knew I had an uncle.'

Jane asked more questions but received little in return; everything seemed to be in limbo. Mr Simpson said that, now he had met Jane, he would place an advert in *The Times* and *London Gazette* seeking information about Walter Walker Dunhaughton.

'And in the meantime, what happens to the house and estate?' asked Jane.

'Well, it seems sensible for you to continue to live there and run the estate until things are sorted out. That could take a long time.' Mr Simpson once again surprised Jane with the clarity of his answer. He seemed to oscillate between long periods of tedious banality and the occasional sharp and concise observation.

The next day Jane moved back to Lainston House. Mrs Squires was only too glad to help her get the house functioning again. She needed the money; Jane coming home was a genuine piece of good fortune for her, if not so happy for Jane. Mrs Squires was a widow and had been struggling financially since Irving's death. She had been living in a rented room; Mr Simpson had told her that it was his role to ensure the estate of Mr Dunhaughton did not spend unnecessary money and, as no one was living at Lainston House, there was no need for a housekeeper.

It did not take her long to light some fires, order groceries from the village shop and bring the stove and ovens back into use. Fresh linen was placed on the beds and in the bathrooms.

In some ways Jane was glad to be home, but she could not disguise her increasing loneliness. She had not really had a relationship with her father; there was no real conversation between them, no rapport, and certainly no demonstration of love or affection. Yet he was all the family she had — or at least knew of. She worried about the uncertainty; what would happen if Irving's brother was found and he claimed the inheritance?

The initial and essential work to set up the house for the three or four hours it took her kept Jane mentally, as well as physically, occupied. When it was done however and Mrs Squires returned to her rented room, to collect her things, Jane was left alone. She felt the absence of her father, a void that permeated throughout the house. Jane shuffled without purpose from room to room, hearing the sounds of happier times as her mother and father laughed or sang. The decibels of the sounds she heard deep inside her mind soared as she entered her father's study and she stretched her arm so that she could steady herself against the wall. Everything had been left untouched with letters and papers untidily covering the desk. Normally, Jane would have set to and sorted the papers but now she could not summon the willpower. She turned slowly and closed the door.

Gradually things settled back to normal. Jane started to understand the finances of the estate. She regularly went to the farm manager of the Barings' estate; he gave her lots of practical advice and came over a couple of times to see for himself what needed to be done.

Jane also went to the bank manager, who was also helpful. The estate had no cash but the bank manager made loans available, which would be used until the sale of lambs in the spring brought in some much-needed money.

Woodly was brought back and Jane spent as much time as she could riding with the hunt. She attended church, the first time she had been since leaving the village, and met the new vicar. She had not once thought of the Reverend Shell, and she realised that she had not replied to his last letter in which he told her of his decision to go to Africa.

Christmas came and went. Jane spent the festive season with Lilly and was delighted when, on New Year's Day, her friend announced her engagement to a wealthy Hampshire landowner. Delighted, but privately worried that her only true friend might become less accessible, Jane was also envious since she had not heard from Lieutenant Handcock. Was she being foolish? Would it lead to anything? Many was the night that she went to bed to read Wordsworth and think of him.

Chapter 25
Following Orders

Jane was not to know that, far away in Pretoria, Lieutenant Handcock lay in a dingy prison cell writing to her:

Dear Jane,

I do hope all is well with you. I am not sure if you are now back in England but I have written to you at the Bloemfontein address you gave me as well.

Things have taken a bad turn for me and The Breaker. All I want you to know is that we are not guilty and were following orders from Kitchener himself.

Look after yourself.

Peter

This undated letter arrived at Lainston House on the 5th of March 1902. The envelope was handwritten and Jane studied it carefully before opening it. She could see it had a Cape Town postmark but she did not recognise who it was from. It clearly was not from Betty or Caroline; the handwriting was scruffy and the envelope dirty.

When she opened it she was puzzled, as there was just one piece of paper, which was lined and badly folded. The writing was in pencil and hard to read. It took her some time to realise that it was from Peter Handcock.

She read the letter, if you could call it that, over and over again, not comprehending what it was saying. Why had he not written more? What did 'bad turn' and 'not guilty' mean? Guilty of what? She noticed that he made no mention of coming to see her. If he was not interested in her then why write at all? Surely, he could have just forgotten about her.

She sat down at the kitchen table, trying to collect her thoughts. There was no address for her to write back. She had so many questions. Why had he not given an address? Did that mean he did not expect a reply — or did he not want one? She struggled with this thought. Why would he write to her if he were not thinking of her? Surely Kitchener himself would not have given orders to a lieutenant?

As she tried to make sense of the note, she began to get annoyed with herself. She was going round and round, asking the same questions.

The following day she showed the letter to Lilly after they had been out with the hunt. Lilly was equally perplexed but said she would ask her father to make some enquiries with the War Office.

It was about ten days later that Jane, who had been out riding with Lilly, was asked by the butler if she could spare his lordship a few minutes. Jane looked at Lilly, puzzled, but Lilly shrugged her shoulders, indicating that she did not know what it was about.

Jane followed the butler into a long corridor and then into the hallway, which they crossed. The butler opened a door and stood to one side as he announced, 'Jane Dunhaughton, your lordship.' He closed the door behind him as he left the room.

The room was a magnificent study and library. A large oak desk with a leather top filled the bay window; the chair in front of the desk looked out onto the gardens, which, although windswept, were still most impressive with ancient yew and oak trees forming a natural end to the garden. Library shelves ran down the whole of the wall to Jane's right; this was the study of a serious, learned man. To Jane's left was a large table, which was filled with more books and papers arranged in a very precise way. Lord Baring was sitting at his desk but rose and walked over to her.

'Jane, how good to see you. I am so sorry about your father. It must have been a terrible shock. I do hope you are coping. You know that we are always here to help if you need us.'

'That is so kind. It was a shock but Lilly and your estate manager have been very helpful. Everything is still cloudy. I have to plod on until affairs are resolved.'

'Yes,' Lord Baring said, inviting Jane to sit down at the table. 'Lilly has told me about the complications with the will. I hope everything is sorted out soon, and in a way that helps you. You have been Lilly's best friend for so many years.'

'Thank you,' said Jane. 'I really do not know how long it is going to take. The uncertainty is quite distressing.'

'I am sure it is,' said Lord Baring. He was in his late fifties, portly with a white beard but with a kind and approachable manner. He looked slightly uneasy as he moved a set of papers from side to side.

'I suppose you are wondering why I have asked to see you.' He looked at Jane directly but did not hold the look for more than a fleeting second and moved his eyes back to his papers. He ran his finger nervously along the edge. 'You told Lilly about a letter you had received from a Lieutenant Handcock in South Africa.'

'Yes, that's right.' Jane realised that this interview was about Peter. 'Do you have news?'

'Yes, I do. But may I ask how you know Lieutenant Handcock?'

'Well, I hardly know him. We were both on a train that was derailed and shot at. We had to wait a few days for a rescue train and we became friends. That is the only time I met him.' Jane looked quizzically at Lord Baring, seeking more from him.

'Jane, I am afraid I do not have good news. Very bad news, in fact. Given the shock of your father's death and all the unresolved issues, I am reluctant to add to your worries. All I can say is that you would be best to put Lieutenant Handcock behind you and try not to think of him any more.' He said this quite firmly as though giving her fatherly instructions rather than advice.

'Why?' Jane replied, sitting bolt upright. All her antennae were fully engaged. 'What have you learned?'

There was quite a gap before Lord Baring answered. Jane was staring at him and he realised that he would not get away with vague, imprecise snippets of information. On the other hand, he had the greatest reluctance to reveal the full contents of the letter from St John Brodrick, Secretary of State for War, which lay before him. He paused not knowing how best to play this. He liked Jane and he knew that Lilly

273

had been worrying about her ever since she had set off for South Africa, even more so after her father became ill.

'It's not good, Jane. Not good at all. I can say I have a letter from St John Brodrick, Secretary of State for War, which tells of the fate of Lieutenant Handcock. I do implore you not to press me further but try and forget all about him.' As he said this, he realised that he was mishandling the situation. In his attempt to lessen the blow, he was simply intensifying Jane's anxiety, compounding her desire for more information which, when it came, would seem all the worse. He wished he could start again.

'Please tell me the truth. I do need to know. He wrote to me saying he was not guilty. Guilty of what?' Jane pleaded.

This was the opening Lord Baring needed. He said firmly, 'I am afraid that Lieutenant Handcock has been found guilty of murder and executed under military law.'

There was a loud gasp from Jane, who recoiled from her tense upright position. 'No, no, that cannot be right.' She looked imploringly at him, willing him to say it was a mistake, that he had confused the names.

'I am afraid it is, Jane.' Lord Baring wanted to hold her, put his arms round her shoulders and comfort her, but his solid, Victorian upbringing prevented him from moving closer. 'He was executed along with another man, Lieutenant Morant. Would you like Lilly to come in?'

He could see that Jane was on the point of breaking down and he knew that he would be hopeless if a woman started to cry in his company. He rang for his butler by pulling a cord at the side of his desk.

Little more than two minutes passed before Lilly arrived, during which time Jane did not hear any of Lord Baring's words. It was good that she did not, for his efforts at comfort were clumsy; well-meant but awkward and contrived. Saying it was fortunate that Jane had not known Lieutenant Handcock longer may well have been true, but it did not provide Jane with the solace she needed.

Jane was not able to function properly; she did not hear words or notice movement. She did not form coherent thoughts or questions. Her eyes wide open saw nothing. Her ears on full alert heard nothing. She did not hear Lord Baring explaining to Lilly what had happened; she did not see Lilly reading the letter from the War Office; she did not hear Lilly berate her father for not informing her first and letting her break the news to Jane. She did not remember being guided out of the study and taken to the drawing room and drinking a very large gin poured by Lilly.

There are different types of grief: grief when your favourite dog or horse dies; grief when a parent dies before you are of an age to fully comprehend; grief when your beloved dies in their prime, and grief when hope and prospects are dashed at the outset of a journey. For Jane, this was the grief that comes when the sun, after a very brief display of warmth and colour, is shrouded with dark grey clouds that bring the prospect of prolonged drabness. She had dreamed of happiness with Lieutenant Handcock. She had seen sunlit uplands but all too fleetingly, and now she saw a deep chasm with torrents of swirling water. Her grief was born from the death of hope.

Chapter 26
Trying to Comprehend

As the days passed and she regained her faculties of comprehension and inquisitiveness, she probed Lilly for more information. Lilly knew what her father did not, that the road to recovery lay with full disclosure, with the ability to interpret and understand. As Lilly provided information, based on the letter she had seen from St John Brodrick, it raised more questions and led to Lilly writing a letter for her father to sign and send to Brodrick with many follow-up questions.

Brodrick was desperate for Lord Baring not to ask questions about the affair in the House and so he did his best to placate him. Brodrick was at a loss to understand why Lord Baring was interested in the matter or even knew about it.

Jane began to put together the pieces of the jigsaw. Breaker Morant, Handcock and a Lieutenant Witton had been arrested for the murder of a number of prisoners in their charge. This followed the murder and mutilation of Captain Hunt, the much-loved senior officer of the Bushveldt Carbineers, by a Boer rebel group. There was a suggestion the murders had taken place as an act of revenge in a fit of violent anger.

It appeared that the president of the military court, a Lieutenant-Colonel H. C. Denny had requested on behalf of the court that mercy be extended to Handcock, Morant and Witton. Kitchener, whose decision it was as commander-in-chief, would not reduce the sentence for Handcock and Morant, though he did for Witton. The executions took place on the 27th of February 1902, at Castle Military Prison in Cape Town.

Jane began to write down her own interpretation of Handcock's letter. He had said that they were acting under orders from Kitchener; if that was so, it was obvious why Kitchener would not commute their sentence. Dead men tell no tales — and they could have implicated Kitchener in the murders. Jane could only rationalise the acts of murder — if indeed such acts took place, which she doubted — if Handcock was instructed to do so by a senior officer or, indeed, the most senior of officers, Kitchener himself.

By the time Jane had put all these pieces of information together, which took many weeks, her grief had turned to anger. She did not hold grudges, she could move on and forgive, but she could not share the public adulation of Kitchener. For her, Kitchener was the man who not only introduced a policy that led to the deaths of thousands of women and children, he had also betrayed the first love of her life. She was certain of this. She could not have misjudged Handcock to such an extent. It was not possible that the reader of *Lyrical Ballads* was a cold-blooded murderer. She believed that the recommendation to commute Witton's sentence must have been based on some reason that had come out in court. But what was she to do? Nothing would bring him back.

Her anger brewed inside her. It was not visible to others for, with great difficulty, Jane kept her emotions in check. She was certain that her instincts were right and a great miscarriage of justice had been committed. She wanted to take it further and, when the opportunity came, she asked Lilly if she could meet with her father. They went along together to see him in his study.

'Will you ask a question in the House about Lieutenant Handcock? I am certain a great injustice has been committed. I — we — don't know the full story and we need to. Will you press for an enquiry? Please?' Jane implored.

'I am afraid I can't, Jane,' Lord Baring replied. 'I can see this has affected you deeply but asking questions in the House will not lessen your grief. I need to pick my fights carefully. I know this is not what you want to hear, but I genuinely feel nothing will be gained by probing further. The court must have had its reasons for reaching its decision. It was just bad luck that you came across this chap.'

Jane was hurt by the response which was far colder than she had anticipated. 'Oh, I see,' she said. She did not try and argue the point but looked sadly at Lilly, who looked incredulously at her father.

As Jane left the room crestfallen, Lilley turned to her father and said angrily under her breath, 'Thank you, Father. That was most helpful. Did you really need to add that last sentence?'

Chapter 27
The World Moves On

Time and events moved on. A peace treaty was signed in May between Britain and the Boers and Kitchener returned to England a national hero. Lilly was married in late June on a gloriously sunny day. Jane was maid of honour and, whilst sharing the enjoyment of the day, could not help pondering her own future and the lack of anyone in it.

She tried to be engaged in village life, attended as many functions as she could, loved riding with the hunt and immersed herself in the affairs of the estate, but her activities felt superficial. She was occupying herself, keeping busy but there was a major gap in her life. Gradually she thought less of Lieutenant Handcock, realising that there was nothing to be gained by constantly fuelling her anger. As always, she was a pragmatist and her grief gave way to the passage of time.

She travelled up to London to watch the coronation of Edward VII on August 9th, 1902. She took the opportunity to visit the Courtneys and stayed with them for two nights, partly to share her experiences of the South Africa trip but also because all hotel accommodation had been booked well in advance. They talked a great deal about Emily, who was convalescing in France and writing her account of the concentration camp scandal.

Lord Courtney and Caroline were scathing about Kitchener but felt the tide of public opinion was very much against them. They were worried about Emily, who had been deeply hurt by the abuse she had received for voicing her concerns about the conduct of the war. She was hurt emotionally and also worn out physically.

At the coronation, Jane struggled to cope with the hundreds of thousands of onlookers. She could not fail to notice the prominence given to Kitchener and the adulation of the public. When she saw him for the first time, albeit from a distance, she could think only of the time she sat by the track transfixed by Peter Handcock.

It struck her then that public opinion is shaped not by facts but by perception. If you perceived that something had happened, then it had. She understood, in a detached, phlegmatic way, the public's view of Kitchener but she could not share it, recognising now what Emily had known so much earlier, that perception was a tool that could be manipulated by those who the public wanted to believe.

She took the opportunity after her two days in London to travel down to Dover and then on to West Hougham. It was here that Edith and Alun Newman had taken up residence when they returned to England. Alun was manager for the Shakespeare Colliery. Jane had been to see them once before, to attend James' christening. They had delayed this service especially so that she could attend. She was made to feel very welcome and she could see that James was loved and well looked after. Alun doted him on.

Interestingly, neither Edith nor Alun made any reference to South Africa when they were with Jane. It was as though they had eliminated it from all their memories.

Nineteen hundred and two passed and then the horrid winter of 1903, when much of Hampshire lay deep in snow for weeks. Jane was becoming restless, dissatisfied with the routine of life at Lainston House, the lack of variety in her days and the absence of new experiences. She often thought of the many new experiences she had encountered in her year in South Africa. She wanted to do something positive, to make a difference and not simply maintain the status quo, but the lack of certainty about her ownership of the estate and the strong pull of inertia prevented any radical moves.

It was June 1903. One day Jane collected her letters from the post office, having been in the village for a few basic foodstuffs. She could see instantly that one of the letters was from Emily; she recognised the distinctive handwriting. She opened it at once, not even waiting to get home.

It was a long letter telling of Emily's life, writing and plans. It ended with an invitation for them to meet in London the following week. As soon as she got home, Jane wrote a short reply saying that she would come up the following Wednesday and they should they meet as before at Claridge's at noon.

It was with a sense of déjà vu that Jane entered the foyer of the grand hotel and waited to meet her friend. She did not wait more than two minutes. The two hugged and embraced in a way that reflected their deep friendship, a friendship that transcended time and distance.

As they enjoyed the splendour of the setting and sumptuous food and service, they reflected on how different it was from the experiences they had shared in South Africa. 'I have nightmares about those train journeys,' said Jane jokingly but with a definite undercurrent of truth.

'I have nightmares about the camps and the children dying,' said Emily. It came across as a slight put-down, inferring that Jane should be thinking of others suffering rather than herself.

Jane, as always, backed away, not wanting to be separated from Emily in their views or anything else. 'Oh, of course. It's just that in order to get to the camps we had to go on those trains.'

'I'm glad we did. Without the fuss we created, they would have had everyone in camps. They did not care a jot.'

'Do you think we made a difference?' Jane asked, desperately wanting a positive answer.

'Yes, I do. I really do. Lloyd George saying that the government policy was like King Herod killing all the baby boys had a massive impact, and the government started to take fright. They were scared of the international condemnation as much as anything.'

'I think that the government was not aware of the policy until you made them aware. I think Kitchener would have been even more brutal if he had not been brought to account,' said Jane, becoming more animated.

'*We* made them aware, Jane. I could not have done it without your help and support.' Emily pushed aside the lamb chops she had ordered and looked at Jane forlornly. 'I think about all those thousands of people who died. From what I have heard, many more died in the camps they set up for black people. The government cared even less for them, and when they burnt the farms they simply herded the blacks into the desert. Oh yes, they set up camps — but they were nothing but places to die. It's a scandal. I am at a loss to know how a Christian country like England can behave in such a way.' She attacked the lamb chops again as though stabbing government ministers.

'What is the phrase: "What the eye does not see, the heart does not feel"?' said Jane.

'Yes, exactly. The vast majority of people have no real idea where South Africa is. They don't really care, as long as England is winning.'

'But they *do* care,' said Jane. 'You have seen that. But they have to be made aware. It's only now that I realise that the vast majority of what politicians tell you is not the truth, it is simply what they want you to hear.'

'I am going back and I would like you to come with me.' Emily was looking directly at Jane, having put down her knife and fork so as to emphasise the seriousness of the statement.

'Back to South Africa? But why? The war is over.' Jane was slightly horrified as well as mystified.

'I need a cause and there are tens of thousands of children who have been orphaned. There are whole communities with no means of earning a living, or making things, or even undertaking simple farming. Everything has been destroyed. I can help them. I am going to set up schools and workshops, help them get back on their feet. Come with me. It will be different and we will be welcome this time.'

'I can't. I simply can't,' said Jane. 'Things have changed. I don't even know if I own Lainston House — and if I don't, how will I live? All that needs to be sorted before I could contemplate going back. How long are you thinking of staying? Your health must be your main concern.'

'I am getting better and the South African climate will be good for me. I won't have to travel on those trains like before,' she said, smiling at Jane.

'I really need to get my position clarified before I can disappear again. And who would run things if I am not here? I am not sure I could go back, though, even if everything was sorted out here.'

'Well, Jane, you know you will always be welcome. I sail next week and I will write to you once I am settled in Cape Town.'

Chapter 28
Return of the Native

The rest of the summer of 1903 passed without major incident for Jane. She was busy, yet not engaged; she occupied time rather than directed it. She was wistful, longing for a transformation — though into what she had not expressly defined; underneath, it was for a partner.

The village saw her as sensible and pragmatic, helpful and caring, tidy and organised, yet behind these public characteristics there was a person whose youth was slipping by in a melancholy routine of lonely nights and respectable days.

It was not her fault that she was uncertain about her status at Lainston House. It was not her fault her father had gambled and drunk, or that he had left her in such an uncertain position. It was not her fault that her mother had died, leaving her unloved. It was not her fault that Kitchener had refused clemency for the first love of her life. These things were not her fault but, as the months passed, she increasingly thought that they were and that maybe she was cursed in some way.

She attended church regularly; occasionally she crossed the garden and lane and entered the church on her own. She sat quietly; whilst not praying, for she felt that would be too direct and selfish, she wished for a change in fortune and for new sparks to rekindle her barely smouldering embers.

It was the 23rd of February 1904 when Jane received a letter from Simpson and Simpson, the solicitors she had seen in Winchester. The letter said little, simply asking her to call in at the office at her earliest convenience. As the only matter she had ever dealt with them about had concerned her father's will, she immediately put on her long fur coat, hat and gloves and took the horse-drawn bus service from the village into Winchester.

Increasingly horse-drawn services were being replaced by petrol-engine motor vehicles but in the main this was in the towns and cities; rural areas lagged behind. There was a service twice a day into Winchester, leaving the village at 9.10 and 11.10, and Jane squeezed in alongside three other passengers for the hour-long journey.

She was nervous as she walked up the high street and stopped at the entrance to the solicitors. She took a deep breath before climbing the stairs and going into the outer office.

It was nearly two years since she had last been to the offices of Simpson and Simpson but it could have been yesterday. Nothing had changed. The same young-looking clerk looked up, peering between the piles of paper on his desk and asking how he could be of service.

Jane explained who she was and held out the letter from Mr Simpson.

'Oh, I see,' said the clerk. 'Just wait a moment.' He disappeared into the inner office. Just as last time, she had quite a long time to wait until the door opened and Mr Simpson emerged, holding out his hand. 'Miss Dunhaughton, how good of you to come so promptly. Do come in.'

They entered the inner office and again nothing had changed. The gas fire burned intensely; the papers were even higher on the desk; the wallpaper looked slightly darker, but basically all was the same.

Mr Simpson's demeanour was also the same, for again he spent ages talking about nothing, or so it seemed to Jane who was nervous about what he was going to tell her. He asked her if she was well, if she was still riding with the hunt, if she was perturbed by the inclement weather.

After ten minutes of inconsequential trivia, perhaps recognising Jane's increasing irritation and fidgeting, he finally said, 'Well, I take it you would like me to tell why I have asked you to come in.'

Jane nodded enthusiastically.

'I have quite definite news. I do not know if it is good news but it *is* news and does move us forward. Your father's brother has been in touch. He lives in India and our advert in *The Times* was brought to his attention. He intends to return to England and look at the estate, with a view to returning permanently.'

Jane winced and slumped back in her chair. She took a few seconds to respond and then said, 'What will happen to me?' It was as succinct a question as she could conceive, and aptly summed up the central issue.

'I am afraid that will have to be agreed between you and Mr Dunhaughton. I have advised him of the contents of your father's will in so much as it affects him. If he decides to take up residence at Lainston House, it will be for him to agree how this will affect you.'

'You mean if he asks me to leave,' Jane said pointedly.

'I would not have put it so directly but it is possible that he may decide to do so. Equally, he may find some other arrangement acceptable. I believe that can only be answered once he has seen the property and estate and met you, Miss Dunhaughton.'

Jane left the offices in a state of shock. It was almost two years since she had become aware of her father's will. It had little if any impact on her; in fact, everything seemed to be improving and matters were being put in order. The farm and estate were on a much sounder footing. Jane had continued to live at Lainston House and spend her time much as she had done before her father's death. If it had gone on much longer, she would have started to forget about the will.

Now the situation had changed totally. She might — no, she would probably — have to move out. Mr Simpson had told her that her father's brother had a wife and two children. They lived on a tree plantation in Darjeeling where he had been most successful; firstly in marrying the plantation owner's daughter and then in expanding the business substantially. Why would he want her to stay at the house?

It took some time for the enormity of the news to sink in. It was raining hard as she entered the high street and she hurried along, sheltering in shop doorways along with scores of others. She had no umbrella, which she now regretted.

It was ironic that, as she stopped in Dixon's the grocer's, she saw advertisements in the window for Darjeeling tea being sold loose and in packets.

She had an hour to waste before the service back to Lainston House, so she hurried, as best she could, in her long coat, some fifty yards until she came to a coffee shop. She went in and ordered coffee and cake. She was totally self-absorbed during the hour, not noticing anything going on, who came, who left, the staff, the coffee or the bill. Nor did she notice the time, for when she finally got up, slowly and dreamlike, she was already too late for the service that had left some ten minutes before.

Jane did not swear; she had never sworn and hated bad language, failing to understand why anyone needed to use profanities. When she discovered that the service had already left, however, she let out a quite audible 'damn'. It embarrassed her that she had uttered such a word; maybe someone had heard! What they would think of her? Where had such a word come from? She hurried away as though there were an odious presence nearby.

At the end of the high street she came to the Old Vine Hotel. She decided that she might as well have lunch and wait in comfort for the next service. She settled down. The log fire was roaring, casting flickering reflections on the low, oak-beamed ceiling. Jane recalled how excited she had been when she met Emily and Edward Hemmerde after the general election meeting. It seemed so long ago; so much had changed. Was it all going to change again?

The melancholy that had been lurking for the last few months was advancing and she found it hard not to imagine the worst. Where would she live? What would she live on? She had some money of her own but only enough to buy a small home; if she used it all for that purpose, she would have nothing left. Finance now seemed to take on a different perspective.

Back at home, she tried to carry on as normal, attend to what needed attending to and keep up appearances, but she found it hard to remain positive. A dark cloud was hovering over her, threatening to unleash a torrential downpour, a downpour that she suspected would have a greater impact than she could yet imagine.

She visited her bank manager and, for the first time, discussed not the estate accounts but her personal account. She had been left money when her mother had died; in the sixteen years since then the money had been untouched, quietly gaining interest that was currently at three per cent. She had been left £1,250; with compound interest this sum had grown to £2,107. Not a fortune, but it would be a major help.

Although depressed by the turn of events over which she had no control, she tried to plan what she would do if she had to leave Lainston House. She concluded that the solution would be to rent a house, thus preserving her capital until she arrived at a long-term plan. What preoccupied her as much, if not more, than where would she live, was what she would do.

At the moment the estate was her life; managing the farm and the staff, looking after the garden and the house occupied her fully. Her church was across the road and, apart from a few weeks spent in London just before she went out to South Africa, she had lived nowhere else. She recalled her thoughts when she was in South Africa that she would like to work helping others not as fortunate as herself.

It was early summer when things became crystal clear. Jane received a letter from Simpson and Simpson; Walter

Dunhaughton was on his way to England and was expected to arrive on the 6th of June. Once established in Southampton, he would travel up to Winchester and intended to tour his estate and look round the house. That was only a week away.

There was nothing Jane could do but wait. She went to see Lilly, who was visiting her family for a few days, and inevitably they talked about the imminent visit from Jane's uncle.

Lilly was mortified when it dawned on her that Jane could soon be homeless. 'Oh Jane, what are you going to do? It's so beastly that everything goes to the men. And just when you are getting everything shipshape! It's your house, you have lived there all your life.'

'Well, it isn't my house. And until women get the vote and change the law, nothing will change. I have been thinking about joining the Women's Social and Political Union. Events like this bring it home just how second class we are.'

'I'm not sure that's a good idea,' said Lilly. 'I have been reading about them and Father says they are not like the other women's groups. They are troublemakers, intent on causing real pain unless Parliament gives them the vote. What is it they keep saying? "Deeds not demands".'

'"Deeds not words",' Jane corrected. 'They believe the talk has gone on too long with no progress, so new tactics are needed.'

'Not if you end up hurting somebody and going to prison,' cautioned Lilly.

'They are adamant that they won't hurt people — other than where it really counts, in the pocket. They are targeting property, not people.'

'But we are property owners,' said Lilly. 'So are you.'

'I thought I was but it appears I am not.'

'Gosh, you really have been thinking about this. Have you been to any meetings?' Lilly asked, becoming concerned.

'No, but I was thinking of going to one in London next week. I probably won't be able to if Walter Dunhaughton arrives.'

'I'm not sure you should join that group. I think they are a bad lot. But never mind politics, when does your uncle arrive? Do you know?' Lilly tried to move the conversation away from militant women's issues. She knew her husband would boil over if he found out she was talking even remotely about it, never mind that her best friend was thinking of joining the most militant women's group. Her husband became incandescent with rage at the prospect of votes for women and she had learned quickly not to go down that path.

'I am not certain of a precise date but he arrives in England on the 6th of June,' said Jane. 'The sooner he comes here the better. I can't stand the worry and uncertainty.'

'That I do understand,' said Lilly, anxious to find some common ground.

It was the 9th of June when Mrs Squires came into the garden where Jane was pruning, weeding and generally passing the time on a lovely summer day. Daisies were coming into full flower, whilst the cherry blossom faded and littered the lawn with fallen petals. Jane had a basket of cut flowers. As Mrs Squires approached, Jane said, 'Please put these in water, I would like to arrange them.'

'A gentleman has called for you, miss. A Mr Dunhaughton. He has come in a motor vehicle.'

It was the last item that clearly fascinated Mrs Squires. Cars were becoming more frequent on the roads but out in rural Hampshire they were still a rare sight. Mrs Squires could not recall anyone having arrived at the house in one before.

'Oh, that's Father's brother. I have been expecting him.'

'I did not know your father had a brother, miss,' said a puzzled Mrs Squires.

'Neither did I,' said Jane, her stomach churning with the worry of what was to come from her meeting.

'I showed him into the drawing room. I trust that's what you wish.'

'Yes, that fine,' said Jane, turning and walking briskly up the garden path and into the house through the boot room. She rushed upstairs, looked at herself in the mirror and brushed her hair before going back downstairs.

She paused and took a deep breath before going into the drawing room. 'Mr Dunhaughton. I am Jane Dunhaughton, your niece.'

He was standing when she entered the room and he walked over holding out his hand. He was about fifty; he was very dark skinned, no doubt from the sun in India. He had a full head of dark hair and a slim moustache. About five feet ten inches tall and of slim build, he wore a light-coloured suit with a waistcoat that housed a gold chain attached to a pocket watch. Jane looked carefully at his face as she approached him to shake hands. She could see no obvious resemblance but what struck her most was how much younger he looked than her father, and the contrast between his dark sun-bleached skin and the pale, shallow look of her father the last time she had seen him.

'Very pleased to meet you. I am sorry that it took your father's death for us to meet for the first time. I did not know you existed.'

'Likewise,' said Jane guardedly. 'It was quite a shock when Mr Simpson told me about you.'

'Mr Simpson?' queried Walter Dunhaughton.

'Yes, Mr Simpson the solicitor.'

'Oh yes, of course.'

Mrs Squires came in with coffee and cakes and they sat down. Jane observed Walter closely. He was confident and assured; he would not be able to say the same about her. They talked about his trip from India and the fact that it was so much cooler in England. Jane asked him about the car; did he have one in India? He said that he did, the same model, a Rover 8 that he had imported from England.

'I suspect you will want to know what my intentions are with the house and estate,' he said finally, standing up and looking quite officious.

'Well, yes,' said Jane nervously. 'It has been quite a worrying time trying to keep everything running smoothly but not knowing what would happen.'

'I suspect you were hoping that I was dead or would never show up.' Walter looked challengingly at Jane.

She was uncomfortable, not used to such confrontational or direct comments. 'I would not say that. It was a shock when I discovered you existed. I have done my best to keep the estate on a sound footing.'

'But hoping that I'd never show up. Nothing wrong with that. I would have thought the same if I had been in your shoes.'

'But I—' Jane was about to protest but was interrupted by Walter.

'No buts. It does not matter, not important. What is important is what happens now. As you know, the estate belongs to me as set out in your father's will. Subject to me looking round the estate and the house, I intend to come back to England with my family. I have a wife and two young boys aged eight and six. They will go to school in England. Can't have them going to school in India. Need to go to a proper school, not some tinpot place run by spinsters and wogs. So, I suspect you are wondering what will happen to you. Well, I have a plan. I said to my wife, Gertrude, that I would meet with you, see what type of egg you were and, if you're a decent sort, we could offer you a job looking after Herbert and Charles until they go off to school in a couple of years' time. Want them to get to know England, local customs, etc. Don't want them standing out like nignogs, do we?'

Jane was completely taken aback, not only by the offer but by Walters's challenging style and language. She had never experienced anything like it and she was not sure she liked it. She hesitated, mumbling more to herself than saying anything substantive.

'Well, what do you say? I'd like to get things sorted then we know where we are.'

Jane regained some composure and quietly but clearly said, 'That is very kind of you and I appreciate the offer. I wonder if I may be allowed to think about it for a few days?'

'A few days?' he shouted 'A few days? We need to move faster than that. How about we look round the house and the estate and when we are done you can let me know what you think? After all, we are family so we should get along fine.'

This seemed highly unlikely to Jane who was in a state of shock, blown over by the pomposity and arrogance of her only relative. 'Yes, we can look round the estate.'

'And the house. I would like to start with the house.'

'Of course,' said Jane, standing up. 'We can start with the hallway.'

'Seen the hallway. Why not get that servant woman to show me round? Even better, I will stroll around by myself. You sit down and enjoy the view. After all, it is my house.' He laughed, thinking he had made a witty remark but to Jane it was anything but. She was appalled at his manner.

He left the room. Jane was dumbstruck.

When he returned, he expressed his admiration for the house. 'Jolly fine, will do nicely. Now the farm. Do you have a farm boss? Not another woman, is it?' He burst out laughing again. 'He can show me round. Drive round in my car.'

Jane went up to her room as Mrs Squires took Walter Dunhaughton down to the farm buildings, where she knew the farm foreman was waiting. When she returned, she sought out Jane and found her with her head in her hands at her dressing table. Jane's eyes were bloodshot and she looked as though she had been physically hit rather than verbally abused.

'Miss, are you all right? You don't look well. Maybe you should lie down,' she said.

'I am fine. Did you want me, Mrs Squires?'

Mrs Squires asked if Mr Dunhaughton was coming to live at Lainston House and would Jane be staying. Jane explained briefly what the position was. She could not say whether Mrs Squires would be needed.

'I am not sure I could work for him, miss. I am not sure at all.'

'That makes two of us, Mrs Squires.'

Chapter 29
A Tribe from the East

Walter Dunhaughton was gone for a couple of hours. When he returned, he bustled through the door as though he had lived there all his life. 'Very fine, very fine indeed. Pity some of the land has been sold. I understand your father was a drunk, had to sell the land to pay his debts. Pity, great pity.'

Jane looked aghast. 'He was your brother and he did leave you the estate in his will!'

'That he did. Didn't really know him. We went to separate schools. Only saw him in the holidays — as he was much older than me, we hardly spent much time together. I knew he would get everything when the parents snuffed it so I cleared off to India. Done all right for myself.'

Jane did her best to remain composed and spent another unpleasant thirty minutes with him before he announced that he had to be off, as he was meeting some chaps in London that evening. Before going, however, he said, 'May have been a bit hasty earlier. Clearly you need time to think about my proposal. I will be in London for three days and then will come back to Winchester. Finalise all the will business. I can call in and you can give me your answer. Once the boys are settled here, Gertrude and I will go back to India then we will come back for the summer holidays. Too hot in dammed India then.'

This obviously raised a great many more questions for Jane but there was no chance to ask them for no sooner had he spoken than he got into the car and bumped his way down the road.

When he had gone, Jane poured herself a gin and sat down, taking a big gulp. She rarely drank and never in the daytime, but some inner force propelled her to the decanter. 'Oh my God, what an unpleasant man,' she thought. 'What am I going to do? My only relative — how rude can you be?' Her thoughts swirled and crashed around and there was no possibility that she could come to any decision.

What she did think was how unlike the father she had known and loved Walter was. 'How could two people from the same family be so different? Father may have been difficult before I went away but I am sure he was ill. I cannot see that man ever being pleasant.' As she sat sipping rather too feverishly at her gin, a clear image of her father formed in her mind. It was an image of a caring sensitive man who loved his only child.

Over the next three days she tried to look at the problem logically. She set down on paper her alternatives and the attractions of each one. There were so many questions that she needed answers to. Could she keep her room? Would she be part of the family, able to use the house as an equal? Would she be at the family table for meals? Would she pay rent? Would she be paid for looking after the boys? What did that mean anyway? What did she know about bringing up boys? If her uncle went back to India for nine months and only came back for the summer, who would run the estate?

Fear of the unknown was her strongest emotion. She disliked Walter Dunhaughton but perhaps she could put up with him if he was not around for much of the year. She had not lived anywhere else and she loved Lainston House. What would happen to Woodly if she moved? Where would she go and what would she do? There was no way she could answer these questions, but the mere fact that she was turning them over confirmed the magnetic pull of the known and the security of the familiar. They were hard forces to break.

Walter arrived back at Lainston House unannounced. Jane had stayed at home, fearing that he might arrive and she would not be in. She could not rationalise why she was so worried about this; perhaps she feared he might simply lock her out.

When he arrived in the splendidly shining Rover, she was at the window and saw him walking up to the house. She answered the door herself.

'Jane, no servant today?' he asked, surprised.

'I was by the window and I saw you come up the path.' She knew immediately that she was on the back foot but she was not confident of the ground on which she stood.

They went into the drawing room and Jane asked him if he would like tea or coffee. 'Coffee for me,' he replied. 'Sick to death of tea, swimming in the stuff.'

Jane went to ask Mrs Squires to make some coffee and then returned to the drawing room.

'Such a nice room this,' Walter said when she came in. 'Light. It's good.'

'I think so too,' she said, not knowing how to start the conversation she desperately needed to have.

She need not have worried for straight away he said, 'Sorted all the will business. It's mine now.'

'That's good. It's best that it's resolved,' Jane said meekly.

'So have you thought about my plan? Rather like the thought that my niece will be looking after my children, better than a bunch of strangers — even though you are a stranger.' He gave a great belly laugh.

Jane did not laugh but took a deep breath and said, 'I need to understand my position. I have many questions. For example, can I still live in the house and will I be part of the family? Will I have to pay rent? If you are in India, will I be running the estate?'

'Good God, what a lot of questions!' He jumped up from the sofa. 'Course you can stay here, that's the whole point. You know the area, know the house, can keep things tickety-boo when we aren't here. No rent — but no pay. Family don't pay each other. What's wrong with that?'

'Nothing. I just wanted to make sure that I understood,' Jane replied.

'That's good then, all settled,' he said. It did not for one second cross Walter's mind that Jane might not be quite so settled. He walked round the room then looked out of the window towards the church. 'You a churchgoer?' he asked, turning towards her and looking at her intently.

'Yes, I am,' she replied.

'This church here, C of E, isn't it?'

'Yes, that's my church,' she replied nervously.

'That's good. Want the boys brought up proper Christians. Worried you might be Catholic or some other heathen rubbish.'

He turned again to the window. 'Well, now that's all settled I will be on my way. Got some things to do in Southampton then going back home. Back in three months with the boys.' With that, he turned and moved towards the door. He opened it and went into the hallway.

'Good to meet you, Jane. Glad we are getting on so well. Makes it all so much easier. I will let you know when we will be arriving.'

He got in his car and, after three attempts to start it, drove off without looking back. He had been in the house less than ten minutes.

Jane knew she had been manoeuvred, herded into a pen and the gate closed before she could escape. Did she want to escape? Perhaps it would all be fine and things would continue as they always had. She could go on with her life and would not have to face moving into a new, uncertain world. Many would envy her. What had she got to worry about?

She did worry, though. She had no real enthusiasm for looking after the children; she was not sure what she was supposed to do with them. Whilst she was most certainly seeking companionship, she had become increasingly comfortable with her independence and with being able to determine her own affairs; she could see that Walter's plan would threaten all of that. The fact that she was placed in this position rankled. She had lived here all her life; why should this unknown person barge in and take over? Why did men all ways get first call?

The days passed. High summer moved imperceptibly into the softening mellowness of September. The geraniums faded whilst the late-flowering dahlias and hydrangeas added drama, their bright colours contrasting with the subdued transformation of the copper beech. The harvest festival at church came and went, as did the last of the area's summer fetes. At these, and at every other opportunity, Jane made it clear that her uncle would be returning and that she would be looking after the children prior to them going to boarding school. She said she was looking forward to it, but she knew that she was not.

The transition from summer to autumn, the cooler evenings and shorter days, the early morning sun no longer waking her, could well have been a script for Jane's mood. The bright summer of enterprise and boldness, dealing with adults commercially and energetically, would be replaced by a dull grey landscape of operating as a tied servant.

Appearances were everything. She did not mention her dislike of her only relative, but she did tell a number of villagers her view that it was not right that she had not inherited the estate. If her mother had been alive it would not have happened. The keen observer would have noticed a hint of bitterness in Jane that began to fester and grow.

On the 1st of October 1904, a letter arrived from Simpson and Simpson saying that Mr Dunhaughton and family would arrive in England on the 10th. After spending a few days in London, they would travel to Hampshire and would be grateful if the house was ready for them. Mrs Squires made it clear to Jane that this meant much more work and she did not know how she would cope. A fourteen-year-old farmworker's daughter was the answer.

The family arrived on the 15th of October, on a beastly day with high winds and lashing rain. They came in two motor vehicles, both Vauxhalls, the first with the Dunhaughtons in it and the second carrying all their luggage.

The Dunhaughtons were not in the best frame of mind, being very cold and wet. Mrs Gertrude Dunhaughton was younger than her husband, considerably younger in fact; she looked no more than thirty though she was in fact thirty-two. She was used to a large number of servants looking after her every need. She had never undertaken any work of any description, was totally spoilt, almost completely uneducated and bigoted. Servants were there to be used. Even though she had no formal training as a teacher, she had managed to instil her personal characteristics into her children, Herbert and Charles. It was soon evident that they were obnoxious.

Gertrude was dressed immaculately. On entering the house, her first words to Jane were, 'You must be Jane. How do you do? Can you show me to my room so that I can change? Have someone bring up the large brown case.'

The large brown case lay in the hallway; the driver had carried it there from the motor vehicle with some difficulty. On being told by Jane that she would be happy to show her to her room but that she did not have anyone to carry the case upstairs, Gertrude gave her a withering look that would have demolished temples. It was hard to convey the utter contempt that went into the look: disdain mixed with incredulity that she could be treated so abominably.

'What do you mean, no one to carry it? You do have servants, don't you?'

'Just Mrs Squires,' replied Jane, 'and she can't manage that case on her own.'

'Well, you can help her, can't you?' It was not meant as a question.

Jane responded in a way that she was to reflect on and regret. Later she wished that she had taken a stand at the first opportunity but, driven by her innate politeness, she avoided direct confrontation and said tamely, 'I will see what we can do.'

It cut little ice with Gertrude. 'Good. Can't stand here on the stairs all day, can we?'

Chapter 30
A Short Journey but a Long Way Travelled

It took Jane just over a month to reach a final decision about her future at Lainston House, a month in which she moved from being a willing, if not enthusiastic, participant in the Dunhaughton scheme through a series of mood changes. These took her inexorably from concerned to worried, from depressed to angry, and finally to determined. She was determined to move on, make her own life and not be dependent on others.

The driving force behind these mood changes was Gertrude's attitude. She was incapable of thinking anything other than that Jane was a servant. Meals at the family table were uncomfortable; Jane felt as though she was intruding and unwelcome. Walter was too insensitive to notice anything other than what Gertrude told him directly, which was always about what she wanted, wanted to do, wanted doing. Jane was simply a tool to help achieve her needs. Never once did they have a conversation as equals in which

Jane's views were genuinely sought or they shared any emotional involvement.

Gertrude's discussions about the children consisted of instructions about what Jane should do with them. Given that Gertrude was lacking depth in any subject and could not focus on anything but trivia and herself for more than a fleeting moment, these instructions lacked any consistency, rationale or substance.

If Gertrude was the major source of Jane's growing unease, the children did not help. They had quickly learnt that being selfish and objectionable would get them what they wanted, and they were masters at practising these skills. Their true forte was lying; they had discovered that there was no benefit from telling the truth and no punishment for doing the opposite. They would say anything: Jane hit them; Jane took their things; Jane broke their toys and then blamed them. Nothing was sacrosanct.

It was just four weeks after the Dunhaughtons had moved in when Jane was aghast to look out of her bedroom window and see Charles and Herbert throwing stones at George, the church gardener. '*Shudra*, be gone, *Shudra* clear off!' they shouted, whilst tossing pebble after pebble over the garden hedge and across the lane into the church grounds.

Jane rushed out of her room and down the stairs out in to the garden. 'Children! Charles, Herbert, stop that at once!' she shouted as she ran towards them.

'Why? He is just a worthless *Shudras*,' said Herbert. Jane did not know this word but could clearly tell it was insulting.

'That is George. He is a good man and you should not throw stones at anyone.' Jane knocked the stones from Charles' hand.

'He is just a *Shudra*. I am going to tell mother about you,' said Charles as he turned and ran toward the house followed by Herbert.

'I am so sorry, George,' Jane shouted over the hedge. 'They are really impossible to deal with.'

'Need a good hiding, they do,' came the reply.

Later that morning, Jane was sat in the drawing room when Gertrude came in. 'Charles says you have hit him. Have I not told you before not to hit the children?'

'I have never hit the children — but they do need to learn not to throw stones at people,' Jane said quite forcibly.

'They would not throw stones at people,' Gertrude said immediately. There was no attempt to gather any more information. She turned, adding, 'You need to remember who you are talking to.'

It was only two days later, on opening the dining room door at eight a.m., Jane was surprised to see Gertrude. Gertrude had never been down so early before. 'Good morning, Gertrude,' Jane politely said. 'Good morning, Walter,' she added, noticing him by the window with his back to the room. He was almost hidden by the fall of the curtains.

There was a frosty atmosphere and only Walter replied. 'Yes. Morning. Not sure there is much good about it.'

'Oh, why is that?' asked Jane uncomfortably.

'Why don't you ask milady here?' Walter moved from the window to look at Gertrude. His lips turned down and he looked irritated.

'For goodness' sake, be quiet,' Gertrude said, incensed by this remark.

If Walter looked irritated, Gertrude looked about ready to explode. Venom oozed from every pore as she turned towards Jane. She hissed, 'Can you not have your food in your room or the kitchen? We don't want you in here.'

Jane shuddered to a stop. It was as though a great chasm had just opened up immediately in front of her and she dared not move. Her feet felt like huge blocks, pinning her to the spot. She stumbled to find the words to respond. 'This is the dining room.'

'Don't argue! Have you nothing to do?' Gertrude responded.

'If you could leave,' added Walter, now looking quite menacing. It was not a request.

Jane looked around the room. She could have cut the atmosphere into slices. It took only a moment for her to decide to leave the room but that moment made her shiver. Cold sweat swept through her like an avalanche gouging its way through a narrow crevasse.

'Oh, my goodness,' she thought as she went back up the stairs. 'It was sometimes difficult with father but not like this.' As she entered her room, she thought, 'This is no longer my home. I am not even a servant.' She slumped onto her bed, not angry but determined and resolute.

As was her way, she did not storm out in a great blaze of anger, or even politely try and reason, but rather she quietly made her own plans and then carefully executed them in a disciplined, organised way. She made lots of lists: the type of house she wanted; where it should be and how to move there; what she could legitimately take from her current home (which was surprisingly little); what she would need to buy, and what she would do with her time. This was by far the most difficult issue to resolve. All the other matters could be arranged; she could make decisions and act. But she was not prepared to sit at home and brood. She needed to be engaged in something worthwhile.

It did not take her long to find a sweet, four-bedroomed cottage with a lovely garden and paddock for rent only a mile from the Barings' estate. The landlord had met Jane at hunt meetings and was only too willing to lease it to her, expressing sympathy for her plight. Jane took a lease for a year with the clear understanding that if she wanted to extend the term that would be fine. The cottage was furnished; if not to her taste, it was more than adequate for the time being.

She arranged for a removal firm to call at Lainston House on the 18th of November at ten a.m. The evening before, she retired early to pack her clothes and personal possessions. It did not take her long; two hours of concentrated activity had all her belongings stored in three large cases.

As she turned out the light, she opened the curtains and looked out into the blackness of the night. It was an appropriate view and reflected her mood.

In the morning she had breakfast as normal on her own at eight a.m. She was always first up; Walter was normally down half an hour after her, but Gertrude rarely surfaced before ten. Jane had said nothing to anyone about her move, not even to Mrs Squires and certainly not to the Dunhaughtons.

After breakfast, she went upstairs to check on the children and ensure they were up and dressed. They never were, but today Jane made no effort to scurry them along. She simply said, 'Time you were both up and dressed. Your clothes are on the chair ready for you. Come downstairs for breakfast when you are washed and dressed.' She knew they would take no notice of her unless she went back and nagged them. She had no intention of doing so.

By eight thirty she was getting nervous, anxiously looking out of the dining-room window.

Walter came in breezily. 'Are the children up?' were his first words. 'Don't want them thinking they can lie in bed all day.'

'Good morning, Walter,' said Jane, ignoring his question.

'Morning. Are they up?'

'I have asked them to get washed and dressed and come down for breakfast,' said Jane.

'You need to be firmer with them. They need some discipline.'

'Indeed, they do.' Jane looked at Walter in disbelief. 'I will go and check on them.'

She left the room, not to check on the children but to escape Walter's company. In her room she closed the door and spent the next hour nervously pacing, looking constantly out of the window, checking if the removal carriage had arrived. She was trembling as she waited. How would the Dunhaughtons react? Should she have told them that she was leaving?

It was nine forty-five when the removal cart arrived. It was an open carriage pulled by a large grey Clydesdale horse, a wonderful animal that Jane was pleased to see looked in pristine condition. Its coat shone and its hoofs were bright.

She dashed out of her room, ran down the stairs, passed Walter in the hallway and opened the front door.

She ran down the path and introduced herself to the driver. 'There are three cases; they are upstairs in my room. Can you help me bring them down?' she asked, clearly agitated.

'Course, ma'am. Lead the way,' replied the stocky driver, a man in his thirties. Jane led him into the hallway and was relieved that Walter was no longer there.

Jane took the smallest case and went downstairs with the removal man. She had never been so nervous in her life, not even when she was on the train in South Africa and being shot at. That had seemed like an adventure but this was a nightmare. Her heart was pumping like a piston as she went back upstairs with the driver for the final case.

As they came down again, Walter confronted them at the bottom of the stairs. 'What's this? What is the cart for?' he asked with his hands on his hips, looking directly at Jane.

'I have decided to leave,' said Jane. 'I am taking my things.'

'What, just like that? I thought everything was working out dandy.'

'I think it is for the best,' said Jane, moving past him as she reached the bottom step. 'Please take the case to the cart,' she said to the driver.

'You can't just leave! You have the children to look after.' Walter's face was growing red.

'No, Mr Dunhaughton. They are your children, not mine.'

Walter exploded. 'What? How dare you? You are employed to look after them and you need to give notice.'

Jane looked at him incredulously. 'Employed? I am not employed by you, or anyone else. I am sure Gertrude will manage and you will soon find someone else.'

'You ungrateful bastard! After all we have done for you!' He moved closer towards her and Jane felt afraid. She had never been sworn at before, nor felt threatened like this. She mumbled, 'It's for the best,' as she turned away and walked towards the door.

'Oh no you don't,' Walter said, as he grabbed Jane's arm and pulled her back. 'You are not just going, taking my things.'

Jane struggled to get free of his grip. 'Let go of me, please! Let go!' She was shouting now, her words coming out in a harsh shrill voice, which made Walter release her.

She rushed out of the door, followed by Walter.

'Everything all right, love?' exclaimed the alarmed removal man.

'No, it's not all right!' shouted Walter. 'Those cases have my things in them. Take them down now.'

'They are not your things, just my clothes. I have taken nothing of yours. Please go, driver. Please,' she said imploringly. It was the last 'please' and her frightened look that swayed the driver to flick the reins. The huge horse inched forward.

Walter reached out and took hold of the horse's mane. 'Take those cases down or you go nowhere.'

The driver jumped off the cart remarkably quickly for such a big man. He squared up to Walter. 'You take your hands off my horse or I will break your arm.' There was no doubt that was exactly what would have happened if Walter Dunhaughton had not released his grip of the horse's mane.

'I don't know anything about what's going on between you two, but you touch my horse again and I will knock your head off.' The driver moved within an inch of Walter and now it was Walter who was afraid. He backed away.

The driver stood like a huge, square rock, eyes fixed on this man who had dared to pull the hair of his beloved horse, his soulmate and his livelihood.

It was Jane's voice that broke the intensity of his stare. 'Please, driver, let's go.'

The rights and wrongs of the argument between Jane and Walter Dunhaughton were irrelevant; the driver was firmly on Jane's side. Even if she had committed some heinous crime, nothing would have changed that. Walter could not have made a more serious mistake than pulling Charlie Boy's mane. The driver had looked after that horse every day since the foal was born in his father's stable some fifteen years earlier.

They moved off, Walter glowering and fuming and shouting pathetically, 'I will call the police.'

'You all right, miss?' the driver asked, looking back as they went down the lane.

'Yes, I am fine. Glad to be away.'

'He shouldn't have touched Charlie Boy. Nobody touches Charlie Boy.'

In the next half hour, as they made their way slowly to Jane's new home, it was not clear who was the more upset, Jane or the driver. It took most of the journey for Jane to stop shivering.

As they pulled into the cottage she was renting, the driver said, 'I don't think he hurt him. He's a tough lad is Charlie Boy.'

Chapter 31
A Knock on the Door

It was February 1905 and Jane was both depressed and annoyed. She was annoyed with herself. She knew that the reason for her depression was her failure to confront the biggest issue facing her — or at least the one that daily tormented her. When she had left Lainston House, a day she did not want to remember if she could help it, she had not secured Woodly's future.

Despite all her meticulous plans, her endless notes and lists, she had not envisaged that the day would go so badly and that she would be afraid to go back and collect Woodly and bring him to her new home. There was a paddock near the cottage and, even though there was no stable, she knew she could stable him in the winter with any number of hunt members, not least the Barings.

As the days and weeks passed, she grew more frustrated at her indecisiveness, her prevarication and cowardice. It gnawed away at her and her demeanour started to change; she saw only problems, she smiled less and, even in the safe environment of church, she was less chirpy. She missed the physical adrenalin of the hunt, the excitement of the chase, the feeling of exhilaration that she obtained nowhere else.

The underlying problem lay in her own character. She sought to avoid confrontation above all else. How could she engage in an act that would almost certainly result in confrontation, perhaps even violent confrontation?

Occasionally she woke with a vivid memory of Walter Dunhaughton holding her arm tightly with a look of real menace. If she went back to Lainston House and asked to collect Woodly, what response would she get? She imagined the encounter, tried to map out the words that would be used; it certainly would not be a conversation. She tried to imagine herself remaining quiet but determined, calm but resolute, but underneath she knew how scared she had been when she left. No amount of talking to herself in the mirror could break the impasse.

The worst aspect for Jane, was how clearly she understood the cause of her depression and changing outlook. She knew what the cure was but she could not swallow the medicine. Her depression was her own fault.

It took a glorious winter's morning and a chance meeting with Lilly's brother, Harry, in Winchester High Street to bring things to a head.

'Hello, Jane, how are you?' Harry asked in a genuine, warm manner. 'We have not seen you recently. Is everything all right? I hope we have not upset you.'

'No, no, not at all,' Jane replied.

'Will we see you tomorrow? The hunt will be leaving from our house. You have to come,' Harry asked, looking for a positive response.

'Well, maybe. I have some things to do. It might be difficult,' Jane said evasively.

Harry could sense that she was holding something back and looked at her intently. 'Is everything all right?' he asked. 'Let's have a coffee and you can tell me what could possibly stop you and Woodly coming out tomorrow.'

Once inside the small coffee shop, Jane suddenly opened up and explained that Woodley remained at Lainston House and she lacked the courage to go and ask for him.

'Oh, that's nonsense! I will go round this afternoon, get Woodly and bring him to you. Lime Cottage is where you are, is it not?'

To say that he was a man of his word was an understatement for that is exactly what he did. Having been told by Mrs Squires that the Dunhaughtons were in London, he went to the stables, saddled up Woodly whom he knew so well after looking after him whilst Jane was in South Africa, and rode him back home where he placed him in the stables. That evening, he called round to Jane's cottage in his motor car and took Jane to see her horse.

The effect was immediate. The burning heat of unadulterated joy dispelled the dank mistiness that had shrouded Jane since she had moved out of Lainston House. Woodly may have been happy to see Jane, but Jane was unable to cope. She broke down in tears, ashamed of her own timidity. She was embarrassed at how easy it had been to solve her problem.

The next day she threw herself at the highest fences, jumped the widest ditches and galloped as if chasing hares. That night, she slept as she had not for months.

She was brought back to earth three weeks later when PC Alan Ormound walked up the garden path of Lime Cottage and knocked on the door. It was just after nine; Jane had finished breakfast and was preparing to go riding with a few members of the Sparsholt hunt.

She was surprised to see a police officer at her door and expressed an audible, 'Oh!'

PC Ormound asked if she was Miss Jane Dunhaughton and, on confirmation of this, asked if he could come inside.

Jane let him in through a small vestibule into the hall and then into the front parlour. It was richly furnished with a dark wood sideboard, a table and six formal dining-room chairs. There was a number of bookcases filled with trivia, photographs, and pictures. The walls had poor-quality prints of famous paintings and the curtains were thick and heavy. The room was as Jane had found it; although functional for dining, it did not make the most of its position and was dark most of the time. It needed redecorating but Jane had not given any thought to this; she had decided that she would make no changes for six months until she knew what her longer-term plans were.

She invited PC Ormound to sit down but he declined, saying he would stand. 'Can I ask what your visit is about?' Jane asked, perplexed as to why the police were visiting her.

'Can I ask if you lived at Lainston House?' PC Ormound asked.

'Yes, I was brought up there. Why do you ask?'

'When did you leave?' he followed up.

Jane was not clear where this was leading. She answered his questions openly but with a growing unease. He asked her if the house was hers and she told him about the will and her uncle moving in, much to her surprise.

'Did you take anything with you when you left?' the policeman asked.

'Just my clothes in three cases.'

'Was that all?'

'Yes. Why are you asking me these questions?'

He ignored her question and asked again if there was anything else, she had taken.

'No, just my clothes.'

PC Ormound finally came to the reason for his visit. 'So, you did not take a horse when you left?'

Jane still had no comprehension where this was going and told the officer exactly what had happened. 'Harry Baring collected my horse from Lainston House.'

'Harry Baring, Lord Baring's son?' asked the officer.

'Yes, we've been friends for many years.'

The officer asked a number of other questions and then said, 'You say the horse is yours. Have you proof of that?'

'I have ridden Woodly since I was a young girl. Everyone in the area knows that Woodly is my horse.'

'Mr Dunhaughton says the horse belongs to the estate and that you have stolen him. He says he wants the horse back and that you should be charged with theft.'

Jane gasped and put her hand on the table to steady herself. 'Oh no, that's not right. Woodly is mine, everyone knows that. Ask Lord Baring or Harry or anyone.' She looked pleadingly at the constable. 'I would not steal from anyone.' She felt her chest tightening and she was short of breath. Surely this could not be happening?

Before she had collected her thoughts, PC Ormound was letting himself out. 'I'm sure there has been a misunderstanding but I have to report back to the chief constable and let him know what has happened.' His last words were, 'Don't worry, miss, I am sure it will all be sorted out.'

Jane went round immediately to the Barings. It was a half an hour walk but she moved briskly, her mind buzzing, her thoughts flitting between worry over the suggestion that she was a thief and outrage that her uncle was calling her a thief. Behind it all, though, was a growing unease that she could not prove that Woodly was hers.

When she arrived at the Barings, she asked if Lilly was in but on being told she was out she asked if Harry was at home. The servants could see how flustered she was and shaking. As soon as Harry came into the hall she started to blurt out what had happened.

'The police have been round to see me. He says I have stolen Woodly. I have not you know. I have not, he is mine.'

'Jane, let's slow down. You need to tell me what exactly has happened. Let's go and sit down. A good cup of tea will do you good'. They went through into the dining room and Harry rang for a servant and asked for tea. He refused to let Jane mumble incoherently by asking her mundane questions about Lime cottage. It was a good ten minutes before he said:

'Now then Jane tell me exactly what has happened.'

'Mr Dunhaughton has been to the police and alleged that I have taken Woodly without permission. In effect he is saying I have stolen Woodly. Everyone knows that Woodly is my horse. I would not steal anything.'

'Of course he is yours and we all know you would not steal. All this will soon be cleared up. I will go myself and see the chief constable. I will tell him I took the horse.'

Jane was reassured and began to regain her composure but it still took a couple of weeks for her to completely return to normal. The shame of being called a thief, of having a police officer call on her, of implicating Harry in these allegations... She had just about recovered when PC Ormound arrived on Tuesday the 4th of April at nine a.m. Again, he knocked on the door and was shown in by a wary and concerned Jane.

He did not waffle or prevaricate but simply said, 'Miss Dunhaughton, I have to advise you that you are to be charged with the theft of a horse which goes by the name Woodly. You are to appear before the magistrates' court on Wednesday 12th of June to answer the charge. The papers are here and I would ask that you sign to acknowledge that you have received them.'

The impact on Jane was shattering. She found it hard to sign her name because her hands were shaking so much. She felt ashamed, embarrassed that she was being tried for theft. She found it hard to assimilate and collect her thoughts as to what she should do.

She asked no questions of the police officer, she just wanted him to go. Had he been seen coming to her house? What if everyone knew?

He asked her a number of questions. Did she know where the court was? Was she able to get there? Did she have a solicitor to assist her? Did she understand the process? Jane nodded to all the questions, having no real understanding of what she had been asked, her mind nothing more than a vacant space.

During the following week Jane barely ventured out; she was afraid of being gossiped about. She worried that the court would have a list of people on trial. Who would see it? She told no one of the charge, not even Harry Baring, which would have unquestionably helped. She did not tell Lilly or anyone in the village. She hurried to the post office for a few basic provisions but otherwise stayed behind closed doors, festering and brooding, worrying and fretting.

She turned over the background to the case. How long had she owned Woodly? Everyone knew he was her horse so how could she be accused of theft? Why was Walter Dunhaughton doing this? Why could he not have simply discussed it with her? What had she done wrong? She approached her problem from the perspective of the victim, failing to tackle it as the accused who had to marshal her defence. She did not try and answer her own question about why Walter Dunhaughton had brought the charge against her.

At the court hearing Jane sat in the waiting room, head bowed, afraid to look up. A clerk had taken her name and ticked it off against a list pinned to a square board that he carried round. She was told her case would be heard in about an hour.

The room was full of different characters: rough-looking men the like of whom Jane had never met before; loose women, whom she certainly had not met; clerks and solicitors; smart men in suits looking pompous and superior. It was a melting pot of society but Jane did not take in any of it and barely lifted her eyes. The worst thing would have been to see Walter Dunhaughton; she assumed he would be there.

The clerk told her that the case would be heard shortly and that she should enter the courtroom. She was led to the dock and confirmed her name and address.

Sat in the dock she could not bear to look at Walter Dunhaughton as he gave his evidence.

'Yes I inherited Lainston House and the farm and estate, all the property of the estate belongs to me. It was all part of the will. The horse, I think Miss Dunhaughton called it Woodly, was part of my inheritance. I was shocked to discover the horse had been taken without any reference to me. As far as I am concerned, it has been stolen.'

Jane was to go into the witness box.

'I promise to tell the truth the whole truth and nothing but the truth,' she said, as she read from the card.

'Do speak up Miss Dunhaughton, we can hardly hear you,' the clerk demanded in an offhand pompous manner.

'Miss Dunhaughton, is it correct that you admitted to PC Ormound that you had taken the horse?'

'Yes,' Jane replied, meekly.

'Is it also correct, that your solicitor advised you personally, that Walter Dunhaughton had inherited the estate from your father?'

'Yes,' Jane replied. This time even more softly with her eyes lowered.

'Do you agree with Mr Dunhaughton that no reference had been made to him about taking the horse?'

'Yes,' she said, nodding her head, shame written all over her face.

'Do speak up Miss Dunhaughton,' the clerk instructed again as she tried to answer his last question. 'Is there anything you would like to add?'

'I have brought up Woodly since he was born and ridden him all his life,' she said, barely audible. 'I have looked after him. Everyone knows that he is my horse. I did not steal him.'

'It is clear that the horse has been taken without permission,' the Justice of the Peace said whilst summing up. 'Whilst I have every sympathy with you, Miss Dunhaughton, the horse was part of the property of the estate and as such, Miss Dunhaughton, you are guilty of the charge and the horse must be returned. As for the sentence, it is clear that you have acted naively but I believe without malice. You mistakenly believed the horse to be yours. As such, I sentence you to a fine of five pounds and three months in custody, suspended for a year.'

Jane had to be helped out of the dock and guided out of the courtroom. It was all a blur; the place was so busy and there were so many people. She had to sign papers and pay the fine. It was fortunate that she had her cheque book, otherwise she would have had to go to the cells whilst payment was arranged. She had her photograph taken in a small room by the clerk and was made to feel inconsequential, a nobody, nothing but a common criminal.

It was late that afternoon, when she was back at home trying to recover from her ordeal, that the very thing she did not want was forced upon her. There was a loud rap on the door and the unmistakable voice of Walter Dunhaughton called out, 'Jane, it's Walter Dunhaughton. I have come to collect my horse.'

She sat paralysed, not wanting to open the door. She was transfixed, afraid of him and afraid of having to let Woodly go. Oh, why did she not have anyone to help her? A second loud rap pierced her ears. She looked around, wondering if she could leave and avoid the confrontation.

'Oh, come on, woman. We have things to discuss.'

She braced herself and opened the door. Walter stood at the entrance, blocking her view out down the path.

'Ah, good,' he said. 'I will come straight to the point. The court has agreed with me that the horse is mine but I'm not an unreasonable man. I am willing to sell him to you. That way it's all proper and sorted. If you want to buy him then he is yours, otherwise I will collect him now. The farmhand will take him.'

He looked over his shoulder, indicating that the farmhand was in the car, but Jane could not see past Walter.

Jane was indecisive. She wanted Woodly, she could not bear to part with him, but this was unexpected. She was unprepared. She had still not accepted that he was not hers.

'Oh, come on now. You lost and he is mine. Do you want him or not?' Walter waited a couple of seconds during which Jane stared past his shoulder like a startled rabbit, unsure what to do.

It was Walter summoning the farmhand to come up the drive that broke the impasse and prompted her to blurt out, 'All right. How much are you seeking?'

'Fifty pounds.'

'Fifty pounds!' Jane exclaimed, alarmed at this huge amount.

'If you don't want the horse, I can sell it elsewhere.'

Jane looked aghast at this reprehensible man. He no more cared for the horse than any of the farmyard animals; he was simply using her, enjoying his command of her, his victory in the court. It struck Jane forcibly what this was about: he could not stand the fact that she had walked out. He wanted to be the decision-taker and to have the power. Making her pay £50 for the horse was simply about re-establishing his position of authority.

'All right, £50. But I need a receipt and a letter from you saying that you have agreed to the sale.'

'All here,' he said, taking the wind from Jane's sails. For a fleeting second, she had thought she was beginning to regain some pride and self-determination but the fact that he had these documents already prepared knocked her back again. This was a plan, a carefully worked out plan to humiliate her.

When he left, he did so with a cheery smile and positively skipped down the path.

Jane did not skip anywhere after she read the *Winchester and Salisbury Journal,* which contained a full report of her trial with a headline: *Well-known local hunt rider convicted of theft.*

No amount of reassurance from the many hunt riders who contacted her, or from Harry Baring or Lilly, could dissipate the cloud of misery that hung over Jane, for weeks.

It was in these weeks that Jane committed herself to supporting the campaign for women's suffrage as best she could.

Chapter 32
When Will the Violets Bloom?

The embarrassment of the court case did not subside easily or quickly. It was not until the middle of the year that Jane began to feel like herself again, that her self-confidence started to return and she stopped thinking that everybody saw her as a thief. No one said anything to her, other than to offer words of sympathy and tell her that she must put the whole thing behind her.

Her inability to shake off the embarrassment was not helped by her lack of purpose. She had lost the oxygen that fuelled her daily life: the running of the estate. She had not found anything to compensate and nothing remotely to measure up to the sense of achievement that had come from her endeavours in South Africa.

The days passed indistinguishably. A ride with the hunt here, pottering in the garden there; tea with the vicar one day, a garden fete the next; the occasional ball where she was always embarrassed by her lack of a partner and where all the other women of her age had children and husbands and households to run. She was existing comfortably but without purpose.

Lime Cottage was no Lainston House but it was pleasant nevertheless, especially on a glorious midsummer morning. Jane had breakfasted in the garden, sitting with her back to the windows of the house and the wisteria-covered walls. Her coffee pot, cup and plate were in front of her on a small wooden table around which were four chairs. Her attention had been caught by the magnolias, which had just come into bloom; together with the daises and lupins, they formed a vivacious bed of colour.

Beyond lay the paddock in which Woodly contentedly grazed. Jane sat in a contemplative mood, thinking of the gardens at Lainston House and Kia Lami. All wonderful in their own way, she thought. She wondered what Caroline was doing at that moment. And Emily, for that matter. At least they would be doing something.

She had woken after a broken night's sleep and immediately started to wonder what she would do that day. 'The days are really long,' she thought. 'I was less lonely in South Africa. I never wondered what to do with my time over there.' She smiled ruefully as she thought of the new experiences, cruel injustices, happy and miserable times, new friends, new sights.

She was not reflecting idly: she was weighing up whether to stay in Hampshire or accept Emily's invitation to go back to South Africa.

'The country is no longer at war. With Emily and the others, I would not be on my own like I am here. I am sure there would be worthwhile things to do helping get the Boer women and children back on their feet.' Her thought process had switched; now she was focussed on finding positive reasons to go.

She did not realise that the positive reasons she articulated to herself were the mirror image of why she was so unsettled. Something to do, friendship, new sights, the possibility of meeting someone special — these thoughts floated through her mind like the embers of a fire shooting out small flickering but enticing glimmers of light. A glimmering light such as Arthur Silverton. Her mind was made up; she would go back.

She enjoyed the days sailing south on the SS *Kenilworth Castle*. She recalled the frustration Emily and she had felt when they first went to South Africa in 1901. It was different this time; she was on her own and could melt away, absorbed in her own thoughts, whenever she wanted. She enjoyed the freedom of not having to think about anything; she enjoyed meals with the other travellers, talking and listening, occasionally laughing. She was not on a mission; she had accepted that it was the need for change that was the reason for the journey. This time she had not embarked on a crusade to save the moral conscience of a nation. If there was a crusade, it was to bring some purpose into her drab, lonely life.

Emily was waiting for her at the docks in Durban. They greeted each other warmly and that night they talked for hours about what had happened in their lives and those of the people they knew.

Emily was saddened to hear first-hand about the loss of Lainston House and Jane having to buy back Woodly. She was appalled that Jane had not fought the case with more resolve — marshalled her friends to support her, employed a lawyer to argue her case. Her outrage began to irritate Jane; nevertheless, there was genuine affection between them that overrode Jane's sensitivity on being so forcibly reminded of her own shortcomings.

Emily was not the person she had been in one way: her health. Her breathing was strained and she struggled to get her breath, especially when eating. She looked older and had lost a little of the vitality that had initially made such an impression on Jane.

Her health had not prevented her from throwing herself into her causes, however, and she was providing schools for children and teaching the women how to spin cloth on machines. Emily had utilised her many friends and contacts in South Africa to help her with premises. Her work was being funded and endorsed by Boer leaders including Martinus Steyn, former president of the Orange Free State, and his wife.

Jane and Emily dined with them on numerous occasions. It struck Jane how ridiculous it was to have embarked on a war with these people who were as approachable and welcoming as any of her friends back home. The fact that the Orange Free State was now part of South Africa had not prevented the Boers from getting what they wanted; they made up the majority of the population and they soon achieved almost all of the objectives they'd had in the war through the ballot box. This topic came up frequently; there was a consensus that politicians rarely had the vision to see beyond the immediate and realise that much of what they proposed, whilst well meaning, would have the opposite effect of what they had planned.

Jane helped as best she could. She undertook clerical work, she taught English in the schools and loved reading poetry to the children. Deep down, though, her heart was not in it. The work lacked the immediacy of what she had done in the concentration camps. She knew that she was only marking time and she had no intention of staying permanently.

It was with mixed emotions that she decided to return home. She had been back in South Africa nearly a year and, although physically involved, she felt detached mentally and emotionally. Her thoughts often returned to the train journey when she met Peter Handcock and the feelings of vitality and exuberance that she had experienced, which were lacking now.

When she told Emily that she had decided to return to England, her friend was not surprised. She felt that Jane was searching for something; what she was doing now in South Africa was unlikely to provide the answer.

'Yes, you are right,' said Jane. 'Things don't seem to be going my way. My mother dies, my father dies and leaves the only place I have known to a stranger. The only man I have genuinely felt something for is dead. I don't have a home to go to and no one to go home to. I am a lost cause.' She smiled, but both she and Emily knew that underneath the self-mockery and stiff upper lip there was disillusion. Aspiration and reality were increasingly separate.

'Where will you go back to?' asked Emily.

'I have written to Mr Thompson, the owner of Lime Cottage, saying I will be back by July. He promised that he would only let the house for a few months whilst I was away and that he was happy for me to go back.'

'Is that what you want?'

'I don't know. I really don't know. The cottage is fine, with a nice garden and paddock, but the days are all the same. I don't have anything to do. When Father died and I had the estate to run at least I had a purpose. I enjoyed going to the markets, dealing with suppliers and meeting people. It makes me sad that it has all been taken away from me. Did you feel angry or sad when you lost all that money in America?'

'Angry,' said Emily. 'But then I realised that staying angry hurts yourself more than anyone else and you have to move on. It's harder for women to do something positive; we are supposed to have children and be good wives whilst the men sort things out.'

'Or mess them up, more like,' said Jane. 'Looking back now, what was the war over here for? Just men's egos, them wanting to feel power. All that suffering — for what? If there were women in Parliament there would be fewer wars.'

'On that we are agreed. When you go back, you could get involved with the campaign for women's votes,' said Emily.

'I will.'

'You should call on my brother, Leonard. He can introduce you to the suffrage movement and he might be able to help you find a permanent position. You are going to need an income, even it is only a modest sum. Believe me, I know how soon savings disappear if they are not topped up. That's why I started with the Conciliation Committee. They paid my rent in London.'

'I am all right for money at the moment but I take your point. In five years' time, my finances won't look quite so healthy.'

Jane left Durban on the 4th of May 1906 and arrived back in Southampton on the 19th. She booked herself into the

New Palace Hotel, which had only just opened in Shirrell Heath. Her taxi was a motor vehicle, the first taxi that she had been in that was not pulled by a horse, and she was fascinated by the experience.

The hotel was simply wonderful, its luxury and opulence catering for the well-heeled residents of the area. There was obviously a great deal of colonial money on show and some of the rooms specifically referenced countries of the Empire.

Jane felt more purposeful than she had in South Africa. She had a plan: she was going to try and get fully involved in the suffrage movement. She believed in that. If she could get a position, so much the better.

She loved the hotel and its luxury so much that she stayed a whole week, wallowing in the deep baths and walking in the huge gardens. It was, though, rather a shock when she came to check out and had a bill of £15 18s 6d.

Jane went back to Southampton and caught the train to Waterloo. She took a horse-drawn cab to the newly opened Bedford Hotel on Southampton Row. The hotel manager at the New Palace had recommended it; whilst it was not as luxurious as the New Palace, it was more than acceptable.

Jane asked for a small single room. She was becoming conscious of living within her means; although her bank account was very healthy at nearly £2,000, she had the rest of her life to live.

Chapter 33
Planting New Seeds

Jane spent a couple of days exploring London, including a visit to the National Gallery. She spent more than four hours mesmerised by the brilliance of the art, the ever-changing styles, the technical sophistication and, at times, the compelling simplicity of some of the works.

She stood transfixed by the Vermeer painting: *A Young Woman Standing at a Virginal* wondering who this woman was, what her life was like, what became of her. She could recognise the brilliance of the art in front of her but was unsure what made it so. It clearly was more than just the technical ability of the artist.

As she wandered away, lost in her own thoughts, she stood in front of Turner's: *Fighting Temeraire* and was brought close to tears. The sheer romanticism, the setting of the sun and the sense of loss as the old was replaced by the new seeped into her, as though the brilliance of the sun's rays escaped from the painting and were absorbed into her inner self. She knew instinctively that the painting was about loss and coping in an ever-changing world. It described her world and it had been painted for her. The painting made her sad and she left the gallery subdued, if not despondent. She had answered her own question, though: great art spoke to you personally.

She had arranged to meet Leonard Hobhouse that evening for dinner at her hotel and, as she dressed, she wondered what he was like. Emily had described him as 'fearfully clever but totally impractical'. She said he was a sensitive and caring person but absent minded.

Jane went downstairs and advised the reception clerk that she would be in the lounge. She waited and waited some more, but after thirty minutes she shrugged her shoulders forlornly and made her way into the dining room.

She had already started her consommé when a balding, grey-suited man, aged about forty-five, was ushered in by the maître d'.

'Miss Dunhaughton, I am so sorry. I am inexcusably late.'

Jane brushed off the apology, saying that it was no problem and that it was very kind of him to meet with her.

'Nonsense, nonsense. Emily has told me so much about you. You have had such adventures, some most shocking. I have just given a lecture at University College and have to admit I quite forgot that I was meeting with you tonight.'

They got on well, even though at times Jane was intimidated by his intelligence and knowledge. She discovered that he was to take up a post in January as Professor of Sociology at University College London and was greatly looking forward to it. She did not have the courage to say that she did not know what sociology was.

His knowledge of the South African war, his views as to the real reasons for the conflict and the real winners, were fascinating. He thought that Milner's imperialist strategy to link the whole of South Africa into the Empire was doomed to fail, and that Kitchener's strategy of concentration camps was a legacy the world would not forget. Then he realised that he was hogging the conversation and invited Jane to set out what he could do for her.

'I am interested in the suffrage movement and would like to get involved in some way,' she said. 'I was interested before I met Emily but recent events have firmed up my views.'

She explained to him about the death of her father, the will and her uncle taking over the estate, and expressed her view that it was not right that it was assumed that property belonged to men. She said that it was because of this assumption that women did not have the vote and that should change.

'Quite right, quite right,' he said. 'Men don't live in a vacuum. They can only survive because of the labours of women — labours in more way than one.' He chuckled. 'Men acquire property not only through their own labour but also by the labours of women. A just, liberal society must see that property is distributed accordingly. It will not be until women have the vote.'

He explained that this was one of the central tenets of his view of liberalism: that individuals acquire property not only by individual effort but also by social cohesion. Jane was fascinated.

As they parted, Leonard promised to make introductions to leading members of the suffrage movement, many of whom shared his political views. He had also taken on board Jane's desire to be actively involved and to have a sense of purpose. He did not mention it, but Emily had said in her letters to him that Jane needed a supplementary income; if any positions came up, he would bear her in mind.

Jane, though, now felt she had a mission and she did not simply wait for introductions to come via Leonard Hobhouse. She had been convinced by his arguments that her view was right and was now supported by clever men; that gave her views the endorsement of being part of a political and economic theory. She could not follow all the arguments, but she simplified the abstract philosophical points back to common sense and expressed them in common language.

On a number of occasions, she said to Leonard, 'So what you are saying is…' or 'So that means…' and proceeded to give a logical and simple everyday example to illustrate the abstract points Leonard was making. He was impressed by the practicality of her approach. That practicality took Jane down the path of writing a list of the things she needed to do if she were to get involved in the suffrage movement. She felt that, if she were to be serious, she would need to be in London.

She sought accommodation and answered advertisements in *The Times* and the *Evening Standard* for apartments to rent, and quickly arranged to move into a fine, two-bedroomed flat in Carlisle Place, Westminster. She extended her stay at the Bedford Hotel whilst she waited for the paperwork to be completed. She had to give references and gave Leonard Hobhouse and Lord Baring, which seemed more than satisfactory.

She spent an afternoon in the London Library, reading as much as she could on women's suffrage and taking down the details of the offices of the various movements that were behind the votes for women campaign. She regularly came across the name Millicent Fawcett, and could not help but wonder what Millicent had written in her report on the conditions in the concentration camps. Emily had been dismissive of the report, saying it was merely a gesture to placate or silence critics, but Jane felt she would like to see what Millicent had actually written.

She also came across the Women's Social and Political Union and read of the arrest of Christabel Pankhurst and Annie Kenny after they had interrupted a Liberal Party meeting and demanded that the party supported votes for women. She followed up the story and saw just how quickly the WSPU membership had grown following the arrest and imprisonment of the two women. Jane could see how the publicity would work in the favour of the movement. She decided that she would offer her services.

The WSPU head office was in Clement's Inn, in the home of Emmeline Pethick-Lawrence. Jane went round on the 7th of June and introduced herself. Emmeline was forty years old, with a pleasant, welcoming appearance. She reminded Jane of Emily with her wavy, swept-back hair and clear complexion.

She made Jane feel very welcome. Emmeline said it was a coincidence that she had called, for just that day she had received a letter from Leonard Hobhouse in which he had sought to arrange an introduction for Jane. This led to a long conversation as to how she knew Leonard, then on to Emily and South Africa and her experience in losing Lainston House. Once Jane had explained how she had done office work for the Conciliation Committee, it was inevitable that an offer of similar work for the WSPU would be made and that Jane would accept.

Things moved quickly; within a week Jane had moved into Carlisle Place. The flat was fully furnished but Jane enjoyed herself buying bedding, towels, vases and other small items to personalise it. She was delighted that she could walk easily from her flat to Clements Inn and, on the 15th of June, she started helping out.

There was so much correspondence and new members were joining every day, so Jane's organising abilities and list-making skills were soon in high demand. She felt reinvigorated and also a sense of déjà vu; she remembered staying with the Courtneys in Cheyne Walk and working for the Conciliation Committee. It seemed such a long time ago but was in fact just five years.

The next few months passed quickly and Jane's commitment and enthusiasm was noticed by all. 'Jane, you positively skipped up those stairs,' said Emmeline, on a rainy day in September. 'How can you be so cheerful on such a dreadful day?'

'Oh, I hardly noticed the rain,' replied Jane. 'I have so much to do and my mind was elsewhere. We have to get those lists to the printers today.'

'Yes, we do, but I never thought we would manage it in time. How have you completed them all?'

'I stayed late last night. I was enjoying the work. Sometimes it just seems to flow. It helps when you believe what you are doing is having a real effect, and I see the circulation going up every week.'

She had always had an underlying interest in the votes for women campaign but her own circumstances now made the cause more personal. She was not a zealot or fanatic but had true conviction, which fuelled a passion that she had not had before. When she had gone to South Africa, she was searching for something undefined. Whilst she was appalled at the treatment suffered by the women and children in the camps and wanted to help, she had experienced these things more by accident than design. Her involvement in the suffrage movement was a conscious decision arising from her own beliefs.

She was excited that she met frequently with the leaders of the WSPU. The Pankhurst family and Annie Kenny spent many hours in the offices, and Jane was impressed by their meticulous planning, the zeal that they brought to the movement and the sheer hard work they put in. She was slightly uneasy with their commitment to acts of militancy and the unwavering belief that rhetoric and debate would not bring results, but she was willing to bypass her reservations, not least because she had a role that was valued. The days passed in a blur.

October 3rd 1906 saw the reopening of Parliament. Jane, together with a large group of women, went to petition the new government. Jane and Mrs Pethick-Lawrence had done much to publicise the gathering, arranging the printing of pamphlets, sandwich boards and adverts to attract as large a group of supporters as possible.

Many hundreds turned up: women of all ages and all classes; wealthy socialites; landowners; millworkers, and Cockney fishwives. They were all united by the suffrage cause. The aim was to lobby the government by speaking directly with ministers inside Parliament, but they were barred at the gates and told bluntly that only a small number would be allowed in. Common working women would certainly not be admitted.

Well-dressed, well-spoken Jane and Emmeline Pethick-Lawrence were perceived as no threat by the police and were admitted as part of a delegation of just twenty, which also included Mrs Pankhurst and Mrs Despard, sister of General French.

There was real tension in the air as they entered the lobby of the House of Commons. Jane was nervous but mesmerised by the grandeur and the statues. She had no idea what the government response would be. She had expected that they would be cold-shouldered or given some platitudes, but had not expected the Chief Whip to be quite so forthright. Marching into the lobby with three of four officials behind him, he stood in the lobby and called for attention.

'Ladies, I will come straight to the point. There is no chance whatsoever of this government agreeing to votes for women. There will be no vote on the matter and your visit here today is pointless.'

'That's outrageous!' shouted one woman. 'We were promised a hearing,' said another. There were loud protests but the Chief Whip simply turned his back and walked away.

All the women in the delegation were incensed at being brushed aside with such contempt. Mary Gawthorpe, in a spontaneous reaction, stood up on one of the sofas in the lobby and shouted out, 'Right, ladies if they will not meet with us, let us make sure they can hear us. We shall have our meeting here and now, right here in the lobby!'

There were cheers of support and encouragement from the delegation who huddled round Mary as she began to speak, urging them to redouble their efforts to secure the

341

vote. Almost in an instant, though, a group of policemen appeared from nowhere, barged through the circle of women which had formed around Mary Gawthorpe, and dragged the diminutive but combative Mary down. They rushed her out of the lobby as she struggled and kicked, trying to escape their grasp.

The group was now high on adrenalin and Mrs Pankhurst jumped onto the sofa. 'Ladies, I urge you not to move until the government has heard our demands. We must stand firm.' She too was grabbed, dragged down and bustled out, only to be replaced by Mrs Despard and then by Emmeline, with the same increasingly violent response from the police.

Jane was aghast at seeing her friend Emmeline dragged by the hair. She rushed to try and stop the burly policemen from causing her real hurt. It made no difference; soon Jane was thrown to the ground. She crashed onto the hard, tiled floor and was dragged by the arms through the lobby doors and out into the street.

A huge crowd had gathered, not all sympathetic to the women's cause. Fights were breaking out, with many of the working-class women who had been denied entry being attacked by onlookers.

The battered group of women were unbroken in spirit and spent the night in the cells singing, encouraging each other and planning what they would say when they came to court. They had many contacts and they all agreed that the best thing would be to plead not guilty of whatever charge they were accused of and demand to be heard in the High Court. They wanted publicity and this was a perfect opportunity.

There were ten upper-class, dishevelled, unkempt and bruised women in the dock that morning, but they held their heads high and they were unafraid. Jane was emboldened by the courage and resolve of the other women and drew great comfort from the camaraderie that had developed.

After the police had given evidence, Mrs Cobden-Sanderson asked to make a statement. She was a slight, delicate women dressed in lilac and grey and her cheeks were a soft dull-rose colour. She was the gentlest-looking English rose but she had deep roots and sharp thorns and would not be gainsaid.

'I am a lawbreaker because I want to be a lawmaker,' she told the magistrate firmly and defiantly.

Hearing this the magistrate, Horace Smith, intervened shouting, 'Silence! I have heard enough. You are all clearly guilty of causing a disturbance. You are all bound over to give a surety of £10 that you will keep the peace. If you do not pay this sum, you will go to prison for two months.'

There was uproar. 'We demand justice!' 'We have the right to speak in our own defence!' 'This is not justice this is tyranny!' were but some of the cries from the women in the dock. Horace Smith would have none of it; all the women who refused to pay or commit to keeping the peace were hustled out of the court and soon found themselves in Holloway Prison.

For Jane, it all happened in a flash. Such was the commotion, she was hardly aware of what was happening. She recalled making no conscious decision not to pay the fine or keep the peace, but was caught up in the moment, followed the group and sought comfort in numbers.

In the police van that took them to Holloway, the women were ecstatic, all deeply conscious that the government had a real problem now. The publicity would result in tremendous trouble for them and in many more women joining the cause.

Despite all of this, the next month in prison was a nightmare. The women were classed as the worst offenders and endured the harshest conditions. The clothes they had to wear were rough and irritated the skin; the food for a group that was used to the finest victuals was simply appalling. There was enough to keep them alive but it consisted of porridge, bread and potatoes. The monotony was the worst part, being cramped inside a tiny cell and having to urinate in a bowl and empty it in the morning into a drain at the end of the corridor.

They did not weaken mentally, but physically the days began to take their toll. Emmeline became quite ill, as did Mrs Cobden, and they were taken to the prison hospital. The doctors were worried; the last thing they wanted was a death inside prison and so the two women were released.

The fury in the press grew to fever pitch at the treatment given out to these women who had been imprisoned for holding a meeting. At last the Liberal government wilted and Gladstone agreed to the prisoners' release.

It took Jane a good month to recover her strength. Never had her own bed seemed so luxurious; never had simple soup seemed so rich and wholesome. It was not only her strength that increased; her bitterness at the treatment she had suffered for simply attending a meeting inside the home of democracy grew day by day. As her discomfort slowly drained away, her anger at the way she and the other women had been treated ameliorated.

Her view of politicians, already low as a result of her South African experiences, was now reaching the level of contempt. If these men thought that they could defeat women by throwing them in prison, they had even less of an understanding of females than she had realised. What really rankled was the fact that it was a Liberal government and it was their sisters that they were throwing into prison. Had they learned nothing over the years?

The next two years passed in a blur. Jane became enmeshed in work of the WSPU. She worked with Emmeline in preparing, editing and distributing *Votes for Women* the official voice of the WSPU. The publication had started off as a monthly magazine but, following the publicity of the arrest and imprisonment of the Commons delegation, circulation soared and it was soon coming out weekly and selling more than 50,000 copies.

'Do you think we are causing the rise in circulation?' Jane asked Emmeline. 'Or are we the consequence?'

'Oh, the consequence,' Emmeline replied, sitting at her typewriter. 'It's unstoppable now.'

'Do you think so? The government seem just as determined not to give an inch.'

'They know if they remove just one brick from the wall their whole house will fall down. That's why they will not budge — but they will have to. We are not going away.'

'It's that that I don't understand. Surely, they don't think we are going away,' said Jane, continuing to fold leaflets and place them in envelopes.

'They don't think. That's the problem. If we could get them to *think,* it would all be over very quickly. Our time has come. There is a tide and we are riding the flood.' Emmeline jumped up, came round the desk and hugged Jane. 'We are nearly there. One more push and I can see the walls of Jericho come tumbling down.'

At this Emmeline danced round the desk, pretending to blow a trumpet. For a fleeting second, but sharply and clearly, Jane saw in her mind's eye the group of Bushveldt Carbineers marching round the campfire singing *Onward Christian Soldiers* and she saw Peter Handcock's laughing face.

'What's the matter?' asked Emmeline. 'You look like you have seen a ghost.'

'I have,' said Jane, a tear coming to her eye.

Chapter 34
Broome Park

Three more years passed and it was spring 1912. Jane was conscious that she was getting older. She had put on weight and her face was puffier. She took little exercise, although occasionally she returned to Sparsholt, stayed with Lilly at her parents' home and rode Woodly.

They rode now in a more restrained way. Woodly, like her, was getting older and he was having occasional trouble with his right front hoof, which seemed to give him pain. Jane was conscious that she had lost some of her nerve when riding; she seemed to analyse risk to a greater extent. She also did not want to put any great strain on her horse.

Lilly now had a daughter but she did not appear to be besotted with motherhood, commenting to Jane more on the excellence of the nurse she had recruited than on her daughter's progress. She avoided any discussion of Jane's work or the suffrage movement. Although she knew of Jane's time in prison, for Jane had written to her whilst she was in Holloway, Lilly never once asked about the experience.

Time and circumstance change attitudes; there was no question that the closeness that had once been present between them was now a thing of the past. Lilly diligently avoided any possibility of Jane meeting her husband. His paranoia about votes for women had grown stronger and reached the point where he had deliberately gone to a Liberal Party-political meeting where he expected interruptions by WSPU supporters in order to attack them. It was with great pleasure, he told Lilly over breakfast, that he had punched one of 'those nasty, dirty suffragettes'.

Jane did her best to keep in touch with Emily but that was not easy. Emily was now living in France and writing a book about her experiences, but her health was poor. Jane was philosophical about this, understanding that friendships that are not regularly re-ignited tend to glimmer and then fade.

What Jane did do religiously was go to Dover twice a year and visit the Newmans. She was always made very welcome and she marvelled at how no one knew that James was not their child. They had a pleasant home with lovely garden, which Jane realised she missed having. They were regular churchgoers and Jane accompanied them to church on the Sundays she was with them. They always quizzed her about whether there was anyone special in her life and Jane shook her head sadly. When she left, Edith and Alun always had the same conversation about how she would have made a lovely home for someone.

It was James, though, that occupied Jane's attention. Year by year she watched his development with interest; now he was an assured, strong and resourceful twelve-year-old, clearly good at maths and interested in science. She was fascinated watching him confidently playing chess, something that she could not fathom, or plotting the stars on paper after looking through his prized possession, a telescope bought as his latest Christmas present. On June 15th each year she sent him a birthday card, for this was the day his parents had chosen as his birthday, the day he was handed to them in Cape Town. This matter, though, was never raised.

What was raised was the question of a career for James. His father, given the interest his son showed in maths, the stars and science, was obsessed with James going into the Royal Navy. He had already projected a glorious career for him, seeing it as the perfect choice given the importance of science and engineering in the Navy. Edith was happy to go along with whatever Alun thought, but she was not quite so happy when she discovered that cadets entered the Royal Naval College, Osborne, at thirteen years of age and were away for much of the year. Nor was she happy that, at the age of sixteen, cadets were placed as midshipmen in the fleet and she would see even less of him, for the Empire now stretched around the globe. Nevertheless, if Alun thought it was right she would go along with it; it was not her place to argue.

For Alun, getting James into Osborne was everything, a real mark of prestige. Every spare moment was spent working on the sort of questions the entrance exam would present. Alun had no doubt whatsoever that his son would pass. James simply wanted to please his parents and was happy to go along with his father's choice of career for him. James had no knowledge that Alun and Edith were not his real parents, and Alun and Edith had convinced themselves that they were.

'I can see that you're concerned about James going to the Naval College. Does it worry you?' asked Jane, as they walked back from church. She was looking at the backs of

Alun and James as they strode away, walking purposefully back to their home.

'He is so young. I don't understand why they have to go at thirteen.'

'I suppose it's just like school. You go away at thirteen to most schools,' said Jane. 'Are you concerned about it being the Naval College?'

'Alun wants him to go. I just hope there is no war. I saw enough of war in South Africa.'

'Have you told Alun about your worry?' Jane turned to look directly at Edith.

'No, not really. It's not my place. I think it's his father's role to decide on these things,' said Edith rather sheepishly.

'Of course it's your role!' said Jane, suddenly becoming animated. 'You have just as much right as Alun to express your view and, at the end of the day, it should be James who decides.'

'James will do what his father wants.'

'Maybe that's because you have not said what *you* want.'

By now there were nearing the Newmans' house and they went inside. Jane went up to the spare room where she always stayed and took off her coat. She looked in the mirror and shook her head in disappointment. Why should Edith simply follow convention and hold back her own views about her son's future because her husband had entrenched views and she did not want to contradict him? Jane knew Edith was a long way from joining the suffrage movement.

Back in London, the suffrage movement had its own problems, which impacted on Jane. Frustrated by the lack of progress and stubborn opposition from the Asquith Liberal government, Christabel Pankhurst proposed a major escalation in acts of violence against property. Emmeline Pethick-Lawrence opposed this, as she and her husband, who were funding the WSPU, thought it would alienate them from the general public. They were shocked when Mrs Pankhurst sided with her daughter and expelled Emmeline and her husband from the union. The whole organisation was torn asunder and many leading members resigned as a result.

Jane was left in a quandary. She hated confrontation of a personal nature. She enjoyed her work and was committed to it, but Emmeline had become her only true friend and she thought the treatment she had suffered, given all they had done for the movement, was deplorable.

'I am going to resign,' she told Emmeline. 'It's not right. I share your view that burning property is not going to win the day.'

'Don't resign because of me,' Emmeline replied. 'Fred and I can stand on our own two feet.'

'But how can I go to Clements Inn if you are not there? It's your house,' exclaimed Jane.

'Well, they will have to move out. Clearly the WSPU cannot stay in our house if we are not welcome.' Emmeline was calm, considered and not bitter. 'These things happen. People have strong views and we are all fighters. The struggle will go on but in different ways.'

'But it is our approach that I like. I think the Pankhursts are doing what they think best, but they need someone to take a more considered view. Also, I don't think I will be welcome any more. They know I am your friend.'

'Well don't forget that *Votes for Women* is still ours. We will still edit and control it, so life will go on. Let's go and have a nice lunch and show that we are still around.'

Over lunch at the Ritz, they discussed the future. Jane told Emmeline about visiting the Newmans and how, after living in London for so long, she longed to get back to the country and have a nice garden. She also explained that she was concerned about her money, which seemed to be going down faster than she would like.

Emmeline said that she would have a word with some of her husband's friends. 'There is no reason why you could not live in the country but come up to London once or twice a week and still be involved with *Votes for Women*. I know you enjoyed running the estate at Lainston House. Maybe there will be similar opportunities. Who knows until you try?'

London was changing rapidly. Horses were disappearing from the streets and trams, buses, cars and bicycles cluttered the streets. The underground was constantly being extended and took ever-increasing numbers of passengers; Jane frequently travelled on it. The two-penny Central London line proved to be the best way of travelling round for her and she often sat looking at the other passengers, wondering what they were doing and where they were going.

She used the underground to go to Selfridges, which had opened in 1909, and which she loved. She had taken Edith and James to Selfridges for a birthday treat in 1909 and they had seen the aeroplane that made the first Channel crossing on display in the shop. James was fascinated, studying it for what seemed like hours.

Jane continued to live at Carlisle Place and continued to work on preparing *Votes for Women,* week by week taking on more responsibility for its production. Increasingly, though, the smoke from the hundreds of thousands of coal fires, the trains, the cars and buses, began to grate on her. She frequently felt unwell and at times struggled to get her breath. Night-times in the summer were particularly difficult, especially if there was no wind and the smoke hung in the air.

It was October 1912 when Emmeline offered a lifeline. 'How would you like to live in the Kent countryside?' she asked, looking across the desk.

'Why do you ask?' replied Jane, fully aware that more would follow.

'Oh, nothing really. I know you have friends in Kent and wondered if you had thought of moving there.'

Jane knew Emmeline well; there was more behind the question than was being offered up.

'I do like the countryside. It seems so clean compared to London.'

'That's because it is,' said Emmeline, looking down at the papers on her desk. She let things drift for a few minutes whilst Jane waited for the inevitable follow up.

'There is an opening for a house and estate keeper at a property called Broome Park. There is a lovely old house near Canterbury, which is being modernised, and a farm estate. The chief steward is fully committed with the renovation project and wants an assistant to run the day-to-day aspects of the house and farm. I know that is something you have done before.'

Jane sat bolt upright. Emmeline had her full attention.

'I just thought it might be something you'd be interested in,' Emmeline continued. 'I can see that the London air is not to your liking and you often talk of the lovely garden you used to have. If you are interested, Fred can make an introduction.'

'I *am* interested but what about here? You need someone to help you.'

'Yes, I do, but you could come up once or twice a week. I don't think the journey will be too difficult but, if it does prove so, I am sure we could work something out. I think it would be good for you to move out of London. I don't think you intended to be here all this time.'

'I didn't. But you have to take conscious decisions to change a routine and, unless something new is presented to you, it's so easy just to carry on. Before you know it, a number of years have gone by.'

'Indeed, I know that to be true,' replied Emmeline.

Two weeks later, Jane travelled out to Canterbury and then six miles south-east to Barham. Broome Park was at the edge of the village and here she was to meet with the steward, Grenville McLeod. He turned out to be a very smart, urbane, well-educated man from the Borders in his mid-forties. He wore a checked brown tweed suit and spotlessly shiny brown brogues, which impressed Jane given the rather muddy lane and entrance to the house.

The house, whilst grand and impressive, lacked charm or gentility and did not seem homely like Lainston House. As they toured it, McLeod asked Jane many questions about her background and experience. She felt at ease with him and spoke openly of how she had managed the family estate and how it had upset her to move away.

'Is that why you became a suffragette?' he asked, taking Jane by surprise.

'It was not the only reason, but I do feel it is time that women's roles were recognised.' She chose her words carefully, trying not to be too controversial.

'So do I,' he replied. 'Half the population cannot be ignored.'

'Oh, that's good to hear,' she replied, slightly surprised.

'Let's have some coffee and discuss the job.'

He led her up six steps on to the upper lawn and then along a gravel path until they reached a south-facing entrance to the house. They went into a surprisingly small entrance hall and then into the drawing room that occupied a good portion of the ground floor of the east wing. It was an impressive room but was almost devoid of furniture, save for a large table and six chairs.

'No one lives here at the moment. The previous owners moved out over a year ago and the current owner lives in Egypt.'

'Egypt?' Jane queried, obviously not following why the owner should be there.

'Yes, that's right, Egypt. Lord Kitchener, the general chap.'

'Kitchener!' Jane gasped, alarm written on her face.

'Yes. You look concerned. Do you know him?'

'No, I've never met him, but I saw what he did in South Africa,' Jane replied but then stopped, cutting short what she was going on to say.

'Clearly what you saw was not to your liking, but why do you blame Kitchener if you have never met him?' asked Grenville.

'It was his policies that caused the suffering and he was the driving force. There were some other more personal issues as well.'

Grenville could see that the name Kitchener had clearly caused Jane a major problem but he thought that Jane was ideal for the job and wanted her to take it.

'He has only been here twice and not for almost a year. He intends this to be his residence when he retires and comes back to England. That is not going to be for a few years. My main job is to ensure that the house is updated and restored to his liking. He comments on all the drawings I send him and is very specific about what he wants, down to the fine detail. All this is done by post. There is every chance you will not see him if that makes it easier for you.

Jane had been thrown by Kitchener's name coming up and she needed time to collect her thoughts.

'Oh, I see. Are there to be many changes?' she asked, buying time.

'Yes, a lot. The house has not been updated for decades and basically everything — bathrooms, kitchens, electricity, gas, the roof, servants' quarters — will all be brought up to date.'

'If I were to work here, would there be a room in the house?'

'Yes, of course. You can take your pick. There are plenty to choose from,' Grenville said, smiling.

He went on to explain that the main work would be in managing the farm hands and running the estate. 'Very similar to what you did at your old home. That's why you would be well suited to the role and you will be out in the country. I understand you like riding and hunting.'

'Yes. How did you know that?'

'Oh, we have been asking around. Everyone speaks most highly of you. Look, I know I have thrown a spanner in the works by telling you Kitchener is the owner but I think you would be very suitable for the role. He will not be living here for a few years, so why not see how it goes?' He looked directly at Jane and held out his hand. 'I would like you to come and help me out. Will you accept?'

Jane hesitated as many thoughts flashed through her mind. She knew that if Kitchener had not been mentioned she would have been more than happy to accept. She saw the outstretched hand.

Jane though felt a cord holding back her hand. How could she work for Kitchener after everything that had happened. What would Emily think?

It was as though Grenville was reading her mind when he said, 'Think of it that you are working for me not Kitchener. When my time is finished here you will be in a much better position to decide if you want to stay.'

Jane was still hesitant. It was as though she were pulling a heavy weight as she slowly pushed her hand forward.

'Yes, all right, let's see how things progress,' she said with a noticeable sigh.

Chapter 35
Liberation

Jane moved into Broome Park in January 1913. It had taken some time for Grenville to organise furniture for the house. He met with Jane in London and they discussed what she would need. They agreed that for the moment she would take three rooms on the first floor of the south wing, an area that was not to be pulled apart during the building works. She would have a bedroom, a sitting room and a bathroom. A temporary kitchen would be made in one of the ground-floor rooms that would be split into two; the other half would be a dining room, which could also act as Jane's study.

'Gosh, it all sounds too good to be true. Is it reasonable to go to so much trouble?' said Jane, clearly delighted with the proposals.

'Believe me, in the grand scheme of things it is no trouble. The house is to be ripped apart,' said Grenville. 'I want someone living on site. We will have a couple of servant girls who will do all the domestic work, cleaning, lighting fires, washing and cooking for the workers. I am afraid a number of them will sleep on site but they will be well away from you. I really need you to get to grips with the estate, find out what needs doing. I don't know much about agriculture, I am a building man.'

Jane asked how long the work would take. Grenville explained that he had planned for just over a year but he knew that this was assuming no major problems were uncovered. This was why he wanted the men on site, not spending a lot of time travelling from London. Some of the work was specialist and required quality tradesmen, not least in putting in the electricity and other utilities.

'Are you happy having a woman working for you? It's quite unusual,' said Jane, trying to tease out more from Grenville.

'Of course I am. I would not have asked you to come otherwise. My wife is always telling me that if I want a job doing well, I should ask a woman!'

'Do you have children?' asked Jane.

'Yes, three. Two boys and a girl. The oldest, Jack, is twelve and Mary is five.'

'You must be away from home a lot,' Jane said. 'Does your wife not mind?'

'It comes with the trade, I am afraid. I have done very well on these sorts of projects. Lots of old wealthy families are having their houses modernised and I am getting plenty of business through referrals.'

'Where is your home?'

'York. My wife is from there. With me being away a lot, it makes sense that she stays there as she has lots of friends in the area.'

After this meeting in the Goring Hotel near Victoria, Jane went back to her flat and then met with Emmeline, who was delighted that things had progressed so well and that

Jane looked so excited. They agreed that it was too much to expect Jane to come up to London every week, but she would be welcome any time to call in and to attend meetings and demonstrations.

'I'd better not get arrested,' said Jane, half in jest but also with a serious undertone. She really did not want to spend any more time in prison, an experience that had frightened her more than she had realised.

'The way things are going, I think quite a number are going to get arrested. I think the Pankhursts want as many women as possible to get thrown into prison. They think the government will not be able to cope if hundreds of women are in prison and they all go on hunger strike.'

'It's terrible what they are doing, force-feeding these women. I think the Pankhursts are right. A lot of people will start to think that government should not be doing this to their own people,' said Jane.

'Let's hope that nobody dies. But sometimes I think that Christabel, in particular, wants there to be a death in prison. Then they really can create a fuss and maximise the publicity.'

'If they think that throwing people like me into prison, not allowing us to defend ourselves in court, mistreating us and generally acting as though we are vermin is going to work, they have got it seriously wrong. There may be a death, or maybe more than one, but increasingly people are thinking that if that's what it takes, so be it.'

Emmeline looked at Jane in some disbelief. 'Jane, I have not heard you speak like that before. Has something happened?'

'A lot has happened — but then nothing has happened. This is supposed to be a Liberal government. Liberal! I never knew that liberal meant let's keep men in charge and things unchanged. I think our future lies with the Labour Party. We need to support Labour and win some seats. Then they might take notice.'

'You really have been thinking about this. You have become far more radical. I must admit I have misjudged you. I always look on you as Miss Dependable, getting on with the work, organised but not really committed. Now I see you truly are.'

'I am, but I must admit that my mood has not been helped by discovering that Broome Park is owned by Lord Kitchener. He did more to cause suffering to women and children than anyone I know. The government simply ignored the facts that Emily presented to them, pretending they were a fabrication. But they weren't. I saw what went on.' Jane moved her coffee cup from side to side and swept her hand across her skirts in irritation.

'I knew that Kitchener had bought Broome Park. Leonard told me. I did not realise it was a problem.'

'Well, the good thing is that he is not living there and will not be for some time. It is a lovely village and I know I can do what is needed and will enjoy the task — but it was quite a shock.'

Emmeline signalled to the waiter for the bill and asked if Jane was still in touch with Emily.

'Yes, but only by letter. She is back in France, writing, but she is not well.'

'Emily was with you in South Africa. Does she feel the same about Kitchener?' asked Emmeline.

'Yes, most certainly,' said Jane.

Emmeline reflected on this for a few moments. She examined her nails closely and ran her thumbs against one another. She looked up:

'I don't want to pry into what happened in South Africa but I have come to know you well, Jane, and I want to see things work out well for you. South Africa is now in the past, and it is the future that is important. Whatever happened in South Africa should not be forgotten but it should not prevent you from moving forward. If I have learnt one thing in my life, it is that forgiveness is most liberating. Don't become trapped in a cage of your own making.'

Chapter 36
Traitors Should Not Queue

January 1913 came upon her in no time and Jane enjoyed the mental stimulus of preparing for a new life. She saw it very much as an opportunity to recreate what she'd had in Hampshire. She mapped out carefully in many lists what she needed to do, lists ranging from the clothes, furniture and equipment, people to tell, letters to write, finding a church and a hunt to join.

She decided not to take Woodly. The last time she had been to see him she had not been able to ride him; his foot was making him lame and he was in some discomfort. She also knew that the Barings treated him wonderfully well, and she was worried about moving him to an area that he did not know.

She made herself comfortable in Broome Park. Her rooms were simply furnished but the views from her windows were gorgeous. Rolling parkland stretched away littered with exotic trees: Austrian pines, sequoia, copper beech and lines of mature lime trees created splendid avenues to walk along. The grounds were neglected, though; the paths were overgrown, many self-seeding sycamores spoiled the landscape, and lots of dogwood and rhododendron had gone wild.

It was the finance that Jane had to get to grips with first. Although Grenville was as pleasant a gentleman as could be imagined, he was very clear about his expectations that the farm and estate should not cost money; they should make a substantial contribution to covering the running costs of the house and pay towards its refurbishment. It was soon clear that they did not, and it did not take Jane many weeks to work out why: the farm foreman was selling much of the produce in the local markets and not putting it through the books. He was also syphoning off a significant chunk of the grain harvest, taking it to a separate grain dealer and keeping the income for himself.

Jane spent a whole week tossing and turning once she had clearly established what was going on. She was hesitant about confronting Abel, the farm foreman, not because she had any doubts about what was happening but because of her experiences, firstly with Walter Dunhaughton when she left Lainston House and secondly when she was arrested at the House of Commons. She had been scarred by these events and the fear of physical assault preyed on her. She did not want to confide in Grenville, however; she wanted to show that she could deal with the problem herself. Eventually she plucked up the courage to tackle Abel directly.

She asked one of the workmen if the foreman would come round to see her. The foreman, Jack, was a pleasant chap, a skilled bricklayer from the Winchester area, and Jane had got to know him by chatting over numerous morning cups of tea. When he arrived, she explained that she had an unpleasant task to undertake and would feel more comfortable if she had someone present when she did it.

Jack asked no questions. He deduced that Jane wanted someone there for personal security and he simply nodded, saying that it was no problem.

When Abel arrived, Jane led him in the kitchen. Jack was sitting at the large table.

'Abel,' she said straight away. 'I have concluded that farm produce is being stolen. I believe that you are responsible. You can either leave now with one week's pay and we will say no more about it, or I can call the police and we will have the matter investigated. Which do you want? I need a decision now.' She looked at him directly, not moving her eyes away from his but holding out a packet that contained £4 10s.

He looked ashen, all the wind knocked out of him. He said nothing as he tried to think what was best for him. To Jane it seemed an age and she started to worry that he might argue, but she did not show this; her face remained set in a determined, no-nonsense expression. It was this that won the day.

Abel blinked and then crumbled. He took the money and turned his back. Not saying a word, he went out of the kitchen.

'Blimey, Miss Dunhaughton, don't think you needed me here. You would have frightened off a whole regiment,' said Jack.

Jane slumped down onto a chair, drained of all energy. It was as though she had climbed the highest mountain and swum the widest lake, all in the same day. 'Believe me, I did need you. It was me that was petrified.'

'You should be on the stage, then!' he said, slapping her on the back rather too forcibly.

Nineteen thirteen moved from winter to spring and then high summer. Jane's life began to take on a regularity and symmetry with which she was familiar and comfortable, if not wildly excited. She made great progress with the farm and estate accounts, just as she had at Lainston House, and Grenville regularly praised her efforts. She made friends, or at least acquaintances, at the local church. She joined the hunt and enjoyed riding, and she made a small flower garden in the area immediately below her bedroom window. She took pleasure each morning looking down on the pontentillas, the daises, hydrangeas and geraniums that she had planted.

She kept up her correspondence with Lilly, Emily and Emmeline, and occasionally she wrote to Caroline at Kya Lami. She was encouraged by the resourceful way in which South Africa seemed to be getting back on its feet.

She went to see the Newmans and increasingly felt a bond growing between herself and James. She did not know any other teenagers and she marvelled at his intelligence, how sound and sensible he was. While she understood Edith's concerns, she began to think that James would fit in well in a disciplined organisation like the Navy. She was worried that she may have gone too far in saying so to Edith, who shed a tear both in joy and worry when news came that James had been accepted in to the naval college at Osbourne and would start in mid-September.

The one area where regularity and symmetry were not evident was in her political and campaigning life, where her views became more entrenched and combative. She recognised in herself a dichotomy: she hated conflict or confrontation in her personal life, yet she was increasingly willing to countenance it when it came to votes for women.

She joined the Labour Party and saw in its policies the natural home for democratic suffragists. She attended party meetings in London and read political and historical texts. She could see that, although she had always tried to see the best in others and to do as she would have liked done to her, a more stringent bitterness was creeping into her character.

She made no progress in finding a soulmate and someone to share her life. In church, at the hunt, in the village, the only men she met were married. Now aged thirty-six, she doubted if anyone would come along. She saw in James something that had passed her by, the chance to have a child. Though she tried not to dwell on it, she occasionally felt sad and empty, particularly when tending to her garden or looking out over the parkland. Her life was devoid of emotional attachment and, as the days passed, she felt it more and more. More than once she re-read *Michael* and thought of what might have been.

The house was far from complete by January 1914, not least because Kitchener had made considerable alterations to his initial plans. Jane had not seen him, even though he had visited Broome Park twice in September. On these visits he laid out precise plans for furnishing the house and engaged an interior designer who had worked with Grenville on a number of stately-home projects. It was not until June 1914 that final preparations were made for the completion of the project and for Kitchener to hold a weekend party to announce his arrival.

Nothing prepared Jane — or indeed the whole of Britain — for the outbreak of war in August 1914. The wonderful summer, the best for a decade, seemed to radiate warmth and contentment, a sense of well-being and prosperity. It was a long time since Britain had been at war and many had forgotten what it was like. Neither did they realise how different this war would be.

At the suffrage movement meetings in central London, Jane found herself speaking up and campaigning rather than taking a back seat.

'I have seen first hand, the effects of war, the suffering and the hardship, not just for the soldiers but civilians too. I have seen long lines of injured in hospital and I do not want to see that again.'

She spoke with conviction and passion to convey the terrible and almost always unforeseen consequences of war.

'As I see it, the women's movement is fundamentally a Christian one that sees everybody as equal; as such, it should campaign for peace and negotiations to put a stop to what I am certain will prove to be a disastrous war. Looking back now, what was gained by the Boer War? How can we justify the large numbers who lost their lives or their loved ones?'

It took a great deal out of Jane to find the courage to stand up and speak in public. It was not something she would ever be comfortable with but she was unshakable in her conviction that everything should be done to avoid conflict. She was not prepared, however, for the divisions within the women's movement. She was taken aback by how acrimonious the debate became and the negative reaction to her and other women who spoke in a similar way. Being accused of being pro-German or unpatriotic by women she had been at meetings with for a number of years was deeply upsetting and knocked her confidence. She had rarely spoken at meetings before and had not for one moment anticipated people with a common cause could be so aggressive.

It was at the NUWSS annual meeting in February 1915, when Millicent Fawcett spoke belligerently of it being treasonable to talk of peace, that Jane broke with the movement. She could not cope with being cold-shouldered; on one occasion, when queuing for her lunch, she had been shoved violently by another woman who told her that 'traitors should not be allowed to queue'.

Chapter 37
An American Calls

Kitchener's eminence in society continued to rise above the dizzy heights it already enjoyed. In September 1914 he was made Secretary of State for War; he now held enormous power. He had furnished Broome Park but had not moved in; he needed to be in Whitehall or in Paris, and was far too busy to enjoy the stately, retired life for which he had bought Broome Park.

It was June 1915 when Jane woke with deep unease in her stomach. As the morning passed, the feeling increased to the point she was almost sick. She knew that she was not ill; she was worried about having to meet Kitchener that day, for Grenville had told her that he would be showing him around the finished house.

She was unsure how she would react when she saw him face to face. She had often thought of asking him about Breaker Morant and Peter Handcock, but she had matured enough to realise that Kitchener was not going to enter a discussion with her on that topic. She had also thought often about Emmeline's comment that she should not be trapped by bitterness, and that forgiveness was liberating. Even so, when she visualised Kitchener holding out his hand when they were introduced a cold shiver went through her.

As it was, she met him in an unexpected moment when she was off guard, tending to flowers in the bed below her rooms. Grenville was walking the grounds with Kitchener and he pointed out Jane.

'Ah, you're the housekeeper, I understand,' Kitchener said in a booming deep voice from about ten yards away.

Jane was on her knees and rose immediately. Before she could respond Kitchener added, 'Look forward to seeing much more of you,' and moved on. He walked a couple of paces, turned and said, 'Wonderful flowerbed.'

Jane hardly had the chance to look closely at him. He was tall but portly, magnificently dressed with a greatcoat draped over his shoulders and wearing a fine, dark-grey three-piece suit. Within seconds, he and Grenville were round the corner; they were followed thirty yards behind, by two other men dressed in dark suits and bowler hats.

Jane was lost for words. She did not know what to make of it. No handshake; it had all been very perfunctory. Clearly, she was not important enough to merit further discourse.

So that was it. So many hours imagining what she would say if she met him and she had not spoken a word. So many hours spent wondering how she would react, and it was over before she even realised it was happening. Maybe it was for the best. She had been advised that there was little to be gained by holding a grudge and everything to gain from forgiveness — but it had been quite difficult.

She expressed those thoughts to Grenville when they met at the end of the day.

'I am sure that is right. You're a churchgoer. Surely forgiveness is at the heart of Christian teaching,' he replied.

'It is, but you need the other person to know they have been forgiven for it to be truly meaningful. I suspect he never thinks he needs forgiving for one moment,' said Jane.

'This is all quite deep,' Grenville smiled. 'I just wanted you to know that my work here is done. Kitchener's secretary will run things from now on. I hope all goes well for you, Jane. You have done everything I hoped for.'

He turned to go out of the room but, as he reached the door, he stopped and looked back. 'By the way, he loved your flowers. If you want to keep him happy, make sure he has fresh flowers on his desk every day.'

***

In June, Jane went down to Dover to visit the Newmans. The trains were full of soldiers embarking for the trenches of northern France, and Dover was far busier than normal. The activity, even though it was on a far larger scale, reminded Jane of Cape Town and Durban docks. There were khaki uniforms and vehicles everywhere.

She found Edith subdued, worried that James, who was nearing the end of his second year at naval college, would soon be sent to sea. Jane tried to play down the danger, saying that the Royal Navy could not be challenged, but she was also worried. The two of them stood in the garden late one evening and heard the guns firing far away across the Channel. They looked at each other for reassurance. They did not find it.

The rest of the year passed uneventfully. There was great difficulty in getting in the harvest, given that so many men were away fighting, and Jane struggled to get machines repaired. But life went on and people coped with the constant news that loved ones had been killed or seriously injured.

She met frequently with Emmeline Pethick-Lawrence. Emmeline had also suffered as a result of her support for the cause of peace and they provided each other with as much comfort as possible, reminding themselves that they were far better off than the troops on the front line.

They were both concerned about Emily, who was receiving even more wrath from the xenophobic public and seemed to be on a path that could see her locked up or charged with treason. They knew she was simply doing what she thought best, with no hidden agenda other than the relief of suffering.

It was in November of that year that Jane received the saddest news. Lilly rang her first thing one morning on the phone that was now installed at Broome, almost certainly at the insistence of the government that thought they might need to contact Kitchener. Lilly said that Woodly was not good and that Jane should come and say her goodbyes.

Jane went straight to the station and then on by a tortuous route to Sparsholt and the Barings' house. She was warmly welcomed by Harry and the staff who were expecting her.

They went immediately to the stables. Woodly was lying down, his head flat on the straw. Jane immediately entered his box and put her arms round him, kissing him on his neck and whispering to him. He raised his head and she rubbed her head against his, telling him how much she had missed him.

His eyes registered that he knew who she was, but he could only lick her hand and would not take the apple she held for him.

She hugged him and began to relive their life together, 'Do you remember when we won the point-to-point? That was a good day, wasn't it, Woodly? How many chases have we won together? You've had a good life. Not because you won races and had nice stables but because you have been loved all your life. Being loved makes every day special. I should have asked you to give me some lessons on how to be loved. Sometimes I think it has passed me by.'

She stopped talking for a few minutes but continued to stroke his ears and rub her forehead against his. When she spoke again, her tone was more positive, as though she were imparting important information that needed to be remembered.

'We may be parted for a short time but when we meet again it will be in a place where there is only love. When we meet it will be forever, so don't worry. I will be coming, and when I arrive I will expect you to show me round and introduce me to your friends. You will do that, won't you?'

She could feel his pulse ticking away very faintly and she wanted the feeling to go on and on, to pass from temporal to eternal and become embedded in her. She remembered the feeling of togetherness they used to have as they rode and it was with her now.

She stayed with him into the evening. The stable was lit by an electric light at the door and by a candle the stable hand brought to her. After two hours the vet arrived and checked Woodly over. When they went outside, he told Jane that there was nothing he could do. Woodly was old and had come to the end of his life.

Back inside, her horse raised his head slightly and licked Jane's hand. Quietly he shuddered and passed away.

Woodly had been loved by all who came into contact with him and Harry, the stable hand, and Jane all shed a tear. They tried to tell each other what a great life he had enjoyed, but it was a very sad household that evening and at breakfast the next day. Harry asked Jane if she wanted to say one last goodbye but she could not bring herself to go back to the stable. Her memory of Woodly raising his head would rest in her mind for ever.

As the day wore on, she found herself reflecting on her life. She could hardly remember a time before Woodly; some of her happiest times had been with him. She brooded on the fact that she now rarely had excitement; she functioned and did what was necessary, but she knew deep down that she was not happy. She rarely laughed and she spent too much time alone. The pain from the loss of Lainston grew rather than diminished; she was deeply conscious that she was now just a servant and she felt unquestionably diminished.

***

The misery of the war continued through the winter of 1915–16. Hardly a week went by without news of more deaths or injuries among the villagers who had gone to war. Jane heard the same depressing news from Lilly in Hampshire. There seemed to be no end in sight, no light at the end of a tunnel.

Women banded together, gave whatever support they could to each other and made the best of things, for there was nothing else they could do. The politicians had no answers but prayed that the massively successful recruitment drive, fronted by Kitchener, would produce enough new army divisions to tip the balance.

Seeing Kitchener's face everywhere she went made Jane wonder if her country needed *her*. Should she volunteer to be a nurse? Over tea at Broome, however, the local vicar pointed out that running the estate and producing food was an even more vital task. He was less straightforward or clear when Jane asked how he reconciled the fact that clergy in Germany would also be calling upon God to help them achieve victory.

In May 1916 there was much talk of a major offensive by the British. Kitchener began to use Broome more frequently, coming at weekends accompanied by young men in military uniform and his secretariat and bodyguards. They were all men.

The number of servants increased but Jane found herself sidelined; it was Kitchener's secretary who arranged for staff to be brought in from London. She did, however, place fresh flowers in Kitchener's study every morning if she thought that he would be staying at Broome.

It was the 8th of May, a bright, early-summer morning, when one of the servant girls came in to her study and said that there was a gentleman asking to see her. She gave Jane a card. It had an address on the Old Kent Road, London and the name Arnold Kayton, agricultural equipment supplier. 'He wants to see me?' Jane asked.

'Yes. He specifically asked for you.'

The servant girl had left Mr Kayton standing in the hallway. Jane apologised, led him into the study and asked what she could do for him. He was about forty-five, almost six feet tall and broad shouldered. He was clean shaven and dressed smartly in a linen suit and boater hat, which he took off and held by his side. He had a small case by his feet.

'I am hoping that I can help you,' he said in a clear, confident voice. He had a distinct accent that Jane could not place. 'I know just how difficult it can be managing an estate, doing the ploughing and getting in the harvest, what with all the men away at the front. My company supplies tractors that can do the work of scores of men. I am touring the area because the government is encouraging farms to buy new equipment so that food supplies can be maintained.'

He bent down, opened the case at his feet and pulled out a printed sheet that showed a tractor pulling a plough. 'You see, the tractor can replace all your horses. It doesn't need feeding, and can plough far quicker than a man and horse. I am sure you know that it takes a man nearly a day to plough an acre using a horse. Our tractors can plough an acre in fifteen minutes.'

Jane was shocked. 'Fifteen minutes?' she asked disbelievingly, then looked carefully at the printed sheet that repeated this statistic. She had read recently about the government promoting the use of tractors and was aware that they were importing them from America, but she had no idea that they could improve productivity so much.

Jane sat down and re-read the information. She looked up and asked Mr Kayton how much a tractor cost and how would one learn how to use it?

'About £450 or thereabouts — it depends on which model you get. The bigger ones are obviously more, but they can do more work. We would show your farm workers how to use the machine. It's not difficult, just like driving a car.'

Jane continued to look at the machine. It would make such a huge difference. 'I am interested, but I would need the landowner's permission to spend so much money,' she said, handing back the pamphlet.

'Oh sorry, I thought this was your estate and farm. No, please keep the leaflet. Who is the owner?' Arnold Kayton asked, almost in passing.

'Lord Kitchener.'

'What *the* Lord Kitchener? The man on the poster?'

'Yes,' said Jane. 'The very one.'

'I would have thought he was too busy to run an estate.'

'He doesn't run it, I do. He is not here very often. He comes at weekends mostly. I would ask his secretary, who controls most things.'

'Well, if you are interested, we could supply a tractor within two weeks. They have been imported from the United States.'

'I am interested. How would I get in touch with you?'

'You have my card, which has our address on it. But I will be coming back to the Canterbury area in two weeks. I could call in and see if you have come to a decision.'

Jane looked again at the pamphlet. She considered it most carefully and then said, 'Yes, do that.'

***

It was on the Tuesday the 23rd of May that Mr Kayton called again. He was driving a small, black, upright car that sat well above its wheels.

Jane had seen it come into the grounds and guessed it was Arnold Kayton's. She had not been able to see Kitchener's secretary as he had cancelled their visit the previous weekend, but she had been thinking a great deal about the farm and tractors. She had called on a couple of the neighbouring farms to ask what they thought. Like her, they were struggling due to the lack of horses and men and were considering the new machines. One of the farm managers said the landowner could not afford *not* to have one, and this argument appealed to Jane. The other farmers had not been visited by Arnold Kayton, though, and did not know anything about the tractors he supplied.

When Kayton arrived, Jane went out to meet him and they stood by his car. 'I am afraid I have not been able to make a decision as Lord Kitchener's secretary cancelled their visit last weekend. He will be coming this Friday.'

'Never mind. I was in the area anyway. Are you still interested?' he asked, looking straight at Jane, who was dressed in a long grey skirt, white blouse and woollen cardigan. She had been hoping that Arnold Kayton would call. Something about him interested her; she had made a special effort with her hair and put on make-up, which was unusual for her unless she was going out.

'Yes, very much so. We really have to do something for I don't know how we will get the harvest in and then do the ploughing. There are even fewer men this year than last. They have all joined my employer's army.' Jane smiled. The joke was rather flat but she had been rehearsing it all morning and she did her best to make it sound spontaneous.

'Well, he's certainly been successful. You have to say that,' said Arnold.

Jane listened carefully. She still could not trace the accent. 'You are not from here,' she stated, probing.

'No. I was brought up in the United States. Pennsylvania, to be precise. I came over to sell the tractors. That's why I have this Model T Ford, which I brought over. Best small car by far.'

They discussed whether the Americans would join the war and other bits of news before Jane apologised for not being able to make a decision. 'Please come inside and have some tea or coffee. It is the least I can do.'

Arnold asked numerous questions about how Jane came to be at Broome; she answered willingly, making it clear how hurt she was that she had been forced to leave Lainston. She explained how it was her contacts in the suffrage movement that had led her to Broome.

'You seem to move in high circles,' he said. 'You have mentioned quite a number of lords and ladies, and here you are managing Lord Kitchener's estate.' He spoke in a teasing, friendly way that invited Jane to respond in a similar manner.

'I don't really know Kitchener at all — I have only spoken to him once. He liked my garden.' She added, 'Actually I am not an admirer of Kitchener. What he did in South Africa was wrong and, whilst I am trying to forgive him, I cannot forget it.'

Arnold pricked up his ears and was all attention as Jane explained how she had been in South Africa during the Boer War and the terrible things she had seen.

'You certainly went through a lot. It has left you scarred, I can tell.' He looked at her sympathetically and held out his hand as though to offer comfort or share her emotion. Jane, just for a second but a noticeable second, fought back the bitterness that lurked beneath the surface of her composed demeanour.

She instinctively took hold of his hand and he gave hers a gentle squeeze before withdrawing and sitting more upright. 'I am sorry, I did not wish to be forward. I just wanted you to know that I understand how you feel.'

'That's so kind,' Jane said, looking away, slightly embarrassed at the way she had let down her guard. She quickly moved the conversation back to business. 'I am sorry you've had a wasted journey but we are very interested.'

'Well, it's not wasted then,' he responded immediately.

'No, I suppose not. If this were my land, I would place an order now but I need his lordship to sign it off.' She stood up, looking more composed.

'But he is coming this weekend?' Arnold asked.

'Yes, that's right. It's not Kitchener I need to see, though, it is Mr Weston. He sorts out all Kitchener's domestic affairs. I am sure I will get an answer for you.'

They chatted some more then Arnold got up, explaining that he had some more calls to make and needed to get back to London. He would call back the following Tuesday.

He did indeed call the following Tuesday. It was eleven thirty a.m. when Jane noticed the black Model T Ford come into the grounds. She had been eagerly awaiting Arnold Kayton's visit all morning. She had thought about him a great deal. She recognised that she had the same feelings for him as she had felt for Lieutenant Handcock. She hardly knew Arnold, but there was something inside her that said that here was a man who shared her views, was kind and sympathetic. She desperately wanted to meet with him for reasons other than to discuss tractors.

It was a grey, nothing, sort of day, and there was a hint of drizzle in the air. Once again Jane had dressed as best she could without looking out of place. She could not recall being quite so nervous before. She was hoping that she could engineer another meeting with him; maybe she could visit a farm where the tractors were working. All sorts of ideas had passed through her mind; her main focus had been to appear plausible even though she really wanted to say, 'Why don't we have lunch?'

Once again, she went outside to meet him and they shook hands as Arnold got out of the car. 'So nice to see you again, Miss Dunhaughton,' he said.

'Likewise. The weather is not quite so nice, though. Shall we go inside?'

They went into Jane's study and she rang for coffee and biscuits.

'I have some good news. Mr Weston has approved the purchase of a tractor. Indeed, he says that Lord Kitchener, as Secretary of State for War, is very keen to promote their use and serve as an example to other farmers. The government is very worried about the manpower shortage.'

'That is good news. When I get back to the office, I'll send you an official order. If you can sign it, we could have the tractor with you very speedily. Who would the invoice be made out to?' Arnold asked, sipping the coffee that Jane had poured.

'To Broome Park Farms Ltd,' she replied.

'So Lord Kitchener came this weekend?'

'Yes, together with his entourage. It is quite a houseful, what with all the civil servants, bodyguards, servants from his London house and quite a few military types.' Jane sounded positive and upbeat; she was pleased with the way the meeting was progressing.

'That must take quite some organising. You must have been busy all week. I can see why Lord Kitchener is keen to have you here.'

'Oh, I don't know about that. He doesn't really know who I am. I have only met him once. He said he liked my garden so I put flowers on his desk each morning when he is here. Mr Weston, his secretary — he is the one I deal with — says Lord Kitchener likes that.'

'Yes, that's a nice touch. I remember you telling me Lord Kitchener liked your garden.' He looked directly at her as though he were saying, 'I listen carefully to what you are saying.'

Jane smiled.

'Will he be coming next weekend?' Arnold asked, looking away in a casual, unhurried way.

'I am not sure. I know he is planning a trip to Russia.'

'Russia?' Arnold said, much more alert. 'How will he get there? The German army are in the way.' He said it jokingly, as though it were impossible to get to Russia.

Jane was keen to interact with Arnold so she replied without hesitation. 'He is going by sea. The Royal Navy are taking him from Scapa Flow.'

'Of course, I should have realised that. Afraid my knowledge of European geography is a bit lacking. I think of Russia as being just a big land mass.'

He stood up at this point and looked more serious, as though the previous conversation had been mere gossip. He looked directly at Jane and said, 'Miss Dunhaughton, I was wondering if you would like to visit a farm where the tractors are being used next week? And I thought, if you have the time, we could go to a show together.'

It was everything Jane had been hoping for. None of the conversation she had rehearsed had gone as well. She tried to look nonchalant but, as she replied, a huge smile appeared on her face.

They arranged to meet at Canterbury station at one p.m. on Wednesday the 6th of June, from where they would travel out to a farm nearby to see a tractor in operation, then go to see the early evening performance at the Marlowe Theatre. Arnold said he would take his car to Canterbury and would bring her home.

The following week was the longest Jane could remember. She was like a child waiting for Christmas Eve. Kitchener arrived with his entourage on the Friday; to some extent that helped take her mind off Arnold Kayton, for she was kept busy. There seemed to be a flurry of activity with people scurrying around, coming and going.

A mysterious group arrived and were ushered in with no formality but great haste. They did not appear in the public rooms but food was constantly requested for Kitchener's private quarters. The staff were kept busy and it was a relief when Mr Weston told Jane on the Sunday morning that they were leaving at midday and would not be back for at least a month. Jane did not like being the housekeeper.

On the morning of Wednesday the 6th, Jane woke very early at five a.m. She opened the curtains to see a bright sunny day that pleased her; she was desperate for it not to rain. She had spent hours wondering what to wear, given that she was going to a farm and then to the theatre. The theatre!

She had not been for years and was looking forward to it and to being with Arnold.

She wore a long dress with a belt around the middle. Her handbag was fastened to the belt around the waist. She looked at herself for ages and steeled herself to say she looked fine. She undressed and put on everyday clothes, then spent the next few hours getting increasingly agitated.

At eleven o'clock she changed back into the outfit she had chosen and arranged for the farm foreman to take her down to the station where she would catch the train to Canterbury.

She arrived at Canterbury station at 11.25, thirty-five minutes before she was due to meet Arnold. She was pleased; she could not have coped with being late or worrying that the train might be delayed. She bought a copy of *The Times,* went into the buffet and asked for a cup of tea. She did not read the paper but turned the pages, her mind elsewhere. She wondered where Arnold lived, where he had been this morning. How long would it take to get to the farm?

It seemed a very long thirty-five minutes and she looked at the station clock regularly and anxiously.

At five minutes to twelve, she left the buffet and walked the thirty yards or so to the station entrance where it had been agreed they would meet. There was no sign of Arnold, just a line of three taxi cabs waiting for fares.

She wondered where he would put his car and if they were actually going to the farm in his car. That would make sense. It was now five minutes past twelve and she looked round incessantly. Every person walking towards the station raised her hopes; she examined every vehicle carefully to see if it was his.

By twelve fifteen she was becoming quite concerned. He had always been on time before. Maybe he had been held up; maybe his car had broken down or he had an accident. She told herself not to be silly; it was only fifteen minutes. The clock continued to tick, though. More people came and went and more vehicles dropped off travellers.

By twelve thirty she was at a loss as to what she should do. Then it hit her: she had got the time wrong. They were due to meet at one p.m. Why had she put herself through this? The thought gave her hope, but she knew underneath that she would never have made a mistake with the time.

She went back to the buffet and bought another cup of tea. 'Back again, love?' asked the woman behind the counter. 'Waiting for someone?'

'Yes, I am. They must have been delayed.'

'Well, you put your feet up. Trains are always running late. They blame the war but it was the same before, so that don't wash.'

Jane sat down now, feeling anything but excited. She was anxious and uneasy. She fiddled with the paper on her lap; she felt cold and shuddered. She had a shawl and she pulled it tighter around her shoulders.

At five minutes to one she went back to the station entrance and scoured the area hoping, praying, that he would be there. She wondered if there was another entrance; maybe he was there. She walked away from the station looking for a turning, but there was only one entrance and she made her way back there.

She waited until one thirty, her fingernails refusing to let go of the tiniest grip of the cliff of hope, but her strength finally failed. Bewildered, resigned, she made her way back into the station to retrace her steps to Broome.

As she looked up at the departure board, she heard a cry from a newspaper seller. 'Kitchener dead. Lord Kitchener dead. HMS *Hampshire* sunk. Read all about it.' The cry rang out again: 'Kitchener dead, Lord Kitchener dead, HMS *Hampshire* sunk. Read all about it.'

She rushed over to the newspaper seller and bought a copy of the London *Evening Standard*. To her disbelief, she read the huge headline: *Lord Kitchener Dead, HMS* Hampshire *sunk, 700 casualties*. She read on about the *Hampshire* having been sunk by a German submarine near Scapa Flow.

The rest was a daze. There was a lot of activity around the newspaper seller and people were talking to each other, having read the news. Someone, a woman, was talking to her and Jane nodded and agreed, to what she had no idea.

It was on the train back to Broome that her worry over what had happened to Arnold and shock at hearing the news of Kitchener's death started to ferment in her mind. Those two ingredients suddenly combined and exploded. A deep shiver ran down her spine and she visibly shuddered.

She knew that Lord Kitchener was going to Scapa Flow; she had seen the itinerary as she put flowers on Kitchener's desk. She had told Arnold. *Oh no. Please not.* A terrible thought ran through her mind. What if Arnold was a German spy? Surely not. She was being paranoid. Should she tell someone? But tell them what? That she had told someone something she should not have known?

When she got home, she went straight to her room and paced up and down. A servant girl knocked on her door and asked if she had heard the news. The girl was in tears, but it was not the loss of Kitchener that worried her. 'What will happen to us now?' was what she asked.

Jane muttered some platitude and told her not to worry, everything would be all right, but the girl could see there was no conviction in the words. She could see the distress on Jane's face.

The night wore on. Jane was mentally exhausted. She had relived every moment of her meetings with Arnold. Had he come to her simply because Kitchener owned the house? To her knowledge, he had visited no other farms in the area.

She jumped from her bed and searched desperately for the card Arnold had given her and the printed sheet about the tractor. Where was it? It had details of his company. She would go and see him. Maybe she was worrying about nothing. Yes, it would all be cleared up in the morning.

First thing, she walked to Barnham and caught the 6.38 train to Canterbury, then a train to London Victoria. She was in Victoria at 8.10 and, as she did not know the best route to the Old Kent Road, she sought directions at the station. She was told to go to The Elephant and Castle and ask from there. She immediately took the Underground and, on arriving, went up the escalator. She was becoming more nervous with every second.

She went outside and saw a single cab waiting for a fare. She said, '215 The Old Kent Road.' The cab driver nodded and set off.

During the seven minutes she was in the cab, her heart was pounding and her stomach churned. What would she say when she spoke to him? Would he be there? What would she do?

She kept thinking of those 700 dead sailors and Kitchener. She might not have had much time for him but she had never once wished him dead.

Her hands were numb by the time the cab stopped because she had been squeezing them so tightly. She could not open her purse and the cab driver had to help her. She found herself mumbling almost incoherently and the cab driver thought she was either mad or ill.

She got out and looked around for number 215. She could see 220 to her right, a store selling cheap, second-hand furniture. Immediately in front of her was a fruit and vegetable shop with boxes of fruit and potatoes outside. She could not see a number. To her left was a general store with bread and tinned goods in the window. At first she could see no number but then she noticed 216 above the door. She looked across the road but there was nothing but a Presbyterian church.

She stood where she was for a minute before going into the general store and asking if they could tell her where 215 was. 'Yes,' came the reply. 'Straight across the road.'

'But there is just a church there,' said Jane, bewildered.

'Yes, that's right. It's my church. I play the organ,' said the big-breasted woman behind the counter.

'But I was told 215 sold tractors. See,' and Jane held out the card she had been clutching since she left Victoria.

'Not here, love,' the shop assistant said. '215's been a church all my life.'

Jane's journey home was the worst of her life. Utter bewilderment, a deep sense of betrayal, rising anger and frustration and total dejection battled inside her. How could she have been so foolish? Why her, what had she done to deserve this? She had hurt no one; she had always tried to help others. She had fallen out with no one. She thought she may have found someone, but she had found treachery. How could she have misjudged Arnold so dreadfully?

She tried to cling on to last remaining threads of hope — some mistake at the printers — but it was hopeless. Her inner voice told her to let go. She let go and plunged into the deepest crevasse of despair.

She cried through the watches of the night, standing at the window, looking out over the parkland as a barn owl fluttered and dived then soared with its prey firmly gripped in its claws.

In the morning she could not bring herself to dress. She lay on her bed motionless, drained of all energy and purpose. She did not have the mental faculty to confront what had happened and to ask herself what she should do now. She was trapped in a prison of gloom, a prison of darkness and despair.

At twelve noon the servant girl knocked on her door. When no answer came, she asked through the door, 'Miss Dunhaughton, are you all right? Are you ill? Would you like anything?'

Jane replied in a wavering voice that she would be down soon. The servant girl said she would put her post under the door.

It was about an hour later that Elsie, the servant girl, heard a low, deep, repetitive sobbing. Initially she was not sure from where it came, but she put down her mop and stood transfixed, listening intently. Her eyes moved round the hallway where she was working and gradually followed the sound. She craned her neck as she looked up the stairs to where the soft but heart-breaking sobbing was coming from.

Elsie knew now that it was from Jane's room; she knew instinctively that the post she had taken up must have contained upsetting news. She did not know what to do. Should she enquire again if everything was all right, or might that cause Jane, who had always treated her well, further distress? Jane might not want others to see her when she was so upset.

Jane lay on her bed for another hour, trapped in her own disillusion. Only with the most forlorn endeavour did she rise and cross the room to pick up the mail from the floor. She saw a Dover postmark and knew it was from Edith Newman.

Dear Jane,

I write because I have heard the terrible news about Kitchener. I know it troubled you managing his estate after your experiences in South Africa, but I also know what a kind and forgiving person you are. It must be so upsetting for you and all the others at Broome Park. The Lord has looked kindly on us for it had been planned that James would have his first posting on the Hampshire. *The plan was changed so that James would join the ship in a month's time. They did not say why it had been changed but you can imagine our relief.*

Please come and see us. You are always in our thoughts and we will always thank you from the bottom of our hearts that you brought James into our lives.

Edith

Jane sobbed when she read the letter. She had been destroyed by the deceit and treachery of men, the violence of war and conflict, cruel twists of fortune, injustices of the law and high politics. Above all, however, it was the loss of all hope and belief that there would be a brighter future, a promised land of love and affection that cut so deep.

She lay motionless, unable to reconcile the endless lists of misfortune that had fallen upon her because of her own good intentions. When had she done anyone any harm? Where was her God, her champion? She had only spoken well of others, and all her work had been done with high hopes, aspiration and integrity.

She had thought all those hopes were dashed against the rocks when the *Hampshire* went down. Edith's letter, albeit short, gave her a slight ray of sunshine, however small, in the depths of her despair.

It was summer 1916.

Jane Dunhaughton was thirty-nine and still unloved.

Postscript

Arnold Kayton, or Gunther Kreggs as he was christened, was a German American, whose parents had immigrated to America in 1900. He was recruited by German intelligence in the United States and sent to England. The decision of the British to import large numbers of American tractors provided the cover for his spying activities.

He was arrested by the British secret service on the 7th of June 1916. They had been following him since his arrival. He was held without trial, as the British did not want to reveal that they knew of his activities or face accusations that they could have prevented Kitchener's death. He returned to America and died in Milwaukee in 1941.

Emily Hobhouse died on the 8th of June 1926 in London. To the end, she campaigned on women's and social matters. To this day she is revered in South Africa, with towns and naval ships named after her. Her ashes were placed in the National Women's Monument at Bloemfontein.

Alfred Milner enjoyed a glittering career after South Africa. He was ennobled in 1902 and held a number of high-profile business positions. As a result of his experiences in the Boer War, Lloyd George appointed him to the War

Cabinet in 1916. He was the architect of the Balfour Declaration and became Secretary of State for War in 1918. He died in 1924.